For Pinkie Kavanaugh

The Lost King
by Ursula Jones

Originally published in Great Britain by
Inside Pocket Publishing Limited 2012

First published in the United States of America by
Inside Pocket Publishing Ltd 2012

Text copyright © Ursula Jones 2012

ISBN 978-1-9084581-2-4

Printed and bound in the United States of America

www.insidepocket.co.uk

THE LOST KING

by
Ursula Jones

The king was pretending to be dead. He lay quite still on his back with his eyes shut. He'd been lying out there for hours amongst the other bodies strewn around the castle courtyard. He didn't know much about what had caused this catastrophe, but he knew he was king. He'd seen them kill his father and he'd watched from underneath his bodyguard's cloak as they dragged his uncle's corpse away. With his Uncle Haakron dead too, there was no one else left to be king but him. The king was seven years old today.

When it happened, the cooks had just given him his chocolate ice cream birthday cake. They had surpassed themselves. It was made in the exact shape of his father's castle, with fireworks leaping out of it. Blue fire ran down the sides from the chocolate battlements. Gold stars shot from the Topmost Tower. His parents and the other kids at the table were laughing. His older sister, Melior, had just said, 'Cut and wish. Go on, silly,' when the tall windows of the Ante-room smashed inwards and glass rained down as the enemy attacked.

Somehow he'd stumbled into the courtyard where Saan, his bodyguard, had found him. But someone had stuck a dagger into Saan's back during the fighting and Saan had fallen forward onto him, nearly squashing him under his huge weight. So it was Saan who took the brunt of the bullets sputtering across the gravel when the enemy mounted their guns on the walls and strafed the yard.

As the fighting raged around them, the little king had gradually pulled Saan's cloak over himself until he was entirely concealed. Saan had been gasping and coughing blood but he'd told him to wait until the fighting had died down. He would know who had won the day by the banners.

'Whoever is the victor will run their banner atop the tower,' Saan whispered to him. 'If it's ours, go straight to the throne room and sit yourself squarely on it. If it's their banner, get out. There's loyal folk out there who will treat you kind. You know the way.' The blood bubbled in Saan's voice. 'I showed you the secret way.' Then someone came by and smashed Saan's head in. The king could feel Saan's blood drenching his own body.

Two men stood so close to him their boots grated on the gravel right next to his ear.

'All kids look alike to me,' one of them grumbled.

'Anyway,' growled the other one, 'how do you tell the king's kid from any other kid? It's a needle in a haystack job if you ask me.'

'Better get on with it,' said the first voice, 'it's urgent.' And the two moved off. So the little king knew someone was searching for him, but who were they? Why were they looking for him? Were they the enemy or his own people?

It was quiet now. He dared to ease himself gently from under Saan and peer out from beneath his cloak. There were bodies everywhere, lying still as stones. One or two, though, were struggling to get up. The little king craned to look up at the Topmost Tower. The banner was there! But whose was it? Who had won the day? As he squinted at the limp banner, a breeze picked up and straightened it out. It was his father's! His father's banner was flying high from the tower. The battle was over; the enemy had been defeated.

The little king felt a wave of relief break in his chest and realised for the first time how scared he had been at the prospect of finding himself alone among the enemy. He wriggled from under Saan, and Saan's body rolled over with a thump. A voice said sharply, 'Watch it, that's my foot.'

He saw a boy sitting up on the other side of Saan and rubbing his ankle where Saan's dagger handle had hit it. The boy was very battered by the battle but he seemed familiar. 'Looks like we've won,' he said and stood up. He was a big boy of about twelve and the little king saw he had the small royal crest on the front of his tunic that all his father's pages wore. 'Let's go, mate,' the page said.

The little king got to his feet too and the page flashed him a sympathetic smile at the mess he was in. The king knew him now. It was Gurmail, a nice boy who was always ready to stop what he was doing to play.

Gurmail looked more searchingly at the king. He took in the distinctive fair hair, soused now in Saan's blood, and the dark eyes looking up at him from a blood encrusted, small brown face. 'Sorry, sir', he said. 'Didn't recognise you.'

The little king knew he must get on his way to the throne room. He nodded at the page and set off across the courtyard, skirting the dead. He turned in the frame of the arched main doorway and looked back at Saan's body and at what was left of his dark face, ashed over now with death.

He put his thumb in his mouth and silently thanked Saan's spirit for saving his life. He glanced sideways up at the god's Offering Table. The fruit and bread that had been on it were stamped to a pulp on the ground. He thanked the god for defending his father's castle. Then he remembered it was his castle now and he turned and trotted inside, heading for the throne room.

The castle was deserted. The wind blew through the stone corridors. There wasn't a window left with glass in it. Shards crunched under his shoes as he made his way quickly to the Ante-room. He pushed open the door and was at once confronted by a crowd of jostling, whispering children.

A man with a kind brown face and deep red hair smiled down at him and beckoned him inside. The hem of the man's robe was rusty with dried blood. The little king held back for a moment, sucking his thumb, then continued purposefully across the roomful of children towards the door of the throne room.

'Is that everyone?' the man asked, then added cheerfully, 'Room for one more,' as Gurmail, the page from the courtyard, came into the room too. The man closed the door and addressed the children. 'Now,' he said pleasantly. 'Now,' he repeated more loudly. The whispering and muttering stopped and the children gazed up at him.

They were all sorts: Messenger Boys, kitchen boys, schoolboys, boys from the butchery or maybe not. Maybe they were just bloodstained like he was. His robe was crimson from neck to toe with Saan's blood. He noticed there were girls in the room too, raggedy looking things with their hair tied back for war.

The man moved amongst the children and took a rifle from one, a sheaf of arrows from another and a hatchet from another, explaining, as he did, that the battle was over now. 'We can lay down our arms,' he said. Then he told them that the enemy had killed their people by the hundreds and that most of the grown-ups were dead. 'Many of you will have lost your parents,' he said gravely. A tiny girl burst into tears. 'Be brave. You will be looked after.' He patted her head kindly, then said sadly, 'Our king is slain.' Most of the children began to cry. The man crouched down beside them, put his arms round several of them and rocked them comfortingly.

'But the king has a son,' the man said, and he smiled suddenly. 'He will be the new king'. His voice grew stronger as he explained that this was what the old king would have wanted. He smoothed the hair back from a weeping child's face. His fingernails were black with blood and he smiled again and stood up. 'The new king will be crowned at once,' he said, 'and we shall rebuild our kingdom. Long live the king.'

'Long live the king,' the children repeated in a tearful murmur.

The man sighed and looked them all over. 'We are all so dishevelled, so battle stained, I scarcely recognise any of you.' He smiled helplessly and was silent for a minute. Then he threw up his hands in mock despair that made some of the older children smile too, despite themselves. 'No,' he said, 'I can't guess. Tell me. Which of you is the king?'

There was silence. The children looked about them and then back at the man who had folded his hands inside the sleeves of his robe. 'Which of you?' he asked again and the little king took a step towards him, pushing his way under another child's arm.

But the little king's robe was gripped from behind, pinning him to the spot. He struggled for a second and the grip tightened. He was almost choking. The neck of his robe was cutting into his windpipe. Someone was trying to prevent him speaking to the man. Someone was preventing him from being king; someone who was in league with the pageboy too, because Gurmail stepped to the front of the crowd of kids now and held up his hand. 'I am the king's son,' he said loudly.

Everyone began to talk at once. With a massive effort, the little king managed to open his mouth to protest and a hand came from behind him and clamped his mouth. 'Your Majesty,' the man was saying. Oh this was so unfair! The little king fought uselessly to free himself from the horrible hand as the man went down on one knee in front of the lying pageboy, who the little king had always thought was his friend. The boy took a deep breath and said, 'That's me all right.'

'My most gracious Lord,' the man said, and the door opened and two enemy soldiers came in. The man wasn't a bit frightened, though. He gestured in the page's direction and the soldiers killed the boy with a single cut to the head.

The children screamed and stampeded out of the Anteroom. They poured over the dead page's body, jamming the doorway as they tried to get out. The little king ran with them. He looked up into a soldier's face and saw he was grinning. The red haired man was prodding the pageboy's body with his foot, saying, 'That's my orders accomplished. Home time.' He was taking off his robe now and asking, 'How do you get out of this thing?' The king saw he was wearing an enemy uniform underneath the robe. It had all been a trick: the flying banner, the pretence that his father's side had won. It was all a trick to catch him and kill him.

So who had saved him from giving himself away? He shot a look behind him but the room was empty of children now. He was alone with the man and the two soldiers. He froze. His robe! It was embroidered front and back with his own royal crest intertwined with his father's. The front may be covered in blood but the back was a dead give-away. He was going to be recognised now.

One of the two soldiers stamped his boot suddenly and said 'Boo!' at the little king, who shot through the Ante-room door followed by the sound of their laughter. 'Dirty little devil,' he heard one of them call after him.

He had to get out of the castle at once. He stopped at the end of the gallery to find his bearings. He wasn't used to wandering about the place. Most of the time he'd stayed with his mother in the king's quarters, playing up on the roof gardens with his sisters, Melior and Lal. It occurred to him he must not think about his mother and his sisters or that they were all dead. He must not draw attention to himself by crying.

Saan had said that the enemy would be guarding the castle gates. To get out unnoticed, he had to leave by the Secret Way in the Inner Court. He leant against the gallery wall and remembered how he used to look down from the roof gardens onto the Inner Court far below. That meant he should go down. But which way was down?

A slimy feeling on his back made him turn round

11

sharply. The stone wall he'd been leaning against was smeared with glistening brown stuff. He held his robe and twisted the back towards the front, nearly ricking his neck to see. His back was covered in the brown stuff. It looked as though he'd messed himself. He sniffed. He stank of chocolate. Someone had smeared his back with chocolate ice cream cake, his own birthday cake. His embroidered royal crest was completely obliterated by chocolate.

The door of the Ante-room crashed open at the far end of the gallery, and the two enemy soldiers came out lugging the dead pageboy. A voice ranted from inside the room, 'How do you know it was him? Kill them all. Kill every child that cannot account for itself. And get this dratted ice cream mopped up.'

The king didn't wait to hear any more. He flew out of the gallery down a long flight of stone steps into a tangle of puzzling corridors running this way and that. At last he found the door to the Inner Court.

From this entrance, he knew you had to turn left and walk twelve arches down. He didn't know what that meant but he'd find out. He took the iron ring of the handle carefully in both hands and lifted the latch. It was a low door that a grown-up would have to stoop to get through, but the king slipped through like a little ghost. He waited for a minute to be sure he was alone.

The Court was in deep shadow. He was standing in an even more shadowy arcade. The stone floor felt slippery wet, but he could not see what was on it. The arcade ran round the Court's four sides in a series of arches. These must be the arches you had to walk down. The centre was open to the air. There was usually a fountain playing there but it had been turned off. The castle towered above the Court, surrounding it on all sides, but at the very top he could see a rectangle of deepening blue sky with a hint of a skimpy crescent moon. He gave a little skip. That was where he was going: away from these terrible enemy people. He turned left and began to count.

Seven, eight; he walked on down the arcade. He could just make out a pile of rubbish ahead of him through the gloom. As he got close he saw it wasn't rubbish. It was people. They were dead and stacked on top of one another at the twelfth arch. A great many people in the castle must have known about the Secret Way. So had the enemy.

He moved even nearer and saw two of the children he'd asked to his birthday party amongst them. Tears came into his eyes as he stared up at the wall of bodies. They were blocking the way out. He must not cry.

Then one of the bodies said, 'Oh, no! Not another,' and clambered upright. It was one of the enemy. The enemy grasped the king by his fair hair. Another soldier came round the pile of bodies. The king could hardly move his head but his eyes were level with the man's scabbard. He saw the foreign-looking pattern engraved in the metal. He saw the pale flesh of the man's fist all covered in blood as he drew his dagger. 'Gluttons for punishment, aren't they?' the man said to his companion, and the king saw his arm draw back to drive the dagger into his ribs.

With a violent slapping, cracking sound, the fountain broke into life. Someone had turned it on and water beat down onto the paving stones of the Court. Both soldiers jumped and turned to look at it, and the king ducked from between them and fled. The soldiers wheeled round, cannoned into each other, fought each other, and long after the king had got clean away, came to a breathless, confused standstill.

The king was trapped in the castle, with everyone on the lookout to kill him. He'd once seen a rat caught in a cage trap. He remembered the gardener dangling the cage over a tub of water, about to plunge the rat in and drown it and the rat, huddled against the bars, making a sobbing sound, knowing its life was at an end. The king felt like the rat.

He crouched in a doorway and put his hands over his ears to keep out the noise of the sobbing; but he couldn't, because it was in his own head. Then, like a single note of music over the top of the sobbing, he heard a voice that seemed almost his father's say, 'What about the old service stairs?'

He remembered them at once. The service stairs had run like mad threads behind the walls of the castle. They'd been used before the proper plumbing was put in. In those days, servants had hurried up and down them discreetly carting away chamber pots from bedrooms. Commodes and bowls of washing water were spirited away, out of sight and sound, to be emptied outside. Even whole bathtubs had been known to make the trip. As if by magic, a servant could appear silently in a room through one of the cleverly disguised entrances, winkle a bedpan from its modest hiding place and, just as magically, disappear with it.

The service stairs had fallen into disuse long ago, but some of the staircases were still there and some of the hidden ways onto the stairs remained open. The only one the king knew about was in his father's dressing room at the top of the castle. He stood up and began the long climb upwards.

It took him ages, hiding in alcoves and cupboards at the least sound of someone approaching. Once he climbed into the niche of an arrow slit window and stood, flattened into its stone angle, while a line of prisoners emerged from one of the lifts and shuffled away with three enemy guards. All the time he could hear a voice shouting in the distance, and the sound of far off cheering blew in through the broken windows.

At last he came to the tall double doors of the Great Room. He had to cross it to reach the final flight of stairs to his father's apartments. The shouting was much louder now. He stretched up, opened one of the doors a crack, and saw a row of the enemy. They had their backs to him.

The windows to the balcony of the Great Room had been opened. They were standing in their dark blue uniforms, looking down at the crowd in the courtyard below. Gleaming sashes ran in a brilliant diagonal across the back of each tunic. Gold epaulettes sprouted from their shoulders like furious hair. The wind picked at the plumes on their shiny helmets and gently shifted the massive tapestries that stretched from ceiling to floor, lining the Great Room with woven pictures that told the history of his father's city. His city.

One of the enemy was talking to the crowd through a megaphone. It was hard for the king to understand him because he was using long words. He crept inside the open door to listen.

'The lying tyrant is dead,' the man said and, to the little king's horror, one of the other men held up his father's head stuck on a bayonet for the crowd to see. 'Let him cure his headache now,' the man said. There was a huge noise of appreciation from the crowd, and the other man jerked the head on the bayonet up and down in the air. Suddenly his father's head swivelled to face the room, and his dead eyes stared meaninglessly into the little king's. Or was there a meaning? His father's head swivelled away again. The little king held onto the rough, stiff edge of a tapestry to steady himself. He must not cry. He must not draw attention to himself.

Now the man was holding up a letter and tearing it up. The letter was from his father; it had the king's seal on it. The man threw the bits of letter in the air and the wind whirled them back into the room. 'Rubbish,' he said, and the crowd roared.

'For that, his castle is taken,' the speaker went on. 'Nothing remains but to exterminate…'

What's exterminate, thought the little king.

'…to wipe out,' the speaker translated obligingly, 'his heirs.'

That's me, thought the little king.

Then the wind blew the door behind him shut with a bang. Two of the enemy turned round in a flash. One had a drawn sword; the other held a handgun. The one with the gun strode across to the doors and pulled them wide open. He looked up and down outside. 'Nothing,' he said to the one with the sword and closed the doors. 'Just the wind.' And the little king, plastered against the wall behind a tapestry, released the breath he'd been holding with a soft sigh.

He edged round the Great Room, slithering sideways behind the tapestries like a cautious crab until he came to the gap occupied by the door to his father's apartments. A piece of the torn letter had been blown there. It was lying on the ground. It was blank. He was on the wrong side of the letter to read it. He must go on.

In two steps he'd be able to reach up to the handle. The crowd outside gave another roar and the enemy officers flooded back into the room, talking excitedly.

The king peered through the chink between the tapestry and the wall and saw a white-gloved hand grasp the door handle. Then the owner of the hand came into view. He was a tall, narrow, pale man with dark eyebrows and a dark moustache. The man was so close to him that the little king could see his own reflection in the bottom gold button on the man's uniform. The man had an important feel about him. He was obviously the boss.

The boss man opened the door. 'Did themselves all right, didn't they?' he commented, looking up the carpeted flight of stairs to the royal apartments. Then a thought struck him and he tugged at the tapestry the little king was standing behind. 'One of the first things we can do,' he smiled at his officers, 'is trash this lot.' One of the men whooped. The boss man smiled again and went up the stairs.

They began at once. The king heard laughter and some tense silences, then some counting in loud unison. One, two, three, and he heard the first of the tapestries crash to the floor accompanied by cheering and jeering. He couldn't risk making the return journey back to the main door. They could pull his hiding place apart at any second. There was nothing for it: with a quick prayer to the god, the king darted across the gap between the tapestry and the door and up the stairs after the boss man.

No sign of him on the landing. The doors to right and left that led to the roof gardens and his sisters' apartments were shut. The door to his parents' room ahead of him was half open. He crawled towards it. He noticed a lighter oblong patch on the panelled wall next to the door. It was where the family portrait had hung: his father and mother, Lal, Melior playing with her skipping rope, himself on his pony, and the baby in his mother's arms. The picture was in splinters in the corner of the landing. He must not cry.

The boss man was in his parents' bedroom. The king could see him kneeling by the big bed, leaning his elbows on the blue quilt. He had unbuckled his sword and laid it on the carpet beside him. The king could see the boss man's profile. His eyes were closed. He had black lashes. His white gloves were clasped together. The boss man looked as if he was praying, except the picture propped on the bed in front of him was not of the god: it looked more like half a gilt wheel.

The way into the dressing room was directly behind the boss man. The little king offered another prayer to the god and crept forward. The king was behind the boss man now. He could see the dust on the soles of his boots and the white skin of the back of his neck sticking out of his gold braid collar as he leant his head forward slightly to pray.

It occurred to the king that he could kill the boss man. He could pick up his sword and thrust it between his shoulders. He nearly did. But then that same voice in his head intervened. He measured with his eye the size and weight of the sword and the boss man. Even kneeling down he was taller than the king. He was huge; he was strong. The little king tiptoed on, opened the dressing room door, went through like a mouse, turned the key soundlessly and withdrew it from the lock.

Hundreds of his father's robes hung on racks. His shoes, lined up in neat rows, held the shape of his father's feet; and a coat, draped over a stand ready to be brushed, looked almost as if his father were there, wearing it. The room had the reassuring feel of his father and of home and safety, and he had to fight with himself not to lie down amongst the clothes and go to sleep. Home was danger now, and he would never wear the royal sky blue robe of office which was kept here in the glass cabinet.

The king pushed his way in amongst the garments. The coat hangers rattled above his head. He leant all his weight against a woollen cloak to slide the clothes along the rack and scanned the wall behind it. Where was the entrance to the service stairs? Somewhere here. He pressed the wall. Nothing happened. He pressed in a different place. Still nothing. And again. Nothing. His heart began to thump. Suppose it never opened? He thought of the boss man praying outside. Then he heard the handle of the dressing room door being tried and the boss man calling out to the men below, 'There's a locked door here.' He heard him shouting to them to come and force the door, and he pressed frantically on the wall again.

Then came the sound of the men pounding up the stairs to the royal apartments. The king began to beat on the wall with the palms of his small hands. Crash! The men were throwing themselves at the door. Crash! The door juddered. Crash! Then a panel in the wall slid sideways. Stinking cold air flowed in from the pitch-dark rectangle it revealed. Crash! The door bowed with the impact. The king stepped into the dark, heaved the cloak into place behind him and pulled the panel shut as the door burst open.

The dark was terrible. He had always been afraid of it. He didn't dare move forward. He stood paralysed with fear, his eyes wide, trying to gain a little light out of that cold, smelly dark. Then a pistol shot was fired on the other side of the panel. He had to get going.

He stretched out his hand and the key he was still clutching grated against a stone wall. So he had a wall on one side of him. He could feel gritty, thick dust under his feet and he moved one foot forward, tentatively scraping it along a surface. He found the edge of a step. Or was it a precipice? A sheer drop into thin air? He wished his sisters were with him. They would know which it was. *'Fluffy white and green and gold.'* It was the nonsense rhyme his sister skipped to. Very, very carefully he lowered his foot, keeping the heel of his shoe pressed against the stone rise. There seemed to be nothing there. The terror rose up in him. The rhyme filled his head and pushed out the fear. *'Fluffy white and green and gold, Yellow magic in a mould.'* Then his foot found something: the next tread. Then the next, and the next one. He was all right; he was on the service stairs.

Down and down he went, very slowly, keeping the rhyme in his head so that nothing else could get into it, repeating it over and over, *'Fluffy white and green and gold, Yellow magic in a mould.'* Not caring about the stench now, or the blackness; just making his way painfully to safety and the kind people Saan had talked about.

Then something dark rushed past his shoulder. He gabbled the rhyme silently again and again. *'Fluffy white and green and gold.'* He grabbed at the wall at his side, and the key in his hands clonked away down the steps ahead of him. How could he have seen anything in this darkness? But he was right; below him the faintest fuzz of light was showing. Then the dark shadow jumped past him again. It was crooked and skinny and it whispered his name in a hoarse voice.

His terror made him press back against the wall. He couldn't move. But he knew he must. He must run away up the stairs. He must. But before he could, the wall he was pressing against moved and then was suddenly gone and he fell backwards through another entrance panel that had opened up in the wall behind him. He fell into silky, sucking-down, choking powder. He was sinking into the slippery stuff, his fingernails scraped on wood as he sank, choking and fighting for air.

Dazzling daylight flooded in from above him and there was a knock of wood against stone as someone opened up the top of wherever he had arrived. He was seized by a fiery-faced Baker. He'd never seen a face so red. It had wide-open pores round the nose and bristly stubs of black moustache and beard sticking out of it. The little king was hauled out, covered in flour. The Baker said, 'Kids! I thought we'd got us a nice rat.'

One of the enemy was standing by – a barrel-chested soldier, who was wearing a revolver in a holster and passing the curved blade of his long kukri knife from hand to hand as he watched the struggling, coughing king. 'Who is this, then?' he asked. 'You said you'd shown me all your boys.'

In one swift rip, the Baker tore the little king's robe off, opened an iron porthole and threw the robe into the roaring furnace behind it. The robe, Saan's blood, the dried chocolate ice cream birthday cake, and the little king's own royal crest intertwined with his father's, glowed brightly and were gone.

'Give him here,' the soldier said. 'A kid can't account for himself, we see him out.'

'He's the second shift,' the Baker replied. 'My boys work in shifts; there's a horde more like him.'

The fiery-faced Baker kept tight hold of the little king squirming in his hands and gave him a reproving shake. 'Hiding in my flour vat! What were you afraid of, boy?' he bawled. 'Nobody kills a baker.' He stared the little king in the eye and emphasised, 'Not even a *baker's boy* like you. You hear me? Not even a baker's boy.' And the king knew what he was being told. The Baker bawled to some unseen person, 'Brad! Clean up this brat and put him back to work.'

Brad turned out to be a tall, brown, skinny boy of ten or so. As Brad led him away, the king heard the Baker say to the enemy, 'His first battle. He's not accustomed.'

And the enemy answered, 'It gets to you, your first one, doesn't it?'

'Yes, well if you'll excuse me,' the Baker answered briskly, 'I've your army to feed.' The enemy took the hint and strolled off to the other end of the Bakery.

The king followed Brad into a room off the Bakery. There were white uniforms of all sizes, like the one Brad was wearing, hanging from rows of pegs on the whitewashed walls. Brad selected a small pair of trousers and a jacket and chucked them onto a bench in the centre of the room.

'Get those on you,' he said. The little king looked at them and wondered how on earth you did that. He was used to his robe; and anyway, someone always dressed him. He picked up a garment and thrust a leg into the first available hole.

Brad sat down on the bench and laughed. He laughed

so much it brought two other curious boys into the small room. They were similarly dressed in white uniforms and soft white shoes. The other boys began to laugh too. The king had put one leg through the neck of the jacket and the other down the sleeve. The three boys rocked with laughter.

The little king spoke. 'What...?' he said, and stopped short. He had meant to say "What's so funny?" but he was frightened by the sound of his own voice. It was the first time he had spoken since Saan had been killed. His voice was high and shrill and terrified.

The other boys seemed to find the single 'What?' even funnier than the antics with the jacket. 'What?' one of them imitated him squeakily, and they all three doubled up with laughter.

The Baker suddenly appeared in their midst and put his raging face close to the little king's. 'Joker!' he rasped. Then he roared at the three boys, 'Get out of here.' He jerked his head at the king. 'This one's in for a belting, and you will be too if you don't clear out,' he roared at them. They left instantly. A floury haze hung in the air where they'd been standing.

The Baker unbuckled his thick leather belt to thrash the king. He slashed it down hard on the bench. 'Scream,' he instructed the king, and the little king screamed. As he did, he realised he'd been wanting to scream all day. 'This,' said the Baker, as he hit the bench again with the belt, 'is the last time I can show you.' He stripped off the king's jacket and put him into the trousers. He threw away the king's shoes. They were pink where the flour had soaked up some blood he must have stood in. Every so often, while he dressed him, the Baker brought the belt down again on the bench and the little king screamed.

'Thank you,' the little king said, as soon as he was dressed. Once more the Baker thrust his scarlet face close to the king's. 'No thanking,' he hissed. 'Nobody thanks here.' He straightened up and glared down at the king thoughtfully. Then he added, 'And no talking, see? Not until you're rid of that posh accent, see? Shut it. You're dumb.' He hit the bench. The king screamed. 'All you can do is scream. And work.'

The Baker was breathing hard now from the hitting. 'You're a baker.' He hit the bench. The king screamed. 'You're dumb. The clamour of the guns has scared you dumb. That's your story, see? And you answer to the name of Reb.' The belt smashed down on the bench once more and the king nodded in reply to the Baker; then he screamed.

But he didn't answer to Reb. The story of the single, shrill, 'What...?' got about the Bakery and it stuck. Soon the little king was known to everyone as Watt, the dumb baker's boy.

∗ ∗ ∗

All this was in the one-hundred-and-tenth year of the Empire. As time passed, nobody bothered to wonder where Watt came from other than the flour vat, or who he was or what he was really called. His Royal City of Khul lost itself and its name too and was known simply as Slave City. And just as its king vanished, so did Khul's greatest treasure. Like the king, it lay unrecognised, a prisoner of ignorance, in the city that was conquered by the Old Country in a single day to become the most far-flung colony of its huge empire.

CHAPTER ONE

'Where?'

The call was as lonely as the grave.

'Where? Where?'

He tugged his father's arm and cried. 'What? What are you looking for?'

Tears of blood spurted from his father's eyes and surged over Watt's head in a tepid wave. He fought the blood but he was drowning; drowning in his father's blood.

Someone took hold of his hand. Someone pulled him upwards. Someone called his name. Someone grumbled, 'You and your nightmares!' Watt opened his eyes. Brad was there in his white baker's boy uniform, pushing Watt back onto his straw mattress on the stone floor. 'You may be dumb when you're awake, Watt, but you can't half holler when you're asleep.'

Watt smiled up at his friend. It was morning and he was safe from his dreams for another day. Every night for the last six years his tortured father had haunted his nightmares, looking and looking for something but Watt could never find it because he could never discover what his father was searching for.

Brad said, 'I came in to give you a call and you fair frightened the life out of me with your shrieks. And crawling like a baby you were. Yous half navigated your room with your flappings and flopping.' Watt smiled again, stretched on his mattress, and looked round the little room that the Baker had allocated him just off the Bakery. It was as far away from the other baker boys' dormitory as possible, and he had it to himself because of his dreams.

'You, lad,' the Baker had bellowed, 'are sleeping solitary. You'll scare my boys witless with your screams and then who'll bake the castle's bread?' He'd explained the real reason to Watt privately. 'In there, you yells your secrets to the walls and not to a pair of ears.'

Brad said, 'Get a move on, Watt. There's a mound of work ahead.' And Watt remembered that today the State Visit began. They'd been preparing the city for the visitors from the Old Country for weeks. The castle was polished as clean as a new pin, and the countless City Inmates who worked there now had been provided with brand new servants' uniforms. An unexpected part of the preparations had been an issue of some spanking new loaf tins to the Bakery – but an unhelpful size for the ovens. The officer who brought them explained to the Baker that His Excellency the Ruler of the Old Country and Seventh Governor of its Empire – also known as the Roc for short – *always* had his own personal loaves wherever he travelled, baked in his own personal tins.

The Baker had experimented and cursed, sent to the icehouse for a cold pack to put on his burning hot head, and at last the loaves from the new tins had come out right: the crust on the bottom was marked with a perfect ROC. The trial loaves were removed, Watt remembered, in case a City Inmate dared to taste one.

Now the big day had dawned. The Roc was arriving.

Watt would have to get up and put on his newly issued Ghosty Boy uniform. Whether it was the baker boys' floury faces or their white uniforms that had earned them that nickname Watt had never discovered; but Ghosty Boys they were. He looked at his crisp new uniform hanging on the peg on the door – a larger version of the one the Baker had helped him into six years ago on the day of the Attack. He was used to it now, but for a long time he'd hankered after his comfortable robe.

Yesterday was the nearest Watt had ever seen the Baker to jittery. He'd called Watt into his office and whispered ferociously that he was to keep himself to himself during the visit. 'No surprise turns,' he'd whispered. 'No king's tricks.' Watt rarely replied to the Baker. They thought it was safer. But he'd no idea what he was getting at, so he spread his hands in a questioning way. The Baker had rasped the explanation, 'I want you to be so unnoticeable you could be took for a flour sack.' So Watt was no nearer to understanding what a king's trick was.

He went over to the basin to wash and stared in the mirror above it: brown eyes, brown face, head shaved bald as a brown egg – the usual picture – but not much like a flour sack. He'd have to practise.

'You ever going to wash? Our shift starts early today,' Brad reminded Watt. Then he whispered, ''tis policy for the day.'

'Policy' was how the Enemy described the rules they imposed on the City Inmates. The dreariest 'policy', Watt remembered, had been when they changed all the City's fun festival days to boring official ones of their own; but the very worst 'policy' had been when they sent away every able-bodied male over the age of seventeen to man their war ships. The Inmates were told they would be back shortly, but they still hadn't returned. Every family was affected. And although Watt and the younger Ghosty Boys weren't allowed out of the castle, Watt sensed the Inmates' grief at the loss of the young men; it hung around the City like poison. Now, every year, these '"Non-Essentials", as the boys were called by the Policy Makers, were taken away in carts across the plain, never to be seen again.

Watt looked at Brad in the mirror in the room behind him. He was sitting on the mattress with his long legs doubled up, long arms wrapped round them and his head resting on his knees. Brad was sixteen now. It would be his turn soon. Watt couldn't bear to think about it. But then Brad sighed deeply and Watt sensed a quite different sort of trouble. Sure enough it came. 'Watt,' Brad said in a tragic voice. 'I'm in love.'

Watt leant against the basin and tried to look interested, though really he was thinking wearily – Not again! Brad had been in love four times already this summer, and Watt had listened patiently to every rapturous detail from start to finish – and there was always a finish.

Being dumb, Watt reflected, had turned him into a sort of listening post. He didn't really mind, but just about everyone in the castle had used him at some time or another to off-load their deadliest secrets because they knew that they wouldn't be divulged to anyone else. It never occurred to them that Watt could write down what they said. None of his friends wrote anymore. Ever since the Attack, kids didn't have school; they worked instead, and the Policy Makers kept tight control of possessions. Pencils were as rare as hen's teeth.

Brad wriggled his prized gap-toothed old comb from his trouser pocket and ran it through the end of his brown ponytail. 'She is fire and ice,' he said, ardently sorting out a tangle.

Brad's words – Fire and Ice – catapulted Watt back to an unwanted memory of fireworks shooting out of his ice cream birthday cake and of his mother and father laughing. He forced his thoughts back to the present. He avoided thinking about his past life. It was over. He was a Ghosty Boy now.

It had taken him a while to learn the baking trade – he'd been so small when he started, his head barely reached the top of the kneading trough – but six years on he was what the Baker called 'adequate'. And while he was becoming 'adequate,' Watt had grown into a slight but tough kid with no voice, a sad, friendly face and a shaved head.

The Baker had decided early on that Watt's fair curls drew 'terrible attention,' as he put it, and he'd bawled out one day at work, 'You look the nits type, lad. I'm not having bugs in the bread. Get those locks took off.' So no one questioned Watt's unusual hairstyle. The rest of the Ghosty Boys prided themselves on their long hair. They tied it up and tucked it under their forage caps when they worked; but on the holidays granted by the Policy Makers, they let it down in more ways than one. Brad was no exception.

'Fire and ice,' Brad repeated with a gusty sigh but Watt wasn't paying attention; he was fighting off memories of his parents again. He wondered why his mother never came into his dreams and whether he'd stand up to it if she did; perhaps it would only make him miss her even more.

Brad could tell he wasn't getting a sympathetic response to the agonies of his love life: his friend's face was a disappointing blank. He put away his comb and said condescendingly, 'But you can't understand the pain of love, Watt. You're only thirteen.'

Watt thought he could certainly understand the pain of hearing about it, but he gave Brad his best listening face. He didn't want to upset him. In between bouts of love, Brad was a good mate; he'd become expert, too, at interpreting Watt's grunts and gestures for the benefit of the other twenty or so Ghosty Boys in the Bakery. Brad was Watt's voice.

Every so often the Baker had called Watt into his office for a hiding, as he'd put it, and while the Baker gave him a phantom walloping and Watt screamed for the benefit of anyone passing the other side of the closed door, the Baker 'had a listen to his words'. But the verdict was always the same: 'Too posh by half!' Eventually, Watt had given up any thought of speaking again.

Watt stripped off his nightshirt and Brad swore. 'That's some wallop you've got there.' Watt grimaced. He'd forgotten about his back. Occasionally, the Baker had to hit him for real. 'Just in case anyone gets nosey,' he'd explained apologetically to Watt the first time he did it. Then he'd belted Watt. 'You forgot to yell, dafty,' he'd said, with a touch of admiration.

Brad swore again and said it was a crying disgrace the way their boss was forever picking on Watt. Watt wrinkled his nose, clenched his teeth and adopted his most stupid grin. It was his special slobbery, spittle-lipped grin. He'd spent a long time inventing it in front of his mirror. It looked awful and it was dead useful. He used it if he was tempted to talk. It either sent people hurrying on their way or, if it didn't, the clenched teeth prevented him uttering.

He couldn't speak up in the Baker's defence because even Brad, Watt's best mate, didn't know who Watt really was. There were only two people in the world who were allowed to know: the Baker and Watt himself. The Baker insisted on it – 'the fewer as knows it, the fewer as tells it,' he'd explained in his rasping whisper, and Watt agreed.

He had seen enough of the sickening punishments meted out to Inmates to know the Baker would be made to suffer unimaginably if the Policy Makers ever found out that he was hiding the king of Slave City right under their noses. The Policy Makers were satisfied they had killed the king. And long may they go on thinking it. So Watt grinned his stupid grin and let Brad rattle on about the brutal Baker.

Brad said, 'You'll have company today. The Over Lord's ordered no one in the castle is to speak unless it's necessary. We're to keep our minds on our work.' Both boys glanced up at the ceiling, as if some invisible eye were watching them. Brad asked in a scared whisper, 'Do you sometimes wonder what he looks like, Watt? I do.'

Watt shook his head. He didn't need to wonder. He knew. The Over Lord was the boss man he'd last seen on the day of the Attack. What he didn't know though, and what nobody else talked about, was why the Attack had happened. Why had the Policy Makers invaded the City?

Once, early on, he'd borrowed the Baker's old stub of a pencil during one of their private meetings and written the question down on the back of one of the

Baker's recipes. But the Baker had shrugged and cursed and quickly rubbed the question out with a bit of fresh bread; so Watt didn't ask any more.

Watt ducked his bald head under the tap to wash. The Over Lord was the most powerful Policy Maker in the City now. He ran it. Watt felt goose bumps rise on his scalp.

* * *

The motorcar lurched and the pewter travelling flask she was trying to drink port wine from clanked against Madame Isabella Porcini's large, perfect teeth. The wine slopped onto her large, perfect bosom. She murmured something uncomplimentary at the back of her chauffeur's capped head, which she could see through the glass screen separating him from the rear seat where she was ensconced.

She brushed ineffectually at the red stain on her magnificent travelling dress and, between bucks and bumps, snatched a second, and this time successful, attempt at a mouthful. She threw back her magnificent head, with its jet-black hair drawn into the nape of her neck in a bun almost the size of a second head, and gargled loudly – quite drowning out the put-put of the engine. She drew down the window, intending a mighty spit. Yellow dust swirled in on her. She pulled it up again and swallowed instead, then almost choked as the motorcar stopped with a jolt. 'What in the name!' croaked Madame Porcini.

The chauffeur slid back the screen and touched his cap respectfully, but his fleeting smirk at the sight of the flask aggravated Madame Porcini. Gargling with port wine was the very best cure for a lost voice and the great Porcini's voice, if not yet lost, was certainly under threat. Her porcelain white throat felt as though someone was going for it with a hacksaw.

She croaked at the chauffeur. 'Why are we stationary?'

'You said, ma'am, to stop as soon as we could see it.'

'See it?'

'Slave City, ma'am.'

Madame Porcini wound a smoky swathe of chiffon around her famous but agonised throat, muffled her legendary mouth and waited for the chauffeur to open the car door.

He left the controls reluctantly and kept the engine idling in case it wouldn't start again. It was a big gamble bringing a solitary car this far from civilisation. There were spare fuel cans strapped to the car's sides and the toolbox was well equipped but, even so, not many would do it. Motorcars were not for an endless trek like this. If they even *possessed* a car, most people stuck to reliable, horse-drawn vehicles for a journey on this scale. But Madame Porcini was not 'most people'.

Her chauffeur pulled down the mounting step for her and, with his help, she emerged from the dusty little car, which appeared even smaller, dwarfed as it was by its magnificent passenger and the quantities of luggage piled onto its rear rack.

Far ahead of them, a city rose out of the endless yellow plain like a solitary pyramid that shook and shimmered in the heat. Beyond it, and almost too misty with distance to see, were the foothills of the mountains that marked the entrance to the Unconquered Territory. Of the City itself, they could only make out the gleam of buildings stacked on its steep sides and four smudgy towers of a castle on the summit that stuck up like fingers trying to touch the cloudless sky.

Madame Porcini regarded it with dark, tragic eyes.

'My god!' she croaked. She pressed a mournful, porcelain fist to her magnificent forehead. 'We are summoned this far from home for such a pig hole!' But her chauffeur's mute nod of agreement irritated her. 'Drive on,' she commanded. 'Powerful men await Porcini.'

* * *

It was just as the Over Lord had ordered. Not a voice was heard in the castle. The only sound was of work.

In the kitchens, the chomp of the cooks' knives on chopping boards mingled with the sound of the kitchen boys riddling the cast iron ranges that heated the ovens. The regular huff-huff from the bellows added to the noisy silence as other kitchen boys flared up the fire under the roasting spit. All that could be heard from the China Room was the clatter of the plates the scullery maids were counting for that night's banquet.

In the Banqueting Hall, the Butler watched over the footmen in their dark brown livery. Only the clink of the silver cutlery broke into the quiet as they laid the long table. On the floors above, uniformed chambermaids whirred carpet sweepers backwards and forwards and silently made up feather beds with linen sheets.

Above them, in the Great Room, another wordless army of Inmate servants prepared for the performance that night by the renowned diva, Madame Isabella Porcini. Seventy spindly gilt chairs with red plush seats were brought up in the lift and placed in rows. A thousand crimson silk roses had been silently sprayed with perfume and hung in festoons from giant gilded urns standing sentinel on either side of a black velvet covered dais. Here the great singer was to give her recital.

Above them all, the Over Lord stood in his Topmost Tower and surveyed the City. His black eyebrows drew together in a frown. Something was wrong. The shepherd boy on the slopes outside the city walls was asleep on the job! The Over Lord's thin hand, as pale as sour milk, reached for the polished brass speaking tube that reared up from the edge of his desk like a cobra preparing to strike. He spoke his orders into it.

Minutes later a sentry's voice from one of the watchtowers down on the Second Defence Wall called through a loud hailer: 'Oi! Scar!' It spoke in the strange enemy accent. 'The Over Lord's compliments and if you want to see another day, wake up!'

The Over Lord smiled again as the distant figure of the shepherd boy jumped to his feet and picked up his crook. The boy was pathetic, not even good enough to be sent away as a Non-Essential.

Scar the shepherd was smiling too. Another day was all he needed. "Another day" was the exact time, Scar calculated, that he had left to live. Scar wondered about his death. Would it bother him when the moment came? And the moment would come. What he was planning to do could only end in death.

He checked his fob watch surreptitiously. The Over Lord was on time as usual: he looked this way about once every hour. The fob watch was the one thing the enemy had missed stripping Scar of on the day of the Attack. The other thing they'd left him with was the scar that had given him his name. It still hurt him six years on, but not as much as the fall of the City hurt him and nothing like as much as the killing of his king and all the king's children.

Most survivors of the Attack had been wounded, but no child had come out of it with a scar like his. It started at the top of his head and ran in a lumpy, fat worm of vermilion flesh down his forehead, across his blinded left eye, through his cheek and jaw and down the side of his body to his left knee. It had taken months in the City hospital to heal him.

He looked up at the City's jumble of stone houses and buildings jostling downhill towards him. Lots were empty. There were few enough Inmates left to live in them, but the Over Lord had cleverly disguised this grim fact. The Empire's scarlet flag, with its emblem of a golden rising sun, flew from every chimney stack; merry bunting criss-crossed each empty street and alley as though prepared by enthusiastic citizens for the Roc's State Visit. The City looked like a perishing fairground.

Scar could see a Policy Maker officer ordering around a little group of Inmates. They were up ladders, trying to sling even more bunting across the library that had been shut these last years. The place was all Policy Makers now. Four hundred of them alone were packed into the garrison next to the castle, and all the best houses had been commandeered to billet their officers.

Scar grinned at the sound of an Inmate Band rehearsing the Old Country's national anthem. They were making a fair old hash of it. Why, he wondered, couldn't the Policy Makers tootle out their own perishing anthem to the Roc themselves? They couldn't wipe their arses but an Inmate had to do it for them.

Scar moved his flock slowly towards the south side of the slope. He was out of the lea of the wind here, and his shepherd's cloak flew behind him, but he needed a good view of the State Visit.

Far off he saw a ball of dust rolling towards the City's main gate. Was this it?

The Over Lord saw it too and picked up his field glasses.

Two mules were pulling an open cart along the track that served as the road to the City. The driver cracked his whip at the creatures as they struggled through the blinding dust. Behind him, a man wearing goggles and a black fedora was spread-eagled over some bellying dust sheets to prevent the wind lifting them off a grand piano roped onto the cart.

The Over Lord lowered his glasses. The Pianist, he thought. What some people will do for a living!

He frowned again as his vigilant eye fell on his god's Offering Table in the castle courtyard. Again he reached for the speaking tube. In no time a Policy Maker soldier was out there organising a huddle of Inmate servants carrying baskets of fresh offerings. Soon the central slab of the Table was piled with fruit and honey loaves. Everything was in hand for the State Visit. For six long years the Over Lord had been preparing for this moment and now he was ready.

Scar was ready too. The Roc's visit would span the rest of the day and all of tomorrow. He was due to depart the following morning. But by then, the Roc wouldn't be going anywhere ever again. Not if Scar had anything to do with it.

CHAPTER TWO

Watt and the other Ghosty Boys were well into the afternoon's work when the first of the guests arrived. With so many extra people to feed, the Baker had decided to use every available oven – even the old brick ovens that he swore baked the best bread. He picked up a peel, a wooden spade-like instrument that was used to push the unbaked loaves into the hot ovens, and gave the furnace a disapproving clap on its side with it.

'You can stick your old iron,' he rasped. 'Bricks is the business, lads.'

The Ghosty Boys weren't so sure. The brick ovens were a fair old nuisance to heat up. You had to put twigs and bundles of reeds and small logs inside and set light to them. Later, you had to rake the whole lot out again in the form of white-hot ash, by which time the bricks of the domed interior had heated to the right temperature. Everybody got burned and bad tempered and the Bakery was filled with smoke and cinders.

The Baker opened up the long shuttered window overlooking the vegetable gardens, and clouds of smoke swirled out. At once, the Over Lord's speaking tube whistled. The Baker tore across the room, waving the smoke away with a bit of wet sacking, dragged the whistle out of the tube and held it to his ear. He was told in no uncertain terms to close the shutters again. The State Visit had begun.

All the Ghosty Boys crammed into the Bakery window that looked down on the eastern edge of the courtyard. The State Visit seemed to consist of a mule cart with a huge shrouded shape roped onto it. Ten Inmate footmen were standing next to it in an abject row.

Then a Policy Maker captain marched into view with five guards – all in their black boots and ochre uniforms – and he ordered the footmen to cut the securing ropes. The shape promptly rolled towards the edge of the cart on little metal wheels.

A man in goggles and a black hat screamed and threw himself at it to prevent it falling. The dustsheets slipped off and draped themselves over him. While he ran about beneath them like a mad mole, the Ghosty Boys gazed at the black, kidney-shaped box on fat legs that the sheets had been covering.

'That,' said the Baker, breathing fierily over their heads, 'is a pianner.'

One wheel of the "pianner" was already off the cart. The captain issued a fusillade of orders. The ten footmen rushed to hold it. They couldn't.. At the last minute, the Policy Maker guards had to put their shoulders to it too. And it was back on the cart.

'Or very nearly,' breathed the Baker, '*was* a pianner.'

Scales. Watt suddenly remembered his sister Lal practising scales. Hours on end it felt like. Clear off, he told the memory firmly. What was the matter with him today? Why did his past life keep invading his present one? It didn't usually. By now the man with the goggles had disentangled himself from the dustsheets and lashed out at the captain with one of the cut ropes. Watt didn't want to watch any longer. No one hit a Policy Maker without getting killed for it. To Watt's astonishment though, the captain merely skipped out of the goggled man's reach and even smiled weakly.

Then the goggled man really pushed his luck and had a go at the five guards – whipping hands, legs, bums – but none of them retaliated. Eventually, he had all six Policy Makers hopping about the courtyard like mountain goats. The Ghosty Boys gave him a faint cheer, but when the captain looked up angrily at the castle, not a boy was to be seen at the window.

* * *

By the time Madame Porcini reached the castle, Watt and Brad had prepared a thousand rolls. They had kneaded a mountain of dough on top of the kneading trough, then left it to rise inside the trough until it nearly lifted the wooden lid off, and then begun kneading it a second time.

They were working alongside identical twin orphans called Sim and Som. They were easy to tell apart: Som had lost two fingers in the Attack and Sim limped. Som had once described to Watt how he'd dragged his twin all the way to the hospital on the day of the Attack. They'd mended Sim's shattered leg and done what they could for Som. It was a mouldy old place, he'd reported cheerfully to Watt, 'but they's kind to us, Watt, so no grumbles.' Watt knew what he was getting at. Kindness had been in short supply that day.

Watt and the other three worked away silently at pulling and stretching the dough, folding it over and in on itself. They were ready to shape it up but the Baker decided the mix was too damp and more flour should be added.

Watt went to collect a couple of bucket measures of flour from the vat that the Baker had plucked him out of during the Attack. Watt had never told the Baker how he'd arrived in the vat. He let him assume he'd climbed in there to hide. He wasn't sure he wanted anyone knowing about the service stairs. Not that he thought they might come in useful; he was too terrified of them for that. It was just that they were the only private thing he had left. He didn't think of them as an escape route either; the Baker had ruled out escape.

Watt remembered broaching the subject years ago during one of their beat-and-scream meetings. The Baker had snorted and said, 'Easier to escape from your own grave.' He'd put his mouth close to Watt's ear and whispered hoarsely, 'There's spies around. And him aloft...' he gestured upwards to indicate the Over Lord, 'he misses nothing. No one leaves the City but he knows. He knows before *they* do, nearly. You make one move, he'll know and he'll have you.' Watt screamed.

'Hold on,' the Baker said. 'I haven't hit the desk yet.' Then he roared so everyone outside his office would hear, 'Nicking currants is a sin I'll not tolerate,' and Watt yelled as the Baker slashed his desk. All the Ghosty Boys helped themselves to currants; the Baker knew it but pretended not to. Currant nicking was a good excuse to get Watt in for a private talk.

The Baker whispered, 'He took the City to little pieces – looking.' Watt reached for the back of a recipe and drew a question mark on the paper. 'No one knows what for,' the Baker answered, and slashed his belt down on his desk. Watt yelled. 'He scoured the place for it,' the Baker whispered. 'Every house, every building. Scoured it. Never uncovered it.' The Baker winked at Watt and said loudly, 'We're honoured, we are, Watt, to have our Over Lord: top brass, military genius, second-in-command of the Empire.' He lowered his voice. 'It's a desirable item, then, that keeps a man of his talent pinned to the task of just looking? That's all he does – looks and watches.'

The Baker stared at Watt intently. 'You know what he's watching for? You know the secret?' Watt picked up the stub of pencil but, before he could write, the Baker put his hand over Watt's. 'You do,' he rasped, 'you keep it close. Fewer as knows, the fewer as tells.' Watt wriggled his hand free and wrote, 'The only secret I know is where you hide the candied peel'. The Baker turned a ferocious grin on him. 'No you don't. I moved it.'

Nothing more was ever said about the Over Lord's search, but the conversation convinced Watt that escape was out of the question. Deep down, though, he knew that one day, he would leave. Not just because the Over Lord would kill him if he were ever discovered; he would go because anyone in their right mind would get out of Slave City. The trouble was, no one in their *right* mind would try.

Watt stopped to stick his head under the big brass tap in the wall. The heat in the Bakery was worse than ever. When he got back, the boys were discussing the man in the goggles with awe. Watt tipped the buckets of flour onto the dough, and they set to work again.

'He's important, that's for sure,' said Sim, 'to get away with hitting a guard. Don't you think, Watt?'

'Or off his loaf,' suggested Som. 'That's our

explanation, isn't it, Watt?'

The Ghosty Boys always included the silent Watt in their talk because they liked him. It gave extra weight to their point of view, too, if it appeared to be Watt's as well. Watt never objected. He couldn't.

'Nah,' said Brad, up to his elbows in dough. 'He's a Pianner Owner, isn't he, Watt.'

'What exactly *is* a "pianner"?' little Sim asked.

'You know we ain't supposed to be talking,' Brad replied, and Watt sensed Brad had hit a problem: he didn't know the answer. But then Brad said with all the lofty authority of his sixteen years, 'A "pianner" plays tunes.' He turned to Watt. 'Right?'

'Get away,' breathed Som, kneading industriously. 'A big black box on wheels plays tunes! Watt and me has our doubts.'

'How's it do it?' whispered Sim.

Brad sighed in mock exasperation. You turns its handle, dafty!'

And Watt smiled his most stupid, spittle-lipped smile.

They'd just shaped up the rolls and left them to rise a second time when a row broke out over a batch of burnt loaves. While the Baker was chasing the culprit round the worktable, whacking at him with a peel and roaring like a bull, they slipped out of the Bakery unnoticed. They crept down the corridor to a window on the south side and were just in time to see Madame Porcini's tiny, dust covered car drive through the gates into the courtyard.

The car wobbled past the "Blood Orange" – the name the Inmates had privately given to the Policy Makers' new red brick gatehouse – and drew up outside the Main Doors. None of the boys had seen a car before. They were fascinated.

A stupendous figure emerged in billowing copper-coloured silk with a red stain on her bodice that looked as though someone had stabbed her in the heart. How she had squeezed into the weird vehicle in the first place defeated Watt. Perhaps it was made of elastic.

Swathes of chiffon floated round her like adoring smoke. She smiled at a little Policy Maker boy approaching her with a bouquet of roses who looked up at her smugly from under his fringe of well-combed hair. Watt was seized with an impulse to swat him. The impulse surprised him. He'd never felt anything but indifference for a Policy Maker kid until now and he'd never considered swatting anyone either; but this kid – well he just had that effect. The woman flung back her head and laughed – rather creakily Watt thought; then she bent and took the flowers in her arms.

She smiled again at a man advancing to greet her. The boys were stunned to see him bow and kiss her hand. Was she a queen? She took a rose from the bouquet and gave it to him. At a word from him, she took another, kissed it and threw it up in the direction of the Over Lord's Topmost Tower.

The man turned to look up at the tower. Watt gasped and stepped back from the window. Brad said, 'What's the matter, Watt?' Watt shook his head – nothing. But it wasn't nothing. The man was the smiling, auburn-haired man who had nearly tricked him into admitting he was the king on the day of the Attack. Why had he come back to the City? The man had been following orders to kill him that day. Whose orders was he following today and what were they?

The lift doors further down the corridor slid open

and Vince, the lift keeper, stepped out.

Vince was a giant, snub-nosed, jolly, boy hater. He hated boys so wholeheartedly that it was hard to believe he had ever been one himself. If anything – and that meant *anything* – went wrong or broke or disappeared, Vince's smile would vanish, as Watt saw it vanish now, and he'd snarl 'Boys!' and lay about him with fists the size of cottage loaves.

Watt gave the others a warning slap on the back and sped off. Brad soon joined him but Vince had caught Sim, the slowest of them. He was giving him a battering for skiving off work, so Som had stuck by his twin.

Watt and Brad ran the length of the front of the castle, then paused for one more look into the courtyard. The yard was filling up with open carriages. There were pairs of passengers in each one, men in plumed, gilt helmets, and lady passengers they could only see as colourful discs of hats.

A red carpet had been run out from the main door to the largest carriage where a man with an outsize blonde moustache and a chestful of twinkling military medals sat utterly still. Watt thought he was a dummy at first; but then Inmate servants lowered the carriage steps for him to get out, so presumably he could move. He remained seated while two lines of Policy Maker guards drew up at attention on either side of the carpet. He just had to be the Roc. Importance beamed out of him. Still the Roc waited while the last vehicle, a neat little closed coach, swept into the yard.

A small, gloved hand let down the window and a girl with a haze of bright hair and a pink-cheeked face, leant out and studied the castle. Watt heard an appreciative noise from Brad and looked round at him. Brad wore that hungry, calculating expression which meant one thing and one thing only: Love. Watt sighed and glanced back at the girl. And for the first time, he almost – not quite, but nearly – saw what Brad meant.

With an ear splitting cry, Vince was upon them. They legged it down the west side of the Castle, slewed around the corner, put on a sprint along the north side, and slid through the big oak door into the safety of the Bakery. Sim and Som were sitting glumly in a corner.

The burnt loaves crisis had been overtaken by another much more serious one: the furnace was giving trouble. None of the ovens were hot enough. The Baker was sweating buckets and praising the god for the existence of the old brick ovens. Everyone else was grimly accepting that it was going to be a long, painful, and smoky shift.

Later, with his face screwed up against the heat, Watt slid the rolls off the peel into the oven and wondered which of them the pink-cheeked girl would pick up and tear into pieces at that night's banquet.

Far above Watt, in the Great Room, the Pianist wept into his piano, where it was now safely parked on the dais. He was tuning it. The Over Lord, a tall, thin figure in dark dress uniform, watched him dispassionately from the stairs that ran up to the old royal apartments. The Pianist straightened up from under the raised lid of the grand piano, giving one of the gilt urns a knock with his rear as he did. Five hundred silk roses rocked dangerously. He wiped his eyes with a red spotted handkerchief.

Without his goggles, the Pianist was an ordinary-looking man from the western edges of the Empire, with a comical twist to the end of his nose and a jutting jaw. He mopped his eyes again, ran a hand over his crinkly, greying hair, and attempted a smile. The Over Lord looked down at him. His tone was icy. 'You're crying, man.'

'Don't let it trouble you.' The Pianist thumped middle C. 'I often cry before a job.'

'Just get it done,' the Over Lord replied. The scent of the disturbed silk roses reached him. It was lavender! What incompetent clowns these Inmates were!

The Pianist blew his nose. 'You'll be paid cash when it's over,' the Over Lord said. The Pianist looked at him levelly over the top of his handkerchief.

'I never accept anything else.' He trailed his finger rapidly from the top to the bass notes. 'Do you mind if I ask you something?'

'Yes,' the Over Lord said, mounting the stairs. 'I do.' He reached the summit and disappeared from sight.

The Pianist said to the empty room, 'I was only going to ask what Yellow Magic is.'

CHAPTER THREE

Fidelis had been given a lovely room at the top of the castle. The first thing she'd done was to take her basket of carrier pigeons out through a French window onto a little balcony to give them some air after their long journey. She'd hoped to have a good view of Slave City from there, but instead she was looking down at a parched roof garden. The three pigeons cooed appreciatively, and she thought what an age it seemed since Mama had given them to her this morning.

Fidelis bit her lip as she remembered the awful tension between her parents at breakfast – which was served so early they'd eaten it by candlelight and Pa's special loaf was still hot from baking. Fidelis was used to her mother and father behaving like strangers to each other, but this morning had been especially chilly. You could have cut the atmosphere with a knife. The only time her parents really got on was when they were talking Empire politics. Then, they were like excited conspirators. She smiled at the thought – not at all like the Roc and my lady, his wife.

This morning, Fidelis had been only half listening because she wasn't involved. Her father was sketching out the schedule for the last lap of her parents' State Progress round the Empire, and they were leaving her behind. She soon *got* involved, though. Her mother suddenly pushed aside her grapefruit, announced she had a migraine and swept off in her long travelling gown to go back to bed.

'Dash it,' the Roc called after her. 'Our party will be short of a lady.' And Fidelis's mother had said something to the effect that she was sure the Roc would have no difficulty in putting that right. 'I shan't,' he retorted. 'I'll take Fidelis.' Fidelis had felt a thrill of excitement because her parents had definitely decided earlier not to include her in the visit to Slave City. She'd wanted to see it so much she'd summoned up the courage to ask them why and the Roc had said the people of Slave City were lying, deceptive, cantankerous devils, that was why. But he seemed to have forgotten that this morning.

Her mother had protested icily that, at thirteen, Fidelis was too young for such a dangerous city. But the Roc had twirled his huge blonde moustache and said, 'Fidelis comes with me. That is my wish.' And that was that. When the Roc said "That is my wish" you did what he said. Fidelis had run up to pack. She smiled again at the memory, but a touch guiltily. She wasn't fooled: she knew Papa had used her as a weapon in whatever the battle was between him and Mama. That was why she was here. Not for her company.

All Fidelis's friends envied her being the Roc's daughter; his was the most important office in the Empire and she was proud of her pa. He was so busy she hardly ever saw him, so she'd been looking forward to having him all to herself as they travelled north. Instead, she'd done the long journey in a separate carriage with her maid, Prudence, the basket of pigeons and – worst of all – with Span.

Her mother had called her up to her darkened bedroom and issued a list of dos and don'ts from her sickbed that dampened Fidelis's high spirits considerably. Mama had ordered the basket of pigeons, too, and explained that Slave City was an extremely backward society. There was no telegraph and no mail. Messages were sent on horseback, but much the quickest way to communicate was by pigeon, and Fidelis was to write every day. Then she'd given her Span. 'But Mama,' Fidelis had protested, 'he's your dog. You'll miss him.' She wanted to add, 'And you're the only person who likes him.' But she daren't say anything so disrespectful.

Span was an elderly, frilly sort of dog with no interest in anyone but himself and a disagreeable tendency to give off small, asphyxiating stenches. Not a welcome travelling companion for eight hours in a tiny carriage. But her mother had said he was a good watchdog, and in Slave City you needed one. The people were untrustworthy, verging on evil, her mother said, and Fidelis felt another thrill, this time of nervousness.

She couldn't see her mother's face clearly in the darkened room but she could tell by her voice that Mama was furious. Fidelis was sure it was because the Roc had overridden her. She tried to lighten things up with a question about one of Mama's favourite topics – correct behaviour. Just before the onset of the migraine, the Roc had been describing the great singer who was to entertain them in Slave City and so Fidelis asked Mama, who was just as much an expert on etiquette as she was on politics, what she should call the diva. 'How do I address her, Mama?' There was such a long pause Fidelis thought her mother wasn't going to answer at all. When she did, Fidelis knew at once her question had been a blunder: her mother's voice was even harsher. 'As *Madame* Porcini. She is not a lady, as you are.'

So Madame Porcini was in Mama's bad books for some reason. Fidelis had curtsied, kissed her mother's cheek and left, dragging Span with her on his golden chain.

Now here she was in Slave City and the biggest surprise of all was that throughout all those dire warnings about the place, neither of her parents had mentioned how beautiful it was. When she'd let down the carriage window and looked up at the great castle it had nearly taken her breath away.

Fidelis carried the pigeons back into her bedroom where Prudence was unpacking the trunks. Every bit of Prudence was registering disapproval, from her sandy chignon, that scowled out of the back of her head like a pugnacious doughnut, down to her black-buttoned boots. Prudence always sided with Mama, so if Mama disapproved of Fidelis coming to Slave City then so did Prudence. Fidelis gave her a wide berth. Conversation with Prudence in her present mood would be like dodging poison darts.

Fidelis sat down at a desk in a corner of the room. It was made of ebony inlaid with mother of pearl and, like everything else in the room, was very pretty. She would write to Mama: that would keep her out of Prudence's faultfinding range – and Span's whiff range too, with a bit of luck. She raised the desk lid and found some writing paper inside with the Empire's emblem of the rising sun embossed in red on the top. She tore a thin strip from a sheet, selected a silver pen from the pen tray, inspected the nib for bits of fluff, thought for a minute, dipped the pen in the inkwell and began very carefully: "Arrived safely." She sucked the end of the pen for inspiration. She would describe the castle. Right at the last word, the pen dropped a wobbly blot of ink all over it and she had to start afresh on another strip of paper.

She rummaged in the desk and found a blotter – a quaint little blue papier mâché rocking horse with sapphire eyes. The blotting paper was wrapped on the underside of its rockers. When you rocked the little horse across your work, it dried the ink. As she took the blotter out, her hand knocked the back of the desk's interior. There was a slight click and a small drawer swung out of the corner. She would never have guessed it was there.

Fidelis leant into the dark interior and looked. Inside the drawer was a beautifully patterned silver button. It was a large button, and there were shreds of silver brocade fabric and pale blue thread attached to the back of it – as if it had been wrenched from the owner's garment very roughly. Next to it was a narrow ribbon of paper. Written on it was:

They are trying to kill us. Come.
Hurry, my sweet, to service.

There was no signature, just three capital L's in a descending pattern which reminded Fidelis of something, but she couldn't think what.

The message was so violent and so tender that Fidelis wished she hadn't read it. She felt she was butting in on someone else's story and she should just put it back. She couldn't help wondering, though, who the message was from. The writing was quite like her own. Was it from a young person? And who was it to? How long had it lain there? And who had owned the desk and its secret drawer?

The bedroom door burst open and with a cry of "Boo-Boo! Guess who?" her father sprang into the room. Span barked with the shock and emitted a whiff. Fidelis was so startled that she dropped the desk lid with a bang. Only Prudence kept her head and curtsied. The Roc's surprised expression on seeing Fidelis was nothing new; her father often looked at her as if he'd forgotten he had a daughter at all. But he'd never shouted Boo-Boo at her before. 'Humph!' was all he said, and he went off to a meeting with the Over Lord.

Fidelis sneaked a look at Prudence. Sure enough she had her "It's not my place to comment" face on, so it was no good hoping she would throw any light on her father's surprising behaviour. Hiding behind a humble servant mask was an old trick of Prudence, but it was the last thing she really was. Prudence may be her maid but Fidelis had worked out long ago that she was her Manners Monitor too. She was there to ensure Fidelis only did what her mother thought proper for her to do; and she was brilliant at it. Prudence could spot an unladylike action at a hundred paces – blindfolded.

With Prudence so unforthcoming, Fidelis got on with the letter to her mother. She took one of the pigeons from the basket and cradled it in her hands. It looked at her calmly with bright black eyes while she set about the tricky task of attaching the message to the ring on its leg. She'd nearly done it when Prudence interrupted her.

'I suppose you've noticed?'

Fidelis gave a guilty start. Prudence always made her feel guilty, even if she hadn't done anything remotely 'not proper'.

'Noticed what?' she stammered.

'The bed.'

Fidelis looked at the bed anxiously. It looked like a fairy tale princess's. It had diaphanous sky blue drapes gathered into a spiky silver coronet high above the carved bed head that fell in soft pleats to the carpet. They were caught back on either side of the pillows with a silver tasselled cord. Was it an improper bed?

Fidelis said hesitantly: 'It…it's rather large, perhaps.'

'Good thing too,' Prudence snapped. Fidelis didn't know what to make of that. Prudence raised her ginger eyebrows and put her bony hands on her hips. Fidelis knew at once that she was supposed to ask why it was a good thing too; so she did.

Prudence's neck was red with anger. Fidelis could see it rising stringily out of the pretty embroidered collar of her long grey dress. The corset underneath the dress was laced so tight, Prudence looked as though she could pass through a keyhole.

'Well,' said Prudence, 'there's only one, isn't there.'

Fidelis was puzzled. 'But there's only one of me.'

'And what about me?' Prudence spat back. 'A lady should always consider the needs of her inferiors.'

Prudence always referred to herself as an inferior whenever she wished to make it crystal clear that the most superior person in this world – and probably in the next one too – was Prudence. It got results: guilt washed over Fidelis. She bent over the pigeon and finished attaching the message. She stroked its rounded head and muttered, 'Sorry, Prudence,' adding in her own defence, 'I thought you had a room of your own.' Prudence glared. 'Like you do at home,' Fidelis said weakly.

'Well, you thought wrong,' Prudence said and gave a

bitter, neglected sort of sniff.

'I'll sleep on the couch,' Fidelis offered. Anything to keep Prudence, if not sweet, at least out of acid drop mode. But Prudence nearly fainted with shock at the proposal. 'Well then, what do you suggest?' cried Fidelis, crawling with guilt. Prudence gave a defeated shrug as though she were submitting to torture. 'We shall have to share. She picked Fidelis's green water silk evening dress out of the trunk and gave it a vigorous shake.

The long, full skirt clapped the air like a pistol shot and the pigeon fluttered out of Fidelis's hands in a panic. It flew about the room, beating against the mirror on the dressing table, whirring round their heads and scattering feathers before it flew out of the French window. 'Now look what you've done,' Prudence said, cannily dodging the blame, and she took herself off to the wardrobe where she clattered the clothes hangers censoriously. Then she rang the bell to order more.

Fidelis ran out onto the balcony but, mercifully, the pigeon was not hurt. The sun caught the pale underside of its wings as it circled the castle's turrets, finding the right direction to fly back to her mother. But then a short, black line came hurtling up underneath the bird. It was an arrow. Someone had fired an arrow at her pigeon! In seconds it would be dead. Fidelis gave a cry of pity but the pigeon suddenly altered course; it had found the south. It flew out over the plain, while the arrow curved harmlessly out of sight.

Fidelis tried to think calmly about what had happened. Her fingers absently traced the pattern of the wrought iron balustrade she was leaning on while she thought – three linked circles, then a break, then three more and another break. The incident demonstrated exactly why her parents had warned her off Slave City. The place was "unpredictable". And yet all the servants seemed rather submissive and sweet and answered her in a silly accent. Why should one of them try to kill her pigeon? And kill it unobtrusively too. No noise from a gun; just a silent, lethal arrow. She would go and ask her father.

But then another, quite different, crisis blew up. Prudence called from the bedroom, 'Here's a to-do. There's no washstand.' Fidelis went in through the French windows to look. There ought to be a washstand with a bowl and a pitcher of water and a slop pail, but there wasn't. 'How am I supposed to get you washed and ready for tonight's dinner?' Prudence complained.

To add to their troubles, there was a knock at the door and a Messenger Boy carrying a weird-shaped flask, like a porcelain euphonium, came in.

'What's this?' Prudence demanded indignantly. 'A joke?'

'It's instead of your WC, ma'am,' he replied in his funny accent.

Fidelis and Prudence exchanged mystified looks. WC?

'The Butler's apologies,' the boy said, 'but we's had so many requests for a po from your party that we's run out. This was the best we could do.' He gave a contrite little bow.

Fidelis thanked him. She'd no idea what he was talking about but no intention of letting the boy see it; it would be "bad for one's dignity", as her mother would have said. And anything that was "bad for one's dignity" was bad for the Old Country and for the Empire and must never be allowed to happen. Fidelis said, 'It's really hot water we're in need of. Could you fetch us some?'

The boy looked at her a little strangely, then opened what she'd thought was a cupboard door. Prudence streaked across the room behind him, stuck her nose through the door, gave a tight screech of dismay and banged it shut. Fidelis caught a glimpse of a room and of a white open coffin inside.

'What is it?' Fidelis breathed.

'I've no notion,' Prudence replied,' but it doesn't look at all ladylike. Don't go near it.'

Fidelis noticed the Messenger Boy suppress a smile. She hated that. Prudence had made them look stupid – worse, Fidelis didn't know why. She was beginning to feel uncertain about this city, what with the disturbing secret message, then the arrow, and now this sinister room. She had to get back on top of the situation and the way to do it was to issue orders that had to be obeyed.

She scrunched up the spoiled message and handed it to him with Span's empty bowl. 'Throw this away and fetch my dog some water.' The boy looked at her uneasily. 'Yes, ma'am.' He went in to the sinister room and came back with the bowl full of water. Fidelis was astonished. Prudence muttered 'Oh, heck!' The boy put the bowl down in front of Span, who ignored it. Fidelis saw the boy recoil. So Span had made his mark.

Once the boy had gone, Prudence jammed a chair under the door handle of the disquieting room with a sniff of contempt for the whole uncivilised place and went on unpacking. Fidelis sat on the chaise and adjusted the hairpins that Prudence had driven into her plait to hold it in a coil behind her head.

After a moment, she gave what she hoped was a ladylike cry of, 'Oh my, Prudence!' Prudence looked up irritably from the open trunk. 'I've dropped the golden

57

locket Papa gave me for my birthday.' She bared her neck to show Prudence that it was gone. 'There, there,' Prudence said. 'It will be in the carriage, mark my words.' Fidelis burst into tears. 'Hush now,' Prudence remonstrated. 'Your father's just below in a meeting with the Over Lord. Don't disturb him.' Fidelis cried even louder. With a tut of anxiety at the noise, Prudence said soothingly, 'I'll go straight down and fetch it myself.'

As soon as Prudence had gone, Fidelis scooped out the locket from where she'd hidden it down her front and stashed it away in the pocket of her bloomers. She'd never dreamed of play-acting before. Something in the City's air had made her do it, she excused herself. She removed the chair and went into the sinister room.

'Oh my!' she said, examining the fixtures. She pulled a chain and was out of the room as quick as blink as water gushed. But she was soon back. 'Oh my!' she said again as she turned a tap and warm water flowed into the coffin-like vessel.

Half an hour later, after a fruitless search for the locket, Prudence came back to find the bedroom empty except for Span. Splashing and singing led her to the terrible little steamy room where Fidelis was lying in a hot bath.

'It's a bathtub,' Fidelis informed Prudence, who was standing in the doorway, her skinny hands pressed into her cheeks in horror. 'I've read about them in anthropology lessons. And that thing,' Fidelis waved a soapy hand, 'is for peeing in.' Prudence gave a moan. 'It's true,' Fidelis said, 'I've tried it.'

'That's it!' said Prudence. 'I'm sending a pigeon to your mother.'

'No, don't.' Fidelis sat up in the bath so fast that water

58

sloshed onto the tiled floor where her clothes were lying in a tumble. 'Don't send a pigeon, Prudence. Someone is shooting them.'

Prudence rescued the clothes from the water, and the locket fell out of Fidelis's bloomers pocket and hit the floor with a ping.

'Shooting pigeons!' Prudence dangled the locket in front of Fidelis. 'Don't lie to me anymore or I shall inform your father.'

CHAPTER FOUR

Once Watt's shift was over, the Baker gave everyone except Sim and Som a freshly-baked Lost-and-Found as a treat. His Lost-and-Founds had a history. Watt's first ever batch of loaves had turned out flat as dinner plates. The Baker had cursed massively, then drenched them in syrup, rebaked them, dredged them in sugar and spice, battered them into crisp bits, and conjured a delicious triumph out of a disaster.

Brad went off into the City, promising to be back by curfew, while Watt and the younger boys went down to the servants' dining room for supper. The twins were sent straight to bed hungry and missed all the wonderful leftovers from the banquet.

Even the Cook's dark, unhappy face broke into a smile as she watched the Inmate servants fill up on undreamed-of delicacies.

Bursts of quickly stifled laughter erupted at all the tables. Watt soon heard the joke from his neighbours: the grand ladies and gents from the Old Country didn't care for bathrooms. Chamber pots was what they wanted. In the end the poor Butler had sent down to the hospital to boost supplies, and back came enough shapes and sizes of vessels to equip a laboratory. Very put out the visitors were.

The chambermaid sitting next to Watt moved right up close. 'Flipping savages!' she dared to whisper in his ear, and Watt smiled in agreement. He dug his spoon into the Cook's biggest treat – meringue and melon ice cream. As it melted and softly exploded in his mouth, he remembered, clear as day, sitting under a tree with his sister, Lal. His other sister was skipping faster and faster.

Fluffy white and green and gold,
Yellow magic in a mould.
Mother made a melon soup,
From a rotten cantaloupe.

They'd all been eating ice cream. Lal had wiped his mouth with her handkerchief and somehow one of her large, silver patterned buttons had caught in his hair. They'd spent ages trying to… Stop, stop, stop, he told himself. What had got into him today with these memories? He must shut them out. They did nothing but hurt.

After supper a Messenger Boy beckoned to Watt, who slid along the bench where he was sitting at table and followed him into a corner. The boy had a pensive look that Watt knew well: there was a secret coming.

'I've had a message took off me, Watt.' The boy was really troubled. 'I'm in a fair old fret,' he whispered. 'It was from the big singer woman to the Roc and a bloke steps up behind me and takes it off of me.'

'Who?' Watt signalled, and the boy whispered back, 'Not one of us, least not as I knows. Not a Split even.'

Watt nodded. A Split was an Inmate who'd gone over to the enemy's side.

'When I asks for it back, he kicks me half round the castle.' The boy shook his head miserably. 'Said he'd kill me if I told. But Watt, if it comes out I ain't delivered it, it's the sack for me and back to the orphanage until I's shipped out as Non-Essential to the god knows where.'

Watt nodded sympathetically. The boy was dead scared.

'And another thing,' the Messenger Boy whispered. 'My mate's gone missing.' He looked round furtively to make sure no one was listening. 'He ran up to answer the Roc's bell and...'

There was a sudden commotion in the doorway of the washrooms that led off the dining room. Watt looked up to see a footman coming out. The arms of his uniform were pushed up. He was wet and calling for help. Other servants went into the washroom. Some came out with frightened, serious faces, while others crowded into the doorway. Then the Butler came in and pushed his way through; in seconds he was out again, soaking wet and calling for a stretcher. Then everyone stood up to attention because a Policy Maker Medical Officer was making his way fast between the tables. He went into the washrooms too.

Shortly after that, the Cook told all the kids to eat up fast and go to bed and not to worry themselves about the fuss and bother. Watt was among the first to leave, but word had already got round: the missing Messenger Boy had been found in the washrooms drowned in a bath.

Watt felt very troubled. Why should the boy drown himself? He was glad when the Baker told him to stay back in the Bakery to help prepare fuel for the brick ovens, ready for the early shift. He'd try to sneak a word with him about it.

The Baker had set a lantern on the table to save the electrics, he said. Electricity was an expensive commodity in the City. Their two shadows shivered and jumped about the whitewashed walls of the long dark room. The last shift had scrubbed the place as clean as a whistle and it still smelt of damp, soapy wood and stone.

Watt opened up the shutters of the big window at the end of the Bakery. There were more stars than there was black in the sky. He could hear the clatter of the scullery maids washing up in the China Room below him. The banquet was over unusually early.

The next shift would come on duty at around two in the morning. He knelt alongside the Baker where the ovens had dried a warm, pale half circle on the scrubbed stone floor, and the two of them bundled up apple twigs. The Baker started to sing very quietly. Watt didn't take much notice. He was wondering if it was safe to discuss the drowned Messenger Boy. But then the words began to impinge:

Ghosty Boy, Ghosty Boy went to town
Saw a fair lady of high renown.
They stole all his bread and cut off his head
And sent him back home in a box of lead.
Ghosty Boy, Ghosty Boy back from town,
Dead as a nail with a broken crown.

The words finished and the Baker went on humming and working. Watt looked sideways at him. The Baker didn't meet his eye. He didn't need to. The Baker was no poet but Watt understood what he was telling him. If he was supposed to be making himself inconspicuous, he shouldn't go romping round the castle in working hours,

63

peeping out of windows at Policy Makers. That way he'd get noticed – and caught. He felt ashamed of himself. He nodded at the Baker, meaning he'd got the message. The Baker gave him a wink and said he was going to get a couple of hours' kip.

Watt went off to his own room without a chance to mention the drowned boy. He lay on his mattress and wondered who would nick a message from a singer to the Roc. Search me, he thought. His mind drifted on to the smug little fellow with the bouquet of roses: still swattable. Then he forced himself to think about the man who'd bowed to the massive woman. He remembered the auburn hair that curled around his coppery coloured face, and his terrifying, kindly smile. What was he doing here again? And then, to Watt's surprise, the fair girl with the pink cheeks floated into his mind. Who could she be?

The noises from the kitchen had stopped. The castle was deadly quiet. It was no good trying to sleep. He felt bad about Sim and Som. He got up and made his way out of the dark Bakery.

Nobody stirred when he crept into the boys' dormitory. He laid the Lost-and-Found he'd saved for them on the end of Sim's bed and crept out. Then he thought for a minute, crept back, snapped it in half and laid the other piece on Som's bed. Why test Sim's loyalty to his twin?

When he got back to the Bakery, there was a line of light showing under the door. He opened it a chink and to his surprise saw the Baker sitting at the far end of the long table with the lamp and a bottle and glass in front of him. Why had he changed his mind about having a kip? As he watched, the Baker drank down a tot in one go, pushed the cork back in the bottle and came towards the Bakery door. Watt cleared out of his way fast and watched from the corner of the darkened corridor while the Baker closed the door behind him and locked it.

Flip! I'm stuck outside, Watt thought. Now what? There was nothing for it; he'd have to run after the Baker and ask for the key. The Baker would tear him off a strip for disobeying him again, but better that than be caught out of his bed after curfew.

He set off after the Baker, but it soon became clear that the Baker was going to a great deal of trouble not to be followed. Watt grew more and more intrigued. Did the Baker have a lady friend, someone maybe he shouldn't be seeing? The Baker worked his way gradually round and down the castle. Watt found him quite hard to tail. He was in parts of the castle he didn't know well. Ghosty Boys weren't encouraged to stray about the building – it was Policy. Sounds of clapping came ringing down the barely lit corridors, followed by a piano striking up. Watt tucked himself into a doorway. When he dared to come out, he'd lost the Baker entirely.

Disappointed, he gave up and started back, only to find he didn't know where he was. He had to stop himself thinking about the Messenger Boy's story of the man who'd come up behind him. There was no point in being scared of something until it happened. But the back of his neck was prickling as if he knew someone was going to jump him. It was a relief when he saw that the Baker had doubled back too and was ahead of him again. He followed him towards the centre of the castle.

For an awful moment Watt thought he was going to the Inner Court, but the Baker passed its low door and went into a tunnel that Watt had never been down. It was narrow and business-like, and Watt guessed it led to the round tank that lay under the Inner Court. The tank held the castle's water supply before it was pumped through the purifiers and around the building. Why of all places was the Baker going down there?

As he hesitated at the entrance to the tunnel, he saw a figure rolling along behind him. The electric light was very dim here, but it looked frighteningly like Vince. Watt scuttled down the tunnel after the Baker.

He came into a shadowy, warm room. A huge cylindrical tank rested on wooden supports surrounded by a criss-cross of hefty wooden beams that buttressed the low ceiling. It was as if whoever had built the room was making sure the roof didn't cave in. The room was all tank. A fat feed-pipe running from the ceiling to the top of the tank made rushing, surging noises as water was fed into it from the Water Terrace reservoir on the roof.

The Baker had stooped underneath the beams. Watt could make him out in the far corner. There was someone else there, too, sitting on the ground by a lighted candle. It was the Cook. As he watched, a third person joined them from that side. So there must be at least one other entrance to the tank room. The newcomer was a young fellow with a badly scarred face. He sat down with the other two. It looked like a witch's coven. Incongruously, the scarred boy brought out a pack of cards and began dealing.

The water in the feed-pipe stopped running, and in the silence the Cook said, 'Curse the queen for her treachery.'

'Curse the traitor queen,' the Baker rasped. The scarred boy nodded violently.

'Curse her,' he said. 'Curse her.'

What on earth was Vince going to make of this trio? Watt wondered. He flattened himself against the dark wall. But with much grunting and squeezing, Vince joined the other three round the candle. 'Cursed be Queen Lenita for her treachery,' he rumbled.

If Watt had had hair, it would have stood on end. Queen Lenita was his mother! What was this? His mother a traitor! Before he could get any kind of hold on this bit of information, the young man said, 'The Roc's here for two nights. What do we do about it? You know my thoughts.'

The Cook put a hand on his arm. 'No, Scar. The reprisals. They'd destroy us all...'

There was a noise in the tunnel to his left. Watt glimpsed a woman in Policy Maker uniform; then the candle went out. He could tell by the quiet, hurried noises that the four were leaving by the other entrance. The woman intruder clumped up the tunnel again, but Watt remained standing in the dark thinking about his mother.

He couldn't remember her clearly any more. He knew she'd had a velvety sort of voice, and golden hair. He remembered watching her brush it as she sat at her dressing table. And her laughter too, of course; he remembered that. But how could his mother be a traitor? The Baker had called her one, though, and the Baker was usually right.

He would ask the Baker about her. That meant confessing that he'd been spying on him, though. Anyway, what was the Baker doing playing cards long after curfew with three other Inmates who were talking very strangely about the Roc?

Watt crept back to the Bakery. The Baker was there, but he was already snoring in his room. Watt lay down on his straw mattress, too troubled to sleep; but at last he dropped off. It felt like one second later that they were waking him urgently for the morning shift. There had been some sort of incident during the night.

CHAPTER FIVE

The Bakery was teeming with Ghosty Boys. The late and the new morning shift were working together flat out. Watt spread his hands in a question at Brad. What's going on?

The Baker stuck his fiery face round the door of his office and rasped at them both to take a crate over to the Sew House. It was a tall wicker crate, nearly the same height as Watt, and it was piled high with bread rolls.

'To the Sew House?' Brad asked, as though the Baker had somehow lost his way.

The Baker gave Watt a hint of a stare and pulled the door of his room slightly further open. Sitting by the Baker's worn desk with its clutter of receipts, order forms and recipes was a Policy Maker officer. The Baker wanted Watt off the premises and so Watt went, crate and all. Brad followed him in a bewildered sulk.

It took them forever to get as far as the courtyard, partly because the crate had silly wheels that steered it in circles but mostly because they had to keep stopping to let troops of guards march past them down the passageways. Something was definitely up, but what?

Watt tried to ask Brad, but Brad was rambling on about his girl.

"I am wracked with love" was the only answer he got

out of him. There was nothing for it but to lug the crate as best he could by himself until at last they got down to the servants' entrance on the east side of the castle. Watt hadn't set foot in that courtyard since the Attack.

Here goes, he thought, and he stepped over the threshold into the sunshine. It felt wonderfully hot on his face. It was so bright that he closed his eyes and remembered at once the crimson patches the sun made behind your eyelids. He'd forgotten how the sun warmed you through your clothes and lay hot on your back like a friendly cloak. It felt as if the sun had got into his mind too, loosening his thoughts almost as if they were thawing out. He opened his eyes, took a deep breath of the balmy air and gave the crate a push. The little wheels went squealing and grating across the yard. There were no Policy Makers around, and the Inmates were at work, so he didn't go straight across to the Sew House, though he was curious to see it. All he knew about it from his past life was that it was one of the most important buildings in the City. It was where the tapestries were woven for which the City was famous. Or had been.

He took a curving route to look at the front of the castle. It was still exactly the same, but the Policy Makers had made a mess of the rest. The First Defence Wall, which enclosed the courtyard and separated the castle from the City, had been clumsily repaired. The holes blown in it during the Attack had been filled with crude hunks of concrete that looked like big, beige scabs on its meticulous stonework. As for the new gatehouse, it was as if a giant tomato had been slung against the wall. His father's oak doors had been replaced with wrought iron gates. The pattern worked all over them was the Empire's Rising Sun. You couldn't budge nowadays for their perishing rising sun that was so horribly different from the real sun.

Brad didn't notice they were heading in the wrong direction. He came gangling behind, still chuntering on about his love life.

'And now,' he was saying dismally, 'she's disappeared. It's as though a candle in my heart has been snuffed.'

But Watt wasn't listening any more. They were passing the god's Offering Table and it was completely bare. No fruit. No honey loaves. Not a single offering on its flat stone top. He was so shocked that he stopped dead. Brad, trailing in the rear, cannoned into him and knocked some bread rolls onto the ground.

'Stupid!' Brad said crossly. He lolloped about, retrieving the rolls. After a surreptitious glance at the Topmost Tower, he blew the dust off them and would have put them back but Watt stopped him and pointed at the empty Offering Table.

Brad looked at the rolls in his arms and then back at Watt. 'You want me to put these on the Offering Table?'

Watt nodded. Brad cast another, much more nervous look up at the Topmost Tower and then said emphatically, 'I'm not doing it.' Watt gave him a pleading look but Brad said simply, 'It may be Policy.'

So it was Policy now, was it, to starve the City's god? That wasn't right. The god relied on people to look after it just as people relied on the god to do the same for them. The Policy Makers' Rising Sun was on the Offering Table too. So they weren't only starving the City's god; they were elbowing it out. Would it put up a fight? No, Watt didn't think that was the god's way. The City's god wasn't pushy like the Policy Makers' was. The City's god was more of an undercover god that kept itself to itself. If he were honest, the god was a touch iffy: you never knew if it was going to deliver. Maybe you had to be in a real fix before it would. Watt took the rolls from Brad. One thing was certain: the god needed sticking up for.

But Brad was looking as though his dumb, harmless friend had unexpectedly lured him in front of a firing squad. Watt jerked his head at him to tell him to move on, and not to be a part of what he was about to do. He should never have asked Brad to help anyway. Brad may be his voice and interpreter but he shouldn't expect Brad to do everything else for him. If he wanted to defend the god, he should do it himself. Brad gave the cart a push and set out for the Sew House. 'I really wouldn't, Watt,' he advised.

Watt took a step towards the Offering Table. He had a quick look to check the Topmost Tower, the Tower where the Over Lord sat and watched them all like a hawk. Then, with a silent prayer of apology to the god, he ran after Brad and put the rolls back in the crate.

The god would have to starve if that's what the Policy Makers wanted. He hadn't the guts to disobey them. Brad swore heartily with relief and raced off with the crate before Watt could change his mind. But Watt knew he wouldn't dare do that. He followed Brad, feeling sick at his own cowardice. He had let the god down, failed to defend it. He'd betrayed it.

The Sew House entrance lay way below outside the First Defence Wall, but there was an iron access door where the end of its roof butted up against the wall. It was marked "Imperial Staff Only". A dreary droning noise was coming through it. Watt gave Brad a querying look, but Brad shrugged and then pressed the entrance buzzer.

A woman's voice answered almost at once. 'Who is it?' She spoke with the Policy Maker accent.

'Couple of Ghosty boys. We've brought you some bread,' Brad responded cheerily into the speaking tube.

There was a puzzled pause; then, 'Some *what*?' the voice enquired.

'Bread,' Brad called back.

'Oh! You mean *bread*!' The woman's voice repeated the word as though she had just solved a riddle. It was unbelievable, Watt thought, that after six years the Policy Makers still found the Inmates' accent as difficult as ever to understand. The entrance buzzed, and they manhandled the crate through.

The heat inside hit them as though they'd walked into one of their own bread ovens. They were standing at the top of a spiral iron staircase; their heads were almost touching the ceiling of a lofty single storey building. The droning noise had become a deafening chirring sound. They were looking down on rows and rows of City women and girls; all of them were bowed over sewing machines and all of them were sewing the same dark blue fabric.

The place stank of sweat. It was pouring off everyone. The girls were dressed in shreds of clothes; they'd slashed their long skirts and taken the sleeves out of their dresses to keep cool. Two or three older men shuffled along the aisles between them collecting the finished garments. The noise of the sewing machines never let up. Nobody spoke to anyone. They wouldn't be able to hear a word that was said to them anyway. Watt tried to imagine coming to work here every day. The Bakery was paradise compared with this place.

A stout slab of a Policy Maker woman beckoned to them. She was wearing the usual Policy Maker women's uniform – a long overall with a leather belt for her gun holster. The overalls were usually ochre yellow, but hers had faded to a dingy mustard with darker sweat patches under her fleshy arms. She was supervising two Inmates at a table cutting out the fabric to be sewn.

Their crate wouldn't go down the spiral staircase so they left it where it was. The floor, when they reached it, was strangely sticky underfoot. The slab woman shouted at Watt, 'How many have you brought?'

'Five hundred rolls,' Brad answered at the top of his voice.

The slab woman snatched up a stick with thongs of knotted leather attached to one end and slashed Brad across the face. He screamed and clapped his hand over his eye. Watt thought she'd blinded him.

'You answer when you're spoken to,' she said and asked Watt again, 'How many?' Watt held up ten fingers and was about to make an X followed by five fingers when the woman shouted, 'Answer me, drat you.' She raised the whip to hit him too but Brad caught her plump wrist and held it tightly. The woman was so surprised that she stood there for a second as rigid as an over-set jelly; then she drew her gun on him.

'He's dumb,' Brad said very fast. His voice rang out into silence. All the machinists had stopped work; some were crouching under their tables to keep out of the firing line. 'Been that way,' Brad said, 'ever since the...' He'd nearly called it "the Attack", but instead he said, "the Liberation". The Liberation was what the Policy Makers called it. The slab woman gave an angry, embarrassed grunt and pulled her wrist away from Brad. Then she twiddled around on bulgy but surprisingly tiny feet and screamed at the silent room. 'What are you all gawping at? Get on with your work. Now!' And she laid into the nearest girl with her whip. The machines whirred into activity again.

'Got anything we can off-load them into?' Brad looked a bit wobbly now the incident was over. There were five red weals on his cheek. The slab woman shoved a crate at them with one of her hefty shoulders. It nearly knocked Watt over. She gave one of the cutters a crack over the head. 'Where's your initiative, girl?' she shouted. 'Cut'

Brad roared over the din, 'How come you haven't got any? We don't usually supply you.' The slab woman bobbed over to him on her little fat feet and took his hand. Brad looked so uncomfortable, hand in hand with a Policy Maker, that even though the woman was as scary as a mad dog, Watt had to turn away to hide a smile

'How come? I'll show you "How Come"' the slab woman shouted. Her face was swollen and magenta with anger. Watt wondered if she would burst like a boil. She marched them both to the end of the room. The floor got stickier and stickier. She pulled back the front doors and they looked down from the top of some stone entrance steps onto a compound surrounded by a mesh fence topped with strands of barbed wire. A couple of flood lamps were slung on posts at each corner. A Policy Maker guarding the high, gated entrance levelled his gun at them until the slab woman shouted at him to stop. They could see more soldiers through the open doors of some sheds. They were sifting through a heap of metal in one of them and the remains of a cooker in another. It was smashed to bits.

The ground of the compound was even more surprising: it was a carpet of flour. There was a mushy, grey pool in the middle with an upturned water keg lying in it. Flour and water: someone had mixed the biggest puddle of glue Watt had ever seen.

The slab woman went on shouting, but Watt didn't listen. He hadn't seen this side of the City for six years. He'd remembered reed beds and acres of yellow flowers and vineyards and maize crops following the river's path for miles out of the City. What he saw now was much the same as the view from the Bakery window – a strip of pasture along the riverbank with horses grazing on it. The rest of the plain was dust. A column of vehicles, moving along it towards the City, rolled out yellow dust behind it like a dragon's tail.

The slab woman cursed when she saw it and dashed back into the Sew House. Watt caught a glimpse of her bare calves rising like two maroon mottled cones from her little shoes, and looked away quickly.

'Waste of good flour,' Brad observed of the glue pool. No wonder we had to bring them rolls. Watt fanned his face with his Ghosty Boy hat. Something else was missing from the landscape, but he couldn't think what it was.

The guard opened the gate for some Sew House girls coming in to work. They murmured in surprise when they saw the glue and then tramped across it to the door.

A girl in a slashed red skirt, with a mass of squiggly black curls and skin that shone like satin, looked up at Watt as she climbed the steps. Her face was expressionless as she put both her forefingers and thumbs together so they met in two circles in a figure of eight. Just as quickly she separated the two circles, rejoined them, broke them again and then dropped her hands by her sides. Then she went inside with the others.

Watt turned to Brad with his "What did that mean?" query on his face. But Brad was gazing after the tangle of curls and the red skirt with an expression on his face which Watt recognised with a sinking heart. It was Brad's "falling in love" look. He gave him a good poke in the ribs and Brad shook his head in a superior, sad way at Watt's question. 'If you don't know what it means yet, then I'm certainly not going to be the one to tell you,' he replied.

Watt could read him like a book: Brad hadn't the faintest idea what the girl had meant either but he wasn't going to admit it. Watt smiled and went on scanning the plain for the missing bit until the slab woman came charging out again, shouting at them to get a move on.

It took them so long to unload the rolls from the crate at the top of the spiral staircase to the crate at the bottom that the slab woman sent two girls to help them. Under cover of the din they found out from them what had happened. The yard had been broken into during the night. The intruders had wrecked the electricity generator and the cookhouse, and the entire consignment of newly sewn garments had been covered in glue. Six thousand garments were completely ruined. The wagons were coming that morning with supplies for the City and to take the monthly batch of clothing back to the Old Country. They were going to have to work non-stop to make up a replacement load. Meanwhile, the convoy's return was postponed to next morning.

'Who did it?' Brad shouted out of the corner of his mouth. The girl turned her back on the room and answered, 'Who knows?' Then she made the same figure of eight sign as the girl in the red skirt.

Watt and Brad exchanged bewildered looks. Brad realised his mistake too late: he'd given away that he hadn't a clue what the sign meant either. But Watt pretended not to notice. Brad could sulk for days if his dignity was dented. Besides, Brad had taken a huge risk for his sake. The slab woman had been ready to shoot him. Now here she was again, screaming at them from the bottom of the spiral stairs to get out of there. Watt was glad they could, unlike the poor girls.

'Sabotage!' Brad whispered as they crossed the quiet courtyard. 'That's what it's called, messing the clothes up like that. Sabotage.' Watt nodded. So that's what was making the Policy Makers so jumpy: sabotage. Someone was standing up to them.

The glue and the ruined clothes made him feel happy. He hadn't realised until then that he'd been particularly unhappy. He'd just thought that the flat, heavy way he felt every day was how everybody felt. But now his spirits were rising like crazy dough and he had an unfamiliar, gleeful sense of daring.

Brad gave him an impatient shake. 'What's got into you?' Watt hadn't realised that he was standing stock still by the god's Offering Table. Sabotage, Watt thought. That's what's got into me. Sabotage! Brad walked on, kicking the wicker crate to keep his mind off his smarting face. Watt let him get well ahead before he felt inside his Ghosty Boy jacket and found the roll that he'd nicked from the crate for his breakfast. Quick as a lizard after a fly, he put it down on the Offering Table. He sent a brief prayer to the god to look after the brave saboteurs and dared a glance up at the Topmost Tower. Nothing.

No reaction. In seconds he'd caught up with Brad.

He snatched off his Ghosty Boy hat and flipped Brad on the back with it. Brad laughed and flicked Watt back with his own hat and they made for the servants entrance, kicking the crate from one to the other.

When they got back to the Bakery there was none of the usual bustle or smell of baking bread. It was stone cold. The other Ghosty Boys were drooping in front of the Baker in a sleepy line. 'What's up?' Brad asked from the doorway. 'Sir,' he added quickly when the Baker turned a ferocious glare on him.

'We've got a blocked chimney, that's what's up,' the Baker rasped.

Brad let out a whistle through his teeth and Watt felt queasy in his stomach. A blockage meant that one of the boys would have to crawl up the chimney, find out where it was and unblock it. That wasn't simple. The chimney divided into different shafts and you could lose your way. Whichever shaft you chose was still hot from the night's baking and it could narrow down to the width of a fat loaf. It was easy for a boy to get stuck up there. But worst of all, the furnace had to be relit at three in the afternoon to heat the ovens for the night's bake. It was Policy. If a boy wasn't down again by three, he baked too.

The last time the chimney had blocked, the boy didn't make it back in time. Watt could remember him: a thin little boy with a walleye. Worly, they'd called him. Towards three, they had called up the chimney and thought they'd heard a whisper of an answer. They'd waited and waited and called again, but that time there was nothing.

Watt could remember the Baker's burning face as

he'd put a light to the kindling. His eyes had glittered with tears and he'd given each boy a tot of spirit to drink. They knew that soon they'd hear bits of the body slide down the chimney into the furnace and the Baker had made them sing as they kneaded the dough to drown out the sound.

'The lots are ready,' the Baker barked out. He held out the straws for each Ghosty Boy to draw. Some of them snatched quickly and others took forever, staring at the fan of straws in the Baker's floury hands as if they could divine the length if they stared hard enough. 'Long, long, long,' the Baker muttered after they'd chosen, and each child sagged with relief. There was a quick ripple of hysterical giggles when Sim and Som tried to choose the same straw and then they were back to 'Long, long, long,' until the Baker held out the two remaining straws to Watt and Brad. One of them had to be the short straw.

It was Brad who got it. Brad went sallow and grim looking, but he took the candle and matches that the Baker was giving him and the small pick on a leather loop to hang around his neck. Then he checked the timekeeper on the Bakery wall: ten past eleven.

Sim and Som started everyone clapping encouragingly, but it was a dismal sound and soon petered out. Brad took off his jacket. His body looked longer without it. He groped in the pocket and found a small roll. It was varnished tawny brown and made in the shape of a heart. He said to Watt in a thin sort of voice, 'Give her this.' Watt nodded.

Ordinarily, he would have smiled and found a way to ask which 'she' he was to give it to. To Red Skirt or to the Fire and Ice girl that Brad had mislaid? As it was, he took the heart and watched miserably while Brad pulled back the round furnace door and crouched to look inside. He was ridiculously tall. His shoulders were broad too. He didn't stand a chance of making it alive.

Watt ran and doused himself to the skin in cold water under the brass tap. Everyone watched this tactless distraction in surprise. He grabbed Brad's arm, thumped his own chest and pointed upwards to show that he should climb up instead. But Brad said, 'Don't be daft. I drew the short straw.' He shook Watt off, or tried to. But Watt wouldn't be shaken off. He pounded his chest again and pointed.

Brad said in the same thin voice. 'You're wasting time.' And the Baker rasped, 'Behave, Watt.'

But Watt held on. Brad shook him violently to get him off. He was stronger than Watt, who began to lose the contest. Then, for the first time in six years, that clear voice in Watt's head came and he knew precisely what to do: he knocked Brad out with a handy peel.

While everyone was still too stunned to stop him, he gathered up the candle, the matches and the pick. Next thing, he was a pair of kicking legs in the furnace porthole door – and was gone.

Sim called out, 'Thanks!' And Som added quietly, 'For the Lost-and-Found.' Then everyone ran to bring Brad round. But the Baker hit the table with his fist. He'd kept Watt safe for six years and now the boy had to go in for stupid heroics that would probably get him killed. He kicked the table leg. Perishing royalty!

Two Policy Maker guards strode into the Bakery.

'Where's the bald boy?' they demanded.

'Bald boy?' The Baker rubbed the toe of his shoe energetically.

'A bald Ghosty Boy,' the Policy Maker guard said.

81

'He was out in the courtyard just now. The Over Lord wants him.'

The Baker raised his eyes to the ceiling. The god works in unexpected ways. 'Hats Off!' he roared. Every Ghosty Boy whipped off his hat. Ponytails of assorted colours tumbled out of captivity. One of the Policy Maker guards stooped and pulled off Brad's hat where he was still unconscious on the floor. The finest ponytail of all was loosed.

The Baker spread his arms in a furious denial. 'There's none of these boys here is a baldy.'

CHAPTER SIX

The soles of Watt's wet shoes sputtered against the hot metal of the furnace floor. He could just about stand up in there. The skin on his face felt stiff where the heat had already dried it. He was glad of his hat. There was enough light coming through the porthole for him to see that he had to climb a few rungs at the back of the furnace into the chimney opening. The rungs were burning hot, so he took off his wet jacket and wrapped it round his hands to protect them as he climbed. At the top, he crawled into the chimney, which sloped back slightly and allowed him to crouch in the opening while he struggled back into his jacket.

Just ahead of him, the chimney turned and ran vertically into darkness. It was less hot now but the surface of the chimney was caked with black, tar-like stuff that had oozed out of the burning wood. It had a bitter smell that caught in his throat, and was slippery too. He would have to watch his step.

He crawled forward and stood up inside the chimney. It was pitch black. The dark, he told the fearful part of himself, is just "not-the-light" – that's all. Encouraged by this thought, he felt around the gooey surface and found that whoever had built the chimney seemed to have anticipated blockages and had provided well-spaced foot and handholds for climbing it.

At first the going was slow but fairly easy. It was just a matter of probing the tar with his fingers to find the holds. But after twenty minutes or so the chimney became much narrower. He could still stretch up and grope for the next niche, but there was hardly enough width to bend his knee sufficiently for his foot to find its hold. Then he thought of wedging his back against the wall and, still using the handholds, inching his way up by bracing his feet against the other side.

It was painfully slow, but he made progress. Soot and clinker spattered onto his head and mingled with the sweat running into his eyes. It stung, but he daren't spare a hand to wipe his face. He'd climbed a good thirty cubits by now, more than the height of a house. Better to press on with stinging eyes than to fall.

He wormed his way up and up. The chimney grew even narrower, and the unending dark began to feel as if it were alive, and against him. "You're lost," it insisted. "Climb down." He climbed up. Then the top of his head hit something solid. He braced himself more firmly against the side and, little by little, worked his feet upwards until he was hanging across the chimney like a baby in a cradle. He felt above him and his hands met hard, brittle stuff.

He scrabbled gently in his pocket, which was still wet from the sluicing he'd given himself, and brought out the candle and matches. The matches were damp, but after several anxious scrapes he got the candle lit. The flame burned low and blue but it gave enough light for him to tilt his head and see the black clinker blocking the entire chimney. He'd found it! He pocketed the matches, lowered his head and gently took the hand pick from round his neck. He gave the clinker block a tentative tap. Showers of crisp, black flakes pattered down onto his upturned face and into his eyes. Some settled in the crook of his body, but a lot more went rattling down the chimney. He picked at the clinker until he'd hacked away as much as he could reach. Then he put out the candle, stashed it away in his pocket and hung the pick round his neck. This freed his hands to ease himself up a little further until he could get at the blockage again.

He did this time and again. The muscles in his legs were screaming to be allowed to straighten, but he knew if he gave way to them he'd drop like lead to the bottom. What he *could* do was to rub his eyes, which felt as though they'd been soused in vinegar; but it only made them worse.

At last he saw a small blue disc far above him. It was daylight at the top of the chimney. He'd broken through. The chimney was clear. Almost without consulting himself, he began to climb towards the light.

He would have reached the top if the pick round his neck hadn't jabbed him in the chest. It made him jump. His hand swept the chimney surface and loosed a deluge of soot on his head. He breathed in a lungful and began to cough. He stopped concentrating on his feet. They slipped and he was falling. His back was grazed raw against the stones but he hardly felt it. His hands and feet scraped the sides of the chimney, frantic to get a hold.

His fingers found a loop of chain in the stonework and fastened onto it. It held. The sudden weight of his falling body on his arm nearly tore it out of its socket, but he hung on until his flailing feet could find a toe hole. There was a crash and the chain slipped downwards out of his hand. With a screech of metal, a shutter in the side of the chimney opened up. He just managed to hook his elbow over its metal edge and pitch forward into the hole.

He fell face down on a human skull. He discovered what it was when he'd recovered enough to light the candle. Panting and scared, he stared at the skull. He'd never seen one before. The candle flame picked out a few bones lying underneath it. Watt stood up. He was all for leaving, but he could see much further now the candle was raised. He was standing on a filthy, stone stairway. Memory rushed him like an ambush. He was on the service stairs where he'd last been on his seventh birthday, trying to escape.

I could do it this time, he thought excitedly. Then a deadening question came to him. What could he escape to? That's what had been missing from the landscape he'd looked at this morning. There used to be farmhouses on the plain and houses and warehouses round the harbour. Now there was nothing but dust. The people out there that Saan had said would help him had vanished.

He slumped down beside the bones and pressed his hand into his eyes. In the brief moment when he'd thought it was possible, he'd allowed himself to admit at last that he had an overpowering longing to be free. Ghosty Boys of thirteen didn't cry with disappointment, but he could hear sobbing.

He lifted his head and listened. Something *was* sobbing. There was something further down the steps making a noise that made his scalp bristle. It must be the crooked, dark shape that had come after him when he was little. That's why there were human bones. It ate people. He daren't move.

The sobbing stopped. There was silence followed by a juicy sniff. Somehow a man-eater that needed a handkerchief seemed less frightening. Watt decided to investigate and started down the staircase. Whatever it was heard him coming and began scuffling about in a panicky sort of way. Watt's confidence increased. He descended quietly in his soft Ghosty Boy's shoes, twisting and turning with the staircase.

He rounded a corner and a bony limb shot out and tripped him. He sprawled head first down the steps and his candle went out. Something jumped heavily on his back and began banging his head on the edge of a step.

The fight was awful. Whatever it was was trying to push out his eyes with its thumbs. Gasping and grunting, they fought like blind moles. Somehow Watt managed to get to his knees and grip the wrists of the probing thumbs. He pushed his assailant back against the wall and received a kick in the stomach. He doubled over with pain and a hand chopped down on the back of his neck. He punched back hard and met flesh. He found an arm and twisted. 'I give up,' a treble voice said at once. He let go. 'For the moment,' the voice added and lit a candle. It was a girl.

She was wild and frightening looking and breathless from the fight. Her hair grew madly out of her head and was henna red. Her blue eyes stared at him angrily out of a brown face. 'You stupid, filthy, lousy boy,' she said. 'Where did you come from?'

He'd got himself involved with a lunatic, a mad girl who haunted these stairs; he must get himself uninvolved, fast. He grinned his special inane grin and pointed upwards. The lunatic girl tore her fingers through her mass of hair and spat back at him. 'What?

What? You mean you're a god?'

Something about her sent his brain scurrying into corners to unearth a piece of information. 'Speak up,' she said and Watt gestured at his mouth. 'Toothache?' the girl ventured. 'Gods don't get toothache, do they?' Watt pointed to his mouth again. Surely she'd understand he was dumb. But the girl grabbed his hand and said. 'Speak. Go on, silly.'

And Watt did; for the first time in six years he spoke to someone who wasn't the Baker. His voice came out faint and husky. 'Melior!' he said.

The girl let go of him and sprang back as if he'd tried to stab her. 'You're a Policy Maker!' she shouted. Watt shook his head, bewildered. 'You talk like one,' she shouted again. Watt was taken aback. He tried her name again, 'Melior', and she shouted, 'Don't call me that. How dare you call me that?'

'Because that is your name.' He spoke slowly and emphatically. It was lovely. 'You're my sister.'

She slapped his face. 'Where the hell have you been all this time?'

He rubbed his cheek ruefully. 'Aren't you at all pleased to see me?'

Just as usual, as if they'd never been apart, Melior took charge. She led him down the service stairs by the light of her candle until they must have walked round half the castle. Then she made him crouch down and hustled him along a short, low tunnel. They had to stoop to get through it. It brought them into a windowless room, empty except for a block of three stone steps in its centre which stopped short at Watt's chest level and went nowhere. He'd barely time to take this before she turned on him. 'Now,' she said. 'What's your name?'

He was confused. She *knew* his name. But she was waiting for an answer. 'People call me Watt,' he said. He could hear it now – the Policy Maker accent. Where on earth had he picked it up? It must be what the Baker meant when he called his voice posh. He smiled at her. 'But you can call me by my real name.'

His sister didn't smile back. 'Sit down,' she commanded. He obeyed eagerly, sitting cross-legged on the floor. He had so many things he wanted to say to her. Melior planted herself above him on the first of the stone steps – and he stood up again. He didn't want to believe what he was seeing: the dirty garment she was wearing was a Policy Maker's uniform. Had his sister joined the enemy?

'Why are you dressed like that?' he asked tensely. 'Whose side are you on?'

'I'll ask the questions,' she said. 'Sit down.' But he wouldn't. If Melior were a Split, she would hand him over to the Policy Makers to be executed, and there was only one way of stopping her. He'd have to kill her. The thought was like a punch in the stomach. He'd been mourning his sister's death for the last six years; within minutes of finding her alive, he was going to have to kill her. And anyway, *could* he kill her?

They were staring intently at each other. She seemed to be making some sort of calculation. Suddenly, she tore open the front of the Policy Maker uniform. Underneath she was wearing a tatty, torn vest. 'Does this look like a Policy Maker's vest?' she asked. 'A Policy Maker's? With their satins and silks? A PM wouldn't be seen dead in this vest. This is an Inmate's vest.' She was undoing more of the uniform. The god! Watt thought, don't let her show me more. 'Or Policy Maker knickers?' she asked.

'I believe you,' he said hastily and sat down again very quickly.

Melior re-fastened the uniform. She didn't explain why she was wearing it, though. Instead, she gave him a grilling, rapping question after question about their family.

It was bewildering until he realised she was checking that he really was her brother. Why was she having second thoughts? She hadn't actually admitted that she was Melior either. Why? She was much less trusting than the eight year old Melior he remembered. Maybe his accent made her think that *he* was a Split. In which case, she would do the killing. Watt shifted his position surreptitiously so he was ready if she tried anything.

'Have I changed so much,' he asked, 'that you really don't recognise me? And if you do, why don't you trust me?' Melior gave him an ironical look. He understood exactly what she meant: trust was not something you should ever count on in their family. She hammered more questions at him.

'What is the history of the City?'

Watt racked his brains. If she'd asked him for a nice nut-bread recipe he might have obliged. But history! He thought hard, and a tranquil memory of his past life came to him: a man with a wide smile. Had he been his teacher? There was a blurred memory of other children and of squeaky slate writing boards. He began uncertainly, 'Once we were slaves...'

'When?'

'Um...' he floundered.

'Oh, go on, go on, go on,' she said impatiently.

'We were slaves. We escaped. We ran far away. We

90

built the City years and years ago to protect ourselves...'
He paused and met her eye. 'We didn't do a good enough
job, did we?'

Melior looked down and picked at her candle's wax
base with her thumbnail. Her face was darkened with
shadows from the candlelight. She looked so sad he
wished he could say something to cheer her up. 'Do you
remember,' he asked, 'how you took my toy elephant?'
She looked up at once. 'It was *my* elephant.'

'It wasn't.' He felt pure rage.

'It was.'

'It wasn't.' He got to his feet. 'You always took my
things,' he said hotly.

'And you always copied everything I did,' she snarled
back at him. 'You tagged after me wherever I went.'

'Well I flipping wouldn't now,' Watt retorted. 'Not if
I was flipping paid to! And if you say I tagged after you
then you flipping well *do* know I'm your brother.'

Melior smiled. 'You sound like a kitchen boy now.'

He hated her. 'I'm a Ghosty Boy,' he said stiffly. 'I'm
going. Back to my friends.'

'Don't go,' she said and blew out the candle.

Little dots of gold danced on the floor and over Melior
where she was crouching on the steps. It was as if his
sister were sitting in a shower of gold. It looked magical.

'What is it?' he asked softly. Melior held her hands
cupped together and the gold flickered over her brown
skin.

'Sunlight,' she answered.

Watt looked up at the ceiling in surprise. The dancing
dots were shafts of light slanting through minute holes
in the ceiling. 'From the god,' Melior said. 'We're sitting
under the Offering Table in the courtyard.'

'Melior,' he asked, 'how long have you been here? What happened to you after the Attack? And where did you learn to fight like that?'

'At the orphanage,' she said.

CHAPTER SEVEN

'The Mothers – well, they were our keepers really, but they made us call them Mother – the Mothers used to pick on two orphans and make them fight.' Melior let the dancing light run through her fingers. 'They all sat round and watched it – the fight – and they'd lay bets on who would win. At first we kids fixed it so no one got hurt; but then some Split told. After that the Mothers locked the loser in the punishment cupboard. Everyone fought to win then because the cupboard was terrible. No one came near you for twenty-four hours; it was black as night, no room to sit down, no food, no water. At first the smell of disinfectant, then the stink of your own mess – they always made you clean up your mess when you came out. The worst was when they forced the little ones to fight, really tiny ones, like my brother.'

'Are you saying that our brother was there too...?'

'He was four. He lost.'

'The god!' It was all Watt could say; he was so sickened and sorry for them.

'When I heard him in there, crying all night, I thought of mother saying to me, "Avenge this, if you can, Melior," and I swore I would.'

'When did she say that?' Watt was surprised by the way Melior talked about their mother without any shame for her treachery.

'During the Attack.' Melior twisted her hands round and round in the little dots of gold. 'You remember how father and Uncle Haakron went to fight? Well, mother ran with the baby and me into the Throne Room and dragged the great Sword of State down from the wall behind the throne. We thought you'd come with us but you hadn't. We ran back into the Ante-room, but you'd gone. She screamed out of the door, screamed your name but you never came, and we ran to the Inner Court. She made me hold her skirt so she didn't lose me. Mother opened the Way. She was half crying. She told me to stand there and she gave me the baby to carry. "This is treachery, Melior," she said, "and don't ever forget it". She kissed the baby and me and said, "Avenge it, if you can, Melior". Then she turned off the fountain, so she could hear anyone coming, and waited by the door. She kept whispering, "He'll come. I know he will. He's been told."'

'Who did she mean?' Melior looked at him strangely. He felt there was a hint of some secret there. Had his mother had a partner in her treachery? Melior said at last, 'She meant you, I suppose. You did know about the Way, did you?'

'Yes. My bodyguard, Saan, told me.'

'Of course. Saan. He always looked after you. Remember when you were so ill they thought you were going to die?' But Watt couldn't remember. 'Saan was the only person who could get you to take the medicine,' she reminded him.

Memory surfaced. The poison had gathered in painful black swellings at the base of his fingers. He remembered the disgusting medicine too. 'It was a cup of a sort of gravy,' he told her. 'Four times a day. Every time I finished a dose, Saan gave me a reward.'

'Of course.' Melior threw him a twisted little smile. 'Saan would do anything for his Baby King.' Watt felt a twinge of warning. His sister was jealous of him – or of his kingship.

He didn't want another quarrel. 'True. He gave his life for me.' She didn't answer. 'Melior,' he emphasised, 'I'm a Ghosty Boy. Khul has no king.' It had a surprising effect. Melior leant down and put her hand on his head – he nearly ducked. 'I'll see you crowned if it kills me!' she said.

His sister had such see-saw responses to things; it left him feeling a step behind. One minute she was jealous of the king, the next ready to die for the king. She was like two opposing people crammed into one body. It must be what she'd been through that had made her like that. But was either of them the real Melior?

She said too brightly, like someone not quite telling the truth, 'I'm sure mother was waiting for you and for Lal too.'

Watt asked, with more hope than he'd imagined possible, about their eldest sister. 'Do you suppose Lal is alive, like the rest of us?' Melior shook her head. 'I've looked everywhere in the City where I'm allowed to go. Lots of it is out of bounds to Inmates. So...'

He didn't let her finish. He didn't want to believe Lal was dead, not now that he and Melior were so alive. His big sister had been his gentle favourite. He said, 'Wasn't she cross when we went into her room and discovered the secret drawer in her desk!'

Melior nodded. 'Poor Lal. She was so much older than us. We must have got on her nerves. Such a fuss, though!'

'She didn't keep it up,' he said. 'In the end, she and I used to send messages to each other in it. Like a secret letter box.'

'I never knew that.' Melior looked annoyed. There was no knowing when you were going to upset her. But he rushed headlong into the question he'd been avoiding. 'Melior, what did mother do? How did she betray the City?'

'I can only tell you what I saw that day in the Inner Court. I was standing by the Open Way with the baby. Mother was waiting by the door. Four enemy soldiers suddenly smashed through it. Mother shouted, "Go, Melior. Run!" and she went for them with the sword. I didn't know she could. I was rooted to the floor, I was so terrified.

'One of them started towards me but mother put the sword right through his neck. I saw the blood arc out of him and I saw him fall. The other soldiers gave a horrible, savage shout and threw themselves at her with their kukris. She screamed at me again, "Run! Run, my darling". She was fighting and stabbing and slashing. Then there was a shot.

'I ran down the secret Inner Way, down a steep rocky passage. The baby was so heavy that my arms hurt. When I was sure no one was following us, I walked. There were wall lights so I could go fast, but after a while they blacked out. The enemy must have hit the main generator.

'Then the ground became wet and muddy and suddenly I was out by the river, wading through the reed beds. We were soaked to the skin. There was a little hut on the end of a jetty, and we stayed there. I watched the battle in the City above.

'The guns never let up all day, nor the bodies toppling over the battlements. Thousands died. Towards evening it went quiet, and father's standard was hoisted on the Topmost Tower. I stood on the jetty and tried to cheer but it was more like crying. The baby was crying too for food. Then these two reed cutters, Triss and her husband, came by in their punt. They took us on board and we went down river to their place. They fed us. I was going to go straight back to the City but I fell asleep.

'When I woke up, the room was full of riverside farmers saying it was all a lie. The City had really fallen to the enemy. Most of them were leaving that night. They said the enemy was butchering the children.'

Watt said, 'Looking for us? The god! They loathe us.'

'There and then Triss dyed my hair red. She said blonde hair was unlucky and I was to keep mine dyed, whatever happened, which was hard to do in the orphanage.'

'Who put you in the orphanage?'

'The Policy Makers. They left us alone for a year. Then they torched the farms and warehouses where all the tapestries were stored. They sent the men away. We never saw Triss's husband again. They dammed the river upstream of the City and took all our water. Triss said that's why they'd conquered us, so that they could take our water supply.'

'The Baker wouldn't agree. He thinks they're searching for something.'

She gave him a guarded look. 'Mother did say one other thing before…before the soldiers came in. She said, "How could they do this to us after we gave them the yellow magic?"'

'What's yellow magic?'

'You tell me.'

Watt said thoughtfully, 'Fluffy white and green and gold. Yellow magic in a mould.' Melior looked at him as if he was on parole from the nearest madhouse. She said almost kindly, 'Who'd invade a City for a nonsense rhyme?' And Watt felt as daft as he'd ever felt. 'Did Triss say anything more about the Attack?' he asked, to get away from the feeling.

'She said the Policy Makers invented a story about us. It was all Mumbo Jumbo, she said, to give them an excuse for breaking our treaty and attacking us.'

Mumbo Jumbo was a new one on Watt. He was glad when his sister added, 'Superstitious rubbish.'

He was going to ask her more, but Melior wanted to get on with her own story. She said angrily, 'Where was I? Oh yes, with the river dammed, the crops failed and then the reed beds dried out. Without the reeds, Triss was destitute. We were starving. The Policy Makers came. Triss just had time to give me the henna before they lifted us into a cart and took us to that big house where the City Dye Makers used to meet.'

'They'd turned it into an orphanage?'

She looked at him witheringly. 'Well, obviously.'

Watt murmured an apology. Melior could certainly put you down.

'We stayed there for three years,' she said. 'They taught us to sing the Old Country national anthem and how to use a sewing machine. They let me henna my hair because I told the matron I had a scaly, contagious disease of the scalp and henna was the only thing that kept it away. She didn't want all the orphans to go scaly so they let me carry on.' Watt smiled a little but Melior didn't.

'Then, when I was twelve, they put me out.'

Watt crouched in front of her.

'What about...our little brother?'

'They made me leave him. He was crying and hanging on to me. Thank the god he'd never grasped who we really were; I think he would have given us away, he was so terrified of being left alone. They sent me to work for a Policy Maker officer round the other side of the City. Army people. They had two horses; very posh.'

'So do you,' Watt butted in.

'So do I what?'

Watt half smiled, apologetically. 'Talk like a Policy Maker, sometimes. It comes and goes.'

Melior looked thoughtful. 'Maybe it rubbed off on me.'

There was an uncertain pause between them while they considered that possibility. Then Melior shoved her hand through her hair and dismissed the whole problem.

'Anyway, they worked me like a dog and I wasn't allowed out. Sometimes, though, the wife would dress me up as a lady's maid and we'd ride round the City in her carriage. I'd look for a way of escape, but there isn't one. The place is alive with guards, and at night they lock the City gates. Then one day I was sent up to the Sew House with a message for the Supervisor.'

'Old Maroon Legs, you mean?' Watt asked.

'Yes, her.' Melior almost smiled, but then she went on angrily. 'It was unrecognisable. All our beautiful tapestry looms ripped out, and those poor girls machining uniforms.'

'Is that what they are? Uniforms?'

Melior nodded. 'The Policy Makers love uniforms.

They have one for practically every occasion and for each official. Then I saw Triss sitting there, sewing. She was so ill looking, I hardly knew her. I told my boss I wanted a job there. The Policy Makers were having another war somewhere to the east and I said I wanted to help with the war effort by making uniforms.

'Whatever for?' Watt asked. 'It's flipping torture, not a job.'

'To be with Triss, and for a bit more freedom,' she replied. 'We shared a room in the machinists' hostel. We were even allowed into the main square between shifts. Triss told me much more than ever I knew about the City, and its history, and how things used to be in father's time. It was wonderful in those days. We were all so safe and well.

She was silent now. He was just wondering whether it would be wise to ask what happened next when his sister slapped the side of the step she was sitting on and swore. The sound made Watt jump.

'And then a Policy Maker put in for me,'

'What do you mean?'

She sighed. 'Where have you been, Watt? They have to put in for special permission to marry an Inmate.' She scowled and went on. 'They're supposed to obtain the Inmate's agreement, but they don't. You might as well spit in the river for all the notice they take of what we say.'

She moved out of the dancing light into the darkness. 'I'm fourteen; I'm too young to be married,' she said fiercely. 'Aren't I?' Watt nodded vigorously. In truth, he was wondering how anyone could be mad enough to want to marry his sister.

She said disdainfully, 'And I would *never* marry a

Policy Maker: especially a *clerk*.' Evidently, despite everything, Melior had still kept a grip on her rank. He wondered what had happened to his own grip.

'I kept putting him off,' Melior went on, 'but then some idiot boy started pestering me.'

'Who was he?'

'An Inmate. Brod I think his name is. No, Brad.' Melior pushed back her wild hair. 'A real idiot.'

'No he's not.' Watt found Brad's heart-shaped roll in his pocket. 'He made this for you. He's a Ghosty Boy.' She didn't take it when he offered it. She said, 'Why don't they all just leave me alone?' It would be tactless to say he didn't know why either. It didn't stop him thinking it, though, and he put the little heart back in his pocket. He was offended for Brad. Surprisingly, Melior noticed.

'You see, Watt, the clerk got wind of your friend Brad and flew into a jealous temper. He decided we'd get hitched that night. He said if I didn't marry him, he'd apply for an E.O.'

Watt was out of his depth again. What was an E.O.? He was blowed if he was going to ask and get put down for it? But how was he supposed to react? A whistle might do. A whistle could express all sorts of things: horror, relief... But he'd never tried whistling before and nothing came out but a slightly wet puff. She looked at him suspiciously. So he swore. He was rewarded with a nod of agreement from his sister. 'Too right. Once the Roc's signed that Enforcement Order, I'd be married, like it or not.'

She clawed her hair with both hands. 'He arranged we'd leave for our honeymoon on the convoy that takes the garments back to the Old Country. I was desperate.

Imagine being married for the rest of your life to a man you can't bear near you. I *had* to get out.

'It was the end of my final shift. The supervisor stayed behind as usual to check the totals.'

Watt asked, 'This was last night, was it?'

She nodded. 'We girls were lined up ready to leave and quite suddenly... I remembered mother with the sword.' Melior said it so softly Watt almost missed hearing it. 'I think those soldiers killed her. Whatever people think about her, it was brave of her to die for her children.' When Watt didn't reply, she finished in a rush and seemed embarrassed that she'd defended their mother. 'Anyway, an idea came to me in a flash.

'I asked Triss to fall over and make a scene about being hurt; and over she went! No questions asked. The guard got her up. All the other girls were crowding round them to see if they could help, so no one noticed me slip back into the Sew House – except Triss. I was so sad not to say goodbye.

'The Supervisor was leaning over the cutting table, totting up the totals of the garments we'd made that day. I thought – even if I have to kill her, I'm getting out of here.'

'And did you?'

'What?'

'Kill her?'

'No. I brained her with the pinking shears. While she was out for the count, I got her uniform off. I tied her up, gagged her, shoved her in a wicker crate, wheeled her into the latrine, and shut the door on her. Then I put on her clothes over my own.'

'It wasn't old Maroon Legs, then' said Watt. 'You'd drown in her uniform.' Melior smiled. 'There's a thinner one,' she explained. 'I went and called to the guard, "The totals don't tally. I'll have to re-check". I'd no idea if I was making sense. "You go on home," I said, "I'll lock up." And he waved his rifle and went.'

'Phew!' said Watt. 'And then?'

'I locked the compound gates, switched off the arc lamps and trashed the place. I wanted it to look like sabotage, you see, not an escape. That would buy me more time before they came after me.'

'So you tipped a sack of flour over the compound, mixed it with a barrel of water and pitched all the uniforms into it.'

'Yes.' Melior was plainly irritated that he already knew the best part of her story, and she wasted no time in regaining the limelight.

'I bolted the Sew House door from the inside and left by the staff door. Then I had to cross the castle courtyard. It's six years since I've been there, but I was doing all right until the guards on the gatehouse saw me and called out to come on over. "Your late night tot's waiting for you," they said. Obviously the stupid woman drank with them after work.

'I blurted out, "Not tonight, boys. Problems with the generator. Got to report it," and I rushed into the castle through the servants' entrance. But I'd forgotten my way about. I couldn't ask for directions. I'd have roused people's suspicions – a lost Policy Maker.

'The first door I dared open, I found myself on a platform facing rows of men and women in full evening dress, perched on gilt chairs. There were candelabra and jewellery twinkling enough to blind you, and a strong smell of lavender.

'A few people started clapping when I showed up;

103

others laughed. A man sitting at a grand piano hissed "Get off, you clodhopper". I was backing out when a big woman, wearing a golden gown and long gold gloves up to her biceps, sailed in behind me. Then all the people clapped. The big woman said to me out of the corner of her mouth, "Clear off, Dusty." The Pianist crashed in with a chord and she began to sing. I sort of trickled back the way I had come, and ran.'

'Did you go to the Inner Court?'

'No. I'd heard they'd booby-trapped the Way. I was looking for the Ante-room, but before I found it I came upon some really creepy looking people sitting round a candle. I left in a hurry.' Watt didn't say he'd been there. His sister didn't care for people to steal her thunder. Nor did he ask her any more about their mother. He wasn't sure where Melior stood when it came to the traitor queen.

'It was dark in the Ante-room when I found it, but I dared to switch on one light. I didn't want to waste my candle.'

'Where did you get that from?'

'I'd walked in on some messenger kids, sitting on a bench in a little room. I ordered them to give me one, and some matches too. They were so scared of me. It was horrible. Anyway, even with the light on it took some finding.'

'An entrance to the service stairs?'

'Yes. Saan had shown it to me once. Could I find it! There were floury handprints all over the wall by the time I did. My uniform was covered in the stuff. I wiped my hands on it to get them as floury as possible and made handprints all over the floor and on the other walls too, so the Policy Makers wouldn't realise I'd been looking for something. Then in I went. One big step into freedom,' she added in a tight sort of voice.

Watt shook his head in admiration. His sister had guts. He'd only dreamed of leaving the City – she was actually going! He waited for her to go on, but she didn't.

'So?' he prompted her. 'Why are you still here?'

'Because,' she said bitterly, 'there's no way out.'

Watt remembered the skull. 'No way out of the City from here?' he ventured.

'That's right,' she said. 'No flaming exit.' Melior knelt on the floor. 'I was sure Saan said there was.' She began to cry miserably.

Watt was appalled. He wasn't used to crying. Some of the little Ghosty Boys cried when they were first apprenticed and shut up in the castle. You just gave them a friendly bash and a honey bun and, in the end, they stopped. Somehow he didn't think a bash would go down well with Melior, however friendly.

He got up and approached her as cautiously as a tamer would a lion. 'Don't,' he said as gently as he could. 'Don't cry, Melior.' But it made her cry even harder. Would she stop, he wondered, if he said the reverse: do cry Melior. He decided not to try it. This was no time for experimenting.

What would the Baker do? Put his fiery face close to Melior's and roar, "Drip tears in my dough, boy, and you'll really get to snivel!" But then Melior was not a boy; she was this problematical thing: a girl. He put his arm round her shoulders. She didn't bite, so he said encouragingly, 'We'll think of something.' The effect was dramatic. She smiled up at him tearfully and said, 'Will you? Oh will you, Watt?'

That put him on the spot. He'd help her willingly.

But the last thing he'd intended was to mastermind his sister's break-out from the City across miles of flat plain under the gaze of a garrison of soldiers and the Over Lord in the Topmost Tower. With one question – Will you, Watt? – Melior had twisted things around so that he had become entirely responsible for her.

He was sorry for her, but that was no reason to lay his head on the block along with his impossibly difficult sister's. This was her adventure that had gone wrong, not his. He heard himself say, 'Of course I will'.

He relit the candle to give himself time to think and to get over the fright of what he'd just done. He had committed himself. Then he said briskly, 'You'll have to cross the plain by night so you're not seen.' Melior smiled at him gratefully. He thought, Well, that's the easy bit worked out. Now how do we get her out of here, let alone the City?

'I'll wait here,' Melior said, 'while you make your plans.' So now she wasn't even going to help him make the flipping plan! 'There's enough for me to eat,' she said. Watt was surprised. 'Look.' Melior climbed to the top of the "going nowhere" steps in the middle of the room and pulled open a hinged, iron panel in the ceiling. An ancient rope ladder tumbled down from inside it and Melior went up it and disappeared into the gap in the ceiling. After a second, her face reappeared in the gap. 'Catch,' she commanded, and threw a bread roll down on his head.

She laughed down at his astonished face. 'Offerings,' she explained, 'from the god Offering Table. I've already eaten all the fruit.' Which explained the neat pile of cores and peach stones he'd noticed by the entrance. Watt picked up the bread roll and turned it over in his fingers. 'I think I put this roll there this morning,' he told her.

Melior wrinkled her nose. 'Can you smell smoke?'

Smoke! Watt ran. He shuffled along the short tunnel, doubled over like a hairpin, shielding the candle with his hand. Out on the service stairs it lit up wisps of smoke wafting towards him.

He ran back the way they'd come as fast as his candle's cringing flame and the shifting shadows allowed him. His feet kicked up years of thick dust lying on each tread of the stairs. It mingled with the smoke, which was getting thicker as he climbed.

Now he could see the small skeleton. The smoke was pouring out of the opening to the chimney, careering up the stairway and drifting back towards him. They'd lit the furnace down in the Bakery. It must be three o' clock already.

They would both suffocate if he didn't close up the hole. He tried to pull up the shutter with his one free hand while the other held the candle. He was coughing and hacking in the billowing smoke. It had opened so easily coming the other way; now it was immovable. Then Melior pushed in beside him and he shouted at her to help him. Together, they heaved at it and with a grate of metal on stone, the shutter closed and cut the smoke off.

'Well, here's a turn up!' Watt choked. 'Now I can't get out either.'

Melior rubbed her streaming eyes and listened while Watt coughed out an explanation about the lighting of the furnace. He picked up the skull. 'I reckon he found this shutter, same as I did. It's a cleaning access, I guess.' He ran his forefinger lightly over the dome of the skull's small cranium. 'And then he got caught like this too, and couldn't climb down again.'

Melior looked subdued. 'I wonder who he is – was,' she corrected herself. Watt smoothed out the sooty Ghosty Boy's hat lying amongst the bones on the steps and laid the skull on it. 'I think he was probably a kid called Worly.'

They looked at each other. Each of them was thinking the same thing: how long before I look like that?

CHAPTER EIGHT

The Roc blinked. A bread roll lying on the God Offering Table had just disappeared into thin air before his very eyes! Thunderstruck, he stared at the empty space where the roll had been. Did the Inmate chappies round here go in for voodoo? Well, if this vanishing roll was a Mumbo Jumbo trick intended to unsettle him, the culprit was going to pay heavily. The Roc was already in a bad enough temper to hang a hundred of them. The City Elders had not only served him a disgusting lunch; they'd pulled a fast one on him, too. No one did that and got off lightly. He glared at the Offering Table. Then he noticed the rising sun emblem of his own god there. That put quite a different complexion on the matter.

He sat in his open carriage and pondered, while servants placed his strip of carpet for him to alight. Was the roll a sign sent to him from the god of the Rising Sun? If it was, he was dashed if he could follow the god's drift. Might a vanishing roll be a warning, such as "*Here Today, Gone Tomorrow,*" for example? The Roc winced. The idea of his death was unthinkable. He could accept other people's without turning a hair. But *him*, die? No fear!

His Equerry opened the carriage door for him and the Roc marched up the strip of carpet. He stopped short in the castle doorway. Could he hear children singing? A heavenly choir of cherubs? Was it another hint from the god of the Sun? 'What's that?' he asked the captain of his military guard.

'Just the Ghosty Boys, sir,' the man replied, 'about their work.'

'*Ghosty* Boys?' The Roc didn't like the sound of that one bit.

'I'll get it stopped, shall I, sir?'

'At once,' the Roc replied and marched into the castle for tea.

His First Minister, immaculate in his frock coat, was waiting for him in the entrance hall. His First Minister was an excellent man but, in the Roc's private opinion, "a bit of a dandy": his purple striped cravat and large ruby tiepin were jolly nearly flashy!

'How was your day, sir?' the First Minister asked, happily unaware of the effect his get-up was having on the head of the Empire.

'Pretty average torment. I toured the water system. And yours?'

'About as entertaining as yours, I imagine, sir. We watched fifty sheep being sheared. The ugly young chap giving the demonstration was quite cut up that I wasn't you, though. He particularly wished you to be present.'

'Very flattering.'

'Mmm. My wife, Lady Joy, lost her hat to the wind.'

'A noble sacrifice,' the Roc said heavily.'

The First Minister bowed and escorted the Roc to the Ante Room where he was scheduled to take tea with the thirty wives of his councillors and some female City Elders. To the Roc's irritation the room had been sealed off by his Spy Master and the tea relocated to the

Banqueting Hall. He turned on his heel and ran slap into his daughter.

Fidelis curtsied. 'How was your day, Papa? Minister?'

'Dire,' they chorused, and they all laughed.

Fidelis's day had been as dire as the Roc's. It had started off quite well. Her father had looked in to say good morning, dressed in full military rig ready for his Imperial tour of the City, and greeted her perfectly normally: there were no Boo-Boo surprises. He'd kissed his daughter and then examined her breakfast tray. 'I'd steer clear of the white stuff,' he advised.

'It's called yoghurt, Papa.' Fidelis only knew because she'd asked the chambermaid who had brought up the breakfast trays. 'It comes from a sheep.'

'And it can jolly well go straight back if you ask me. Perfectly beastly on toast. Enjoy your sightseeing.' And he was gone. From then on the day went downhill.

Prudence took forever to get her ready. Fidelis could hardly stand still for excitement by the time Prudence was tying the bow of her bonnet under her chin. They were on the point of leaving when word came back through the Roc's Equerry that their sight-seeing trip was cancelled. After a whispered conversation with Prudence at the door, the Equerry left. Prudence pursed her lips and locked the bedroom door. 'It looks like rain,' she explained.

Fidelis glanced out of the French window at the glorious weather and back at Prudence, who shrugged. In fact, the Equerry had reported the Roc as saying that driving through the City and lines of Inmates silently waving flags was like cantering through a morgue, and could turn deuced nasty. His daughter was to stay put.

'Is Papa in danger, Prudence?'

Prudence said of course he wasn't and helped her out of her cape and bonnet. Why couldn't she go out then? She'd been longing to. Well, if she couldn't see the City, she'd explore the castle. But that was forbidden too. Prudence recited a long list of things the Roc's daughter could not do alone. Exploring castles scored high. Peeing seemed to be the only thing that was allowed, Fidelis thought dismally.

'We'll just have to do our embroidery instead,' Prudence said with a sad sniff. But Fidelis wasn't fooled. She could tell by the glint of revenge in her eye that Prudence was getting her own back for the lie about the locket. Prudence loved embroidery and she knew very well that Fidelis didn't. Every stitch was an agonised, stab-in-the-dark of guesswork: would it be right or wrong? Today it was usually wrong and Prudence (just as vengefully) snipped it away with her little silver scissors, assuring Fidelis that a true lady always embroidered perfectly.

Fidelis dabbed at the blood pricks on her work and longed for the day when she turned into a lady. She could tell it was fun, too, when it happened – the councillors' wives never stopped laughing, so it must be. But for Fidelis, turning into a lady was like trying to fit into a dress designed for someone else: bits of her had to be cut away entirely. In other places she needed patches.

Fidelis sat up straight (as a lady should) and re-threaded her needle. She was working on a portrait of Span for her mother's birthday. One birthday had already gone by and the prospect of the portrait being finished by the next was fading. She'd done most of his body and one leg but his tufted toes were miserably difficult. He was hardly an appealing sitter either, she thought, pushing her chair out of his range.

The morning crept on. The pigeons cooed longingly from their basket and, time and again, Prudence unpicked Fidelis's stitches. Eventually lunch was brought up by the Butler and a small, round-faced Messenger Boy who stared curiously at Fidelis's work. Fidelis smiled.

'What do you think?' she asked. 'Anything like?'

'Oh yes, ma'am,' the little boy said appreciatively, ''Tis a fine jam roly-poly yous sewed.'

The Butler looked aghast, Prudence looked outraged, and Fidelis knew she was expected to have the boy whipped for insolence. But he was such a cheerful little boy and, now she came to look at it, the picture looked much more like a jam roly-poly than any dog.

'I'm glad you like it,' she said. 'I'm particularly fond of jam roly-poly. Are you?' The Butler smiled and Prudence did the opposite and the Messenger Boy said seriously, 'I eats every crumb, ma'am.' Fidelis laughed and gave the little boy an Old Country coin. His awed gasp showed it was a valuable tip and he told her proudly that he'd nearly saved enough to buy the materials to make a kite. So she gave him another one. Prudence looked ready to pass out with disapproval, but kept her down-turned mouth tight shut in front of these inferior servants.

The afternoon went by exactly like the morning, except that Span went to sleep. But Span was no slacker: even in his sleep he could exude. At last, the hours crawled to teatime. Ordinarily Fidelis would have felt shy about going to a grand tea party; today she couldn't wait to get away from the embroidery.

She was dressed in the pale blue voile her mother had had made for her. Prudence had chosen a blue velvet ribbon for her hair, and had even given a grudging "Hmm" of approval when she'd tied it, so Fidelis thought she must look more or less all right. But when the First Minister had gone ahead of them to the banquet hall, her father said, like a slap in the face, 'Don't wear blue, sweetheart. Blue's their colour.'

Fidelis hurried away to change, feeling ashamed without understanding why. She wasn't to know it was one of the City Elders at the lunch who had infuriated her father. Instead of reading out the speech of welcome that the Roc's Equerry had prepared for him, the old man had substituted his own speech and asked permission for the City Dyers to make the blue pastel dye again that the City was once famous for. It had made the Roc look foolish and set him against blue – for life. It had also sent the old man to the cells.

Fidelis selected a different coloured frock. It was quite a fight to fasten the back without Prudence. She was confused, too. Her father's uniform, though hardly visible for gold braid and piping and medals, was undoubtedly – well, it was blue.

The Roc marched off to the Banqueting Hall. At least he'd settled the vanishing roll's hash; there was a perfectly rational reason for its disappearance which he'd look into later. It wasn't like the Roc to procrastinate. If he'd been a superstitious man, or investigated there and then, life would have turned out differently for Watt.

* * *

'Any chance we can break out of here the way the bread roll came in?' Watt asked. Melior shook her head. They were sharing the roll in the room below the

Offering Table. It was dried to a crisp by the sun, but they were hungry. They were scared too, and depressed, but neither of them said so.

'There's just a little flap,' she explained. 'I think it's for getting rid of the old offerings.' They climbed up the rope ladder and squeezed into the hollow interior of the Offering Table to examine the small chute and the lever which opened the base of the Offering Tray. It was ingenious, but no use to them.

Watt jumped down. 'Let's take another look.'

'No!' Melior was determined. 'I've searched until I'm sick.' But Watt insisted and led the way with much more conviction than he really felt. He held the candle high to light the way for Melior trailing listlessly after him.

There wasn't a sign of a way out. Every step Melior took behind him seemed to say "I told you so". She only came to life when she recognised the exit to the Anteroom.

'I'll show you my handprints, shall I?'

'Better not,' he whispered as she put her hand on the panel to open it. 'There could be someone on the other side.'

He was right: the Spy Master was there, looking intently at the floor. Who had walked all over it on their hands, and why? He would have given his eye teeth to know the offender was almost rubbing shoulders with him. The Spy Master was rarely puzzled. He was too good at his job. But this afternoon, he was just that.

He'd come a long way since he'd stood in this room and ordered the soldiers to kill the little king. He was head of Intelligence for the Old Country and its Empire now, and one of the Roc's loyal team of experts. He straightened his russet tweed jacket that so exactly matched his hair and considered the problems before him.

Who had sabotaged the Sew House? How had a Supervisor been found this morning bound and gagged in a latrine in the locked Sew House when the night before she had spoken to the gatehouse guards as she went into the castle? He'd interviewed the woman in the City hospital. All she'd say, over and over, was, 'He came up behind me and hit me.' The Spy Master smiled. He was sure she knew more than she was telling and just as sure that he'd get it out of her.

The next puzzle was the message on the carrier pigeon that his men had recently shot down.

'Yesterday Effected Lost Locket
Other Worse Misdemeanours Artful Guile,
Improper Cleansing Prudence'

The Spy Master had read and reread it. It didn't make sense. It had to be in code.

Undoubtedly, the message was the work of the people responsible for the handprints, the sabotage at the Sew House, and the supervisor in the latrine. Who were they? And what were they planning? He ordered the Ante-room sealed and went to see the Over Lord. He summoned the lift.

Vince rose slowly into view and drew back the lift gates for him. The Spy Master stepped inside and nodded his head upwards. Obediently, Vince pressed the top floor button and the lift juddered into motion, carrying them aloft in silence. After a bit, the Spy Master said, 'Well?'

'They had a meeting last night in the tank room,'

Vince replied. 'But one of your lot disturbed us, and they fled.'

The Spy Master swore.

* * *

Meanwhile, Watt was being cheerful for two. It was hard work keeping Melior's spirits up when she was hell bent on keeping them low. He called over his shoulder with what he hoped wasn't too obviously phony cheeriness, 'There has to be a way out if Saan said so. My bodyguard was always right.'

Melior stopped and looked mildly interested. 'How on earth did you become a Ghosty Boy?'

It was the first question Melior had asked him about himself. Maybe they were getting back to the Melior he remembered, a Melior who wasn't so completely self-absorbed. 'I'll tell you while we search,' he said.

When he'd finished his story, she looked at him in a funny way. It was exactly how the Baker looked at a loaf he suspected was under-cooked and soggy in the middle. 'What are you waiting for?' she said. 'The flour vat is your way out of here. Slip back into the Bakery. It's all right for you.'

It was a crazy idea but Watt said tactfully, 'You can't climb down a red-hot chimney into a roaring furnace, you know, and pop up smiling. The Policy Makers would realise there was another way back. They'd find the service stairs in no time...and you'

'Of course,' she said lightly. 'Silly me.' It was another of Melior's tests. She'd been testing whether he would stick by her. He was no nearer finding the old Melior. She still didn't trust him. Part of him felt upset by that, and another part of him wanted to give her mass of red hair a flipping good yank.

They were standing at the foot of a flight of steps on a flat square rock and the red hair was temptingly close. But then he saw a brass light switch in the wall, level with her head, and flicked it on. A blue light glowed, revealing a ceiling made of pure rock at this point, like the roof of a cave. Then, very slowly, more dim blue lights came on up the entire staircase. They could see properly at last.

'You could have been electrocuted doing that,' Melior scolded him anxiously.

He'd scarcely a moment to enjoy the idea that his sister actually minded him being electrocuted before she added, 'And then what would I have done?' At least you knew where you were with Melior, he comforted himself: you were last.

'Blow out the candle to save it,' she instructed. For once Watt didn't obey her. Next to the switch there was a straight, dark crack running down the wall. 'Don't get your hopes up,' he said, trying to keep his voice level, 'but there's just a chance we're on to something.'

He pulled away swathes of cobwebs so heavy with dirt they sagged across the wall like hammocks. More dirt cascaded onto their feet as he brushed the surface with his hands. 'Found it,' he said.

It was an arched door. The silver pattern inlaid in its wood was the same as the motif on the Offering Table: a series of joined circles, then a space, then another set of circles, and so on. They both realised at the same time that the door didn't have a handle.

They tried every way to open it. They were kneeling and pulling it with their fingertips curled under the bottom where there was a wider crack when Watt, whose head was pressed against the door, heard a muffled sound behind it. It was a sound he'd heard so often coming up from below the Bakery. 'Stop trying,' he told his sister. 'This is just the door to the kitchens. You can hear them washing up.'

He felt weak with disappointment. He blew out the candle and started up the stairs. 'Come on,' he said in what he knew was a ridiculously optimistic voice. 'Better luck next time.' Melior followed without a word.

Not long after, he trod on the key he'd dropped six years earlier. It was covered in layers of thick, felt-like dust, but he put it in his pocket. For some reason he was glad to have it back. 'Don't keep it,' Melior said at once. 'They will have changed all the locks.'

Watt was getting thoroughly tired of Melior ordering him about on petty details but leaving him to cope alone with the overall planning. It would be daft to fall out with her, though. They were trapped here and they needed to look after each other. When he'd told her his story, he'd left out the creeping, hurrying thing with the hoarse whisper that lived on these stairways. He didn't want to scare her, but he hadn't forgotten it and nor had he forgotten that it had whispered his real name. It knew him. He replaced the key as he'd been told and allowed himself a sarcastic "Happy now?" Melior sat down on a step and pulled her fingers through her mad hair.

'I shouldn't have got you into this, Watt.'

'Nothing but a pleasure,' he replied tersely. She handed him back the key with a gulpy sniff. He was terrified that she would cry again. It was most peculiar the way she plummeted from Bossy Boots to Weeping-Wreck with no stages in between. He supposed that was girls for you.

She sniffed again. 'We'd both still be happily slaving away for the Policy Makers instead of dying on a servant's stairwell if that dratted clerk and the Brad boy hadn't singled me out. All because I'm a girl.' There were definitely tears now. Great big fat ones welled out of Melior's incredibly blue eyes.

He had to act fast. What would Brad do? Brad, who may not know how a piano worked but knew every detail of how a girl worked. Except, Watt suddenly remembered, the dark girl in the red skirt. The only girl to baffle Brad! 'Melior,' he asked brightly, 'what does this mean?' He joined his forefingers and thumbs in a figure of eight and then pulled them apart.

Melior stopped crying at once and said in a shocked voice, 'Everyone knows what that means.'

CHAPTER NINE

Fidelis missed the beginning of the tea party, but one of the laughing councillors' wives filled her in on events. An Inmate band, who were supposed to entertain the party from the musicians' gallery above with delicate Old Country airs, had deafened them all with a raucous medley of their own on trumpets, bass drums and cymbals until the Roc had ordered them to come down for a tea break.

He'd sent for the Pianist to substitute. There wasn't a piano up there for him to play, but the Roc had ordered him to use his musical know-how and that was why (the lady was sobbing with laughter by now) Fidelis could hear him up in the gallery, playing some spoons.

Fidelis listened and could just distinguish a tiny clicking through all the laughter, like a death-watch beetle. She shuddered slightly at such a sinister thought.

But now the laughing ladies, dressed in their beautiful white lacy gowns and broad brimmed hats, drew her towards the table where the Butler and a troupe of servants were stationed behind silver teapots and hillocks of scones and buttered teacakes. Soon she was laughing and talking and eating along with the rest.

I'm being a lady, she told herself, sipping her cup of tea. And it's very boring. The dreadful thought popped out before she could censor it. There was no time to feel the usual guilt: Lady Joy practically elbowed her into a platter of apple turnovers as she drew Lady Evangeline aside to whisper, 'That trollop Lady Honor has had the old man buttonholed for a full five minutes.' It took Fidelis a couple of seconds to realise that by "the old man" Lady Joy meant her father. 'Get in there, Ev,' Lady Joy hissed. 'She could ruin us.'

Lady Evangeline finished her jam tart in one gulp. With a chilling patter of laughter, she galloped across the Banqueting Hall to the Roc's side and began chatting. It even looked as if she trod heavily on Lady Honor's white satin shoe. Fidelis was interested. Prudence had never included toe trampling in her rules for ladylike behaviour. And what did Lady Joy mean about being ruined?

Lady Joy gave a gasp of surprise when she noticed Fidelis, which she quickly changed to one of admiration. 'What a perfectly delightful frock!' Fidelis smiled gratefully. 'Red is such a bold choice for the afternoon,' Lady Joy went on. 'I declare, ma'am, you'll set a brand new trend!'

One look round the room told Fidelis what she was getting at. Every other lady was dressed in white or the palest of pastels, except for the Elders who wore deep blue robes. Fidelis stuck out like a blob of blood. She blushed with embarrassment. So now, she thought, I'm red all over.

* * *

'It's the sign of hope,' Melior said, drying her tears on her sleeve. 'The sign of the loosed chain.' Watt saw at once that it wasn't a figure of eight that his fingers were making, but two links in a chain. 'Our forebears were chained together to slave night and day for their masters.' Melior reached up from where she was sitting on the service stairs and pulled his fingers and thumbs apart. 'One day they broke their chains and ran away here to freedom.'

Watt grinned down at her. 'I thought it was something to do with sex.'

Melior snorted with laughter. Soon they were both giggling uncontrollably, like they had when they were small.

'Sex!' Melior laughed and leant back against the wall, which opened up noiselessly behind her.

She grabbed at his legs to save herself from falling backwards. But at the same time, Watt dived to catch her arm. Melior screamed his name as he sailed over her back and out through the gap in the wall.

She's used my real name, he thought. She must trust me at last. Then he landed head down in one of the abandoned drums in the musicians' gallery. The noise was thunderous. Everyone in the Banqueting Hall stopped talking and looked up. Melior just glimpsed her brother, stuck upside down in a huge drum, before the panel swung shut again.

Her scream of "Avtar" reverberated about the carved stone ceiling of the Banqueting Hall. In the terrible silence that followed, Fidelis whispered to Lady Joy, 'What is Avtar?' But Lady Joy was as white as an iced bun and seemed struck dumb.

Watt ripped the drum off his head and looked back. There wasn't a trace of the panel in the wall. A chink behind him made him whirl round. Shreds of drum skin flew about. He was face to face with the "pianner" owner, who was holding two silver teaspoons in one hand and boggling at him.

The Pianist couldn't believe his eyes. Had a bald and blackened fiend really materialised in the drum kit? And if so, what should he do about it? He never found out. The fiend raised the great drum and rammed it down over his head, plunging him into darkness and pinning his arms to his sides. Then the fiend was off like a firecracker round the musicians' gallery and out of the exit.

Watt had a quick view below him of many ladies in white looking upwards in horror, like a field of stricken lilies, and of the Roc, holding a teacup midway to his mouth which was rounded in an O of surprise. Blazing among them, he saw the fair girl, whose cheeks weren't pink anymore but as scarlet as her dress.

Then he was gone, so he didn't hear the excited whispering amongst the Inmate servants and musicians of 'Avtar, Avtar, Avtar,' which swept through the hall like an echoing sigh. One of the Elder women said, 'The god has spoken,' and the Roc gave her a hunted look. The Butler clamped a plate of muffins to his fluttering heart and murmured, 'Avtar, the King.' The murmur was taken up, rolling through the Banqueting Hall like a wave. 'Avtar, the King.'

The Roc clapped his cup back on its saucer. Thirty hats swivelled as the ladies dragged their gaze from the gallery to the Roc. 'Carry on, ladies,' he said. Before they could obey, a large drum, wearing black shiny shoes, leaned over the gallery parapet and said hollowly, 'Let me out.'

All the hats swivelled up to the drum. 'Ladies,' the

Roc repeated. The hats swivelled back and the ladies snapped into action, laughing and talking as though nothing whatever had happened.

The Roc sent two guards to investigate the talking drum. Then he wrote a note, which he folded and placed on the silver salver that a small, round-faced Messenger Boy held at the ready. 'Take that to the Over Lord.' He found the boy a coin. 'Buy yourself some sweets.'

The boy looked anxious. 'Sir, I'd sooner keep it, please sir. I got exactly the cost to make a kite to fly now, sir, with this – if that's all right with yous, sir.' The Roc said it was perfectly all right with him, and the boy ran off to the Topmost Tower.

The Over Lord was staring out of one of the windows, his thin white hands clasped behind his uniformed back. There was a bloodless look to him these days. The life had drained out of him in the six years since the little king had crept by while he prayed. His spare body was all bone, as if he had paid for his conquest of Slave City with his own flesh. By contrast, the Spy Master lounging in a leather armchair, radiated well-being, from the top of his tawny head to his handmade brogues.

There was a knock at the door. The Over Lord ignored it and sat down at his mahogany desk. He fingered the message the Spy Master had found on the pigeon.

'Yesterday Effected Lost Locket
Other Worse Misdemeanours Artful Guile,
And Improper Cleansing Prudence'

'It could be a call for civil disobedience,' he suggested. 'A carefully orchestrated dirty strike. Like the mess they made of the Sew House. It's not a summons to open revolt, I think; it advises prudence.' The Spy Master smiled. 'There's no one left here to lead a revolution anyway. I've seen to that.'

'The ingratitude of these people,' the Over Lord said bitterly. 'We have given them civilisation and they repay us with puddles of glue and filth like this!'

The knock at the door was repeated, and the Spy Master opened it. The small, round-faced Messenger Boy looked up at him from the threshold.

'Message for Sir the Over Lord, sirs,' he said, holding the folded paper on the silver salver carefully with both hands. 'From His Excellency the Ruler of the Old Country and Seventh Governor of its Empire, the Roc.'

'Come in,' the Over Lord called. The boy trotted over to his desk and reached up to place the salver in front of him.

The Over Lord looked displeased as he read the note. 'There's been an incident at the wives' tea party.' He held it out to the Spy Master. 'Coincidence, isn't it?' he said grimly. 'Just when we were talking about leaders?' The Spy Master took it and read.

Tea: Cries of "Avtar." Source unknown.
I am calling emergency meeting.
Agenda: What are you doing about this?
How do you intend to catch the culprits?
Remember, sir, that from one hairline crack
an Empire can crumble. The Roc.

The Spy Master looked up from the paper at the boy. 'Did you read this?'

'No, sir.' The small, round-faced Messenger Boy was quite hurt by the suggestion. The Spy Master gave him a teasing wink. 'Oh surely? One peep?'

'Messengers don't peep, sir,' came the firm answer, and the Spy Master smiled again.

He went and looked down onto the Roof Garden at the bottom of the tower and pushed the window wide to take a deep breath of air while he considered the Roc's disturbing message. He turned and patted the small, round-faced Messenger Boy kindly on the head. 'Upsy-daisy,' he said, and threw him out of the window. He watched the boy wheel through the air calling for someone until he hit the gardens.

The Over Lord said, 'I wish you wouldn't do that sort of thing. It hardly builds bridges.'

The Spy Master shrugged and held up the Roc's note. 'The fewer mouths there are to blab about King Avtar and leaders, the better.' And he shut the window.

'You're right.' The Over Lord's attention was all on the message the pigeon had been carrying. 'This is a crude code.' He was blocking out the end of each word. The Spy Master watched over his shoulder. 'Another coincidence,' he commented.

'An extremely unwelcome one.' The Over Lord held his handiwork out at arm's length.

Y E L L O W M A G I C Prudence

CHAPTER TEN

Watt threaded his way towards the kitchens. The Castle was teeming with servants and visitors and he was very careful to keep out of sight. He didn't know much about the Empire or the Roc or why they wanted him dead, but he did know they were sure that they had killed him, so they wouldn't ignore Melior's scream of his true name – Avtar. If the Piano Man had seen enough of him to give a description and they could attach his face to the name, he was in deep trouble. He had to get out of the City. He wondered how much longer he would have waited to try if Melior's attempt hadn't forced him into it. He almost smiled. She'd said he always tagged after her, and here he was doing it again. He must calm down and plan their escape.

He whisked into what turned out to be a picture gallery to avoid two very grand looking Policy Makers in frock coats processing towards him from the other end of the corridor. It was a big, dank room and it smelt of mildew, as if no one much went in there. It was a murky old place too, which was all to the good because a minute later, the two men came in as well. Watt hastily sidled behind a statue of a bloke on a rearing horse.

The men strolled about in silence looking at the pictures of battles. Watt stood stock still, tensed to run.

One of them lit a pipe and he got a brief view of his paper white face in the light of the match and of his striped purple neckpiece with a big, red-jewelled pin. Watt prayed they weren't ardent art lovers; there were hundreds of paintings to look at. They could be here for hours, though how they could see them in the gloom he couldn't imagine.

They paused frighteningly close to him in front of a naval battle. In their dark frock coats they were almost invisible in the half-light. Their white faces seemed to be hanging in the air like two dingy moons. The pipeless moon said quietly in his posh accent, 'The Over Lord assures me we're on course for a success. Brilliant idea of his to lure Porcini here. The man's a born strategist. I'd never have believed the Roc would oblige him with a State Visit.'

'It was the Mumbo Jumbo that did it. What do they call it: the "King's Touch"?' the pipe moon said. Avtar pricked up his ears. Mumbo Jumbo was the expression Melior had used. But the "King's Touch"? What did that mean?

'Pity he failed to lure the Roc's wife here too, though,' the other one said. 'Alma's a knowing bitch. How genuine was that migraine attack of hers? It's certainly weakened our plan.'

'What weakens the plan more is Lady Honor.'

'My wife?' Watt could hear that the pipeless moon was really surprised. 'My wife knows nothing of our intentions.'

The other moon relit his pipe. The smoke made Watt want to cough. He pressed his palms over his mouth to stop himself. He couldn't follow the conversation but it was obviously secret. They'd come in here to talk, not to look at pictures. It reminded him of the snatched private sessions he had with the Baker during the pretend beatings; if the men found him eavesdropping, well – they may be old and posh but they were Policy Makers – he'd be dead.

The pipe moon said even more quietly, 'Lady Joy tells me that the Roc is taking a lot of interest in your wife. You know what he's like. Can't resist a pretty woman. I don't suggest Lady Honor will respond, but if she did feel it her duty to do so, it could be catastrophic for us all. There will be no guards on the Roc's apartment tonight to stop her visiting him. What if she arrived just as we were…you know what…you follow me?'

'I'll see to it.'

'Do that, sir, immediately.'

Watt got the feeling that the pipeless moon was feeling ordered about by the way he tried to score a point with his next question. 'Suppose anyone notices there are no guards on his apartment? The Roc's Equerry for instance? How could the Over Lord possibly square it with them?'

'With the Roc's own reputation. You said yourself the Over Lord is brilliant. He'll simply say the Roc himself ordered the guards taken off – for total privacy. Believe me, the man knows what he's doing. The Empire will be in safe hands.'

The men strolled towards the statue where Watt was hidden and stared up at it. Watt flattened himself behind it, scarcely breathing. 'Precisely what is the King's Touch?' The pipeless moon was trying to change the subject. There was silence and more clouds of awful choking smoke before the pipe moon answered, 'What it says it is. The native chappies here called it something else, though. "Yellow Magic".'

The door was thrust open with a bang and a servant ran in to tell the moons the Roc wished to speak to the pipe moon urgently. They left at once. Watt waited behind the statue, trying to make sense of what he'd heard.

What in the name was the Yellow Magic? His mother had talked about it during the Attack. She'd said the City had given the enemy Yellow Magic. Was that a bad or a good thing? She'd spoken as if it were a powerful gift. Surely there was no such thing as magic. Then there was the rest of the moons' conversation. It wasn't just the Inmates who disliked the Roc. The two moons certainly did. What beat Watt, though, was how anyone could possibly like the Over Lord.

He sighed. Time to get on. Melior was relying on him.

He hung about in the passage outside the open kitchen doors. He had the beginnings of a plan but if it was to work, he had to reach the washrooms on the other side of the kitchen and the staff dining room without being seen. But in the afternoon the place would be bustling with cooks and kitchen boys preparing the evening meal. He stole a look round the door jamb and could hardly believe his luck. The kitchen was deserted.

He spared time for a quick inspection of the wall for any sign of the entrance to the service stairs. It should have been quite a noticeable doorway. There was nothing but wall, though – hung with copper utensils and a timepiece that said it was four-thirty.

The place was peculiarly quiet: he could hear the sizzle of melting fat as it dripped onto the flames from a half sheep roasting on a spit. It looked weird, too. The cooks had downed their mixing bowls and whisks and gone. The three big sinks of water in the China Room were covered with beige scum. A drying up cloth had been dropped on the floor. He couldn't understand it.

The windows were too high to see out or in, except for one small low one he had to pass. It overlooked the east side of the courtyard. He crawled under it, then stole a look over the sill. The entire kitchen staff was standing out there. Was it a fire practice? He hadn't heard the alarm. They were shading their eyes and looking up at the Topmost Tower, still as statues. He gave up guessing and thanked the god for his luck.

He opened the staff dining room door a crack. There was a scullery maid in there. She seemed to be asleep on a bench with her face buried in her arms resting on the table top. He took a chance she wouldn't hear and crept into the room. He'd nearly made it to the washroom door when she looked up.

She seemed not to see him. Her face was slimy with crying. Watt's heart sank. More tears! The woman said, 'They didn't have to kill him.' She looked appealingly round the empty room and tried to wipe her face with her apron. 'Haven't they killed enough of us yet but they need to murder my kid too?'

Her mouth opened in a funny, scrunched way. He thought she was going to scream, but instead she sobbed without a sound – on and on. Watt had never seen crying like that. Then words jerked out of her. 'He was so little to be hurt so bad – all alone.' She shook her head as if she couldn't make herself believe what she knew was true. Then she said, 'Help me. Help me bear it.'

Watt dithered. Was she talking to him or not? If she wasn't, he shouldn't draw attention to himself by answering. Besides, what could he possibly say to comfort her? On the other hand if she was asking him for help, it would be plain cruel to ignore her.

He went and put his arm round her shoulders and she turned and hugged him. Her wet face was pressed against his midriff and she rocked backwards and forwards. It was a bit embarrassing and it didn't seem much use just to stand there rocking, so Watt said, 'We'll have our revenge one day.'

The woman said, 'That won't bring him back,' and laid her head in her arms again and wept.

Watt slunk off to the washrooms feeling silly and inadequate. So much for Avtar and his first kingly proclamation, he thought. Of course she was right. Revenge didn't correct the wrong that had been done. It just gave the avengers a bit of a lift.

He stripped off what was left of his Ghosty Boy uniform. He didn't go into the communal shower the boys usually used; he bolted himself into an individual cubicle. The hot water stung the scrapes on his back where he'd fallen down the chimney and opened up some of the cuts on his arms again, but he didn't care. He washed until he was shining with cleanness; then he waited with the hot water splashing down on him.

He thought about his fall into the drum and about Melior all alone on the service stairs. He hoped she'd keep her nerve until he came up with an escape plan. If only they had somewhere safe to escape to, though. His knowledge of the world outside the City was discouragingly scrappy. His last geography lesson had been six years ago. Perhaps Melior had learned more from Triss.

An Inmate servant came in and began to shave. Watt waited, keeping the water running. Then some boys came in. It was the end of their shift, apparently. In muted voices, they told the man that a Messenger Boy had been thrown out of the Topmost Tower and killed by someone they called the Spy Master. Watt felt terrible that he'd made such a lousy job of comforting the poor kid's mother. The man cursed worse than Brad could and went out. Watt stood under the shower and thought, helplessly, That's all we can do, curse about the things they do to us – or cry.

The boys undressed and were soon mucking about in the communal shower. Watt was out of his cubicle in a flash. He nicked one of their towels to dry off with. Then, working at top speed, he selected garments for himself from the boys' uniforms. They were Messenger Boys. They'd hung everything up very neatly, so he was able to be quick. He even found a left and a right shoe that fitted him from two different boys, and he was just as lucky with the white gloves. He wanted this to look like a practical joke, not as though someone was kitting themselves out with a uniform. He had difficulty with the cap. They were mostly too big because of his lack of hair. Then he found a smaller one. He pulled it well down to hide his shaved head. He checked the mirror and didn't recognise himself for a second or two – the peaked cap changed him so much it was almost as if he had hair. He shot out of the washroom with his Ghosty Boy clothes wrapped up in the towel.

The scullery maid had gone. He sauntered past a few staff laying tables for supper. He held his breath. Not one of them even glanced at him. He was just another Messenger Boy coming out from his shower.

Watt's heart sang. Messenger Boys could go anywhere in the City. Under the pretext of carrying a message to someone, he could go exactly where he wanted to. This uniform was a passport out of the castle. He was inching towards an escape plan.

He'd hoped to throw away his Ghosty Boy uniform in the kitchen boiler, but he couldn't. The room was full of busy people again, staggering about with pails of milk or plucking countless chickens or stirring steaming saucepans, and he didn't want anyone asking questions.

Several carp ogled and twitched in a tank of water he was passing. These Policy Makers could certainly put away some food! Watt was imagining the girl with the fair hair and the red face sinking her teeth into a chunk of mutton when the Cook's voice said from behind him, 'Get a move on.'

Watt jumped. He was standing and staring at the fish tank. 'It's crowded enough in here without you taking up room counting the fish,' she said

Watt touched his cap. It was difficult to break the habit of six years and speak to her. He managed to say, 'Sorry, Lady Cook.' The Cook gave him an appraising look and he realised his mistake at once. He was talking like a Policy Maker again. He had to have a go at an Inmate accent. 'I's never beheld a carp afore.' Not bad, he thought.

She smiled the smallest of hostile smiles. 'Ain't never seen a carp afore. How come you knows what they are, then?' She folded her arms and looked him over in a very unfriendly way. She obviously thought he was a spy – an outstandingly clumsy one. Watt longed to tell her he was on her side. On impulse, he made the sign of the loosed chain. She looked at him as though he was a maggot she'd found in a cabbage and said coldly, 'You get along, youngster, or you'll be in the soup with your daft finger twiddling.' She nodded at a cauldron of the stuff lurching by.

Watt went. He'd made a fool of himself again. What kind of a king was he? At the first opportunity to speak, he'd said something crass and now he'd done something dangerous. So no more pathetic attempts to curry favour, he told himself fiercely.

He was practically out of the door when a kitchen boy ran up behind him. 'Oi, you.' He offered Watt a large gateau. Watt cheered up; he was starving. He tucked his bundle under his arm and peeled off his gloves, which the boy obligingly held for him while he took the cake. 'You got a wigging from the old cow,' the boy said, 'so I nicked a gateau from her larder for you. Her biggest. What you say to cross her then? I saw yous both a-talking.' He had spiky brown hair and eyebrows that met in the middle over friendly, dark eyes.

Watt wiped his fingers on the towel wrapped round his clothes and grinned back. It was his special slobbery, wet lipped grin. It didn't send the boy away, but it gave Watt time to think. There was something too friendly about those dark eyes, something too chummy about the boy. Had he seen him making that sign to the Cook? Watt broke off half the remaining gateau and handed it to him.

'I'm happy to split it with you.' The boy stepped back as if he'd stung him. He said angrily, 'What's your name?'

'What's it to you?' He'd guessed right. The boy was a Split.

They were beginning to collect a few looks from the kitchen staff near them. Watt shifted his position. He couldn't wait to knock the Split's teeth out. He bunched his fist as the boy moved in on him. Inside his head an icy voice said, 'Get out of here. Get out.' And he pulled himself together.

The Messenger Boys in the shower would be discovering their clothes were missing right this minute. If he hung around, he'd be caught.

'Got to go.' he said and walked out of the kitchen. But the kitchen boy wanted a fight. He came after him and grabbed his shoulder. Watt tore himself away muttering, 'Another time,' and loped off. It was too bad he'd left his gloves with the Split.

And it was too bad for the Split, too. A group of indignant Messenger Boys swarmed out of the kitchen in search of their clothes and caught him red-handed with their gloves. And while Watt was already well on his way to the servant's exit, they took them back a bit roughly.

He wasn't pleased with himself. In the last few minutes he had practically written a guidebook on how *not* to behave like a king. A king on the run, what's more. He'd been better at dealing with people when he was dumb. And then he thought – why am I suddenly calling myself king? Just when I'm going?

CHAPTER ELEVEN

'Don't go,' the Roc said.

Fidelis had given Prudence the slip after the tea party and sneaked away to visit her father in his rooms. The Roc was resting in full uniform on his huge bed while he signed each paper his Equerry passed him.

'I didn't mean to intrude, Papa.'

'You aren't, my love.' The Equerry handed him the final paper. 'Hmm. An Enforcement Order, eh?'

'For a clerk, sir,' his Equerry murmured. 'Though it's questionable what good it will do. The young lady he wishes to marry has disappeared.' The Roc smiled as he signed the Enforcement Order. 'Bride's nerves.'

The two men laughed. Fidelis looked down at the carpet with its pattern of joined and half circles. The laugh was the sort adults do when they think you don't know what they're talking about; and even if you *do* know, it cuts you out, as if you weren't in the room. She smiled, though, exactly as the Roc's daughter should, in reply to the Equerry's departing bow.

Her father settled back into his pillows with a drowsy tinkle of medals, so she got her question in quickly before he had a chance to nod off. 'What's Avtar?'

'Avtar? It's what the son of these people's king was called. He's dead.'

'They don't seem to think so.'

The Roc smoothed his moustache. 'If he isn't, someone is going to have me to answer to. Kings!' he exclaimed. 'Who needs them?' And he closed his eyes.

'Papa,' she asked quickly, 'why are we here?' She'd meant why is the Empire here, bothering with a miles-from-anywhere city. She'd begun to think it was something to do with this blue colour thing of theirs, but her father replied, 'We're here as a cover.'

He opened his eyes briefly and smiled at her surprised face. 'Wild horses wouldn't have dragged me to this dump, but my dear old pal, the Over Lord, asked for my help. He badly needed the Spy Master back at work in the City. But these Inmate chappies get deuced windy if they think they're under surveillance, so I came up with a watertight excuse for him to bring in top flight security – a State Visit. Now the Spy Master is on the job and the Inmates haven't the foggiest that the Over Lord has caught on to their dirty tricks.'

'Goodness!' Fidelis was surprised. 'What are they up to?' Her father stifled a yawn. 'Hasn't your mother gone into all this with you? In your politics lessons? The king and things?' Any minute now he would tell her not to pester him and send her away. There was only one way to make her father go on. Fidelis felt a bit guilty about taking it, but she did. 'Mama doesn't seem to want to touch on the king of Slave City.'

It worked. Her father's eyes opened at once. 'Oh doesn't she indeed,' he said grimly. 'Well, we overthrew him. That's what we did.'

Fidelis was uncertain what that entailed but it sounded unpleasant, which was troubling. There was an uncomfortable silence; then her father said, 'You see, Fid, it wasn't personal. It's politics. He could cure people.'

'Cure them! But surely that's wonderful – isn't it?'

'Exactly what we thought. He could cure diseases that had never been cured before. Even healed war wounds. Half dead soldiers crawled into his City and before long...' her father snapped his fingers, '...cured!'

The conversation was beginning to sound more like a fairy tale than real life, and Fidelis could only murmur, 'Astonishing!'

'Too right. Could save us a fortune. The Empire loses more men *after* a battle from wounds incurred during combat than we do men killed outright. The cure could cut down our losses immeasurably.'

'But how did the king do it?'

'Good question, Fid, and it's just what we asked him. Sent an ambassador. Admiral of the fleet. Tell us your secret, Your Majesty. We were ready to pay. Have it for free, says the Slave King, you're welcome to the answer; and he wrote down the formula. Back came the admiral with the sealed envelope. Opened it up. Inside – complete and utter nonsense!'

Fidelis understood at once that this was a massive insult to the Empire. She wondered if she dared ask about something so grave and formed her next question carefully so her father could refuse to answer if he wanted to, without getting angry. 'Can you say what sort of nonsense, Papa?' The Roc was only too happy to say.

'Lot of rot! Yellow Magic. Seaweed. Jelly. Repulsive! Damned cheek.' The Roc's medals jingled aggressively. 'Nobody rebuffs the Empire, Fidelis. If the Slave King wouldn't give us his cure, then the Empire would take it anyway. And in we went.' Her father didn't say any

140

more, but snuggled into his pillows and shut his eyes as if he'd finished the story.

'But Papa,' Fidelis asked, 'Why hasn't the Empire *got* the cure, then? We haven't, have we?' There was a pause before the Roc said slowly, 'Slightly tricky one that, Fid.' He opened his eyes. He looked almost bashful. 'We couldn't find it.'

'You mean they'd hidden it?'

'The Sun knows where if they had,' her father replied. 'There wasn't a sign of it. Not a dicky bird. The Over Lord and our army took this City to pieces trying to find it. Started with the hospital, naturally. Vile place. Eventually, we got rid of the medics and gave it a good scrub with carbolic to clean the place up. Certainly no cure there. Or anywhere else as it turned out. Rum do.'

'And the king wouldn't tell you what it was.'

'He couldn't. Eliminated – along with the rest of his line. That's war for you.'

Fidelis hadn't seen this side of her father before, and she wasn't at ease with it. He seemed almost cruel. Her father must have sensed what she was thinking because he said, 'We had to do it, Fidelis, for the Empire's sake. Uncivilised upstart, that was the king of Slave City for you. Altogether a bad thing.' Fidelis knew that when her father said, "Altogether a bad thing," it really meant, "Will not be tolerated under any circumstances". But she couldn't help thinking it was a shame for everyone's sake that the king hadn't had a chance to reconsider giving up the secret of the cure. The Roc was inclined to agree when she put it to him because, as he admitted, some odd rumours had begun to fly.

'What sort of rumours, Papa?'

'For one: that there *wasn't* a formula.' The Roc

frowned his disapproval. 'For another: that it was the king himself who had been doing the curing. One touch of the jolly old royal finger and you were fit as a fiddle again. "The King's Touch".'

'But surely that's nonsense.'

'Agreed. Sounded like Mumbo Jumbo, voodoo even. Trouble was, it seemed to be true. People had been cured. And now nobody was getting cured. It looked as if we'd killed the goose that laid the golden egg. Bad show.'

'So why did the Over Lord need the Spy Master here again?'

Her father gave her that surprised look as if he'd forgotten she existed and smoothed his moustache again. 'He's had hints that the healing has started up again recently. Wanted the Spy Master to investigate. If anyone can find the cause, it's my Spy Master. It can't be the king. He's dead. Who then, or what, is doing it? Useful to get our hands on the answer. That's why you and I are here, Daughter, and why the Empire is here: for the "King's Touch".' Fidelis smiled. Her father seemed to count her as one of his team of sleuths now, so she dared another question.

'Are you thinking perhaps Avtar survived, Pa? And he inherited the secret gift?'

The Roc closed his eyes. 'Could be. If he has, we'll catch him, clip his wings and use his talents – voodoo or not. But it's equally possible some troublemaker is just claiming he has survived. As soon as I've recovered from those disgusting scones, I'll have a word with my friend the Over Lord. Queen Lenita has given me sufficient trouble as it is without her brat Avtar resurrecting too.'

'Lenita!' That's an Old Country name, isn't it? Fidelis was startled. 'Was she from home?'

142

'She was,' her father answered, quite venomously for him, which surprised Fidelis. Her father rarely gave anyone a clue what he was really thinking, but for once it was crystal clear that he thoroughly disliked the queen. It didn't seem to be preventing him going to sleep, though. Fidelis wished he wouldn't; she was curious about Queen Lenita.

Out of the silence her father suddenly said, 'I'm wondering whether Haakron's behind this whole thing, though. Too bad your mother invented that migraine; I could do with her view on it.' Fidelis bit her lip and said nothing. Invented or not, the migraine was part of the war between her parents and she couldn't take sides. Her father said lazily, 'If Haakron is behind it, that would be a worry.'

Fidelis still waited in silence. Her father might sound half asleep, but if he described something as "a worry" then, for once, she *did* know what he was thinking: it meant it was a very serious matter and it was better not to ask him questions that he may not want to answer.

The Roc didn't say any more, so Fidelis didn't either, though she was longing to. She thought Haakron might be "politics". But though she could have as many politics lessons as her mother had time to give, she was strictly forbidden to take part in politics themselves. She waited until it was obvious her father wasn't going to say any more, then she said, 'I think I'll take Span for a walk on the Roof Garden, Papa, sir.'

'Do that.' Her father was almost asleep.

'Until later then, Papa.'

The Roc opened his eyes. 'You look nice, sweetheart,' he said, 'in red,' and closed them again. Fidelis smiled broadly. 'Lady Joy wouldn't agree.'

'Old witch,' was her father's only comment.

'Pa? Could Lady Honor ruin Lady Joy?'

'No,' said her father. 'She's a ruin already.'

Fidelis laughed and paused in the doorway. 'Papa, someone shot at my pigeon to Mama.'

'That's not possible.'

'An arrow, Pa,' Fidelis insisted.

'You probably saw a hawk after it.' He sighed deeply and snuggled his head into the pillow. His medals gave an appreciative clink. 'The whole secret service is protecting you, my love. Don't give it another thought.'

'All right, Papa.'

But the Roc was asleep.

They were scraping the Messenger Boy off the Roof Garden when Fidelis got out there. She had to stop Span eating bits of him. They told her there had been an accident: a child had fallen out of a window. There was an upturned cap on the ground beside the mess, and someone had placed the two Old Country coins that she had given the small round-faced Messenger Boy inside it. She hurried Span back to her own apartments. She was shaking with the upset of it. She remembered the little boy's serious "I eats every crumb" and felt cold and nauseous.

'That will teach you to stuff scones,' Prudence said maliciously. 'And take that dress off before you vomit on it. Whatever possessed you to wear red to afternoon tea when I'd put you in your blue? I nearly died of shame.' Before Fidelis could finish telling her about the Messenger Boy, she was sick – on Prudence.

For once Prudence didn't put her through a guilt session; instead, she made her lie down on the chaise with a bowl beside her in case she was sick again. Then she showed Fidelis the gown she intended to wear to the ball that evening. She hummed and hawed for so long over whether or not it would be too saucy to attach a teeny little rosette to the neckline that Fidelis gradually began to feel better.

Prudence was in such a chatty mood that Fidelis thought she might get her to throw some light on the Haakron mystery. Was it "politics"? She asked offhandedly, 'Do you know about Haakron, Prudence?'

'No.'

Prudence's mouth shut tight as though it would never open again, which convinced Fidelis Haakron was "politics".

There was nothing for it, Fidelis thought. She would have to ask Mama. After all, Ma was the family expert on politics. She would send Ma a pigeon. It couldn't come to harm now that the whole secret service was guarding them. And you never know, Ma might send an answer back that could be useful to Papa.

As soon as Prudence was engrossed in sewing on the teeny rosette, Fidelis sat down casually at the little desk and took a scrap of paper. What was the shortest way of asking – what is Haakron? And – why would it be a worry to Pa if a Haakron were behind a scheme to remind everyone in Slave City of Avtar, their king, who is dead?

She dipped her pen into the inkwell and wrote.

* * *

Watt was on his way to the servants' exit when he ran into the Butler who, naturally enough, wanted to know why he was roaming the corridors. The Butler rested his hands on his knees and bent to look under the peak of Watt's cap. 'Who in the name are you, anyway?'

Watt thought fast. 'A substitute, sir,' he replied. 'Sent up from the town.' The Butler's face saddened.

'You heard about the poor little blighter?'

Watt nodded. The Butler whispered, 'That makes two of my boys lost now. Stay vigilant, child, and watch your step.' The Butler straightened up and pressed a hand to his heart. 'Off you go to the Duty Room.' And Watt had to obey him.

There were a couple of boys there, sitting on a long bench facing a row of bells hanging high up on the opposite wall. The boys eyed his bundle of clothes in surprise, but before they could ask any awkward questions, two of the bells suddenly jiggled and then jangled and they both rushed off.

He had to get rid of the bundle. He could never explain away a charred Ghosty Boy uniform if he were caught with it. The only other door in the Duty Room was marked "Butler's Pantry" and had a private feel about it.

When he found the light switch inside, the little room fairly gleamed with shelves of silver and gold objects. There were several tins of metal polishing powder lying about and, best of all, there was a sideboard cupboard that he could push the clothes into – except there was no room. It was full of peculiar little glass dishes. He lifted a lid and saw there was a skin of poisonous-looking gelatinous stuff under it. They all had the same skin on them. Some were mouldy. That was a disappointment; the dishes were labelled things like "Avocado" and "Pineapple" – and he was so hungry.

He closed the cupboard and looked around for a

hiding place. Then, right at the back of a stack of ewers and candlesticks, he saw a silver-backed hairbrush. He knew whose it was at once. It was his mother's. He didn't touch it. If he touched the brush she must have held on the very day of the Attack he knew he couldn't trust himself to go on ignoring the broken, bleak feeling he had about his treacherous mother.

There was a bulging blue cloth bag of cleaning rags hanging on the back of the pantry door and he stuffed the clothes into the bottom of it. Then he remembered Brad's heart-shaped roll and dragged them all out again to retrieve it. He got back into the Duty Room in the nick of time. He'd hardly closed the Butler's pantry door when the Butler himself came in and perched on his high stool.

Watt examined the Butler's mild looking face from under the peak of his Messenger Boy's cap. Did the Butler know he had the traitor queen's hairbrush? Surely he wouldn't give it houseroom if he did? But it had been well polished, as if the Butler were looking after it. So the Butler must scare about his traitor mother. What did that make the Butler?

A chambermaid and several boys joined him on the bench. Watt sat and fumed. There could be no sneaking away, but he had to get out and into the City. Someone out there must know a way out for Melior and him.

One of the bells hanging on the wall rang and the girl hurried off. Each bell was numbered in blue figures; presumably that's how you identified who was calling for you. He noticed she took a special servant's lift and remembered he must do the same. He found he was nervous.

When the next bell rang, one of the boys jumped up,

but the Butler said, 'Let the new fellow take that one. It's a lady. Start him in easy, eh?' He sent the boy with Watt to show him the way, so Watt had to go.

They took the lift, and the boy led him to a door and left him to it. It was a perfect opportunity to clear off. Then he wondered if by any chance the lady who'd rung was the fair-haired girl with the red face. He knocked on the door. There was no answer. He knew he ought to be making a run for it, but he opened the door a little.

CHAPTER TWELVE

'Avtar is dead as a dodo.' The Spy Master looked thoroughly disgruntled.

'He might just as well not be,' the Over Lord answered sharply, 'because someone is using his name to stir up trouble. They must be crushed or they'll land us both in extremely hot water.'

The two of them were making hasty preparations for the emergency meeting the Roc had called. The Over Lord waved the Roc's note at the Spy Master. 'The Roc has just about accused me of destroying the stability of the Empire. The Sun! He's had people executed for less. So let's go after these trouble makers.'

'We are,' the Spy Master said. 'I've put the Band inside for...questioning.' He meant "torture", but the Over Lord preferred to be kept in the dark about his methods. 'I'll pin it on them temporarily, until I find the real culprit. I guarantee I'll have a confession from a musician before the Roc joins us.' He smiled. 'That should satisfy him.'

The Over Lord paced round the windows of his tower. 'Good. Our priority is to keep the Roc sweet until we're rid of him tomorrow? But suppose for one minute that, unbelievably, Avtar survived.'

'Impossible. I've had every suspect boy in the City

taken out.

'Suppose he has, though? The King's Touch.' The sheer power of such a thing made him pause in his pacing and grip his desk. 'I'd give a lot to have that in the cells.'

'Sorry to disappoint you. My people are thorough. He's dead.'

'Suppose, then, that the Roc merely *believes* he is alive. The two of us will have failed in our duty in his eyes. We'll be jailed for life, even end up on the gallows rather than...' The Over Lord broke off. 'Well, suffice it to say that is far from the destiny I am planning for us. Let's hope those hints I fed the Roc that the old king's magic is being worked again aren't going to backfire on us. It's uncanny! No sooner do I invent it than it comes into being.'

A bonfire in the terraced gardens caught his eye. Some Inmate servants were burning the thousands of silk roses that had adorned Madame Porcini's recital. Surprisingly, the identity check that the Over Lord had put out on the buffoon who had blundered onto the concert platform last night ahead of Porcini's entrance had produced no result.

'Any idea if that Supervisor was fully dressed when she was discovered in the latrine?' he asked.

The Spy Master gave him a shrewd look. 'Ah!' he said. 'The attacker disguised himself in her uniform. Let's get an enquiry over to the City hospital.'

'Why's she in that mouldering hole? Why not our garrison sick bay?' The Spy Master shrugged. 'She'll be so frightened of catching something lethal, she'll tell me all she knows to get out of there.'

The Over Lord was unconvinced. 'I think the time

has come to get my Man in about this.' The Spy Master agreed happily enough. He'd always been curious to know more about the Over Lord's "Man".

The Over Lord looked at the orange flames of the bonfire and thought carefully about the figure who'd barged onto the dais. 'It's my opinion we're not hunting a "he". We should be hunting a red-headed girl,' he said. 'Young. She'll lead us to the heart of this insurgency.' He picked up the speaking tube. 'I'll put out a general alert for her. You catch her.'

The Spy Master smiled. 'If I have to take this castle apart.'

'Her too when you catch her,' the Over Lord said. 'She's getting in my way.'

* * *

The room Watt looked into was in darkness. Out of the dark he heard, 'Is there no port in this pig hole?'

'Port?' Watt asked warily, wondering who on dry land would have need of a port. A bedside lamp came on and a strapping great lady, wearing a maroon nightcap and a taut satin nightdress, reared up in the bed.

'Port,' she croaked and flumped back into her pillows.

Watt closed the door behind him and looked wildly around the room for anything that would give him a clue about her port. Was she an admiral of the fleet or something? He remembered meeting an admiral in his past life who had come to visit his father: a majestic man who'd been rowed up the river by twenty sailors. But the admiral had worn a simple uniform. This room was festooned with gowns and colourful shawls. There were hanks of silk stockings and long, gold and silver lamé gloves draped over a chair. A lather of lace petticoats spewed from the open top of a trunk. Definitely not a sea-going wardrobe!

'Port,' the mound of a woman repeated, 'or I'll never get another note out.' Of course, this must be the singer whose concert Melior had walked in on. The singer opened vast dark eyes and looked at him beseechingly, and he recognised the woman he had watched arrive in the funny little vehicle. 'Port,' she said.

'You want a port,' he made a guess, 'brought to you?'

'What else?' Feeling rather pleased with himself, Watt turned to leave. The Butler would surely know what it was she was asking for.

'And while you're here,' the woman croaked, 'empty my jerry.' She gestured at a glass container that looked more like a tuba than anything else and it was full of – oh, the god! It was full of pee. The tuba must be one of the hospital's more imaginative contributions to the chamber pot shortage. She saw him hesitate. 'Time was,' her voice creaked, 'men would have killed to empty Porcini's piss.'

'I've no doubt,' he replied politely and wondered how on earth she'd got it in there in the first place. Was she a distinguished contortionist as well as a singer?

Watt gritted his teeth and picked up the tuba. She waved an ivory hand at what must be the bathroom door and he went in. While he was juggling to turn on the light with his elbow without letting any of the wretched stuff slosh over him, he noticed a blue shape floating in the dark. As soon as the light was on, it disappeared. He got rid of Porcini's piss in the toilet as quickly as he could. It glugged and spat back at him as he emptied it, so he had to slow down.

There was something troubling about the ghostly blue shape. He didn't flush the lavatory. He needed time to experiment. He turned the light out again. There was the shape. Or perhaps it was more of an outline, really. With the light on again, it dissolved into nothing. But he'd fixed where it was positioned in the room. Perhaps it wasn't floating. It seemed to be located between the bath and the wash basin. He turned the light off and it sprang into being again: a three-sided oblong shape, like the frame of a mirror or a door. Then he realised what it was.

Watt flushed the lavatory, turned on all the taps hard and called through the bathroom door, 'Just clearing up, um, Lady Porcini.' He accepted the parrot-like squawk that came from the other room as an assent and locked himself in the bathroom. It took him seconds to find the entrance to the service stairs.

When it opened, the blue light from the staircase shone into the bathroom. We must have been crazy to leave those lights on, he thought. How many more places was it leaking through these old, disused panels? The whole secret of the service stairs would be blown apart if anyone else noticed it.

Watt climbed through onto the stairway and whispered his sister's name. There was no response. Using some of the Baker's best curses, he tore down the stairs as fast as its twistings and windings would let him. Melior was nowhere in sight. He passed Worly's bones: the skull was gone. What was going on?

He reached the sealed doorway to the kitchen and flicked up the brass light switch. He hated the dark that came. 'Melior,' he whispered blindly into the black stairwell. She didn't reply. There wasn't time to grope his way round to look in the room under the god Offering Table. He took a deep breath and shouted his sister's name at the top of his voice. He waited in the dark for her to answer.

The scullery maid, whom Watt had tried, and failed, to comfort, lifted her head and listened. She was up to her elbows in washing up suds. 'Hark!' she said. Two trainee maids working with her listened too. On the service stairs, Watt almost screamed, 'Melior!' a second time. And faint as a baby's breath, the name filtered through to the listening scullery maids.

'Who's Melior?' one of the trainees whispered.

'She was the old king's daughter,' the scullery maid whispered back. 'That was my boy's voice a-calling her.' For the first time since her son's murder, she smiled. 'Him and the little princess, they's playing,' she said gently.

Watt stood and listened to the silence. There was no doubt about it; Melior was not there. He worked his way back to the bathroom and closed the panel behind him. He was terrified for his sister. He brushed down his uniform and noticed that his hands were shaking.

Why was the skull gone? Had the thing on the service stairs been biding its time until it was ready to kill again, then reached out and taken her? He couldn't face thinking about what it would do with her or where it had taken her.

He turned off the taps he'd left running and went back with the empty tuba. Madame Porcini had donned a floating maroon robe trimmed with orange ostrich feathers. She was seated at a table on a round mushroom shaped stool. Her sloped desk was open in front of her and she was scratching a pen across a paper. Large portions of Madame Porcini flowed over the edges of the stool. The ostrich feathers bounced slightly in time to her writing. A sob broke from her as she wrote, which set the feathers trembling more violently. The amount of crying he'd met with that day! It should be banned.

Madame Porcini blotted the sheet, folded it and placed it in an envelope. Then, with the tongue that had brought tears to the eyes of emperors, she licked the flap, stuck it down and addressed it to The Roc.

'The Roc first, Port second,' she said. 'Pronto!'

Just as she was about to give it to him, she withdrew the message. 'And it's *Madame* Porcini,' she corrected him. 'I am no aristocrat.' She said it very sweetly, but she might just as well have said "I am no piss pot". She threw back her magnificent head. 'I am an Artist.' Watt bowed deeply and took the message. She held her ivory hands round her magnificent throat and hardly seemed to notice him leave.

As soon as he found a window with a deep recess, he slipped into it out of sight from the corridor. He opened the message and read:

Dearest Jamsie Wamsie,

You do not answer my letters. What have I done to deserve your disdain?

I shall sing one aria only tonight and retire to my chamber. Alone.

Tomorrow I depart. My motorcar is ordered for dawn.

Farewell,
Your humble and adoring,
Porcini
P.S. This pig hole has broken my heart.

Watt replaced the paper in its envelope. His reading wasn't up to much. Recipe language was what he was used to. Words like "disdain" were tricky, but he got the sense. The Roc wasn't talking to Madame Porcini and that was upsetting her very, very much.

He tucked the envelope into his belt. He would go and find Madame Porcini's motorcar and stow away on it. The motorcar was the way out of the City. It was so unfair: he'd found their perfect escape route, only to have Melior disappear. Then he told himself to face up to it: his sister hadn't disappeared, she was dead. She was as dead as he'd thought her to be after the Attack. But this time he felt even lonelier without her. The new, explosive Melior he'd met today may have been exasperating but she had banished all the grief he'd felt for the previous Melior, who'd become an adored but patchy memory. His beautiful, hard-hearted sister, who had suffered far more than he had, was lost forever.

Fingers dug hard into the back of his neck. He squirmed and wriggled but they held him tight. The message was pulled from his belt. He remembered the frightened boy whispering how a stranger had robbed him of a message from the singer to the Roc so it was almost a pleasure to hear Vince's voice rumble, 'Lingering, Messenger Boy, could cost you your post.'

Vince examined the envelope. Then he slapped Watt on the cap with it. 'Where you'll need to take this,' he said, 'is the Topmost Tower. The Roc is meeting the Over Lord there. I'll set you on your way.' He was as good as his word. He took Watt to the top of the castle, just outside the South East Tower, then stood and watched him walk out onto the flat roof.

The prospect of coming face to face with the Over Lord scared Watt so much that he could not think straight. This was the man who knew everything about everyone. The Baker had said he'd killed half the kids in the City, searching for the old king's children. Suppose the Over Lord became suspicious of a Messenger Boy he didn't recognise? He had to get out of meeting him, but how? He looked about for inspiration.

The Policy Makers' banner clinked in the wind where it was flying high above him on the summit of the Topmost Tower. It was always windy up here, he remembered. Everything else was the way he remembered it too: the four towers at each corner; the flat roof with the tessellated battlements on three sides and the rectangular void in the centre. If you looked over its stone parapet you could see past floor after floor of windows right down to the Inner Court. He had once tried to time how long it took his spit to hit the fountain at the bottom. Oh stop reminiscing, he told himself, and get yourself out of this.

The Water Reservoir Tank that was sunk into the whole run of the south side of the roof had altered: it had green islands of slimy-looking pondweed floating on it now. The walkway was different too: there were Policy Maker guards posted there now, not his father's. Shut up, he shouted inside himself, and think. Diagonally opposite him was the Roof Garden and ahead of him, the Topmost Tower. His brain had seized up.

Way below, a flock of sheep moved slowly after the small figure of their shepherd outside the City walls. He'd give the world to change places with a sheep now. Well, you flipping can't, he told himself, so think. Vince was still watching him, so there was no escape. Was he going to go the same way as Melior? He walked over to the Topmost Tower, twisted the iron ring of the handle, pushed open the door and went in.

CHAPTER THIRTEEN

Melior opened her eyes. She was lying on her back in the dark. She didn't know where she was or how she'd got there. All she knew was that something terrible had happened and her head was hurting. But then memory came surging back and she wished it hadn't.

She had seen her brother fall into a drum. When she'd dared to open the panel again, a babble of happy talk burst in on her, and there was a Policy Maker guard standing over the drum while another guard pulled it off. So they had caught him and they would kill him because she'd just told the whole castle who he was by screaming his name. She closed the panel and burst into tears.

She hated herself for betraying him and hated herself even more for wondering if she'd done it on purpose. Did she dislike him? Surely not. On the other hand, did she know how to *like* someone? The other girls in the Sew House were always telling her that she was cold and stand-offish and rude – but that suited her: it fended people off and kept her secret safe. Only Triss knew who she really was. But surely even Morag – as Triss had renamed her six years ago – even horrible Morag wouldn't betray her own brother. Admittedly, he was so infuriatingly cheerful about every calamity that came his way that she'd been ready to hit him. But not to *betray* him, surely? Besides, she'd been counting on his help to escape. No. She'd screamed his name because that *was* his name. But she might just as well have pushed him into his grave.

She cried harder then because she was going to die too. She'd end up as a cluster of bones, like Worly. She'd told her brother there was plenty of food; what she *hadn't* said was that there was no water. She cried more. Perhaps I could drink my own tears, she thought, and cried even more. She'd had no idea one pair of eyes could produce this much water.

And where – the practical question penetrated her despair – where did the water go? Where did the servants who carried the chamber pots up and down these nightmare stairs empty them? They'd even manhandled whole bathtubs of water, so the legend went, so where on earth did they throw it away? She stopped crying. They must have missed something.

They had. Neither of them had bothered investigating four broad steps that descended from the platform outside the door-with-no-handle because they ended at a blank rock-face. Melior went down them now. When she reached the bottom, the noise her feet made changed. It sounded hollow.

She shovelled away at the dust with her feet. It didn't take her long to uncover a round metal trapdoor. She stubbed her toe on a tongue-shaped strip of iron, which turned out to be a hasp. One end was hinged onto the centre of the trapdoor, and an eyelet in the other end slotted over a hefty staple driven into the rock floor. There was a metal peg on a short length of fine chain next to it which was supposed to be pushed through the staple and hold the hasp locked. But it wasn't. It was lying on the floor.

She fitted her fingers into a handhold and heaved, and the trap opened with a rending sound of loosed dirt and squealing hinges. She rested it open against the rock face and looked down into a black hole. It smelt. So this is where they chucked the stuff, she thought.

She lowered the candle into the hole but she couldn't see the bottom. What was visible of the rocky sides in the quivering candlelight was caked in powdery, dried scum. A pale spider hurried into hiding in a crevice and just before the candle flame keeled sideways and went out, she saw some pallid ferns that had taken root. There was obviously life down there, but what had blown the candle out? Air, or something else?

Then she noticed there was a dirty bit of cord knotted to the staple. It hung down into the hole and disappeared out of sight. She was scared there might be something gruesome hanging on the end, but she pulled it up. There was masses of it. It lay in mucky coils round her feet. Why was it there? Was this a pit with nothing at the bottom but old bath water and excrement, or did it go somewhere useful? A test was what was needed.

She raced up the stairs. 'I'm sorry, Worly,' she said to the skeleton, 'but you of all people would understand.' She took his skull, went back and dropped it down the drain hole. There was silence, then a noise of bone against rock that went clattering on into the distance. But no splash; just more silence. It must go somewhere. It was the way out.

Then the hole began to make an unearthly, thin screaming that made her flesh crawl. Melior clapped the lid down and ran. She would sooner risk going back to

161

the Sew House than go down to whatever was screaming at the bottom.

When she opened the panel into the Ante-room, it was full of Policy Maker guards. Some were scanning the walls. Some were down on their knees scrutinising her floury handprints with magnifying glasses. 'It's a girl's prints all right,' she heard one of them say. 'What's the betting they're our red headed suspect's?' She closed the panel noiselessly. The god! They were onto her. They might find the panel at any second and come flooding onto the stairs after her.

She ran back and opened up the drain hole again. She'd seen what the Policy Makers could do to Inmate girls. She'd seen girls driven mad, girls made pregnant, girls disfigured. She'd rather face the screaming thing, which anyway was silent now.

She slung the cord back into the drain and it slithered away into the dark. She yanked on it hard to see how well it was tied to the staple in the floor. It seemed good enough. She stowed the candle and matches in her pocket and started on the business of getting into the drain. She nearly fell backwards and clung to the cord with her knees round her chin. But she'd done it. She whispered, 'Goodbye everything,' and snatched at the lid with one hand. It nearly knocked her out as it came down on her head. She began to lower herself down the drain. It was black as night and the air was fouler by the minute, but she kept going. Then the thin screaming began again. It was much closer. Melior froze, spinning slowly on the rope in the dark. Then she thought she heard her brother, Avtar, calling her name and told herself savagely not to go raving mad. She must force herself to go on down towards the screaming.

The cord started to swing. It lurched more and more violently as the maniacal creature at the bottom pitched it around. She tried to climb up again to get away, but her head smacked against the rock. She remembered how she'd seen stars, and that was all. Where was she now?

Melior groaned in the darkness, then propped herself up on one elbow and lit her candle. A monstrous face was hanging over hers. It licked its lips. She lost consciousness again.

The candle was still there when she came to. So was the face – or a part of a face – still looming right next to hers. The thin screaming came out of it.

Melior shut her eyes and waited for the thing to strike. It didn't. When she dared open them again, the half-face licked its mouth and said, 'Where's that rope go to?' There was the briefest hesitation before it said, 'Ma'am.' Melior closed her eyes again. She could hardly speak she was so frightened. 'Where am I?' she whispered.

'The god knows.'

Melior's eyes flew open. If the face knew the god then it must be an Inmate of some sort. The crying noise came again and a lamb stuck its head out from the face's shirt.

'Oh,' she said limply, 'it was only a lamb.'

'My lamb,' the face said.

'Who are you?' Melior asked.

'They call me Scar.'

Melior held up her candle and saw the other half of the face was a young man's of about eighteen. He was dressed in a shepherd's thick cloak and a brimmed hat, and he had his shepherd's crook. He was half-standing beside her where she was lying at the bottom of the drain. His head was pressed against the rocky ceiling of a tunnel entrance.

Scar gave the rope a tug. He'd had no idea this place existed until today, when he'd gone after a lamb he could hear crying. Its mother was going frantic, running round the gorse that grew in a thick patch on that side of the hill. He'd pushed his way in and come to a cluster of juniper bushes which were so prickly that he'd had to lie flat and worm his way in at their roots. Then the ground dropped away unexpectedly into a dry pebbly channel. The evergreen junipers grew over it so densely no one could possibly have guessed it was there. He'd scrambled along it on all fours, but as the channel cut deeper into the hill he could walk upright over moss and squelchy mud until he came to a cave entrance. It was sinister; there was a child's skull lying outside it, but he could hear the lamb bleating inside so he had to go in. He passed more scattered bones and a bundle of rags before he found it.

As soon as he came near, the little creature began jittering about. He could just see that it was tangled in some rope hanging down from a shaft. He heard a scream above him and grabbed the lamb before something he thought was a great bat landed beside him with a sound like a single thump on a pillow.

Next thing, this Policy Maker woman with cascades of scarlet hair and the brightest blue eyes he'd ever seen had lit a candle right under his nose and then fainted. She was out for a while; long enough for him to remember where he'd seen her before. She was the woman who had walked in on the meeting in the Tank Room. She had the look of an Inmate, but her uniform was a Policy Maker's. She was the worst sort of all. She was a Split.

He couldn't imagine where she'd come from, but he intended to find out. 'Where's that rope go?' he said. She answered him with another question.

'Where's that go?' She nodded at the tunnel entrance.

Scar hated Policy Makers for what they'd done to him and to the king and to the City. His one eye blazed down at the woman. 'It would be nothing but a pleasure to kill you, Policy Maker,' and he drew the knife he kept hidden in his boot.

'Hold on, hold on,' Melior said. Her mouth was dry with fright. 'I'm no Policy Maker.'

'Convince me.' Scar pressed the point of the knife to her throat. Melior gabbled a version of her story, calling herself Morag – how she was running away from the clerk.

All he said at the end was, 'You talk like a Policy Maker.' Melior swapped to her Inmate accent. 'I worked for the Chief Medical Officer. I picked up their talk.' He kept the knife pressed into her throat. 'You're lying, Morag. You're a Split and a spy.'

Melior lost her temper. She raged at him that he was an impertinent, clod-hopping shepherd with as much sense as one of his own stupid sheep and that he'd no right to be threatening her with knives. 'Can't you see, you gormless peasant,' she stormed, 'that I'm on the run and I need help, not a slit throat, silly?'

Scar's one eye widened. 'Princess Melior!' he said, as though he could hardly believe it. 'That's who you sound like!' And he repeated "Silly!" just the way she had said it. Melior made a note never ever to call anyone "Silly" again. That's how her brother had identified her.

'Who's Princess Melior?' she asked guilelessly.

Scar smiled. It didn't do anything for his face –

smiling. 'We used to play boats on the fish pond together. Our fathers were friends.'

No one got through Melior's guard that easily. She said, 'This is the first time I've ever set eyes on you.'

''Course it isn't,' he said almost childishly. 'I served in the Royal Household. Remember?'

'No,' Melior argued back. 'For the god's sake! Who'd forget *you*?'

Scar pulled his hat further over his shattered face and turned away into the tunnel.

'Come on,' he said. 'It's my duty to help you.'

Even Melior realised she'd been tactless, but she didn't apologise. She'd learned not to in the orphanage. It looked weak, and admitted that you were in the wrong, which put you at a disadvantage. However, she needed his help, so she followed him and tried to make amends by giving a bit of information.

'The rope goes up to the castle,' she said to his departing back. All he said was, 'Would you mind hurrying, Princess Melior? The Over Lord checks this side of the hill from the Topmost Tower once an hour. If he sees I'm missing, he'll investigate and we'll be done for.' Melior hurried.

But when Scar looked back she was crouching over the rags and scattered bones he'd passed earlier. She was holding a piece of rag and weeping.

'What is it?'

She couldn't speak for a minute and he waited impatiently. At last she said, 'Lal. This is her dress. See? The blue and silver brocade material. This is one of her silver buttons.' Melior put her head in her hands and screamed, 'These are her bones. The god! I can't bear it. This is my sister. She must have tried to get out this

166

way.' She screamed again, pressing the fabric between her hands. 'She almost made it.'

Scar looked at the bones. 'These are sheep's bones.'

'How could a sheep have been wearing Lal's dress?' Melior wept.

'I'm a shepherd. I know a sheep's bones.'

'And I know my sister's dress.

She pulled away when he tried to help her up. 'I can't leave her.' She was gathering the bones. 'We must bury her.' She was screaming again now. 'For once I'm going to do the right thing.'

'Then save yourself. It's your duty, Princess Melior. You're the last of the Royal House of Khul, the sole survivor...' He stopped. For some reason, that had made her cry harder. He looked at his watch. They had ten minutes to get out of here. He tried again. 'I saw Lal on the day of the Attack'

'Where?' She choked with crying. 'Tell me.'

'Only if you come with me.'

She glared up at him through her tears. 'It had better be good.'

CHAPTER FOURTEEN

Watt waited at the bottom of the Topmost Tower, holding the heavy door ajar so that he could watch Vince outside. Vince took his time but, at last, he rolled away into the South East Tower and Watt came out onto the Roof Garden. He'd escaped a meeting with the Over Lord.

He set out in search of Porcini's motorcar. If anyone asked where he was going, he was delivering the message he was carrying to the Roc's apartments.

He passed a spread of red sawdust that had been shovelled over the Messenger Boy's blood to soak it up. How could he have been so stupid to talk about avenging the poor kid's death? What was really needed was to stop the same thing happening ever again, but he couldn't. He was powerless.

He jogged along the broad central path of the Roof Garden, which was withered and scruffy now. It had been full of children playing when he was little. He remembered weaving his toy horse around the big urns placed at intervals on either side of the path. The miniature orange trees they held were mostly dead, but some were still gamely sprouting a shock of leaves and blossom at the top of their broomstick-like trunks. He jogged on, moving in and out of the shadows they cast in the early evening sun. They looked like big black lollipops lying on the gravel path and on the patchy yellowing grass that flanked it.

The fishpond had dried up, so the carp were gone. So were the roses that had rambled along the parapet overlooking the Inner Court. All that was left of them was a scraggly tangle of twigs. A few of the herbs his mother had planted had not quite given up the fight to stay alive, but it was a losing battle. The place was baked hard as a brick now and was just about as inviting.

He noticed a drab little lump of feathers in amongst some parched lavender. It was a dead pigeon. He picked it up. There was an air gun pellet in its chest. Without a moment's hesitation, Watt took off the message attached to its leg and read:

Haakron? A threat to Empire?

The sweet scent of the lavender mangled his thoughts as he tried to understand. Haakron a threat? Haakron was his uncle, his uncle who had been killed during the Attack. He'd been dragged away dead by the feet. Watt had seen it with his own eyes. Was it possible he had survived? Surely he was dead. But if Haakron was thought of as a threat to the Empire – the whole huge, powerful Empire – then he must be alive, very much so. And if he was alive, where was he?

A fern with a wodge of damp earth clinging to its roots splattered at his side. He looked up. The girl with the pink cheeks was waving commandingly at him from the balcony of what had once been his sister Lal's apartment.

Fidelis had been brushed and spruced and squeezed into corsets, then seated in front of the mirror while her hair was battened down into submissive little coils. Prudence stood behind her, her tin box of tools for subduing people's hair wide open on the dressing table. Her mouth was full of vicious hairpins, which she rammed one by one into pin curls, saturating each lock of hair in a mixture of sugar and water so that when it dried it would be set crystalline rigid.

Next, Fidelis had been hooked into her green water silk dress. A spotted candy-pink scarf had been tied round her head in a stiff bow that stuck out above her ears like a pair of spread wings. It was to stay there until the curls were dry. 'About an hour,' Prudence said, and Fidelis had gone to wait out the hour on her balcony.

The dress was tight and the pins tugged at her scalp. She was wondering drearily if she could bear this for a whole hour when she saw a Messenger Boy, crossing the Roof Garden below her, stop his jogging run and pick up a dead pigeon: her pigeon. Fidelis panicked. She must get the message back. If it should come out that she'd been meddling in politics, her father would be angrier with her than he'd ever been in her life.

The boy was standing stock-still. There was no one else around. She uprooted a potted plant and slung it at him to get his attention without the guards at the other end of the roof hearing. It landed at his feet and he looked up at her in a dazed sort of way. She signalled to him to wait there for her.

Luckily, Prudence was lying on the bed with a slice of cucumber over each closed eyelid, preparing herself for the ball, and Span was in a pungent sleep, so Fidelis was able to tiptoe out of the room to the Roof Garden.

At first she thought the boy had cut and run, but then she saw him squatting in the round shadow of an orange tree, holding the dead bird. He appeared to be studying every feather. 'You there,' she said, and he looked up.

Watt saw the pink-cheeked girl was wearing an extremely silly hat. Fidelis saw a flash of amusement come and go on his face and thought what a sight she must look in her awful scarf. She said coldly, 'I think you have my carrier pigeon. Give it to me.'

The boy passed her the dead bird. When she saw the pellet wound, Fidelis felt a stab of shame. So much for our secret service, she thought. But the message was gone. She panicked again.

'Did you take the message?' she asked, just as coldly. The boy took his time to consider the question, then shook his head. 'Are you sure?' Her voice was curt to cover her fright. He nodded.

Watt was unsure of his moves here. He'd never had to lie to a Policy Maker before. It felt much the safest to play dumb again. When he talked he just seemed to act out his guidebook on "How Not To Be A King". The girl said, 'Are you *really* sure? The message was private. To my mother.'

Watt noticed playing dumb resulted in receiving information. He wondered why on earth this absurd looking girl's mother should know if his uncle was a threat to the Empire.

Her green dress rustled as she crouched down beside him, and the pink wings flapped as though she might take off. She smelt of perfume – some sort of flowers that quarrelled with the lavender. She said earnestly, 'I would like the message.' He shook his head and held his fist clenched. She may look a harmless joke, but she was a Policy Maker and she could have him shot for taking the message. She only had to summon the guards and he'd be just another patch of red sawdust in seconds. 'Why don't you speak?' He grimaced at her stupidly. 'Is it that you can't?' she asked gently. Watt nodded.

'But why?' she asked. 'Why didn't your king cure you? Watt almost asked her what the flip she was talking about. Did she think his father had performed miracles? 'Or was dumbness something he couldn't work his voodoo on?' she asked. This alarmed him. Was she a crazy person? She certainly had a lot of ironwork sticking out of her head through the pink scarf. If it was to keep her brain straight, it wasn't working.

She was close enough for him to see that her eyes were steel grey and rather beautiful, and he suddenly saw that she was very frightened. He'd never seen that in a Policy Maker. She looked so scared he almost felt sorry for her. She said, 'I'll tell you a secret.' And he thought – Like they all do. 'No one must know I sent that message,' she went on. 'No one must see it except Mama.' Then she said "Please" so unhappily that he thought the kindest thing was to give her the message and run.

Someone asked, 'Can I be of assistance?' They looked up. The Spy Master was smiling down at them.

* * *

The Over Lord's greeting of 'Ah! My dear eyes and ears,' to his *Man* was so effusive that the Spy Master wondered if the Over Lord was beginning to feel the strain. 'A drink?' the Over Lord suggested, with a smile that gave him a look of his old self for a moment.

The tot was accepted happily. Once they'd all three settled and taken a sip, the Over Lord asked solicitously, 'Are you well?'

'Good enough,' his *Man* replied.

The Over Lord put his own drink to one side. 'Trying times for you,' he commented sympathetically.

'A State Visit,' his *Man* responded, 'brings its pressures.' The Over Lord gave him an understanding nod. 'Yes. I hear you had trouble with the furnace today.' The Baker turned watery eyes on him and rasped, 'What can I do for you, sirs, this evening?'

The Spy Master was lost in admiration. Even he hadn't had an inkling the Baker was an agent. No wonder the Over Lord had been so clued up about the so-called Resistance Movement. The Baker was at the heart of it.

They were interrupted by a guard with a message. A clerk had reported an Inmate called Morag missing, and her sweetheart with her. The clerk had requested permission to take in her room-mate, Triss, for questioning. Morag had not been seen since she finished last night's shift in the Sew House.

'Aha!' the Over Lord said. 'The Sew House again. I think we're on to something.' But to everyone's surprise, the Spy Master, who had been looking over the Roof Garden, suddenly excused himself and left. He had spotted Fidelis with the Messenger Boy and the pigeon.

'Anything on the identity of the sweetheart?' the Over Lord asked the guard, who gave the Baker a spiteful look and replied, 'One Brad.'

'Rolls!' the Baker objected. 'Brad's down the hospital. Broke his stupid head. Pranks,' he rasped. 'My boys will

173

get up to pranks.'

The guard was dismissed.

'Which reminds me,' the Over Lord said. 'One of your boys was meddling with the Offering Table this morning. A bald one.'

The Baker shrugged. 'Half the kids round here is baldies. For the nits.'

'Nits?'

The Baker leaned across the desk to the Over Lord.

'Head lice. We've a plague of head lice.'

The Over Lord drew back hastily. He gave the Baker a small purse of coins from his desk drawer, and the Baker listened while he described events at the Roc's tea party and the very regrettable scream of the name "Avtar".

The Baker took a sip of his drink, then rasped, 'There's a story going round that Avtar survived the Liberation.'

The Over Lord gripped the edge of his desk. 'The Sun!' It was like a prayer for mercy.

The Baker went on. 'They say that he's disguised as a servant boy.' He laughed. 'And here's the rich bit. They say he's acting like he's dumb. "Avtar The Dumb", they're calling him.'

'And the King's Touch?' The Over Lord could hardly get the question out. 'What do they say about that?'

The Baker didn't answer directly. He put his head on one side and gave the Over Lord a meaningful look. The Over Lord groaned. 'He has it.'

'There's talk of him leading an insurrection,' the Baker said. 'What better time, sir, to overthrow the Empire than when all its leaders are gathered in the City?'

'What better time indeed,' the Over Lord replied quietly.

CHAPTER FIFTEEN

'Can I be of assistance?'

Watt and Fidelis looked up. Watt saw the auburn haired man smiling down at them. His instinct was to run for his life but he forced himself to stay put.

The Spy Master saw the Roc's daughter in an unbecoming hat, holding an interesting looking pigeon.

'Can I be of any assistance?' he repeated, adding a sardonic, 'My lady.'

Fidelis said, 'I found this pigeon and we were just going to bury it.' Watt was impressed. This was no crazy person. She was so poised, you'd never have guessed that she was dead scared, and you'd certainly never have known from the sound of her that she was lying. The man held out his hand for the bird and Watt flinched involuntarily – the man was lethal.

'I'll see to it, my lady.'

Watt had never heard a Policy Maker woman called "my lady" before. She must be posh. Whatever she was, "my lady" didn't want to hand over the pigeon.

'We wouldn't dream of troubling you, master, sir,' she replied.

'How thoughtful.' He gave her his most radiant smile. 'But I must remind my lady that this boy is a messenger, not a grave digger. He has his work. And you, my lady, are none other than...'

The pink-cheeked girl broke in with a formal,'You are right, Master Spy Master.'

Watt crouched at the man's feet thinking – so that's his job; he's the Spy Master that the boys in the shower room were talking about. He's just killed a kid and he's chatting and smiling as if he were at a garden party. He must be really used to doing it.

The girl went on, 'I shall be forever in your debt, master, for your guidance.' They spoke to one another in a way that was quite new to Watt. Evidently they couldn't just come out with it straight, like – "Give me that pigeon". And "No, I'm keeping it". Instead there was this polite dual between them, with icicles for weapons.

The girl stood up behind him with a rustle of silk and handed the dead pigeon to the Spy Master over Watt's head.

'Where's the message?'

Watt could tell from the way he asked that the Spy Master would kill a hundred boys to find it. The god alone knew what he'd do to him if he discovered it hidden in his hand. Or to the girl for that matter.

Watt eased himself upright and stood facing the Spy Master, eyes downcast, like a good servant, hands behind his back. He heard the girl say innocently from behind him, 'Message! I found none, sir.' Slowly, Watt very slightly uncurled the fingers of the hand holding the message, but would she notice it? And would she dare take it?

The Spy Master laughed. Watt's heart began to bang. He'd learned on the day of the Attack that the nicer the Spy Master appeared to be, the more dangerous he was. Sure enough, he said, 'You, boy. Did you find a message?' Watt shook his head. And still the girl didn't take the message. She said, 'Sir, it's of no use to question the boy, Master, sir.' Watt felt her fingers touch his hand, felt her take the tiny piece of paper from him as he unclenched his fist. She went on smoothly, 'He is dumb.'

'Dumb he may be.' Watt saw the Spy Master's eyes glint merrily. 'But he can show me his two hands. Now!' He snapped at Watt. Watt jumped and spread his hands out in front of him. The Spy Master flicked a glance from Watt's empty palms to the girl and said, 'I amuse you, my lady?' Watt could hear by the pink-cheeked girl's voice when she replied that she was trying not to smile, and he prayed Lady *Pink Cheeks* wouldn't mess them up at the last minute.

She said, 'Oh, Master Spy Master, sir. Even at your most severe, you can always make us ladies smile.' The Spy Master positively preened. Watt relaxed a little. This girl knew exactly what she was doing: she'd crawled, and it had worked. She'd knocked the man off course with a simpering compliment. Did all Policy Makers do this? Think one thing and say another in a flowery fib? And might it be a handy way for a king to carry on? It had certainly got them out of trouble.

The Spy Master said, 'My Lady Fidelis.' Watt was thinking Fidelis was rather a nice name when he went on, 'If a message were to come to light, so to speak, it would be in the interest of the Empire to show it to me. If someone were to *hand it in to you*, for example. Understand?'

A chill of fright went through Watt. They weren't out of trouble at all. The man knew he'd passed her the message. He heard Fidelis behind him reply steadily, 'I can assure you, sir, I am as aware of my duty to the

Empire as any of us.' The Spy Master rewarded her with a little bow, as if to say – you won that point, don't expect to win another. Then he changed tack abruptly. 'Show me the letter you're carrying, boy.' Watt gave him the letter from Porcini with its loopily written address, and Fidelis said sharply, 'That's to my father!'

The god! Pink Cheeks is only the Roc's daughter!

'Quite right, my lady,' the Spy Master agreed. 'In this uncertain City all your father's correspondence goes through the tightest of security, namely myself.' He bowed again. 'I look forward to the pleasure of seeing you again, my lady, at the ball this evening.' He turned to go. 'Perhaps without the hat.'

Watt didn't smile. The hat was a riot, but it would be cruel to laugh at someone who had just saved his skin. Besides, it was rotten of the Spy Master to remark on it – that was like judging a loaf before it was cooked. Even he had worked out by now that the pink hat anchoring down the ironmongery was some part of a "getting ready" ritual.

The Spy Master said languidly over his shoulder, 'You, boy. Come with me. You may be needed to carry this letter on to his Excellency.' Watt could do nothing but obey. It felt like following a python.

He stole a grateful look back at Fidelis, but she was trying not to cry about the hat jibe. People cried so much more than he'd realised and for such big and little reasons. He gave her a quick, comforting smile and dared a conspiratorial wink of thanks. She returned it with a watery flicker of an eyelid before she ran back the way she'd come.

Watt followed the Spy Master as he strolled on, pausing to toss the dead pigeon over the parapet down in the Inner Court. It smashed in a flurry of feathers onto the parquet floor that the Inmates had been laying all day for tonight's ball. Then the Spy Master hit him a real crack on the jaw. It felt as though his head had snapped off his neck.

'Dumb are we?' the Spy Master asked agreeably and then beat him up. The Baker's training held good. Not a word came out of him. Watt caught glimpses between punches and kicks of Policy Makers hurrying by. But no one tried to stop it. The Spy Master kicked him round the Roof Garden until the world was nothing but pain.

It was over as suddenly as it had started. The Spy Master was helping him up. He looked quite shame-faced as he pulled Watt to his feet. 'Sorry, boy.' His apology was muffled and he couldn't meet Watt's gaze, but at least it was an apology. 'You really are dumb, aren't you?'

Stop! The cold voice in Watt's head cut in as he opened his mouth to answer. The Spy Master was watching him like a cat about to pounce. Watt spat out a gob of blood. The man had nearly fooled him again. He nodded at the Spy Master. Yes, he was dumb all right.

'How do you communicate then?' the Spy Master mused, and dragged him to the parapet. Watt wondered if he was going to throw him over. 'Ink!' he commanded. Watt fumbled for the small bottle all the Messenger Boys carried, while the Spy Master took the pen clipped into Watt's top pocket, then spread Madame Porcini's letter face down on the parapet. He handed Watt the pen. 'Tell me your name, boy,' he said kindly, 'or I will kill you, I promise.'

Careful, careful, the voice warned him. If he finds out you can write, he'll know you can read. If you can read, he'll know you've read the message the Fidelis girl took from you. He'll hurt you far more to find out what it said.

Watt had no idea why the Roc's daughter was writing to her mother about his Uncle Haakron, but he would protect Haakron from the Spy Master at all costs, particularly as it seemed his uncle was standing up to the Empire. He took the pen and wondered what he would do if he genuinely couldn't write his name.

The cold voice said – if he's promised to kill you, you would try and look as if you could write; so Watt drew a squiggle. The Spy Master hit him on the back of his head so that Watt's face hit the stone parapet and his nose bled. He did another squiggle. The Spy Master hit him again. And so it went on and on. At last the Spy Master said, 'That's enough, imbecile,' and picked up Porcini's letter, covered with squiggles and Watt's blood.

Watt leant against the parapet and wiped the blood off his face with his sleeve. The last of the evening sun touched the dead rambling roses. Down in the Inner Court, darkness had already arrived and Inmate servants were lighting hundreds of candle lamps strung along the arcades. It looked beautiful. It was strange that while he was being hurt so much, other people's lives went on so pleasantly. The Spy Master led him towards the Topmost Tower: the last place on earth Watt wanted to go.

They'd practically climbed to the top of the narrow stairs when they met a man coming down. He stood aside to let them pass. It was the Baker. He touched his forelock to the Spy Master. He never so much as looked at Watt.

The Spy Master led Watt into the Over Lord's room

where he was at his desk writing to the hospital about the supervisor's uniform. He seemed thinner and weirder than Watt remembered. He said, without looking up, 'That Baker's certainly worth his weight in gold. He's filled me in on this Avtar business.'

Watt's whole world swung around and rearranged itself. The Baker, *his* Baker, his protector, was in league with the Policy Makers – a Split – and informing the Over Lord about him, what's more. Treachery was the very last thing he would have dreamed of from the Baker. It left him feeling desolate and deserted.

The Over Lord looked up. 'Ah!' he said regretfully when he saw Watt. 'Didn't realise you had company, my dear Spy Master.' He sighed. 'The boy's heard too much. Can't put the Baker at risk. This will have to be another of your window jobs. Pity. Two in one day. Not good for morale.'

Watt reckoned he had half a chance of getting out of the room alive if he took the emblem of the rising sun on the Over Lord's desk and bashed him over the head with it. But what about the Spy Master? He was a killer; he'd half killed him already. But amazingly, the Spy Master just said, 'Oh the boy's not a problem,' and took the Over Lord's letter. 'Do you want this delivered to the hospital?' He tossed Porcini's letter onto the desk saying, 'Another of Porcini's scrawls.'

The Over Lord gestured at Watt. 'For goodness sake!' he remonstrated.

'I tell you, the boy's not a problem,' the Spy Master repeated, handing Watt the letter for the hospital. The Over Lord shrugged and ripped open Porcini's letter. 'This is all shaping up very nicely.' He looked quite animated. 'Porcini leaves at dawn,' he told the Spy

Master. 'We must ensure her car is made spick and span.' There was something peculiar about the way he said that last bit, but Watt was so glad not to be hurtling out of the window that he couldn't give it much attention.

Then the door flew open and the Roc swanned in, dressed to kill in full military uniform. His moustache was waxed to fine points at either end like daggers.

'I say, you fellows,' he said. 'Do you suppose Haakron is too far north of here to have anything to do with this Avtar business?'

Watt saw the Over Lord deliberately conceal Porcini's letter to the Roc under a pile of papers. But then the Roc was addressing him. 'Look lively, lad. Clear out and deliver your message, can't you!' Watt nodded and ran.

The Roc seated himself with rigidly creased care. 'Avtar,' he said. 'First: could he be alive? Second: if he is, has he got his father's dratted cure hidden up his sleeve? Third: Haakron.' He paused to reflect. 'Confound it! Do you think that boy understood what I said just now?'

'Oh, I'm sure he'll deliver the message, sir,' the Spy Master said.

'No,' the Roc replied. 'I meant did he understand what I said about Haakron?'

The Spy Master smiled. 'It really makes no odds what he did or didn't understand.' The Roc looked doubtful, so the Spy Master continued soothingly, 'He's illiterate and he'll never repeat a word. The boy's dumb.'

The Over Lord pushed back his chair so violently as he stood up that it fell over. 'What did you say?' The question came out in a crazy whisper. The Spy Master looked at him in surprise. 'That he's dumb, that's all.'

'Dumb!' The Over Lord almost screamed.

The Roc raised his eyebrows. 'Are you feeling quite

183

fit, old man?' He seemed the picture of concern. But the Over Lord wasn't taken in. The Roc hadn't got where he was by worrying about people's health. The Over Lord was in an anguish of frustration. He had to hunt down the boy immediately. The King's Touch was a source of infinite power that he must have. But how could he set the hunt in motion with the Roc sitting there? He couldn't reveal that he'd let Avtar, the City's king, slip through his fingers. That way lay his own destruction.

CHAPTER SIXTEEN

'Lal was in the Ante-room.'

Scar led Melior along the dried up waterway as he talked.

'The Policy Makers had rounded her up with a crowd of other kids. An auburn-haired man was there pretending to be one of us. I knew he wasn't but he was convincing; probably had slave forbears. They were looking for Avtar. The auburn-haired man asked which of us was the king because they wanted to crown him. And Avtar steps forward. Then there was a sort of quiet scuffle round him. I don't know what was going on. There were tall kids in front of him. Lal kept bobbing in and out of my sight. So did Avtar. I was scared stiff that the auburn-haired man would notice. But then another boy said he was the king. He was much older than Avtar but the Policy Makers hadn't done their homework so they took his word for it. And that was that. I didn't see Lal again.'

He turned back to Melior. 'You have to wriggle under these juniper roots here out onto the hillside. Don't cry. Watch yourself, it's prickly. I'll go first; as soon as you're through, hide under my cloak. We have to look like one person to the guards on the second defence wall.

Once Melior had wormed her way through, Scar

practically tucked her under his armpit and they walked down the slope in the setting sun together with Melior concealed by the cloak. It was peculiar to be hugged by someone who plainly wasn't very keen on you, but that was the price of freedom, Melior told herself. The lamb inside his shirt wasn't on her side either: it gave her a prod in the jaw with its hoof.

'Would you mind not moving from there?' Scar said and walked away, leaving her under the shelter of a jutting blade of grey rock.

Scar kept talking to her without looking at her, explaining that she was in the only place on the hill where the guards and the Over Lord couldn't see you. It had taken him years to discover that, and he wanted to keep the secret.

Melior sat still as stone, looking down the scree below her and at the river on its glinting way eastwards to the sea. Scar had reminded her of her father's day when, "Would you mind?" was how the City people had asked someone to do something for them. It avoided giving an order. No ex-slave wanted to be commanded to do anything. Everybody had the right to reply – yes, they *did* mind. But it was pointless to dwell on the old days. She had to think about getting off this hill without being seen.

Scar was making a big show of reuniting the lamb with its mother now for the sake of the guards up on the wall. The ewe and her lamb played their parts perfectly with lots of overjoyed bleating. '

'What happened to the boy who said he was king?' she asked him.

'What do you think?'

'They killed him?'

'That's more or less it.'

'Serves him right for trying to be king.'

Scar shot her a surprised look. 'I like to think he was trying to save the little king's life.'

Melior hadn't thought of that. But if it was true, then the boy's sacrifice had been for nothing because of what she'd done to her brother today.

'There's a gibbous moon tonight,' Scar told her. 'Wait until it sets just before dawn; that's when it's really dark. The guards can't see a thing.'

It was all too easy. She was to go down onto the plain, take off on one of the garrison horses tethered there, and she would be free. But what about her brothers? They wouldn't be. She'd given Avtar away to the Policy Makers, and she was leaving her little brother to fend for himself. She felt ashamed. It was a horrible feeling that she'd never had before; it made her want to bury herself under the rock she was sitting by. She just nodded agreement to Scar. She was too ashamed to speak.

He wandered off with the flock. When he came back, he shoved a sandwich in her hand as he and the flock passed her, and she ate it gratefully. 'What was your real name, Scar?'

'I forget,' he called back. The snub was justified. She swallowed a mouthful of sandwich and said, 'Forgive me, Scar.' She couldn't quite bring herself to say what for, but she'd been insanely stupid to assume he'd always had that mangled face. The Policy Makers had hacked their way through most of the children in the City, searching for Royals. He'd obviously been one of their victims. She asked very formally, 'Would you mind telling me your story?'

But evidently Scar did mind. Instead, he said, 'Do

you remember how we two disobeyed the rules and went walking down the side of the Water Reservoir Tank on the castle roof? Do you? We got into a fantastic row.' Melior tried in vain to remember. 'You dropped your toy elephant in the water. I nearly managed to fish it out for you, but it suddenly sank. We never saw it again.'

'So it *was* my elephant, wasn't it?'

'Well, actually,' Scar said, 'it was Avtar's.'

'You boys!' Melior snapped. 'Always ganging up.'

Scar wasn't going to be put off. 'Poor Avtar. He didn't half take on about his elephant.'

Melior said, 'Avtar's been captured.' Scar was so stunned he actually turned to look at her. 'Avtar! Avtar is *alive* still? Praise be! But when was he captured?'

'This afternoon,' Melior said. 'And it was all my fault.' When she'd finished telling him what had happened, he looked so angry she was quite glad he had to keep his distance from her. 'The god! Why did you shout his name?'

'It just popped out,' Melior wailed, and burst into tears.

Scar got up and walked off around the hillside. Melior could hear the bleating of the sheep following him going further and further into the distance. She began to think he'd abandoned her for betraying Avtar. But towards dusk, he came back with the flock and stood some distance from her.

'All right,' he called to her quietly, 'this is the plan. I've told the Over Lord that I'm staying out in the fold tonight to tend a sick lamb. I'll let it get a bit darker, then I'll climb up into the castle the way you came out and see if I can rescue him.' Scar's voice sounded grim. 'They'll have him in the cells.' Melior knew he meant they would be torturing him. 'What does he look like now?' Scar asked.

'He was a Ghosty Boy.'

Scar seemed extremely surprised, but he didn't say why. 'His head is shaved,' Melior said, and told him the little she'd discovered about her brother. All he said was, 'Let's get on with it then. Do exactly as I say.' And Melior obeyed him.

Scar led his flock round the rock. As the sheep came past her, she grasped a ewe. It was newly shorn so there was no fleece to hang onto, but she got hold of it round its neck. It kicked and bucked and then fell on its side where it lay panting, unable to get up. She held it hidden, stroking its head, while Scar moved the rest of the flock away through the dusk to the fold. She waited.

He was alone when he came back. He was pretending to be looking for his lost sheep. He took his time. She was very nervous about this bit. Scar walked slowly behind the rock to join her, and then they moved at a tremendous speed. She took his cloak and hat, put them on and grabbed his crook while he righted the ewe. Then she stepped out from behind the rock onto the bare hillside with the ewe following behind her.

Would the guards watching from the second defence wall be fooled into thinking that she was Scar rounding up the sheep? She tripped on his long cloak and sent a prayer to the god that it wouldn't make them suspicious. There was no shout from overhead. She straightened her shoulders and strode off to the fold where Scar had told her to wait until it was dark enough to go down and steal a horse.

She felt a bit less ashamed now because in a very small way she was repairing the damage she'd done: she was helping Scar try and rescue Avtar. But another part of her felt wretched because she was deserting her other brother. When they'd come to the orphanage to separate the two of them, they'd nearly snapped his fingers, unbending his small hands from round her arm that he was clinging to. 'Now then, Felix,' the matron had said, 'we don't want a crybaby do we, Felix?' And the matron had held Felix down as he struggled to follow her. 'Come along, Felix,' they'd said to him. 'You're a big boy now, Felix. You don't need your sister Morag anymore.' And he had cried that he did. She remembered him calling and weeping as they led her away. She'd blocked her ears because she couldn't bear to hear his calls rise to a terrified scream, over and over. 'Morag, Morag'. The sound would haunt her forever.

Scar squatted on his heels under the rock and watched Princess Melior striding through the twilight with the ewe trotting after her. She was on her way. The god knew where. He dug out his pack of well-used cards and shuffled. A thought struck him: while he was in the castle, he may even have time to kill the Roc too.

He'd planned to stick his knife in the Roc when he came to watch the sheep shearing demonstration. But the Roc hadn't even turned up. Maybe the god was giving him a second chance to skewer the swine.

Princess Melior would soon disappear round the curve of the hill. He watched her go in the deepening twilight; then he cut the cards and turned one stack face up. It was the Queen. The card had been renamed after the Attack. It was called the Traitor now. He glanced back at Princess Melior. She'd gone.

He wondered why she had shouted her brother's name to the entire castle. Like mother, like daughter?

He'd very nearly told her his own old name, Gurmail, when she'd asked; he was perishing glad he hadn't now. The less she knew about you, the better.

He checked his watch, though it was hard to see. Coming up to seven o'clock. Time to go.

CHAPTER SEVENTEEN

Watt raced down the Topmost Tower's steps trying to make sense of the tiny bits of information he had about his Uncle Haakron. When he reached the entrance, a hand came out and yanked him behind the open door. The Baker cursed in his ear.

'We're in a mess,' he rasped. 'Where've you been? I thought you were dead.'

'Let me go, you traitor.'

'Traitor?' The Baker looked so genuinely startled that Watt understood how he'd deceived him all these years. He was really good at it.

He pushed a purse of coins into Watt's hand. 'I'm no traitor, boy, but I've blundered badly. We've got to get you out of here. They're after you.'

'You should know.'

'Listen. I'll cause a diversion. Can't think what, but you'll recognise it. The god knows how you'll do it, but we'll try and get you out. Brad can't help. He's down the hospital for the bash you gave him.' The Baker peered at Watt's face. 'Looks like someone's had a go at you too.' Watt jerked his face away as the Baker put up a hand to his cheekbone.

The Baker swallowed unhappily and went on, 'Stay hidden. Then meet us in the kitchens tonight. And whatever you do boy, talk. Talk your head off!'

'I don't believe you,' Watt said. 'You've betrayed me to the Over Lord and you'll betray me again.' The Baker looked so stricken that Watt was almost tempted to take it back. 'Don't you see?' the Baker said, 'I thought you were dead.'

Neither of them could say another word because half a dozen guards came running out of the deep twilight across the roof. The Baker shoved Watt further back behind the door and darted out to lean against it. The leading guard skidded to a stop. 'You seen a Messenger Boy?'

'Yes,' the Baker said calmly. 'Just passed me now, going that way.' He pointed across the Roof Garden. Watt heard the guard say, 'Half of you follow him. You others, get down to the hospital in case he's gone there with his message.' And he heard them run off.

The Baker waited a second, then released him. 'Clear off,' he said. 'They're on to you. You heard the man. Good luck.' And he pushed him out onto the roof. 'Not that way, idiot,' he rasped as Watt set off across the Roof Garden. Hardly knowing who to believe, Watt changed direction and ran towards the South East Tower. The watch guards on that section of the roof took no notice of a scurrying Messenger Boy. They remained facing the darkening plain.

More guards were tramping up the steps of the South East tower. Watt cursed himself for believing the Baker and dodged back, groping his way between the edge of the roof and the Water Terrace Reservoir. There was no balustrade, not even a rail to mark where the roof finished. He got down on his knees and crawled along the copper-lined strip between the black oblong of water and the drop into the courtyard, hundreds of cubits below. He wished he could step into the air like a bird and fly safely out of the City. His hand slipped on the smooth copper and he very nearly did step into the air.

Concentrate, he told himself and lay flat on the strip to give his heart, which had threatened to jump out of his mouth, time to go back to its usual place. The copper was still warm from the day's sun. It was comforting to rest there, feeling the warmth against his bruised cheek. He mustn't go to sleep.

He glanced behind him and saw a beam of light coming from the Topmost Tower and cutting into the near darkness. It travelled across the roof where the guards were standing, picking out their ochre uniforms and moving on to the North East Tower. Then it began to move across the reservoir towards him. In seconds he would be caught in the cone of light. He shoved his hat in his pocket, rolled over and dropped into the Reservoir Tank.

The water was freezing. He snatched a breath, and ducked under the surface and was gone. The light swept over the spot where he'd been lying. The water filled up his ears noisily and seemed to be trying to fill his head too, but he held onto the breath and thanked the god he could remember how to swim. He came up again in time to see the light moving on towards the South West Tower, scrupulously picking its way over every dark surface, probing and seeking. He took a huge lungful of air and then tried to stand on the bottom. It was impossible. He had to keep swimming.

The light swerved on across the Roof Garden and repeated its circuit. Watt braced himself as it hit the water again and ducked. Again the light missed him and he took the opportunity to swim towards the south west end where he could get out between the sweeps of light and make a run for it down the steps of the Tower.

He heard the great gong sounding the seven o'clock dressing bell down in the entrance hall, and the light cut out immediately. Evidently the Over Lord had to get himself all dressed up for the evening.

Watt swam quietly to the south west end and trod water until he reckoned it was safe to climb out. He put up his arm to grab the edge of the tank. He couldn't reach it. His fingers met the metal sides of the tank, nothing more. There was nothing to grip hold of to hoist himself out. He had trapped himself in the water.

He turned on his back and tried to float to give himself a chance to calm down and think what to do, but his uniform was heavy with water. He had a brief view of a sky already filling with stars, then went under. He came up spluttering to the surface. His choices weren't very heartening: he could either swim slowly about the tank until he couldn't manage another stroke, or he could call to the guards on the far end of the roof and give himself up. He wondered what a king would do in his position. Watt swam.

He'd no idea how long he'd been in the icy water – it seemed an age – when he felt a sudden and frightening change. He was being dragged towards the centre of the tank. An undertow was trying to pull him into the middle, and he swam hard against it. He knew what it was. One of the maintenance Inmates had opened the valve that allowed the water stored up here on the roof to flow down the pipe to top up the Great Tank underneath the Inner Court. He would be sucked down into the tank and drowned in a ton of water. He swam more and more frantically just to stay in the same place. He knew he could not keep this up for long.

CHAPTER EIGHTEEN

The soup was iced. It looked like piddle. Fidelis dipped her ladle-sized, golden soup spoon into it and tried some. It had the texture of phlegm. How on earth were all the other eighty diners at the long candlelit table putting it away so cheerfully?

Her elbow nudged the Over Lord sitting next to her and she apologised. He treated her to a chilly little smile. She was seated between him and the Spy Master. They'd both been very attentive, but she could tell they were bored stiff by her already and the banquet had hardly begun. It would have been better if her mother had been sitting there, not her.

She was glad of the roar of talk and the clash of busy spoons; it covered the silence between her and the Over Lord, which lengthened as she wracked her brains for something to say. No one else was at a loss for words. Opposite her, a laughing row of ladies, dressed like glittering goddesses, chatted to the elegant men next to them. Fidelis looked down at her green water silk dress. It was very plain.

It had been an altogether embarrassing evening so far. Madame Porcini had swirled in looking tragic and glamorous in tangerine silk shot with scarlet and decorated with glistening crimson beadwork. Her headdress was an exotic fan of feathers. And pinned to her magnificent breast was a massive corsage of trembling hair ferns and bobbing wild cherries.

Porcini had taken her seat beside the Roc, but the Butler had murmured something to her and she'd had to get up and be reseated towards the bottom of the table between the Pianist and a wiry man wearing a tight black suit and a white tie. The Spy Master told Fidelis he was the conductor of the orchestra for the ball that night.

Fidelis knew that what had happened to Madame Porcini was a snub. It meant Madame Porcini was out of favour with her father, and she wondered why. One or two people exchanged meaningful looks. Lady Joy, resplendent in puce satin and amethysts, actually winked at Lady Evangeline, who was supporting a tiara under whose weight a lesser woman would have buckled. Somehow or other, Madame Porcini was the forbidden "politics" too.

Fidelis could see that Madame Porcini was smouldering with fury. If she'd been a volcano, puffs of threatening smoke would have been coming out of her ears. She wasn't touching her soup; if she had, Fidelis was sure it would have boiled. She saw Madame Porcini say something to the Pianist that caused him to lay down his spoon and look at her in alarm. There was a quick, sparks-flying dispute between them; then the Pianist threw down his napkin and raced out of the Banqueting Hall.

By this time the silence between Fidelis and the Over Lord had become unbearable. Fidelis felt as if she'd been struck dumb. She heard herself pipe up, 'Over Lord, sir, how good and kind your servants are here. I met a Messenger Boy earlier on and he was most helpful, even though he was quite, quite dumb.'

The Over Lord had a spoonful of soup progressing nicely to his lips. To Fidelis's surprise, that's where it stopped and where it stayed. He seemed immobilised by what she'd said. It was not the effect she'd been aiming for at all.

The Over Lord turned the strangest, dead sort of look on her. 'Where did you meet this boy, Lady Fidelis?' He spoke so quietly she could hardly hear him over the beating of golden soup spoons and the din. Before she could reply the Spy Master chipped in, 'You mean you met him *again*, Lady Fidelis? Where?'

The Spy Master was smiling at her so broadly she could scarcely see anything of him but auburn curls and teeth. All the better to eat you with, she thought, and picked up a bread roll. 'Oh...' she began nervously, but the hand holding the roll jerked against the rim of her soup plate and tipped the lot into her green water silk lap.

The Over Lord's and the Spy Master's chair legs screeched on the paved floor as they half rose, with a flap of white napkins, to prevent their uniforms being splashed. Too late! They were both polka dotted with piddle green phlegm. Both of them looked very pained and fed up with her. Most of the diners had stopped talking and were craning up the table to see what was going on. The silence was cringe-making. Fidelis went poppy coloured with embarrassment.

The Roc, who had been chatting cheerfully to Lady Charity, called down the table, 'Go and change, my love. These things happen.' So Fidelis crept out of the Banqueting Hall, praying that Prudence would not consider it her duty to follow her. She couldn't have born a guilt session with Prudence.

She heard the Pianist playing somewhere as the lift creaked up to her apartment on the top floor. He was going over and over the same twiddly trill of notes. She held her soupy dress away from her legs, but she could feel it had gone through to her petticoats. The lift came to a stop and she drew back the folding cage gates and stepped into unknown territory.

Where was her apartment? Instead of the Roof Garden with its globes of lamps lighting the bushes, she was in darkness. The half-moon was reflected in a dark rectangle of black water ahead of her. She had taken the lift to the wrong tower. And, Oh, the Sun! Something was threshing about in the water, making white foam as it floundered around. Was it Span? She ran to the edge. Her evening slippers slipped on the smooth metal surround and she nearly went in too.

She strained her eyes and saw a bald boy flailing about in the water. He was swimming hard towards the edge where she stood but, inexplicably, he was moving slowly away from her. Then she saw that there was a dent in the water behind him. It was turning and swivelling in a dark whorl, like a giant version of the water running out of the bath she had taken. The boy was being tugged towards the hole in the water.

Fidelis knelt down on the edge and called, 'Hold on.' The boy's desperate eyes focused on her. She saw him make a huge effort and, very briefly, hold one finger to his lips, then go on frantically swimming again. It cost him: he was dragged much nearer the swirling indent in the water. She understood at once. She was not to call for help.

Fidelis stood up, took off her white cotton stockings

and knotted the feet together to make a rope. Then she lay on her stomach and, holding firmly to one end, cast the stocking rope out to the boy. He tried to snatch it but it fell short. He missed it and was pulled even nearer the spinning hole where the surface of the water was gliding fast over its lip and spiralling downwards.

His end of the stockings sank. She pulled them in and tried again. The same thing happened. Fidelis gave a sob of frustration. She daren't try a third time. He'd be swallowed up if he stopped swimming once more. Then she had an idea.

She took off her calico petticoat and hurriedly bunched the waistband and the hem together on one side, securing them with the end of the stocking rope. Then she threw the petticoat out over the water. The skirt billowed out and fell with a faint splash. The air underneath it buoyed it up long enough for the boy to reach the hem. She saw his fingers wrap around it and the petticoat was pulled taut. His other hand came up and clung to the waistband.

Very gently she began to pull him towards her. The knot of the stockings was strained and thin, but it held. Little by little, the boy was towed away from the sucking vortex of water until at last she was able to hold him tight against the side of the tank. He seemed half drowned.

Minutes passed before the whirlpool hole in the water grew smaller and smaller and then filled in. Without the noise of the water's rushing descent, that she hadn't even noticed until it stopped, Fidelis could hear herself gasping with effort. The boy never moved. Was he dead? But then he looked up at her and tried to smile, and she saw it was the dumb Messenger Boy.

'Are you all right?' she whispered, and he nodded

just once, fighting for breath and kicking slightly to take the pressure off the makeshift lifeline. He seemed a long way below her. The water level must have dropped a lot. She looked down and he looked up and both of them wondered how on earth they were going to get him out of the tank. If Fidelis tried to pull him up by her stocking rope she would fall in too. The edge was wet and slippery, and anyway she wasn't strong enough.

They both looked about for inspiration. The edge of the flat roof was useless. They both looked at the other side, where the parapet wall surrounded the central void. Its broad flat top was supported by a continuous stone carving of Slave City's emblem: the two chain links followed by a broken one. Fidelis leaned over and whispered slowly down to Watt – he noticed she talked to him as if he were daft as well as dumb – 'We need to tie the stockings to something firm so that you can climb up…'

Watt whispered back, 'How about using one of those stone chain links under the parapet top?'

Fidelis jumped and gave a squeak of surprise. 'I thought you were…'

'Sh!' Watt whispered. 'I know, I know.' His teeth were chattering with cold. 'You thought I was dumb. I'll explain later.' Fidelis nodded silently and walked the stocking rope over to the parapet. It didn't reach the first link, even if Watt held his end above his head. She looked down at the Messenger Boy in dismay and he gave her an encouraging smile. 'We'll think of something,' he said. And Fidelis did.

She stood on her end of the stockings to free her hands, and hoicked one of Prudence's ferocious pins out of her hair. What the deuce, she thought, the dress is ruined anyway. She stabbed a hole in its waist with the hairpin and ripped the green water silk skirt away from its bodice.

Watt thought it made a flipping terrible racket, and she obviously thought the same. She crouched down, peering fearfully at the guards over on the far side. Apparently none of them had heard, and she quickly made another tear down the back seam so that the skirt became one long piece of silk.

She gestured for him to let go of the petticoat, pulled it up, wrung it out and knotted the beautiful water silk to it. She ran and tied the stocking end to a stone chain link, while Watt swam to the corner nearest her. She dropped the silk skirt end down to him. It reached him easily.

'Climb up, can you?' she whispered over the edge. And he did.

Water pattered out of the stockings and petticoat as they took his weight. He hauled himself up hand over hand, pressing his feet against the side of the tank. As soon as his bald head appeared over the edge, Fidelis seized the shoulders of his uniform and hauled too. He slid over the edge and lay face down, shaking with cold.

Fidelis sat nearby with her arms round her knees, waiting for him to recover. Pools of water were spreading out over the roof from his sopping clothes. If Prudence could see me now, she thought, sitting next to a strange servant boy in nothing but my bodice and my pantaloons, she would probably faint dead away for a week.

At last Watt recovered enough to turn on his side to face her. He felt tired out now, and his arms and legs ached. He looked at the thoughtful, pink-cheeked girl in her frilly trousers. How muddling it was that one of the enemy, of all people, should have saved his life. 'Thanks,' he whispered. And she smiled at him.

'I owed you a favour,' she said very softly.

He sat up slowly. He was exhausted, but he took off his jacket and squeezed the water out of it. The pen and ink he carried were lost, but he still had his cap and the letter from the Over Lord, though it looked more like a lump of dough than a letter. 'Even so,' he said quietly, 'you've ruined your lovely dress.'

She looked down with a shy smile. Then she said, 'It wasn't that lovely.' And she told him about the ghastly soup incident and how she'd splattered the Over Lord and the Spy Master. He began to laugh quietly, which made her see that it was just as funny as it was awful, and she laughed too.

'Why wouldn't you let me call for help just now?' she asked. But Watt was ready for that. He didn't want to lie to her, but he had to. 'You get into a terrible row,' he said. 'Anyone who pollutes the water.' She looked pointedly at the pondweed on the dark surface and then back at him. He said lamely, 'I was in trouble.'

She remembered the Over Lord's frozen reaction at dinner when she'd mentioned the dumb Messenger Boy. 'Can I help?'

He was thoroughly confused by now. He couldn't stop himself liking her. She was such an interesting mix: gentle, and yet sometimes flipping haughty. And he loved her ladylike recklessness. But the only way she could really help him was by not existing, by turning time back so that the Empire had never killed his family and swallowed up his City.

He moved over to crouch beside her and she saw now that his face was terribly bruised. 'No,' he said. 'It's very kind of you to offer but no, you can't help.'

'I'd like to.' She looked at him earnestly. She was very pretty. 'I'm sure I can. I have...' she hesitated to come out with it direct. 'I have influence.'

'The best way you can help is to pretend you've never seen me, my lady. Forget me.' And he was gone.

CHAPTER NINETEEN

Fidelis shoved her wet underclothes, and what was left of her dress, under the mattress where Prudence would never find them, then quickly changed into the only frock left to choose from: the hateful yellow organza. She pushed her head through the neck and was groping around to find the armholes that scratched her armpits until they felt as if they were being filed, when she suddenly knew that there was something wrong with the room.

She stood stock still with the bright yellow net hanging over her like a tent. Everything seemed quite normal. Then it came to her. No whiff!

'Span?' She called. 'Span.' The dog wasn't there. She was frightened for him now and ran to the balcony to call him. She called and called, and then ran out of the apartment and down onto the Roof Garden.

As soon as she'd gone, Vince shot out of her bathroom like a bullet with Span under his arm. He kept his hand over the dog's nostrils and wished he could do the same to his own as he held the stinking thing's jaws together to prevent it barking. Vince had been counting on the girl being downstairs having her dinner while he stole her dog. He'd only just managed to hide in her bathroom when she'd come back to her room. He got himself down to the lift long before Fidelis remembered her bathroom and rushed back to look, but it was empty. Then she ran down to ask the guard posted at the bottom of the little staircase if he'd seen Span. But there wasn't a guard there, so she hurried back to the Banqueting Hall for help.

By now Vince was in a rare old come-and-go. He'd reached the lift with the dog still snorting for breath under his arm. In order to press the descent button Vince let go of Span's nose. And Span bit Vince's arm, not hard but very hard. Vince dropped him with a howl of pain, and Span took off. He ran as fast as his elderly legs would carry him down the spiral staircase of the North West Tower, with Vince in enraged pursuit. The Over Lord's instructions had been clear. Kill the dog. There were to be no watchdogs in the Roc's apartments, the Over Lord had said, not even that burnt out mutt; and now here was the smelly tyke on the loose. Several storeys down, Span shot out into a corridor and cut along it at full pelt. Vince closed the gap between them fast, his huge feet preparing to stamp on the dog and snap its spine. Span tucked in his tail and ran for his life, took a left turn and collided with a trio of guards who were part of the massive search the Over Lord had set in motion for the dumb Messenger Boy.

All three guards managed to fall over Span. Down they went like a set of skittles, followed by Vince who flattened them under his brawny bulk. By the time they had all stood up again, the dog was nowhere to be seen.

Vince scouted around for him, but Span had vanished and Vince had to give up. He had other important work to do. He set out for the garrison yard.

Meanwhile, Span followed his nose to the friendliest

smelling place in the castle and arrived in the kitchens, where the Cook gave him a bone. He took it into the corner of the fireplace by the empty spit and the warm embers. He couldn't eat it. He lay next to it, trembling.

By the time Fidelis got back to the Banqueting Hall, the ladies had withdrawn to take coffee and the men were deep into their port and brandy. Her father was telling a silly story about a vanishing roll, and Fidelis stood unnoticed in the doorway. Then the Roc's Equerry cracked a joke at the expense of the clerk and his bride-that-got-away, and her father remarked pointedly that the bride would have to be brought to heel. 'Can't have the lady running circles round us. Very undesirable.' Fidelis knew that the Over Lord was being got at. "Very undesirable", was the Roc's code for, "not allowed."

The Over Lord obviously knew that too because he promised the bride would be found. 'She'll stow away on the Product Convoy,' Fidelis heard him explain. 'The runaways always do. I've ordered the Convoy should be searched before it leaves. We'll winkle her out.' He raised his glass. 'To the clerk's honeymoon.' And there was a roar of bawdy laughter, which cut out sharply when the Roc said, 'Ah! Fidelis.' She curtsied in the doorway and the whole table of gentlemen rose to their feet.

Ordinarily that kind of elaborate attention would have made Fidelis self-conscious but she said, 'Please be seated, sirs,' and down they all sat and listened to her story of Span's disappearance.

The Over Lord was immensely kind and issued orders for search parties to be organised. The Spy Master was just as kind: he escorted her to the Ante-room to join the rest of the ladies. As she went through the door he was holding open for her he murmured, 'My lady,' and tweaked a strand of pondweed off the back of her hair. He handed it to her with a ravishing smile and bow. 'More unusual headgear, my lady.'

To her own surprise she kept remarkably cool, even though she was stuck with the telltale evidence of some truly unladylike behaviour. Worse still, there was nowhere remotely ladylike in the dratted yellow organza frock to conceal it. She smiled back, however, and said her search for Span had taken her far and wide. The Spy Master seemed happy with the explanation. But then he went straight up to inspect the reservoir Water Terrace as soon as the Ante-room door closed after Fidelis.

There was no sign now of Melior's handprints in the Ante-room. It had been cleaned up. There was just a group of well brought up ladies forcing down some filthy coffee. The exception was Lady Zoë, who Fidelis understood to have a wicked past – it was rumoured she'd been a dancing girl – so she was free to lift the ebony lid off one of the silver coffee pots and tip her cup back into it. She held the lid open for Fidelis. 'It tastes of feet, dear child.' So Fidelis followed suit, wondering, as she did, what daredevil escapade had enabled Lady Zoë to know what feet tasted of. She could feel Prudence beaming an outraged glare across the room at her and was very careful not to meet her eye. Fortunately the old Butler diverted Prudence's attention by pouring her a refill and she had to get through a second cup.

'Lady Zoë,' Fidelis asked on impulse, 'did you know the Lady Lenita?' She was longing to know why her father disliked Lenita so much.

'Queen Lenita,' Lady Zoë corrected her. 'Yes. I knew her. Nobody talks about her, Lady Fidelis. Particularly to your father.' And that was the end of that.

Then Lady Joy barged in on the conversation. Did they know that poor dear Lady Honor had taken to her bed after a fall? A broken rib, it was said. Lady Zoë said that yes, thank you, they did know. So Lady Joy went off to see "poor, dear Lady Honor". She trundled away, unaware that she was dragging the pondweed in the rear on her puce satin train where Fidelis had quietly dropped it. And instead of feeling guilty, Fidelis was trying not to laugh.

Lady Zoë didn't appear to notice, but something made her unbutton. She said, 'About twenty years ago, a delegation of independent states came to the Old Country led by the king of Slave City. This was before your father was elected the Roc; he was a handsome young cavalry officer then and in charge of organising the conference, which was supposed to be about trade but everyone knew it was really about water. We wanted some of their river-water and they said we wanted too much. Fortunately, the conference ended in agreement and the celebrations lasted four days – you know the sort of larky things the Empire lays on, dear child: regattas, races, picnics, banquets and above all, dancing – a ball each night. The Lady Lenita was just eighteen then and the beauty of the Old Country – everyone said so.' Lady Zoë stopped.

'Oh don't stop there,' Fidelis begged.

'I haven't stopped. I just wanted to say that Lenita wasn't simply a Beauty, and she wasn't simply clever either, she was above all– how shall I put it? She was nice. Not just nice to her friends either; to people like me, too, people from the wrong side of the track.' Lady Zoë chuckled, 'This was before my marriage shot me over to the *right* side, like being fired out of a cannon!

But perhaps it was my background that made me watchful, made me notice that Lenita was dancing a lot with the Slave King, playing croquet, eating sorbets... It was as plain as the nose on my face that they were in love. Anyway the delegates all left, the Slave King left and when the dust had settled, we all realised that Lady Lenita had left too, and I seemed to be the only person who wasn't surprised, not to say completely scandalised.

'She'd run off with the Slave King?' Fidelis breathed. Lady Zoë nodded and looked miserable and Fidelis felt sorry she'd made her talk about it. 'Do you miss her very much, Lady Zoë?'

'Yes, but it's not that. I wish I'd stopped her. If I had, she'd still be alive.'

Fidelis wasn't sure what to think about Queen Lenita now. She'd understood she was wicked and disloyal but here was Lady Zoë describing somebody quite different. 'Why shouldn't I talk to Papa about her?'

'He was betrothed to her.'

'Engaged!'

'More or less.'

'And she jilted him for the Slave King?' Lady Zoë nodded. Fidelis pictured her father, the young cavalry officer, left in the lurch. She said soberly, 'Pa wouldn't like that.'

'Nobody does,' Lady Zoë replied.

Fidelis wondered if her father had been completely truthful when he'd said he liberated the City because of the King's Touch. Wasn't he getting his own back on the Slave King, too, for stealing his girl, Lenita? She sighed. Politics and personal things could get very mixed up. Lady Zoë looked contrite. 'Now I've made you miserable. Cheer up. The Roc recovered and got

211

engaged all over again. Funny he chose a girl from the same family, isn't it? Lenita's distant cousin.'

Fidelis smiled. 'And then he married Mama. Third time lucky!'

'Me and my big mouth!' Lady Zoë said. 'Have I let a skeleton out of the darned cupboard? The Lady Alma is the distant cousin in question.'

'*Mama* is? *My* Mama?'

'Mmm.'

CHAPTER TWENTY

'You! Messenger Boy! Stop!' Watt fled. He hadn't expected a guard to be posted on the servants' exit. He ran towards the Main Doors, the only other way out of the castle he knew. He'd have to move. They were well and truly after him.

He mingled with the scurrying servants and was soon lost amongst them as they carried dishes to and from the Banqueting Hall – *my* Banqueting Hall, he thought angrily as he hurried past the happy roar of Policy Maker voices. But then his soggy trouser legs reminded him that, but for a Policy Maker, he would probably have drowned by now.

The two Inmate Footmen on duty at the Main Doors seemed very surprised to see him. Watt was in too much of a hurry to ask why. One was thin and the other was fat, and neither of them would unbolt the doors for him.

'It's Policy,' the thin footman said dourly.

'But I've a message from Porcini,' Watt lied.

'Must stick to our orders,' the fat one said. He had so outgrown his brown velvet uniform that unlikely bits of his body bulged uncomfortably over his tight collar. He looked at Watt with throttled, protruding eyes, and winked. 'Only names on the guest list allowed in.' Watt lost no time in asking, 'Any orders about who you can let *out*?'

'Pass, genius,' he smiled and opened the great door. They told him to look sharp with his message from the "Singing Mountain", as they called Porcini, and not to come back that way because they couldn't let him in again. Watt didn't mind because he wasn't coming back to his castle. He was off to hide away in the Singing Mountain's car, and now he had a destination: his Uncle Haakron.

He crossed the courtyard to the garrison. He was pretty sure Porcini's car would be garaged in the mews behind it. He didn't think he'd been there during his *past* life, but he remembered the way in was along a short tunnel that cut through the building at ground level. It was dark, but he soon found it.

Laughter overhead made him look up. Some Policy Maker kids in dark blue cadet uniform were leaning out of a first floor window. Watt rubbed his cheek where the sting of a dried pea had hit him. 'Got him!' one of the boys said, and they all laughed again.

Then a much smaller cadet pushed in between them, and Watt recognised the fair-haired kid he'd wanted to swat. Another pea from their peashooter hit him just under the eye. 'Hold yer fire, mates,' he said. 'You'll have me eye out.'

The other boys laughed uproariously at that, but the younger boy didn't; he looked down at Watt and studied him closely. His sallow little face had an intense, questioning expression that Watt found himself returning. There was something about the kid that Watt very nearly placed. Before he could, the kid disappeared from the window. Watt didn't wait for the third pea to hit him; he ran through the tunnel followed by the boys' jeering laughter.

He arrived in a much grander, more spacious place than the narrow tunnel had led him to expect. The smell of horses and hay was everywhere. He was standing in the corner of a big parade ground that was enclosed by the castle on his right, and by lower stone buildings on the other three sides. It reminded him uneasily of a huge version of the Inner Court. A few flood lamps cast broad wedges of light across the square, and he moved back quickly into the gloom of the arcade that ran all the way round.

He shivered in his wet clothes and took stock. Someone was playing a concertina inside what must be the barracks building. Men's voices joined in the chorus from behind the shuttered windows. The garrison seemed in a very relaxed mood, so at least they weren't hunting him here.

On his left was the Roc's fleet of carriages, parked under the arcade with their empty shafts sticking up like artillery guns. There were a dozen or so shadowy carriages in there too, with the horses harnessed up. Presumably they belonged to the guests who'd come in from the City for the ball. One of the horses was taking a drink from a stone trough. It looked up with the water dripping from its nose when it noticed Watt in the semi-dark, and blew down its nostrils in a friendly sort of way.

He crept in among the carriages. It was the most likely place to find Porcini's car. The buildings opposite him were nothing but stabling; he could hear the horses kicking against their loose boxes. He could hardly see a thing. All that the lights in the arcade were lighting up was the filth caking the bulb. That was why he practically trod on a Policy Maker soldier squatting at the base of a carriage wheel, cleaning his gun.

'Hello, hello.' He took Watt by the wrist. 'What have we here?' he said, pulling him down beside him. Watt could smell the horse dung on the stone floor and the beer on the man's breath as he looked him over. Midges were dancing round their heads and, as Watt brushed them away, the guard trapped his other wrist expertly in the same hand. 'What you doing here, Messenger Boy? Don't you know the Over Lord has ordered all your kind back to your quarters to be counted?'

This was bad news. It explained the footmen's surprise at seeing him, too. Watt thought about his answer. The Baker had said, "Whatever you do, talk." But although the Baker might feel like a friend, he acted like an enemy. Watt decided to play dumb and shook his head. The guard's grip tightened and he called into the gloom, 'Tonight's our lucky night, chums.'

Three more guards shambled out of the darkness and stood in an amused semi-circle round Watt and their friend. They were all drinking from tin mugs and took occasional pulls at their booze while they waited to hear what was so lucky about tonight. The guard grinned up at them. 'This little lad doesn't have anything to say for himself, do you lad?' Watt shook his head. One of the other guards said through a belch, 'There's money in this for us, you know.'

'Less of the "us",' the first guard said. He put his other arm round Watt. 'I found the little lad.'

His friends laughed. One of them put down his mug purposefully on the top of the carriage wheel. Another one said, with a sly sort of look at the others, 'You sure he's dumb?'

It felt as though the guards were gearing themselves up for something. They weren't amused now; they were looking down at him speculatively, almost as if he were something to eat. 'Shall we find out?'

Watt was suddenly scared stiff. He tried to stand up to get away – anywhere – but he was walled in by their thick legs. Hands pushed him down and tore at his clothes. The god! They were stripping him.

'Course he's not dumb,' a scornful treble voice said, and the fair-haired kid stepped into view.

There was an instant change amongst the guards. They lost interest in Watt and turned into a bunch of grinning oafs. The kid must have been all of seven years old, but they greeted him with exaggerated respect. Watt's captor even saluted. 'Evening, little Masterpiece.'

'What makes you so sure he can talk, Masterpiece?' another one asked and crouched down to buff the kid's small shoe with his coat sleeve. The kid treated them all to a fastidious stare, which made them all guffaw with admiration. 'He spoke to me and some of the boys a minute ago.' He looked down at Watt disdainfully. 'Didn't you?'

Watt had no alternative but to answer with a muttered, 'Yes.'

All four guards groaned in disappointment. The kid smiled and patted the one shining his shoes on the head as if he were a dog. 'Thought you were all going to claim the Over Lord's reward for capturing the dumb Messenger Boy, didn't you?' he said.

Watt's heart began to wallop. The Over Lord was much closer to tracking him down than he'd thought. What was really muddling was that when the Baker had told him to talk, it had been the right advice.

'Can I go now, sir?' he asked the guard who was still holding his wrists like a vice. 'I've a message for Madame P's driver.' The soldier pushed him away so hard that Watt fell and cracked his head on the stone floor. The guards and the kid all laughed.

He got up and walked away up the arcade as quickly as he could, rebuttoning his jacket as he went. His legs were trembling. He'd been terrified. He was soon aware that the kid was following him, though. He stopped and let him catch up. 'What is it?' he asked the kid shakily.

'The driver is usually hanging around the car.'

'Where is it, then? Do you know?'

'He moved it to a hay store. I saw him.'

'Show me where.'

'Why?' The kid looked up at him with a complacent smile and Watt felt a stronger urge than ever to swat him. He managed to reply evenly enough, 'So I can do my job, that's why.'

'My pa says, never take orders from an Inmate.'

Watt grimaced inwardly. 'Who's your pa?'

'Head of the garrison,' the kid said proudly.

'Wow!' Watt said, thinking it was no wonder the guards had grovelled.

'Too right.' The kid looked at Watt imperiously. 'Wow!'

Watt said carefully, 'I'm sure your pa would approve if you ordered an Inmate Messenger Boy to deliver his message.' The kid thought about that for a minute while Watt waited, hardly able to contain his impatience. At last the kid said, 'OK. Deliver it,' and waved a small hand at some double doors halfway along the next arcade.

Watt touched his hat politely and walked on. To his annoyance, the kid followed him. 'Do you know this dumb Messenger Boy?' He gave Watt a crafty, sideways glance. 'If you tell me where he is, I'll share the reward with you. Bargain?'

Watt quickened his step. 'Sorry, sir. I can't help.'

But the kid kept up with him. 'You're useless, aren't you? I should have left you to those guards.'

'I'm grateful you didn't,' Watt said, and he meant it.

'I could still call them over.'

This kid was fast turning from saviour to monster. 'They're skittish tonight,' the boy said, sounding, Watt was sure, like a midget version of his father. 'They're at a loose end. Pa says they've been taken off guard duty on the Roc.'

The kid grabbed his cuff so tightly then that Watt had to stop walking. 'Breathe one word about that, you scurf-bag, rat-crap Inmate,' he hissed, 'and I'll definitely put them back onto you.'

Watt was pleased to see that he looked worried. He'd let out one of his "Pa's" secrets by mistake. Watt knew the secret was true, too; he'd overheard the moon-faced Policy Makers say the same thing. The kid said threateningly, 'They'd *love* a session with you.'

Watt stopped himself from punching him into the middle distance and adopted a shocked tone instead. 'Is that the only reason why you rescued me from them? In case I knew the dumb Messenger Boy and you could go shares in the reward?' It took the kid by surprise. He wasn't used to having his motives questioned, let alone judged.

'I suppose it was.'

They walked on. He looked at Watt sideways again, but it was in the way that he'd first looked at him from the window – in a distant puzzled way, as if he were trying to place a misfit of a thought. He said haltingly, 'It felt like a different reason at the time.'

For a minute the kid looked so distressed that Watt nearly asked him what the problem was. But then his expression changed. 'Maybe it was for the glory.'

'You've lost me.'

'His name's Avtar.' The kid spat the name out and Watt's stomach did a somersault. The god! Was this the Baker's work too? They knew everything about him.

The kid ranted on quietly. 'Now he's going to rise up against us, and all the scummy Inmates will follow him and he'll take the City from us because as soon as we kill them, he'll cure them and bring them back to life with the King's Touch.'

If it hadn't been so weird, Watt would have smiled. Was this the Mumbo Jumbo the Policy Makers had invented that Melior had talked about? 'Quite a miracle worker, this Avtar, then,' he said, but the kid was too fired up by the prospect of his clash with Avtar to notice the irony. 'Yes. And if I stopped him, everyone would say that I'm a hero.'

They'd reached the doors now and Watt wanted to be rid of him. 'I wish you all the luck you deserve, sir,' he said. The kid gave him a penetrating look. He suspected Watt was mocking him. He was right.

Watt touched his cap and said servile things about hoping the Sun would shine on his venture. He laid it on thick. He mustn't offend the kid or the dangerous little freak might set his pa's guards on him again. 'I'll bid yous goodnight, sir,' he finished.

The kid laughed. He looked quite human while it lasted. Then he yawned. 'The name's Felix,' he announced. Watt touched his cap again and lifted the latch of the door. Felix said he was missing the cadet's feast and seemed about to leave, then changed his mind. 'This other person they're talking about in the barracks?'

Watt forced himself to look attentive like a good servant.

'Person, sir?

'The clerk's bride, Morag.'

'She's dead.'

Felix stared at Watt, then he backed away from him, whispering and whispering – calling him strings of the foulest names Watt had ever heard. Then he turned and ran off into the dark. It gave Watt a fair old shock. The kid's eyes had been full of tears.

It had been a day for tears. Fidelis's tears over her pink scarf, for instance. She'd talked about the king curing people, too. What in the name had the Policy Makers got into their daft heads with their King's Touch?

He stood with his hand still on the latch. Something was jabbing at Watt's memory like a bird stabbing and stabbing the ground for an elusive worm. The jabbing had happened earlier that day with the moon-faced Policy Makers, and now something that Felix had said had started it again.

With a jolt, Watt saw his birthday party, saw his father striding out of the Ante-room to fight the invaders. He saw him, on the move but static, like a painting, looking back and yelling the question at his queen, 'Where were the guards?'

So there had been no guards on the City walls that day. Watt shivered. That's what his father was asking in his nightmares when he kept crying – 'Where? Where?' And Watt still didn't know the answer. Where *had* the guards been that terrible day? One thing was certain: no guards meant danger and death. Whose death this time?

He stared at the ground without really seeing it. He missed his father. He missed his whole family, even though he'd scarcely known them. He realised he'd always missed them. Then came the cold, reasonable voice in his head. Get a move on, it said. Get out of the City.

He went into the hay store, shut the door behind him and found a light switch. Porcini's car was there all right. The bales of hay had been piled up on top of each other to make room for it. The place must have been used as a workshop at some time because there were wood shavings and sawdust on the floor.

Watt examined the car's shiny maroon and black bodywork. It was very impressive at close quarters. The machine was a gift of a getaway. All he needed now was to find somewhere to hide. He peered in at the spare wheel next to the driver's seat, then walked round to the rear. There was a promising wooden trunk bolted to the luggage carrier. "Tools" it had lettered on it in gold.

It appeared smaller inside than it did from the outside but, if he got rid of the outlandish tools, he might just about scrunch up in there and close the lid on himself. He didn't have time to try. Someone was at the stable door. Watt only just hid behind the bales of hay before Vince came in.

CHAPTER TWENTY—ONE

Vince worked fast. Watt couldn't begin to guess what he was up to and he wasn't going to ask; Vince was a friend of the Baker's and so no friend of his. He watched him from his hiding place through a gap in the hay bales as Vince chucked all the tools out of the trunk, then spread a tablecloth on the floor as if he were preparing a midnight feast. A peculiar one. There was a very fat liquorice stick, which he took from a wicker basket and laid on the cloth along with a little butter churn. Then came a dial with part of a broken timepiece, a wooden tray, several small bags of flour, some wire, and an odd thing that Watt couldn't place.

Vince put the churn on the tray, poured jet-black powder from the flour bags into it, and jammed the lid on. Then he wired the liquorice to the churn. The next part was tricky, judging by Vince's exasperated grunts as he put together the wire, the dial and the odd thing. What in the name is he doing, Watt wondered. The answer came to him in a rush of memory. Saan had once told him that the odd thing was a kind of cartridge. So he's making a bomb, he thought in amazement. The black powder was gunpowder and the liquorice must be a stick of dynamite.

Vince set the dial on a figure, but Watt was too far

away to see – somewhere between a six and nine? Then Vince pushed his penknife down the side of the tool chest and prised up the bottom: he had made a false base. It explained the sawdust and wood shavings, and why the box looked smaller inside than out.

Vince took his bomb on the tray and loaded it into the bottom of the toolbox. Then he set the clockwork going. It began to tick. So it was a time bomb, due to detonate in the early morning. He watched Vince pack layers of hay and what looked like cotton wool all round and on top of it. Then, very delicately, he lowered the false bottom on top and gently replaced the tools. All Watt could do was look on while Vince put an end to his hopes of escape.

Vince closed the toolbox, cleared up and, with a final glance around, switched out the light and left. In the dark and the silence, Watt could just hear the ticking of the bomb's timer.

He was depressed. He hadn't a clue how to take the time bomb apart without blowing himself to smithereens. He was suddenly aware of how sore his face was where the Spy Master had hit him, and how cold and wet and tired he felt. He'd been on the move since six that morning and yet he was no nearer getting out of the castle grounds than he had been all those hours ago when he and Brad had watched the Product Convoy driving towards the City.

The Product Convoy! Why hadn't he thought of it before? He'd go and hide on the Convoy and in a few hours he'd be on his way out. He groped his way to the door and headed back to the tunnel. But not the way he'd come; he went in the opposite direction, walking past the rows of loose boxes. He didn't intend to run into those sinister guards again.

He planned as he walked. He'd use the message he was carrying from the Over Lord to get through the gatehouse and into the City. He would have liked to say goodbye to Brad at the hospital but he couldn't – they were looking for him there.

He was well down the arcade that butted onto the castle when he saw two jumping flames spring up ahead of him. A Policy Maker captain had put a light to a pair of flare torches on either side of a massive wooden door. It was another entrance into the castle and there was a sentry guarding it. He'd have to pass him to get to the tunnel. It was impossible.

The sentry was standing to attention, listening to the captain. Watching from the shadows, Watt saw the captain put his hand out palm downwards at about the same level as the man's chest, as though he were describing something's height. A boy's height? *His* height? Then the captain marched off across the Parade Ground, leaving the sentry on guard.

Watt decided to creep back the way he'd come. Better to keep an eye out for the sinister guards than tangle with an alert sentry. And then the noise began that changed Watt's life.

∗ ∗ ∗

At a signal from Lady Evangeline, the ladies put down their coffee cups gratefully and filed out of the Ante-room. Fidelis wrenched herself away from a fascinating conversation with Lady Zoë and followed them down to the Inner Court. The ladies were all looking forward to the ball and their mood was catching. Fidelis felt a ripple of excitement. Her very first ball! There was a great deal more laughter as each lady ducked through the little door where Avtar's mother had stood and fought their invading soldiers.

The laughter gave way to a buzz of pleasure as the ladies wafted into the Inner Court to join the gentlemen and saw the ten thousand candle lanterns twinkling prettily round the arcades. The polished sheen on the new floor promised good waltzing and the orchestra was ready and waiting.

Also waiting was Madame Isabella Porcini, looking thunderously tragic as she prepared to sing her final song before the ball got under way. The Pianist was at his piano looking harassed, as well he might. Madame Porcini had said at the beginning of dinner that she wouldn't be singing the song they'd rehearsed but a different and extremely difficult one instead. He'd had to leave the table at once to practise the accompaniment. He was starving hungry and nervous.

Everybody else quailed at the sight of Porcini, but the Roc pulled up a little gilt chair, sat himself down bang in front of her, folded his arms and fixed her with a stare over the top of his rapier waxed moustache. The rest of the party stood bunched behind him. Fidelis noticed there was no snide laughter and winking from the ladies now. Not one of them would have dared to say boo to the singer's face. The Pianist made a hesitant start, recovered, and swept into the opening of Porcini's song.

And Porcini sang. She sang as she had never sung before, though her heart and her throat ached. The crowd was silent. The only movement was an almost imperceptible fluttering of the ladies' bedizened gowns as a light breeze moved across the Court like a ghost.

The Spy Master, who was up on the roof looking for clues to explain the pondweed in Fidelis's hair, heard the song and said to himself – after tonight's business, that's it. I shall go home and grow roses.

Porcini's song was the sound Watt heard in the garrison yard. The song was so sad it made you unhappy, and at the same time so beautiful it made you glad. It made him feel extra sharply alive. It ended too soon and there was complete quiet.

An approving shout from the audience broke the silence, followed by clapping and cries of what sounded to Watt like "Uncork, Uncork", and more clapping. Then some quite different, jigging sort of music struck up, and Watt knew she wouldn't sing any more. She'd said so in the letter she'd written to the Roc which he'd never received.

He sighed with disappointment, then looked up above the harsh floodlights. In the glow from the half-moon, he could see hundreds of tiny clouds, like fluffy cobbles, fanning across the sky. It was lovely; just the night to break free. But he didn't move. The argument he was having with himself pinned him to the spot.

No one would ever hear the great Porcini sing again because she was going to be blown to bits, unless he warned her not to get into her car. He considered running to tell her chauffeur, but he'd no idea where to find him. He knew exactly where to find Madame Porcini, though: in her room.

But why spoil Vince's plans? And what were his plans? Watt couldn't see any good coming out of killing Madame Porcini – least of all for Slave City.

But why, argued Watt, should he save Madame Porcini when he was half way to saving himself on the

Product Convoy? Why should he risk sacrificing that opportunity? She was not his responsibility. It was sheer chance he'd seen Vince plant the bomb. So why should he do anything about it? If he did, and was caught, the Over Lord would kill him. But on the other hand, Madame Porcini very definitely *would* be killed if he didn't warn her. Maybe he should toss a coin for it. He smiled – the Singing Mountain versus the Runaway King.

At last he moved; his mind was made up. When he judged he was close enough, Watt slipped his hand up to the bolt of a loose box and swung open both halves of the door. He'd expected the horse to come shooting out like a charger on the battlefield. As it was, he had to tiptoe inside and give the sleepy beast a shove from the rear. After that, it all went to plan. The horse trotted out and set off on a joyful canter round the floodlit Parade Ground.

Odd soldiers emerged from the dark arcades and ran towards it. All eyes were on the loose horse, and the sentry did exactly what Watt wanted: he went round to block its escape through the tunnel, leaving the door unguarded for Watt to dodge into the castle.

He'd never been in this part before. It was starker and more businesslike, and there were plenty of people around still working. There was a steamy hot smell of laundry, and it wasn't long before he passed a semi-lit room with lines and lines of sheets hanging up to dry. There were kids in there turning a huge clothes mangle. He passed what must be storerooms with notices on them like "Preserves" and "Salt House" and "Spices".

Outside "Confectionary", he ran into three delivery boys of about his age. One of them poked a hole in the corner of a carton they were loading onto a trolley.

'Oh dear, oh dear!' he said, with a false concern as he wriggled a sugarplum out through the hole. 'Who is the owner of this pretty thing?' The other boys shook their heads in mock mystification. The first boy grinned and recited a quick dip, touching each of them, including Watt, on the chest.

Dip, dip. Dip and ladle,
Baby's dying in his cradle.
Mouldy melon, mutton broth,
Mix together, skim the froth.
Baby drains a brimming beaker,
Up he jumps and cries 'Eureka!'
Y-O-U-R-S spells yours...

He gave the sugarplum to Watt with a sympathetic, 'Spirits up, mate.'

Watt was happy to take it. He was hungry, but he must look flipping downhearted if the delivery boy thought he deserved cheering up.

He went on his way, wondering what in the name "You reek er" meant. It sounded like a dressed-up way of calling someone a stinker.

The Boot Boys he passed next weren't at work; they'd left the heap of shoes they were supposed to be polishing and gathered round a young Messenger Boy. They looked as if they were reading his palm, which seemed odd.

The Delivery Boy's dip had set a memory stirring. It was definitely something to do with his old life. He explored the memory unwillingly. Memories hurt. Then it came to him. The boy hadn't completed the rhyme. He remembered playing "Chase" up on the Roof Garden with his friends and they'd used the dip to choose the Chaser. But he couldn't think how the rest of it went, and gave up trying.

There was another crowd of kids hanging round the lift. A little black-eyed laundry girl was examining another Messenger Boy's hand. 'It smells like cooked meat.'

'Feels like it too,' the Messenger Boy said. 'They told us it would soon stop hurting, but it ain't yet.'

'What they want to do a thing like that for?' a butcher boy asked mutinously. The group leaned into the Messenger Boy as he lowered his voice. 'Butler reckons they's searching for someone.' The kids looked at each other in excitement as he said, 'Yous know who!'

He noticed Watt, a fellow Messenger Boy, on the outskirts of the group and summoned a smile for him as he held out his hand. 'What number are yous, mate?' Watt realised it wasn't the boy's palm they'd all been looking at; it was the inside of his wrist. There was a number 40, newly branded on it.

Watt was so angry at what the Over Lord had done, at the cold-hearted cruelty of it, that he couldn't reply. The man was actually prepared to burn the other kids' flesh to find him. He felt guilty, too. It was wrong to try and save himself if it was at the expense of other Inmates. His guilt forced the question out of him: 'Why should you lot all suffer on account of him – of you know who?'

The butcher boy put his fist under Watt's nose and told him to shut his flipping gob. The Messenger Boy said very quietly, 'It's only him as can win the City back for us. That's why.'

Their faith in him gave Watt a shock. How could they believe that someone of their own age, faced with a garrison of four hundred enemy soldiers to overpower and no army of his own to do it with, could possibly win back their City? But he smiled at the Messenger Boy and hid his unbranded right hand inside his coat, as if it hurt. Then he gave him the sugarplum. 'Compliments of Avtar,' he said and stepped into the lift.

They were thrilled. Their awed whispering at the cheek of what he'd dared to say faded as the lift juddered upwards.

> *'Now my story ain't so tragic,*
> *Thanks to swigging Yellow Magic.'*

That was it! The last bit of the rhyme. He'd remembered it. And there was that perishing Yellow Magic again. What was it?

He reached Porcini's floor and was on the point of knocking on her door when a troop of guards came out of the stairwell and called to him to stay put. Watt's heart crashed into his wet shoes. Here he was, the only Messenger Boy in the City without a number branded on his wrist. The Over Lord had laid a trap for him and he'd walked straight into it on his do-gooding mission. He wasn't going to save Madame Porcini's life; he was going to chuck away his own, like yesterday's stale loaf.

Then he remembered the Over Lord's message. It would prove that he was on serious business and they'd leave him alone. The guards were all round him now. He felt in his pocket – but the message had broken into hundreds of saturated pieces.

231

CHAPTER TWENTY—TWO

The prison cells were gruesome – hot and terrible. No one was allowed down there except on official business. But Scar had his pack of cards. If anything could get him in, the cards would.

He'd climbed up onto the service stairs and arrived in the Ante-room. But the Butler had come in almost at once with a team of Inmate servants to clear away some used coffee cups, and Scar had to skip into the Throne-room. Except it wasn't the Throne-room anymore, it was a bar. Scar was outraged.

The smell of liquor and tobacco smoke turned his stomach. He could hardly cross the room it was so crowded with leather armchairs and small tables. He was looking for the great Sword of State, but it had gone from where it used to hang above the throne. So had the throne. There was a jerry-built counter there now, stacked with dirty glasses and, behind it, rows of shelving laden with bottles.

He found the Sword, though. It was rusty and had snapped in two just short of the hilt. It would take a tremendous blow to do that. The two pieces had been mounted on the wall, and a lock of fair hair, that was stiff with dust, had been suspended from the point like a hunting trophy. Scar read the inscription below it:

Lenita, a lady who in a moment of moral
vitiation and of tergiversation congruent
with the weakness of her sex, forsook her duty
and conjoined with the slave king of Khul.
She was duly put to the sword
opposing her own people.

Why not just write "Traitor," Scar thought. The Policy
Makers had such a roundabout way with words that it
was hard to make out their meaning. But they obviously
hadn't a good word to say for Queen Lenita either, even
though she'd turned the City over to them.

Some joker had drawn a girl's face on the wall under
the curl so that it looked like the face's hair. The drawing
had sweeping eyelashes and a sexy grin. Scar spat on it
and left.

Down in the cells, two bored jailors greeted him with
suspicion until Scar sat down to deal the cards and play
several rounds of City Skelter with them for high stakes.
He let them win every game to soften them up. 'Poor old
Scar,' they commiserated, pocketing his money. Then,
exactly as he'd intended, they asked what they could do
for him.

None of the Policy Makers that he played ever noticed
that Scar was brilliant at cards; freaks didn't possess
skills in their view. So Scar would either win or lose a
game, depending on which result would get him what he
needed from his opponent. His spirits rose when one of
the men agreed to show him round the cells.

The man lit a lantern and led the way down a half-
finished passageway that was newly blasted out of the
rock. Brown water seeped out of the ceiling and spread

menacingly down the walls in carroty orange stains. The cells were the only part of the castle the Policy Makers had expanded. 'Can't show you the new interrogation room,' he apologised. 'There's an old geezer in there being done over for a speech he made to the Roc. Pity. We've got some nifty new equipment in there.'

The man led him past cages with lumps of clothes inside that Scar could hardly identify as human beings. The place stank. A thin Policy Maker woman with a bandaged head was lying on the floor in one; in another, six people were crammed together, whimpering. The man told Scar they were Inmate musicians who'd messed up a tea party for the Roc and had their fingers crushed for it.

The sickening tour seemed to go on forever, but eventually they reached the last cage. 'The Nursery,' he announced. Ten or so frightened Inmate boys shaded their eyes from the sudden light of the lamp and retreated to the back of the cage, a terrified little gang. A tiny boy screamed at the sight of Scar. 'Can't account for themselves,' the guard explained to Scar, and wagged a mocking finger at the boys. 'So tomorrow morning we're off to the Land of No More, aren't we lads?' The boys began to moan and beg. Scar wanted to strangle him. The light faded out of the cage as the man walked away with his lantern, but by then Scar had made sure there wasn't a boy in there with a shaved head. But if Avtar wasn't in the cells, was he dead already?

* * *

'You seen a dog?' one of the guards surrounding Watt questioned him. Watt was so relieved he forgot he should speak. 'A little 'un?' the guard persisted. Watt pulled himself together. 'Not a sign, mate,' he said. 'Sorry.'

The guards looked hot and irritated. 'You see it,' they grumbled, 'take it to the Roc's daughter. It's hers.'

'Will do,' he replied. ''Scuse us, fellers,' and he walked into Porcini's room without knocking.

She was spread-eagled across her chaise longue, panting. The feathered headdress shuddered and the wild cherries on her breast bounced with each breath.

'You came quick,' she croaked suspiciously, 'I only just ring for you.' Watt smiled blandly in reply and Porcini said, 'I want a doctor. The best.' Watt decided whoever answered the bell could fetch a doctor. 'Listen, Madame Porcini,' he said earnestly.

Porcini heaved herself into a sitting position to object. 'Boy, Porcini rings. You fetch.'

'Someone's put a time bomb in your motorcar.'

Porcini gaped. She had a singer's mouth – the size of the furnace door. Watt knelt by her side to stress the urgency of what he was saying. 'Don't get into it. You'll go up with a bang half way home.'

Madame Porcini flumped back onto the chaise longue, which was shunted backwards by the impact. Watt shuffled after it and its mighty passenger on his knees.

'Do you understand, Madame Porcini?'

Porcini closed her mouth and her eyes. 'This make no sense,' she murmured. Her eyes opened abruptly. 'Who in this pig hole would kill Porcini?' Watt didn't want to go so far as naming names. He said indecisively, 'Probably an Inmate.'

'What does this Inmate gain snuffing Porcini?' she

asked accusingly. 'You are an Inmate. Why do you tell me?' She obviously didn't believe a word.

He tried to explain. 'I heard you sing.'

She smiled. It was like the sun coming out.

'You want my autograph, darling?'

There was a knock and a Messenger Girl came in. She looked very surprised to see another messenger not only present but on his knees to Porcini. She bobbed a curtsy, though, and asked what she could do for Madame. Porcini sat up and spread her arms wide. 'A doctor,' she said hoarsely, 'before I die!'

The girl looked very scared. 'Oh, ma'am,' she said, 'all the Medical Officers are at the ball dancing and drunk.' Porcini did another of her crash landings on the chaise and retreated further from them both. 'Dancing and drunk while an Artist dies,' she grieved. 'I have sung...' her voice broke in a sob, '...my farewell to this world!' A tear rolled out of the corner of each magnificent eye.

Watt said quickly to the girl, 'Run down to the hospital. Blow the perishing PM doctors. Fetch an Inmate doctor and some stretcher-bearers.' Then, as an afterthought, 'Strong ones'. Porcini's eyes opened and flashed him a coquettish, offended look before flapping shut again. The girl nodded, and then Watt had another idea. 'While you're there, find a Ghosty Boy called Brad. He's a patient. Tell him there's a mate needs him urgently.' Brad had contacts. There was a slim chance he could wangle him past the gatehouse guards and down to the Convoy. 'What's the time?' he asked the startled girl.

'After eleven.'

That meant the Baker would be having his kip before the late shift got underway, and the Bakery would be

236

empty. 'Tell him to meet his mate in the Bakery. Quick as you can, if you don't mind.' And the girl ran.

Watt returned to Porcini. Several more tears were crowding out of her eyes. Girls really were criers, he thought. Crying was part of their everyday life, not the rare and shaming incident it was for boys. He was against crying. It solved nothing. He tried to think of something to stop her. He said, 'The Roc never received your letters, Madame Porcini.' And Porcini reared up like a mad horse.

'What?' she cried and clutched her throat in agony.

'Steady,' Watt warned. 'And I don't think any of the Roc's letters get delivered to you either.'

'Then it is not the Roc who is quarrelling and bombing Porcini,' she said. 'If it was Wamsy, I would go willingly to my doom!'

'No, don't do that,' Watt advised hastily. 'All the letters are delivered to the Over Lord and the Spy Master. They take them off us Messenger Boys. They've drowned one of us.'

Porcini's eyes narrowed and she gave a low whistle – a very good one. She put her hands to her temples and said slowly, 'This spells danger. There is danger to the Roc, I think.'

'And to you,' Watt stressed.

But Porcini dismissed this with, 'I am a pawn.'

Watt hadn't heard of chess so he'd no idea what a pawn was. He thought she'd said she was a prawn.. He wondered if she was delirious. He'd never seen anything less like a prawn than Madame Porcini. Then she said, 'And danger to his daughter.'

That shook Watt. The girl had just ripped her clothes to bits to rescue him and now she was in danger. The god! It was an unfair world. Porcini was deep in thought now, and a silence grew between them. When she spoke, her voice was quieter and even more hoarse, and there was sweat on her ivory forehead. 'What more do you know of this pig hole, darling boy?'

It was not an easy question to answer. He'd thought he was going to all this trouble solely for Madame Porcini and not for Policy Makers who would kill him as soon as look at him. His problem was that some Policy Makers were proper people more than they were Policy Makers. Fidelis, for instance. He liked Fidelis a lot, so he said, 'The Head of the garrison says the guards have been taken off the Roc's apartments, and I overheard two big cheeses in a picture gallery say the same. They're in on it.'

Madame Porcini rose to her feet. One hand was pressed to her chest, the other was flung sideways in a tempestuous gesture. 'They are going to murder them!'

Watt felt his scalp prickle with fright. 'Who?'

'The Over Lord and the Spy Master and the pig hole cheeses. They are going to murder the Roc and his daughter.' And she fell to the floor in a faint.

The noise was stupendous. Air ballooned under her flaming skirt, which then slowly subsided around her immense form. The feathered headdress wobbled and, quite unexpectedly, Madame Porcini's hair fell off. Another baldy, Watt thought, and very tactfully pushed the wig on again. He sat next to her on the floor. He'd wait with her until the doctor came. Then he'd meet Brad. He patted her magnificent, unconscious hand comfortingly. 'You'll be all right, Madame Porcini,' he said. 'You really will.'

He sat holding her hand. The words she'd spoken beat

like a pulse in the silent room: "They are going to murder them." The Over Lord and the Spy Master are going to murder them. He had a vision of the pink-cheeked girl's anxious, concentrated look as she'd dragged him to safety in the reservoir. The silence pressed in on him as he sat and waited in the dishevelled room. They are going to murder them, he thought, and with Madame Porcini out cold, the only people who know about it are the Over Lord, the Spy Master, the cheeses – and me.

CHAPTER TWENTY—THREE

It might be her first ball, but Fidelis could tell that
something was going wrong with this one. People were
leaving. At least ten gentlemen had already excused
themselves to the Roc. Her partner was one of them.
He'd steered her to the edge of the floor and with a
sickly grunt of apology in the direction of her father,
he'd flown.

Fidelis sat down with the other woebegone ladies who
had been deserted and watched the remaining dancers
mournfully. It was a fast polka. Round and round the
couples plunged. Fidelis loved the polka. This one
seemed to be going on rather a long time, though. The
dancers were puffed and hot. By the look of Lady Joy,
there was a fifty-fifty chance of her bursting out of her
amethysts! And still the couples danced and plunged.
Fidelis glanced at the orchestra sawing away at their
instruments – but without the wiry conductor! He had
disappeared too. She had to hand it to his players: they'd
carried on without him, and they only stopped when the
last couple admitted defeat and left the floor.

More people withdrew in a hurry and Fidelis went
and found Prudence to ask her why. Prudence was
sitting fanning her face. Her long nose was red from the
frenzy of the polka.

'They've got the runs,' Prudence said bluntly.

'The runs?'

'Upset stomach,' Prudence snapped as Lady Evangeline made a fast exit through the little door in a streak of diamonds. Prudence's mouth turned downwards in a hoop of disapproval. 'It's my opinion they've caught something in this filthy place,' she said. 'But what can you expect with all those bathrooms?'

'Or could it be the water?' Fidelis suggested in the bathrooms' defence. Fidelis was rather keen on the bathrooms. 'Could be,' Prudence agreed grudgingly. 'It's only the gentry has caught it. The natives haven't, that's for sure. But then they're used to their mucky ways. There's more servants standing around this ball than there are guests.'

The Butler, who was gliding about keeping an eye on things, hid a smile. He'd been pleased enough when he'd arranged for all those silk roses to be sprayed with lavender; but that was minor compared with this, and he offered a little prayer of gratitude to his old father for the wonderful legacy he had left his son.

The Butler's father (nicknamed Thunderbags) had been an apothecary and had sold a variety of remedies to the citizens. He'd been a great favourite with the old king, which was just as well because his cough drops were, to say the least, chancy, and his poultice for warts was so dangerous it had finally been banned. But the remedy that had really made his name – Thunderbags – was his powder for constipation. Large stocks of it remained after his death and the Butler had never had the heart to dispose of it, though he had no real use for it. Now he had!

The god he'd been nervous! He'd spiked every guest's

plate with the stuff. He'd steered clear of the Roc – that could be treason. But as for the rest: some people had got a dose in their cold soup; others in their carp sauce or capon stuffing; most had consumed it disguised in the strong gravy that came with the roast mutton; while just a few had their sorbets tampered with. The gentlemen's port had fair fizzed with the stuff, and the Butler was terrified they'd notice; but by that time, the gentlemen were so full of wine they were past doing anything but drinking more. He'd gone to town with the ladies' coffee and bunged in the whole of the last packet. He'd noticed a couple of them surreptitiously pour it back, but the rest had politely drunk it all up. The Butler hid another smile.

The Policy Makers had killed old Thunderbags during the Attack. They'd killed the Butler's wife and family and his baby granddaughter too. It wasn't a fitting revenge, the Butler thought – what was a night of diarrhoea compared with the loss of a life? But it was revenge of a sort, and it was sweet.

✳ ✳ ✳

Scar hung about in the tunnel by the Water Tank. Now he'd drawn a blank in the cells, he wasn't sure of his next move. He could do with someone who knew the castle better than he did.

Like an answer to a prayer, Vince passed the far end. Scar whistled to him, and Vince tiptoed heavily down the tunnel to join him.

'What are you doing here, Scar boy?' he asked. 'You're supposed to be spending the night outside the City walls.'

Scar grinned. Only the Over Lord knew where Scar was spending the night – but somehow, old Vince knew too. Vince knew everyone's business. He was just the man to help him.

He pulled his collar down towards him until Vince's great ear was level with his mouth and breathed, 'I'm looking for Avtar, the king. I need your help.' He spoke so quietly, Vince had to bend his head to hear him. 'He's here in the castle. I had it from his sister.'

Vince's eyebrows shot up. 'Easy now, Scar. Tell old Vince what exactly you're on about.' He drew Scar further down the tunnel. 'There's guards coming out of the walls tonight. If they catch us in conference we're fair done for.'

'His sister says Avtar's been captured.'

Vince's sunny face was unusually solemn. 'It's the first I've heard of a capture, Scar.'

'That's cause for hope then. I know we're looking for a Ghosty Boy.'

'But the gossip is Avtar was a Messenger Boy,' Vince argued.

'No.' Scar whispered back. 'A Ghosty Boy.' He chuckled. 'That's going to surprise the Baker. I can't wait to see his face when he hears he's had a Royal hiding away in his Bakery all this time.' He gave Vince a friendly poke in the chest with his finger – it was like poking a rock garden. 'I want you to call a meeting with the other two. It's our duty to find Avtar alive or dead.'

Vince nodded agreement and smiled his twinkly smile, then asked, 'But where's the sister, Scar?'

'Safe enough,' Scar whispered. Vince cocked an enquiring eyebrow, and Scar couldn't resist whispering proudly, 'She's in the sheepfold, pretending to be me.'

Vince laughed silently and punched the air.

They arranged that Scar should stay hidden in the tunnel and that Vince would round up the Cook and the Baker. 'I'll be a while. Cookie may be off duty,' Vince warned. He rolled away at a stately pace until he was out of Scar's sight; then off he went like the clappers to the Duty Room where he found a Messenger Girl and sent her into the ball to tell the Spy Master he was needed very, very urgently.

CHAPTER TWENTY-FOUR

The Spy Master's men took Melior prisoner so expertly she never even heard them coming. They gagged her and dragged her from amongst the frightened sheep, and brought her back into the City. Scar's cloak fell open during the skirmish, and at the sight of a Policy Maker woman under arrest the handful of Inmates out after curfew vanished into the dark. No one wanted to know.

As the four men carried her steadily up towards the castle Melior felt so tired and overpowered and defeated she couldn't attempt to get away from them, even though one of their beefy bottoms was within easy kicking range.

They were approaching the crossroads where the hospital stood when four stretcher-bearers came into the light, sagging under the weight of a mountainous orange figure. A lanky boy on his way out held open the entrance doors for them and they tottered inside. In a dreamy, indifferent way, Melior recognised the lanky boy as the awful pest Brad. Then a man broke out of the darkness and attacked him.

He threw Brad into the street and laid into him. There was raging shouting, and a knife flashed. Two of the men holding Melior ran and separated them, but Brad had already been stabbed in the arm. Melior registered through a weary fuzz that it was the clerk who had the knife. He was screaming abuse at Brad, screaming that he was going to kill him because Brad had stolen his girl. Then the clerk saw Melior and he broke free to smother her in kisses.

Melior had a close up view of his lips, like little pink worms embedded in his jowl. Strands of his fair hair got in her mouth. His eyes, that reminded her of the currants in the puddings at the orphanage, burned with passion. 'Where have you been?' He was almost crying. Scar's hat was knocked off her head and he clasped Melior so tightly it took the combined strength of the Spy Master's men to pull him off her.

So now all four men were holding onto the clerk, and no men at all were holding onto Melior. Given a sliver of hope, she was her old self and bolted.

She had about forty seconds start before they all realised what had happened and ran after her, including the lovelorn clerk. But Brad sidled off home to the castle. His arm hurt and he needed his bed. He was so tired he wasn't sure he could answer the unknown mate's appeal to meet him.

* * *

The Bakery was in darkness when Watt crept in to meet Brad. He savoured the familiar smells of the place: the scrubbed, clean soapy one that mingled with the sharper smell of the burnt fuel from the Baker's old brick ovens. They made him feel homesick for the warmth and the safety the Bakery had meant to him until now. But how wrong he'd been to trust the Baker.

The hum of the flames in the furnace changed to

a higher pitch as the wind soughed outside. It swung back the shutter of the big window, letting in enough moonlight for him to see that the floor was covered with hundreds of bits of white paper swirling in the draught. He picked up a piece fluttering against his foot.

The room darkened again as the clouds tattered across the moon, but he'd had time to see what it was, even though the paper was ripped to bits. It was one of the Baker's recipes: his Lost-and-Founds. It was puzzling; the Baker normally guarded his recipes as if they were sacred. Then the moonlight came back more brightly and he saw the Baker himself, sitting at the far end of the worktable with his usual bottle in front of him and his hand around his half empty glass. There was a second glass on the table, so he must be waiting for someone to join him. Watt had just decided he'd better go before they arrived when the Baker leant forward across the table and dropped his glass over the edge, where it smashed on the stone floor. Darkness fell again as the moon went in. Watt had never seen the Baker the worse for drink before, but that must be why he was sitting in the dark shredding his flipping recipes. Best to leave him to it. Then he heard a scratching, swishing noise coming from his own room. It could only be Brad waiting for him out of the Baker's sight.

He crept round the Bakery, keeping well against the shadowy wall. As he drew level with his chair, a gust of wind swung the shutter back again and a shaft of bright moonlight fell across the Baker. There was a knife sticking out of his back. The murderer had driven the knife in up to the hilt. Watt had to press his knuckles into his mouth to stifle his scream of horror at the sight of it. He stood there aghast. He tried to think who he could call for help and for what sort of help. Then the noise coming from his own room started up again. He ran across to the door and opened it.

The room was lit as bright as day by a storm lantern on the floor. The noise was Vince, tearing Watt's mattress apart and searching through the straw. He twisted round at the sound of Watt's shocked gasp and shouted, 'You murdered the Baker. It was you, wasn't it, Messenger Boy?' and rushed Watt. Watt pulled the door shut in his face. He heard Vince slam into it on the other side and fall, and he ran out of the Bakery and straight into Brad.

Brad's legs folded under him and he sank to the ground. 'You keep off, you Spirit you,' he shrieked, 'or I'll have the god on yous.' Watt was completely nonplussed for a second. Then it dawned on him: Brad thought he'd been burnt to death when they'd relit the furnace. He thought he was seeing a ghost.

There wasn't any time to explain. He heaved Brad up and said, 'Shut it. Run. Help me!' Somehow that set Brad's long legs working. Watt ran, dragging Brad behind him, to the only safe place he could think of. He ran back to Madame Porcini's empty room and closed the door. As soon as they'd got their breath back Brad panted, 'The god protect me! What help yous needing? Why's you a haunting me?'

Watt clapped his hands loudly. 'Look,' he reassured him. 'I'm solid. I'm alive.' He dug out the heart-shaped roll to prove it. 'You gave me this. Remember? To give to your girl. I didn't burn to death.'

'Thank the god,' Brad said and burst into tears. Watt knelt opposite him.

'Brad,' he began, 'the Baker.' But Brad didn't hear him for crying. They were all at it – this useless crying business. He watched Brad in silence. Then Brad's face opposite him began to spring patches of mist. He thought he was going to pass out, or that he was ill like Madame Porcini. Then the heat of the tears running down his face, the pain in the back of his nose, and the piggish sounding sobs coming out of him made him admit that, for the first time in six years, he was crying too. He was crying for the Baker because the Baker hadn't deserved to have his life cut off like that. His life had been the one thing that he could truly call his own. Everyone's life was like that and no one had the right to take it away, not even to pay back treachery, not even to pay back the worst sort of treachery, the sort Watt had experienced when the Baker, whom he trusted, had betrayed him to the Over Lord. And Watt realised he was crying because he cared much, much more about the Baker than he'd ever understood until now. He loved him.

Brad said tearfully, 'What's up with you, Watt? We's rejoicing, ain't we?'

Watt managed to get out, 'The Baker's dead. Murdered.'

'The boss?' Brad's tear-filled eyes were staring at him in disbelief. 'The boss murdered?' he asked. Watt could only nod. 'The poor old boss,' Brad said, and cried more.

And so did Watt. His throat ached with trying to stop, but he couldn't because everything was over and changed and different. The Baker was gone and nothing would ever bring him back. The Baker's invention – the dumb boy – was gone too. It wasn't Watt sitting here crying; he was Avtar now, though beyond the name he didn't much know what that meant. What he *did* know was he'd have to be more careful with this flipping love.

It could blow up in your face, love could; it went hand in hand with treachery. The Baker had shown him that – and his own mother. Love didn't work.

Handkerchiefs. That's what they needed. He set about searching for some. Porcini had stacks of them; she had stacks of everything. She must have a history of lost luggage; almost every item she owned had an understudy. His most interesting find of all during his search was a little barrel of biscuits by the bed.

He hesitated to give the magnificent silk handkerchief to Brad because the trembly old Inmate doctor who'd come with the stretcher-bearers had said that Madame Porcini probably had diphtheria. They'd all put on masks and white cotton gloves, and given Avtar some too. Diphtheria, they told him, was catching. People died from it.

Madame Porcini opened her eyes briefly and said, 'The King's Touch. That will cure me, doc.' It was the same daft Mumbo Jumbo Fidelis and the kid Felix had talked.

'Hush, Madame,' the old doctor replied. 'There's no king. He is gone.'

'Then Porcini is a gonner too,' she whispered. The stretcher bearers hushed her and battled to put her onto the stretcher but their united strength couldn't shift her. Then Avtar suggested they tried rolling her onto it. Thanks to him, her wig had stayed put too. As they moved off with her, she held Avtar's gaze with dark, sad eyes. 'Tell Wamsy, never forget Porcini.'

He touched her hand. 'You'll be all right, Madame Porcini,' he encouraged her.

The old doctor had delayed to write a message for Avtar to take to the Over Lord. It was just what he needed. He could use it as a passport out of the castle in place of the message that had fallen to bits.

But then the doctor's trembly hand stopped writing. The old man gave him a very professional look and said, 'You should get that seen to.' He frowned at Avtar's blank reaction. 'I'm talking about your face. Yous been in a fight?'

Avtar shook his head. 'A PM had a go at me.'

The doctor made a "tsk" noise of irritation. Before Avtar knew what was happening, the doctor's medical case was open again and he was in Porcini's bathroom having his face bathed. It was a weird feeling. It was soothing but it was dangerous. It made him feel looked after, and that was something he mustn't expect in the castle. He mustn't soften up. The doctor said, 'Stand still. I'm not going to eat you. I can't do much for the black eye, but this will calm down the rest.'

As the doctor was putting on the salve, Avtar said, 'I never heard of the King's Touch until today. Today it's cropped up three times.'

'It's a PM fable.'

'Mumbo Jumbo?'

'Worse. It's the City's greatest loss. But we don't talk about it. Ever.' He snapped the lid back on the jar of salve. 'There, that should feel more comfortable.'

Avtar thanked him. He sat on the edge of the bath and wondered why no one talked about it if the loss was so great. The doctor washed his trembly hands. Any minute now the old man would be off, leaving him in the dark about the City's loss.

'No one dares talk,' he said to the doctor's back. 'That's our trouble. I reckon talk can be stronger than a secret even. If someone talked to me about the City's

251

past, I'd understand why things are like they are now. Maybe even change things.' He smiled at the doctor, who was looking in a hurry to leave. 'I'm no Split.'

'You sound like one.' He was packing his bag. 'Getting people to talk is how they operate.' He was going.

Avtar had one more try. 'You can make a half decent loaf if you know the recipe. But if someone just hands you a bag of flour and a twist of yeast, shows you a tap and says, "But we don't talk about it. Ever." – you'd be in a fair old confusion.' The doctor hesitated then said suspiciously, 'You know a deal about bread making for a Messenger Boy.'

'I've a mate in the Bakery. Brad.'

The doctor brightened up at once. 'Brad. We've got him down at the hospital for a sore head. Said he did it in a prank. All fibs. Some Mohock gave him a slap.' Avtar didn't interrupt. He just added Mohock to his stock of new words. 'Nice lad, Brad.' The doctor put his case down and sat on the edge of the bath next to Avtar.

'Look,' he said, 'I don't know the entire answer to what you's asking. But believe me, there's no such thing as the King's Touch. There was a group of people: the king, and that old rascal Thunderbags – he was in on it and a lot more. They're all dead now. Killed. I'd been away from the City for a long time. The king encouraged us to study elsewhere. I came back, though, to find out what this thing was that everyone was talking about that could save lives. It had saved the little crown prince Avtar when he was mortally ill. I chose my time badly. I arrived the day before the Attack. Thunderbags took me up to the laboratory the next day. The people working there showed me some mould and said it had extraordinary properties. It was Lenita, they said, who'd first noticed it.'

'My moth... the queen, you mean?'

'Yes. She noticed the stable boys were using a mould to cure saddle sores on the horses.'

The doctor hadn't bothered to curse the queen. He'd talked about her quite naturally, which was even more confusing than this mould talk. 'They'd just showed me the mould,' he said. 'It was white as a rabbit's scut and had a furry look. Thunderbags said it turned green as it got older; he was explaining how it was the first stage in the process of making the cure, when the enemy attacked. I was cut to pieces. Then I was requisitioned to care for Policy Maker casualties. I didn't get down to our hospital for weeks. When I did, I was too late. The nurses told me the Policy Makers had destroyed the Yellow Magic utterly.'

'Yellow Magic? Where does that come into it?'

'That was the City's nickname for the mould cure. Apparently, in its liquid form, it went yellow at a certain stage in its development. But the Policy Makers said it was filthy and we were ignorant savages, and they scrubbed the place clean of it. They wouldn't believe a mould could cure anyone.'

'It does seem a bit far-fetched.'

'That's science for you.'

Avtar didn't say anything. He'd been fair peppered with new words today. The doctor went on, 'It was a brilliant piece of observation on Lenita's part, and its development was masterly.'

The doctor looked sad and worn out now, and more trembly than ever as he sat hunched on the bath edge. 'No one knows now what the mould was, or how they grew

253

it, or how they nourished it, or how they administered it. Some of us – I can't say who – are trying to find it again, secretly, of course. But it's all lost.'

'Maybe not. How's this for Sigh Ants?' And Avtar recited the skipping rhyme and then the dip that had so recently, almost against his will, pushed their way back into his memory.

The doctor was looking a bit dazed when he finished, so Avtar repeated it.

Mouldy melon, mutton broth,
Mix together, skim the froth.

'Don't you see what they are describing?' he asked. 'It's the making of the cure, only they've used the nickname for it – Yellow Magic! The rhymes aren't nonsense at all. They're like a recipe for the cure. Us kids' games have preserved the method. So there's your Yellow Magic back.'

The doctor laughed and said the mutton broth must have been used as a nutrient. He hurried out to Porcini's desk, grabbed paper and started to write; but he stopped and said, 'For the god's sake, child, don't breathe a word of this to anyone. The Policy Makers have been looking for this cure for the last six years and you appear to have it in your head. They'd give gold for you. A cantaloupe did you say?' And he groped for more paper.

'Just write the rhymes,' Avtar advised. 'Then if you're caught you can say you're a part time poet. And by the way, they made you drink the gravy four times a day.' The doctor gave him a quizzical look. The dose, Avtar realised too late, wasn't in the rhyme. 'The crown prince wasn't the only one to benefit,' he explained smoothly.

'I did too.'

The doctor was ready to rush off with his pockets full of paper and had to be reminded to give Avtar the message to the Over Lord. Before he left, he said, 'This is a magnificent service you have done the City. Thanks to you, we're one huge stride nearer to recovering the greatest piece of knowledge in the world.'

Avtar was shocked. 'You mean that's not it found?'

'Don't be disappointed. Your rhymes have given us the *process*. That's invaluable. But now we have to wait for the mould to recur so we can use it. The Policy Makers were very thorough in eliminating it, but we must pray to the god that somewhere in the City that vital, particular type of white fluffy mould has survived. Myself, I think your cantaloupe might be a clue.'

Avtar was disappointed, but he didn't show it. He said, 'Good luck doctor. Remind the Butler he can get all the melons he needs to experiment with from the castle vegetable gardens. There's stacks growing there.'

'The Butler?' The doctor was all flustered.

'Oh go on,' Avtar told him. 'I know he's in on the search.' The doctor laughed again and asked, 'Who were your parents? You remind me so much of someone, but I can't think who.' Avtar put on his best Inmate accent. 'There's not many of us in this City as remembers their parents.'

He read the doctor's note when he'd gone. It said, "Prepare the City for a major health alert..."

* * *

'You ever going to hand out those kerchiefs?' Brad asked in a voice that still had a quake in it. Avtar looked down at the handkerchiefs he was holding and shrugged. Madame Porcini's handkerchiefs were freshly laundered. Health alert or not, he'd share them out. Brad blew his nose and tried to stop crying. Avtar said, 'Vince saw me in the Bakery, Brad. He thinks it was me that killed the Baker.' He wiped his face and thought what a snotty mess crying made of you.

'Vince will kill you back,' Brad said. 'They was mates.'

'I know. That's another reason I have to leave the City.'

But Brad didn't want to consider leaving the City; he had too many questions to ask. He said Watt was safe enough here for the moment. He wanted to know how in the name he'd got from a chimney into this posh bedroom, and changed into a Messenger Boy, too. They shared the biscuits while Avtar explained Madame Porcini to him and the plot to murder the Roc. He looked completely at sea. 'Why's everybody getting murdered?' he asked.

'Well, I think someone must be trying to take over the Empire. The Over Lord is my guess, with some powerful mates behind him.'

'And?'

'And nothing.'

'Nothing? Dough balls! Where's the miracle come in?'

'Miracle?'

'You *talk*.'

'Don't be daft. I could always talk,' Avtar said.

Brad was livid, and Avtar could see why. Brad had worked his socks off interpreting for him for years. 'And all the time,' Brad said indignantly, 'yous could speak as good as the rest. What's your game?' So Avtar explained that the Baker hadn't wanted him to give himself away. Brad looked totally uncomprehending. 'You see,' Avtar said, after a minute of wondering whether he should, 'I'm the king.'

'Oh, yes,' Brad replied. 'And I'm the gingerbread man.' Avtar smiled. He didn't make much of an impression as a king. Even his own sister hadn't rated him. 'Joking apart,' Brad said, firmly dismissing his friend's claims as fantasy, 'I've got perishing blood coming out of my arm like out of a hosepipe.'

'The god! Why didn't you say?'

Brad grinned. 'Too busy bawling my eyes out and talking, mate.'

Avtar made Brad take off his jacket, and ripped up a towel from the bathroom to make a bandage. Brad said it didn't hurt, but it obviously did; so Avtar asked how it had happened, to take his mind off it. Brad described the fat-faced Policy Maker's crazy attack. 'And here's the bit that will break my heart forever.' Brad's face was tragic. 'My girl – you remember my girlfriend?'

'Which one?' Avtar asked absently, busy with the bandage.

'Which one?' Brad snatched his arm away in a huff. 'The *only* one.' But he was too keen to tell his story to keep up being offended and quickly gave it back. 'Would you credit it? She was a Policy Maker all this flipping time. Fancy me falling for one of *them*! She'd been arrested by four PM blokes, though, and Fatty Face goes for me with a knife and says she's his girl and I'd stolen her!'

'What colour was her hair?' Avtar asked tensely. Brad reckoned that now Watt could talk, he asked some really nit-picking, daft questions. What had hair to do with his drama? 'Same as ever it was,' he answered sourly.

'But what colour?' Avtar almost yelled at him.

'Red,' Brad replied in an injured voice, 'and I'll thank you to keep yours on, mate. That's if you had any. Red. You know, Morag with the red hair.'

Avtar sat down on Madame Porcini's bed and put his head in his hands. 'Oh, the god!' he said. 'She's alive and they've got her.'

Brad decided his friend was a darn sight moodier, too, now he could talk. What was all this grief over a Policy Maker? He bounced down beside him. 'Dunno why you're so low about a Policy Maker, boy. Anyhow, those dopey guards let go of her and she beat it.'

'Where to?'

'Into the City. How should I know?'

But Avtar was up and organising busily. 'Brad you have to go and find her.'

'No I flipping don't! Can't you get it into your head? I'm through with her. She's a Policy Maker.'

'She's my sister,' Avtar retorted. 'She needs help.' He was taking his jacket off. 'Swap clothes.' And he put on Brad's jacket.

'You're littler than me,' Brad protested. 'What do you mean "your sister"?'

Avtar was scuffling through Porcini's little desk to find her pen and ink. 'You can go anywhere as a Messenger Boy. Get on with it, Brad,' he commanded. 'Tell them at the gatehouse this message is for the hospital.' Deftly he altered the doctor's message so that now it appeared to be from the Over Lord to the hospital instead of the other way round. Brad, who'd been thinking of pointing out that he was the eldest and should be the one handing out the orders, thought better of it and did get on with it.

'These trousers are all wet,' he complained suspiciously. 'What yous been doing in them?'

'And your coat's all bloody,' Watt retorted. But then Brad found the key and the Baker's purse in Avtar's jacket pocket and grew even more suspicious. Avtar took the key, saying it was a keepsake. 'Hang on to that bread roll,' he instructed Brad. 'My sister will need convincing that you really are bringing a message from me. She doesn't trust people easily. Show it to her. She knows I had it. And ask her whose elephant fell in the water, too. That should do the trick.'

'Elephant?' Brad looked completely bewildered. 'Now what you perishing playing at?' he cried as Avtar advanced on him with Madame Porcini's make-up case. Avtar told him to shut up and painted a magenta forty-two on his wrist. 'All Messenger Boys are branded. It's a new trick of the Over Lord,' he explained as he did it. 'Now, as soon as you've found Morag, both of you are to hide on the Product Convoy. They're loading it right now and it leaves early tomorrow. Tell her – if you don't mind – that I'll join her as soon as I can.' He didn't add that he hadn't a clue how.

'How?' Brad demanded. He was taking off the jacket. 'You're sending *me* out the way yous were going to go yourself, aren't you?' They were struggling now – Avtar to keep Brad in the jacket, and Brad to get out of it. 'You and your perishing self-sacrifices, mate. Last time you fair near killed me with that clump you gave me round the head.' Brad was winning the jacket fight. 'Hospital said I'd an awesome old skull to survive,' he lied. Avtar hung on to Brad's lapels like a terrier.

'But, you've a better hope of getting through than

me. You've only got *one* maniac hunting you: the clerk. I've got the whole flipping army after me.'

'Why?'

Avtar roared at him. 'Because I'm the perishing king, moron!' Brad took him by the shoulders and roared back, 'You're off your flipping loaf. It's Vince what's after you.'

On cue, Vince came into the room and closed the door behind him. The boys' fight froze. Vince was breathing hard with suppressed rage. It had taken him some time to follow the trail of blood Brad had splattered between the Bakery and Porcini's room. Now he made straight for his quarry – a Messenger Boy – only it was Brad, not Avtar. Brad dodged away from him with a yell of fright and Avtar shouted, 'Vince, it wasn't me killed the Baker. We're on the same side, I swear.' Brad dodged as Vince plunged again, and Avtar sent the chaise longue careering across the room at him, like a missile. It crashed into Vince's legs and he stumbled backwards. Then Avtar knocked the electric lamp over, and the room blacked out as it broke.

Something hit Brad on the head and bounced him across the great bed. There was a splintering crash of wood and he slid flat onto the floor. Then came a second, bigger crash. Then silence.

He crawled to where he thought the door was and found a light switch. There was nobody in the room except him. The bathroom door was hanging off its hinges so he could see it was empty too.

Then Vince sat up in the bath and shook his head as though he was seeing stars. He climbed out, and as Brad watched, he smashed the wash basin into a thousand splinters of porcelain. Then he kicked the mirror so it frosted over with criss-crosses of cracks.

Brad didn't watch any more. Vince was mad. He thanked the god Watt had escaped ahead of him. He checked the message was still safe in his pocket, then slipped into the corridor and went to look for Watt's sister.

CHAPTER TWENTY-FIVE

Waiting endlessly for Vince made Scar fidgety, so he went off to the kitchens to look for the Cook himself. There were only some scullery maids there, though, finishing a mound of drying up, and an old, frightened dog in the inglenook. Even the City's dogs were scared to death these days.

The maids said the Cook was off duty. 'Gone home, I reckons,' one of them told Scar over her shoulder as she trudged into the China Room with a stack of coffee saucers from her waist to her chin. There was nothing for it but to go back to the tunnel and wait. At least he'd meet up with the Baker.

On the way back, he had to dodge into a lift with a chambermaid to avoid eight guards marching in his direction. She opened the wicker hamper in her arms and smiled gleefully at him over the lid. It was full of toilet rolls. He left her giggling her head off.

Halfway down the tunnel, a slight grate of a boot in the dark ahead sent him running back the way he'd come. A pistol shot nearly burst his eardrum and bullets ricocheted off the walls as the guards waiting for him fired.

Scar began weaving back and forth to confuse their aim, but it made him lose ground. His scarred leg ached with the pace he was going at. More bullets scraped the wall by his shoulder. He could hear boots just behind him, and someone shouting, 'His head! Aim for his head!' They were close, very close.

But just as he raced past the little door that led to the Inner Court, the Lady Mercy sped out of it. A bullet thwacked into the lintel by the Lady Mercy's nose, and the Lady Mercy screamed the place down.

Two of the guards held up for a few valuable seconds that allowed Scar to pull ahead. The other six skidded to a halt with such a flurry of sparks from the studs in their boots that the Lady Mercy was lucky to escape with her gown unsinged. The Spy Master came out of the Inner Court and gave them a dressing-down about the use of firearms in the presence of ladies. None of them took it seriously since he'd ordered them to kill the shepherd boy whatever the cost. Meanwhile, the Lady Mercy was pressing the lift buttons repeatedly, but no Vince descended to her rescue. With a moan, she scooped up her train and took the stairs like a steeplechaser.

The two other guards reported back to the Spy Master that they had followed the shepherd to the Ante-room where he seemed to have disappeared into thin air.

The Ante-room again! And where had he heard *that* recently – disappeared into thin air? Of course, the Roc and his absurd story of the disappearing bread roll. Was there a connection? Before he could make one, the Spy Master felt an unpleasant twinge in his intestines. He was never ill, he reminded himself. He felt another twinge and strode off to his rooms in the South East Tower to find his medicine chest.

✳ ✳ ✳

Avtar paused outside his sister Lal's apartment and swore to himself that this was the very last thing that he would do for a Policy Maker before he concentrated on his own escape.

He'd got away from Vince by the skin of his teeth, through the entrance to the service stairs in Madame Porcini's bathroom. It had been depressing to step into his father's Robe Room again; it was an office now. The bedroom was even more depressing. The sheet on the bed had been turned back ready for the Roc to climb into it. A carafe of whisky and some sandwiches were waiting for him on the bedside table. Avtar ate the sandwiches and had hidden the plate under the bed. He'd considered doing something gross to the whisky, but resisted on the grounds of shortage of time.

There was a low light burning in his sister's room and a woman, with a long nose and ginger hair that stuck out from under a lace nightcap, lying in the bed. Where was the Roc's daughter? Had he got the wrong room?

The woman turned over and groaned; then she sat bolt upright, swung her feet over the side and dashed into the bathroom. Avtar, hidden below the foot of the bed, almost laughed at the sight of the towel spread on the floor next to him, with the Roc's daughter's ruined green dress on it and her waterlogged petticoat and stockings. He'd got the right room.

He looked about. It was exactly as it had been when Lal had slept and played there, and left him messages in her secret drawer. He stole over to her desk and felt for the release point. The little drawer slid open; inside was what could only be a message from his dead sister. He took the thin strip of paper over to the light. There was no time to read it. Noises coming from the bathroom signalled the long-nosed woman was about to reappear. He put the message in his pocket, slid behind the blue curtains and went out onto the balcony.

The wind was up and the clouds were flying thick and fast across the half-moon. He leant on the railing and looked out over the Roof Garden while he thought about his sister, Lal, and about their mother who had betrayed them. He was ashamed of his mother. He was even more ashamed of himself for not believing she was a traitor. But was she a traitor? The old doctor hadn't cursed her; he'd called her brilliant. And hadn't the Butler kept her hairbrush as a memento? Was it just because she was his mother that he didn't believe she was a traitor? It was weak of him to let his feelings for her smother the facts. He'd warned himself off love already tonight. It would keep sneaking in, though. But what *were* the facts? Why, he wondered, did no one ever come out with what she'd actually done? How had she betrayed the City? He remembered suddenly and clearly the way she'd said his name – Av-*tar* – with the stress on the end. No one else said it like that. And her voice had been – so kind. He closed his eyes.

'Av-*tar*!'

A blast of wind and the sound of glass shattering over on the opposite walkway brought him to his senses. He tucked himself out of sight behind the potted plants and greenery growing across the railings. Stupid! He'd been standing in full view of anyone looking this way…

The Spy Master cursed. He could have sworn he'd seen a white shape on the balcony of the Roc's daughter's apartment. As he'd cupped his hand against a pane to get a better look, the window had burst open wide with a violent blast of wind and he'd very nearly fallen out. His medicine glass had fallen from his hand and smashed to pieces below. Close shave! By the time he'd recovered, there was no figure there. Trick of the moonlight...

Far out on the plain, the sky flashed with vivid lightning. Avtar counted until he heard the thunder. Then he sat and waited for the Roc's daughter. He wondered what time it was. Midnight? He felt tired. He'd been on the go since early that morning. He dozed.

* * *

The more she thought about it, the surer Fidelis was that she could be doing something more useful. She'd danced precisely two-and-a-half dances the whole night and there didn't seem much likelihood of dancing any more. The number of available partners was dwindling by the minute. Two thirds of her father's cavalry had gone down with the "Runs", and the other third looked distinctly seedy.

Perhaps she could fake the "Runs", get out of this boring ball to go and hunt for Span. Her mother would be broken-hearted to lose him. Fidelis wasn't sure her play-acting would be up to it. She wished she had the courage to try it, though; the Over Lord's search for Span hadn't produced results.

He was sitting watching the dance, too, she noticed, with a face like a gargoyle. Maybe his partners had all forsaken him like hers had. Or maybe he was next in line for the "Runs" – he certainly looked more than ever like a convalescent vulture. She caught his eye and he gave her a sticky leer. Yes, he'd be off next, no doubt about it. Lady Joy had gone long ago and at a life-threatening speed. Even so, her husband, the First Minister, had managed to overtake her.

Fidelis wondered about the Messenger Boy. He'd never told her why he'd pretended to be dumb. What sort of trouble could it be that he was in? If only I knew, she thought, I'm positive I could help him, quite positive. Of course, there was one sure-fire way to find out and that was to go and look for him and ask him. She was positive she could help him. But it was out of the question. She could almost hear Prudence's voice – a lady doesn't go running after Messenger Boys. Oh no, no, NO!

An awful grimace of pain twisted Fidelis's face. Then another. She sprang to her feet and ran. To her extreme satisfaction she collected several sympathetic glances on her way out. Not bad, she thought, not bad at all...

The Roc knew he had to declare an end to the ball before it was finished off for him. His own partner, the sturdy Lady Evangeline, had just sprinted out of the Inner Court in a streak of diamonds and left him capering round the floor on his own. The Chief Medical Officer had diagnosed a serious case of collywobbles when the Roc had asked what the deuce was the matter with everyone. 'Probably the water, sir. We're just not used to it like the locals are,' he'd said with a cheeriness that should have won him a medal if the Roc had only known what gripes the Chief Medical Officer himself was suffering.

The Roc sat down and took the whisky the Butler served him. Was there a hint of mockery about the man? The Roc's moustache stiffened with suspicion. That would never do. He sipped his whisky and pondered what excuse he could invent to call a dignified halt to the wretched romp. Dash it, he thought. We can't be caught caving in to our bowels! We'd be the laughing-stock of these Inmate laddies. The Over Lord was no help. Drooping on a chair, it was impossible to recognise the morbid fellow as the same chap he'd been best pals with at Military School.

A violent blast of wind spiralled down into the Inner Court and blew out most of the candle lanterns, leaving the dance floor grim and smoky. The square of sky overhead brightened briefly with lightning, and distant thunder rumbled. The Roc hastily announced the last waltz. 'Before we get rained off,' he explained. 'Don't want to catch our death!' The Over Lord didn't join in the waltz. Not because he was ill – he'd hardly touched his port. The Over Lord was nervous. He excused his nervousness with the thought that it's not every night you plan to assassinate the Head of the Empire – and murder his daughter. And that is what he was going to do.

CHAPTER TWENTY-SIX

Melior ran round a corner, opened the first front door she came to and slammed it behind her. There was a woman inside, writing at a table. She had several small dishes with silver lids in front of her. She looked up in alarm as Melior broke into the room, then snuffed out the candle. Melior leant against the door in the dark and listened. Her own gasping breath nearly drowned out the sound of the Spy Master's men running on past the house and down the road. She'd fooled them.

She considered her next move. She'd seen the woman before. She was one of the four shadowy people she had disturbed in the Tank Room the previous night. Melior remembered her clearly because hers was the only face their candle had lit up. But whoever the woman and her sinister companion were, she was going to have to appeal to her.

'Help me.' It came out as a muffled whimper because of her gag. The woman's voice replied coolly, 'What?' Melior pulled the gag down. It was tied so tightly it felt as if her nose nearly came with it. 'Help me.'

'Why?' As cool as before.

Melior remembered what she'd learned from Scar. 'If you don't mind,' she panted. The voice said more helpfully, 'There's a bolt top and bottom on that door.'

Melior felt for the bolts and shot them across. The woman kept her waiting an unnervingly long time before she relit the candle.

The dishes and her writing had vanished from the table. The woman looked Melior over and said, 'What can I do for you, ma'am?'

'Ma'am?' Melior repeated blankly, and then understood. Scar's cloak had slipped back and the Policy Maker uniform underneath was showing. 'I'm in disguise.'

'As what?' The woman smiled grimly. 'One of us or...?' "One of them?" she left unsaid.

'I'm a runaway,' Melior said. 'There's a clerk has me marked for marriage.' She stopped short. Someone was screaming down the road. A window was smashed, then came the sound of front doors being kicked in. The men had worked out she'd taken refuge in a house and were searching the street. They would be here any minute.

'There's plenty of girls has endured worse than a clerk,' the woman said. 'Don't involve me.' And Melior knew that she would turn her in as easy as spit.

Gunfire sputtered. Melior's voice shook with fright as she said rapidly, 'Give me a knife then if you won't save me so I can kill myself before they reach us.'

The woman said, 'You calm down my girl and clear off while you've time. I can't take on your trouble. There's folks as is relying on me. Important folk.'

It crossed Melior's mind to tell the woman that she was Princess Melior and you don't get more important than that; but she didn't. She had trained herself to keep her secret too well. Instead she risked a confession. 'In the name of the god, help me. I'm running for my life. This is my Supervisor's uniform. I sabotaged the Sew

House.' And the woman took the candle and steered her out of the room.

They were in what seemed to be a disused laundry. Like most of the City, everything in it had been smashed and abandoned. The woman hurried her between shattered stone troughs and tangled heaps of brass taps. The walls were mad: they'd been stained all over with every different shade of blue imaginable. Melior's cloak caught in a splintered wooden vat and the woman tore it away and pushed her towards a narrow flight of blue spattered stairs at the far end.

'What is this place?'

'A Dye House.'

'Die House?' Melior clenched her fists. She'd punch her way out of this if she had to. 'This is where we made our blue,' the woman said. 'The blue that was the envy of the world.'

'Oh! A *Dye* House.' Melior floundered on up the staircase behind the woman, trying not to cry with relief. The woman led her through a room that was a rainbow of swatches of different coloured fabrics hanging on the walls. 'My family were Master Dyers.' She blew out her candle.

Melior heard a door opening and felt air on her face. 'Crawl,' the woman instructed. They crawled out into the open, one behind the other, over a wooden bridge that spanned an alley far below them. Melior had a frightened hysterical urge to giggle as they trundled head to tail, but agonised screaming from the houses they were leaving behind stopped the laughter dead. If they could do that to an innocent person, what would they do to her?

The bridge linked the woman's house with a tall block

opposite. Once inside, she drew Melior through several dark rooms and out onto a tiny landing before she dared relight the candle. She gripped Melior's elbow. 'Who sent you to me?'

'No one.'

The woman stared at her intently. 'You came from the castle?'

'The sheep pens.' Melior could tell the answer troubled her, but the woman didn't explain why.

A ramshackle ladder took the two of them up through a trapdoor into an empty pigeon loft. Their feet scuffed up layers of bird dropping that filled the loft with dust that caught in Melior's throat. The woman wouldn't move until she'd stopped coughing; then she led her through interconnecting attics, over the heads of the sleeping occupants of the houses. They squeezed round heaps of junk and precious hidden things. At one point, they passed what Melior was sure was her father's state robe in a cracked glass case.

They were streets away from the woman's house by the time they tiptoed by a dump of dismantled iron bedsteads. Melior recognised the dusty blue bedspreads piled into a box. 'We must be in the orphanage attic.'

'Tis closed now.' Unintentionally, the woman answered the question Melior daren't ask. 'The children are gone.'

'Where?'

'The god knows. The darkest were taken out over the plain in carts; the palest were given to Policy Makers to parent. 'Tis Policy. Hurry.'

Melior followed without a word. Phoelo, her little brother, was pale. It was unbearable to think who might be his mother and father now.

'We're here.' The woman pushed open a skylight and the wind rushed in through the dark, circular opening. 'Climb onto the roof,' she whispered. 'Keep off the skyline. Go downhill – the length of the street. Second bit's easier. The library roof is flat. And 'tis shut down – so no guards. Go right. Third bit's hard. The roofs stop. There's another skylight. Getting through that is your difficulty, but others have done it afore you. Your way out is on the ground floor. See that cloak stays closed round you; anyone gets sight of what's underneath, they'll do you in and no questions asked.

'Who are *they*?'

'Don't know. Safer that way. Any trouble, tell them Cookie sent you.'

'Give me a leg up, if you don't mind,' Melior asked politely. The woman did as she was asked, and the window clicked shut on her dark, anxious face. Melior mouthed a thank you down through the glass, but the woman had gone.

The tiles creaked ominously under her weight, so she lay face down and gripped the roof ridge with both hands. There was hardly enough moonlight to see. But she could tell she was high up. A monstrous flapping of wings over her head, like an eagle descending on its prey, made her cower. When she dared to look up, the flapping turned out to be nothing but four Empire flags licking and curling in the wind as they flew from the chimney stack. It was a perilous thing to do, but she let go of the ridge with one hand for long enough to stab a couple of fingers up in their direction.

Out on the plain, sheet lightning flickered in the sky. Then came faint thunder.

She began her journey, easing sideways, arm-stretch

273

by arm-stretch, while her toes pushed against the complaining tiles. Time and again the wind billowed under her cloak, nearly lifting her off the roof before letting it collapse with a stinging slap on the back of her legs. But she reached the Library. It was fairly rattling with Empire flags, and she bent and ran low across its heavenly flatness, finding her way by the patchy light of the moon dipping in and out of the clouds.

All too soon she was back on steep roofs again. The houses ran downhill, which meant that she had to keep lowering herself from one roof level to the next. That was difficult enough. Sometimes the drop was much more than her own height, but chimneys were worse. She negotiated them with a mix of agility and prayer. The wind never let up. It was out to get her.

Then the row of houses opened up around a small square, with strings of bunting criss-crossing it in bobbing lines. And there was the clerk marching about officiously from one doorway to another. She clung like lichen to the tiles, willing him not to look up. He'd acquired a truncheon from somewhere and was beating it against the walls as he searched for her. She hadn't thought it possible to be so petrified by someone she despised so much. The wind parted his lank hair from behind and blew it upright like a halo. As he lifted his head to tuck it back behind his chubby ears, he was looking straight up at the roof she was on. Then a voice from the next street called him and the clerk ran to answer, taking plump, manly strides. Melior shuffled away, shuddering with relief.

At length the buildings came to an end. The skylight she had to get through was halfway down the roof. All she had to do to reach it was to lie flat again, which she did, and then slither gently down the roof until she was level with it. Easy. Except it wasn't. She couldn't do it. Couldn't? *Daren't*! She'd been clamped to the roof like a leech for ages and now she daren't let go. What if she missed the skylight and slithered past it over the edge of the roof? She would be killed. Capture would be preferable. Even marrying the clerk would be preferable. Or would it? Melior let go of the roof ridge.

Annoyingly, she stayed put. She gave an impatient wriggle and did exactly what she'd feared: she slid down in a rush. She was really frightened, and her legs were bruised by the frame; but she was there, bunched over the little window with her cloak half-strangling her and her heart banging. The wind blew as if it were seeking its last chance to get her off the roof, and then the first big drops of rain tapped onto the tiles. Lightning flickered and she wrapped the end of the cloak round her fist and waited. Under cover of the thunder that followed, she smashed the glass. She untied the cloak one-handed and it flew like a windsock until she managed to stuff it through the skylight onto the floor below her to protect her from the broken glass as she landed.

More lightning showed her out of the empty room to the top of a staircase. There was a light on each landing, and she could see through the iron banister rails that every storey, right down to the ground floor, was deserted. She hurried down to the bottom. No indication of the way out, though. She chose the nearest door. It closed behind her. It was icy cold and dark.

She held her hands out in front of her and stepped forward. Her fingers met something cold and damp which moved under her touch. Instinctively, she drew her hands back. The stuff was still there when she put them out again. It was softly solid. This time it recoiled from her and then came closer. She turned away from it, but after another couple of steps the cold damp was there again. It brushed her cheek. She turned in the other direction. It bumped into her and withdrew. Somebody whispered, 'Stay where you are.'

Brilliant lights flooded on and she saw she was walking amongst rows of skinned carcasses suspended from chains in the ceiling. They began to sway about and crash into each other more and more violently. Their chains screeched as someone pushed their way through them towards her. The carcass in front of her was hooked sideways with a meat cleaver and an old man glared at her round the red flesh and the silvery sheen of the ribs. She just had time to take in the stained gabardine that reached to his kneecaps, the grizzled chest hair sprouting between its lapels, a flaking toenail thrusting through a frayed hole in his dirty canvas slippers, before he raised the cleaver over her head and she screamed.

'Cookie sent me!'

The old man left without a word, setting the carcasses swinging so heavily it was almost impossible to follow him. She hoped that was what she was supposed to do – follow him. He went outside into a yard where the rain was coming down hard now, turning the ground to muddy mousse. She could just about see the outlines of sheds and high walls as she squelched after him past a pen crowded with sodden, wide-eyed calves. She guessed they'd been brought in on the convoy. Their coats were steaming in the cold rain as if, by a merciful accident, they'd skipped several stages in the Policy Maker abattoir and were already cooking.

The old man unlocked a small door in the boundary

wall and said in the same whisper, 'Just afore dawn, go down to the Product Convoy. 'Tis held up, delayed by saboteurs. There yous asks in the last truck for the Head Driver. You hear me, girl? The Head Driver is who'll take you out safe.' He shoved Melior through the door and closed it after her. She heard the key turn in the lock.

'Thanks,' Melior murmured, 'for your hospitality.'

The rain was sheeting down. The candle lamp in the empty street had misted up as the water splashed over the hot glass. Melior pulled her wet cloak round her and wondered where in the name she was going to hide until dawn. Then, a horse ambled out of nowhere through the driving rain and into the light. It was drawing a carriage without any help from its driver, who had slumped sideways. He managed to pull up next to her and groan, 'Morag?'

'Master,' Melior answered automatically. It was the Chief Medical Officer. His face was grey. His eyes were screwed up against the rain and his mouth was puckered with pain. 'For pity's sake, Morag,' he moaned, 'drive your mistress and me home. I believe we have dysentery.'

As Melior climbed up beside him and took the reins she glimpsed a mound of peach silk on the floor of the carriage. The mistress was obviously in a bad way.

'The Sun!' the Chief Medical Officer moaned. 'What I'd give for your Yellow Magic now.' Melior remembered her mother sobbing just before she died "How can they do this when we've given them the Yellow Magic?"

The man almost spat at her. 'You selfish pigs!'

'Walk on,' was all Melior said. The horse pricked up its ears and headed for the posh side of the City and a dry stable; and for safety, as far as Melior was concerned. Whatever names he called her, there couldn't be anywhere much safer to hide until dawn than the house of a high-ranking Policy Maker.

CHAPTER TWENTY—SEVEN

The only person who hasn't got the "Runs" is me. The thought pleased Fidelis. She could tell by the groans coming from behind every bedchamber door she passed that the "Runs" were no joke.

There were some healthy enough guards around, though. They were looking for someone too, and she was careful not to collide with them. The Roc's daughter shouldn't be out alone without a troop of cavalry chinking along in her wake and Prudence grousing in the rear; and she certainly shouldn't be looking for a Messenger Boy. She turned a corner and ran slap into a particularly frazzled looking lot.

She smiled graciously and veered off in another direction calling, 'Span, Span' so they'd think she was searching for her dog. But the guards told her that *they* were hunting for her Ladyship's little dog and that her Ladyship should retire for the night. They called the lift for her; dutifully she pressed the going-up button, and that was that.

As she stepped out onto the ground floor, she noticed her play-acting was improving by leaps and bounds.

There wasn't a soul about apart from two footmen lying asleep by the main entrance. She could hear what Prudence would have called "a heck of a storm" outside them but the only sound here in the passageway was the tap-tapping of her dancing shoes and the rustle of her dress. Being alone did interesting things to her thoughts: they came jumping up with no trimmings. She wanted to find the bald-headed Messenger Boy – now. A burst of friendly laughter coming from behind a door sounded promising, so she opened it and stood smiling on the threshold at more Messenger Boys than she'd bargained for.

They were all sitting in a line on a bench. They stared at her impassively, without a word. The Butler, who'd clearly just been crying with laughter too, climbed down from his stool and waited for his orders with his head bent. Incongruously, he was holding a jar of healing salve. None of them spoke.

Fidelis said pleasantly, 'I'm looking for a boy...' Someone guffawed. Fidelis stopped in embarrassment and flushed pinker than ever. 'A Messenger Boy,' she corrected herself and the entire room stood up. 'No, I mean a particular one.' They all watched her, blankly attentive and not at all like the comical, charming servants she'd grown used to. Their attitude was so unexpected she couldn't deal with it. 'It doesn't matter,' she stammered, and the Butler ushered her out as though she were a bad smell.

As soon as the door closed behind them there was another burst of laughter from the room and a silly falsetto voice imitated her, 'Aym lookin' fer a Boy.' And then louder laughter. Fidelis had never been subjected to such a blast of dislike before. It made her shrink inwards on herself. She didn't dare look up at the Butler, walking beside her, in case he was jeering at her too. The Messenger Boys couldn't have made it plainer that they were charming and polite to her because they *had* to be, not because they wanted to be.

She thanked the Sun she'd never found the bald-headed Messenger Boy. It would have been unbearable to hear it from him – that not one of them could stand the sight of her, including him. The Butler put her into the lift and sent her upwards into her own world feeling as flat as a pancake.

* * *

The Roc was in a worse mood than ever: he'd had to undress himself. His Equerry, who usually did it, had been struck down by the dratted collywobbles and the Inmate servant who had been sent to replace him hadn't the foggiest idea how to set about it. He'd ordered the stupid man to pour him a glass of whisky and dismissed him. After a bit, the Roc discovered *he* hadn't the foggiest idea how to undress himself either. His collar tried to garrotte him, and he nearly did the splits attempting to pull off his long boots. He did eventually locate the route into his nightshirt, but he gave up on the rest and got into bed in his boots and breeches. In seconds, he was asleep.

* * *

The Over Lord was not asleep. Thunder grumbled and thumped round the Topmost Tower where he lay straight as a tombstone on his truckle bed. His melancholy eyes were on the symbol, fixed to the wall, of his God of the Rising Sun. The wind howled, and the rain drove like stones against the black windowpanes. It was a good night for it – for murder. Tomorrow he would be appointed the new Roc. Any opposition, though highly unlikely, would be crushed. He had back-up.

He'd conquered his nerves – or so he thought. In fact, it was the minute drop of Thunderbags' cure he'd drunk at dinner that had banished them. It hadn't affected him like everyone else. The Over Lord's gut was as rigid as his mind.

He raised his pale hands in supplication to the Rising Sun and prayed to his god to deliver the boy king, Avtar, to him tonight. Far greater than the power of the Roc was the power to cure your friends and cast aside your enemies. With Avtar's healing gift in his control, he would not only rule the Empire, he would be lord of the world.

The Spy Master was waiting in an armchair in his rooms. He was fully dressed under his velvet dressing gown and ready for action. He was also asleep. He had overdone his medicine for the twinges in his stomach. He'd drunk half a bottle of kaolin and morphine. The kaolin had stopped the "Runs", but the morphine had got to him. He was woken by the sound of his own sheath knife falling from his hand. He must stay awake. He was the Over Lord's lieutenant and this was the greatest night of his life. He fell asleep again.

Fidelis came into her apartment very quietly so as not to wake Prudence. She didn't need a Prudence lecture now. She turned on a lamp. The first thing she saw was her ruined dress, petticoat and stockings piled accusingly on a towel on the floor. She gave a guilty gasp. The next thing she saw, which nearly made her scream, was a brown hand beckoning her from low down between the curtains. She retreated to the door. The curtains parted at the bottom and the bald-headed Messenger Boy stuck his head through and whispered fiercely, 'Where in the name have you been? I've been waiting hours!'

Fidelis was so outraged to see him in her room uninvited that she forgot she'd spent the last two hours looking for him. Besides, she was still smarting from the treatment she'd had from the boys in the duty room. It was hard to be haughty in a whisper, but she managed it perfectly. 'How dare you?'

'Cut that out,' he whispered back. 'This is urgent.' He pointed at the bedside lamp and Fidelis switched it off, leaving nothing but a nightlight burning low on the dressing table. Prudence never stirred. Fidelis tiptoed to join him, gathering up her rustling skirt to squeeze next to him. He helped her with it, almost impatiently shoving the mass of fabric behind the curtains.

They had to open the French windows a little to make room for them both. She could just see that he was wearing a different uniform now, but she could hardly hear what he was saying for the roaring of the wind. The rain was pattering onto her buttercup yellow organza and though she was really pleased to see him, there was no doubt about it: this boy was very good at spoiling her dresses. She leant nearer to hear.

As Avtar whispered his warning, the wind dropped momentarily and far away he heard the high, thin voices of the Ghosty Boys singing their lament. So it was two am. The new shift had come on duty and found the Baker. The wind howled again and drowned them out.

Fidelis's eyes grew rounder and wider as she listened to him. At last she whispered back, 'How could Madame Porcini *know* the Over Lord and the Spy Master are planning to kill us?' Avtar gripped her arm and put his finger to his lips, then peered through the curtains. Something had come into the room.

A squat, faceless shape was inching towards the bed where Prudence lay. Avtar remembered the thing on the service stairs and went numb with fright. The shape leapt like a frog to the side of the bed; then Prudence's limbs began to thrash and flail as it held a pillow on her face to smother her.

It thinks she's Fidelis, Avtar thought.

'Oh! Poor Prudence!' Fidelis cried. Before he could stop her, she ran across to the other side of the bed to tug the pillow away The shape sprang onto the bed. Fidelis's scream was cut short as it took her throat in a stranglehold. It pushed her to her knees and buried her head in the bedclothes.

Avtar forgot his terror; rage took over. He broke from behind the curtains and charged the shape, punching it again and again where he thought its head would be. He was shouting at it to stop what it was doing. But it wouldn't. It turned and bit him like a dog. Fidelis was putting up a desperate fight, but the shape was deadly strong. It grunted rhythmically as it bent over her, forcing her head deeper into the bedclothes.

Avtar ran round to the other side of the bed, jumped up behind it and pushed the shape with all his strength. His push, combined with the thing's own weight, sent it bellyflopping onto the bedroom floor.

He clawed at the drapes over the bed and ripped down the whole structure. As the thing tried to get up again, he swung the drapes at it like a thick rope. The little silver coronet whirled round on the end and hit the thing hard. It went down again in a tangle of blue fabric and lay still as a corpse.

Then all the lights snapped on. The Roc said from the doorway, 'You devil!' and fired his revolver at Avtar. Fidelis screamed at her father, 'Not him, not him,' as Avtar smashed onto the floor.

The Roc, resplendent in his nightshirt and boots, said in a plaintive, sleepy voice, 'Who then?'

Fidelis's voice was hoarse with pain. 'That boy saved my life and you've killed him!'

As she spoke, a monstrous looking figure walked in behind the Roc and put the point of a knife in his back. It was the scarred young man. He yanked the Roc's head backwards by a handful of his fair hair and said, 'You're the Roc, aren't you? Drop your gun.' The Roc must have known a knife when he felt one because he said, 'I am,' and threw his revolver on the floor.

The man laid his knife across the Roc's throat and said over the Roc's shoulder, 'My name is Scar.' His scarred face was as close as an embrace to the Roc's cheek. 'And this is a present from Slave City.'

'Don't.' Fidelis begged. 'Don't kill him, please. He's my father.' It was a useless appeal. One eye glared back at Fidelis. The knife shook against the Roc's throat. She said quickly, 'Wait! Imagine if it was your father.'

'I don't have to imagine. Your lot did just this to my father when you invaded.'

'I'm sorry for that. But you know how it feels, then.'

'And so will you, lady.' Scar jiggled the Roc's head

by his hair. 'I'm here to kill Sir Piss and Glory here. It's my duty.'

The cold voice in Avtar's head said "Get up. Who needs an army to free Khul? Think of the Baker's Lost-and-Founds. Get on with it before he cuts his throat. Get up." And he did. It gave them all a tremendous shock – they'd all thought he was wounded, or even dead. Fidelis gave him a frightened half-smile of relief and Scar jumped so hard that a thin red line of blood appeared on the Roc's throat where the knife had gone in.

'Hold on, Scar,' Avtar said, 'there's something you don't know.' He began to talk. He had to go carefully. One shift of the blade and it would all be over. But for once he could *do* something: he could talk the two men round. It made him feel unkind and exultant and terrified all at the same time. He told Scar everything he knew about the Over Lord's plot. He could see the Roc trying to get a look at him; he was interested too, all right.

'So kill Sir Piss and Glory,' Avtar warned Scar, 'and you won't be doing your duty; you'll be doing the Over Lord's dirty work for him. He'll top you, and the Empire will roll on with another Roc, and another and another.'

'Too right.' The Roc could barely open his mouth.

It was courageous but unhelpful because it made Scar angry. Avtar cut in fast, 'Shut up, Roc, and listen to us. This is what Scar and I propose. You agree to give us our City back and my friend here won't cut yer throat. How about that?'

He'd no idea if Scar would keep to the bargain, or if the Roc would agree to it, so he went on talking hard to persuade them both. 'Mind you,' he said to the Roc, though he was directing it as much to Scar, 'we'd want the City of Khul back just as it was, with the river flowing like it used to; and just as peaceful and full of happiness, with us all doing what we're good at: inventions, and weaving stories into beautiful tapestries.' As he described it, Fidelis gave him a questioning look, as if she understood at last how they must feel about the Empire. It encouraged Avtar. Maybe he'd convinced her father, too.

'Now that's not much skin off your nose, is it, Roc?' Avtar asked. 'One little City in the whole of your great big Empire? That's all you'd be giving up to call your throat your own again.' There was no answer. 'I promise. Word of a Ghosty Boy.'

But the Roc was silent. Avtar had never imagined that the perisher was ready to die for his Empire. 'Agreed?' he asked, and hoped he didn't sound as scared as he felt. How long would the knife wait? Still there was silence. Then Fidelis broke it. She almost sobbed, 'Of course he agrees!'

'I'm all right, Fidelis,' her father said. 'It's all right. I agree.'

'If you don't mind,' Avtar said to Scar, 'let him go.'

Scar took the knife away, and Avtar relaxed. He'd done it! But he didn't like *how* he'd done it. He wasn't used to parents. He hadn't meant to play on Fidelis's fear, and on the Roc's feelings for her. He'd forgotten that they loved each other. Love had cropped up again in an unexpected way. But at least no one was dead and, above all, his City was free.

But then the Roc took Scar's wrist and laid the knife against his own throat again. 'I agree on one condition.' All Avtar's jubilation vanished. This man was hard as iron. He'd taken the lead by doing that with the knife. Scar was looking thrown, even a bit foolish. The Roc said, 'I'll restore everything in the City as it was, but no more than that. There's a strong likelihood that one of Lenita's boys survived. Avtar. He is not to be crowned. If he is, or if he comes within a hundred miles of Khul, we take back the City.'

Scar said, 'Then I'm cutting your throat.'

The Roc smiled. 'Go ahead, Scar.'

'Wait!' Avtar stopped him with his voice.

'You can't agree to that,' Scar said. 'Avtar is the king.'

'I can agree, and I do.'

But the Roc said, 'That's all well and good, Ghosty Boy. I grant you're a tough negotiator. But King Avtar's not here, is he? He might not agree. You've no authority to speak for the king, have you?'

His face was a blank. Avtar couldn't tell how much he knew.

Had the Roc guessed who he was and laid this trap so that the only way to seal the freedom he'd just won for his City was to admit that he was its king? It would lose him his crown and probably his life. He remembered how happy and light he'd felt when he'd thought that saboteurs were standing up to the Empire. That's how every single person in Khul would feel if they were free people like the branded Messenger Boy and the trembly doctor, the scullery maid and the boys with the sugarplum, and Sim and Som and the old Butler. He may be a learner king, but he was beginning to see how it worked. A king had power, but not the sort of power the Over Lord wielded, or even his ferocious boss, the Baker. A king's power lay in the power of what a king stood for. That was the power that the kids he'd met round the lift had so much faith in, and it was the power that Saan and the Baker had given their lives for. He stood for Khul. He'd always understood that, as its king, he was born to rule. He'd been wrong. His real purpose was to *serve* his people, whatever it cost him. 'I have the authority,' he said. 'I am Avtar, Slave King of Khul, and I agree to your terms.'

'You abdicate?' The Roc's eyes were laughing with victory.

'I abdicate. Khul is free. Take away the knife, if you don't mind.' The Roc let go of Scar's wrist but the knife stayed put.

'How do we know he'll keep his word?'

'He has to, he's the Roc.'

Scar took the knife away.

'Thank you,' Avtar said. And he was no longer a king.

There was a flat empty moment, and then Fidelis surprised them all. 'And now can we all stop point scoring and playing politics and get down to the fact that the Over Lord intends to murder us?' she said angrily. A mellifluous voice answered from under the blue bed drapes on the floor 'Bright idea, young lady, but you're out of time.' The speaker stood up and pulled the hood from his head. It was the Pianist, and he was holding the Roc's revolver.

He was an expert assassin. In seconds he had Fidelis and the Roc lying face down on the floor. 'You too, Good Looking,' he said, forcing Scar to his knees. 'And take a tip. If you're going to kill, do it fast. As for you, little Mr King,' he told Avtar, 'you know far too much. I haven't forgotten that drum either.'

Avtar knelt next by Fidelis while the Pianist explained that his orders were not to use guns. He could have been about to play a sonata, not murder them. 'Though no one would hear a shooter in this weather,' he said, drawing a dagger that was sharpened to a wire thin point. 'Ready?' he asked Avtar.

Fidelis said into the floor, 'Thank you for trying to help us.' Avtar couldn't reply. He'd won his City's freedom, only to have the Pianist take it away. It was shattering. The dagger was frighteningly close now. He felt weirdly surprised that he was going to die. He reached out and touched Fidelis's hand. It was a way of saying goodbye. It was also a way of distracting the Pianist sufficiently to stop him noticing Prudence, who was creeping up from behind the dressing table where she'd taken refuge.

She was pale and unsteady, but not so unsteady that she couldn't bring her entire box of instruments to make people's hair behave thwacking down on the Pianist's head.

The Pianist crumpled. The Roc was up in a flash and treading on his fingers to make him let go of the gun. Scar wrenched the dagger from him. 'Not my hands, not my hands,' the Pianist pleaded, and let go of the gun.

The Roc's recovery from his second brush with death within minutes was breathtaking. He manhandled the Pianist over to the chaise and sat down beside him. He made a bizarre figure with the blood from his throat turning the lace collar of his nightshirt scarlet. 'Now,' he asked, 'what were your orders from the Over Lord?' The Pianist shook his head. The Roc drummed his fingers on his revolver. 'Don't be a chump,' he said genially. 'Surely you can see that if you don't co-operate you're no use to me and I'll kill you?' Now that, Avtar thought unadmiringly, is the kind of ruthlessness that makes you Top Policy Maker.

The Pianist's eyes filled with tears. 'You and your blasted Empire,' he said thickly. 'Your blasted brass bands and polkas. Your nursery rhyme music! It's only murder that brings in money. How can an Artist make a living from a nation with the musical taste of a cow pat?' Evidently the Roc had been called far worse things. He simply came to the point. 'How much were they paying you?'

The Pianist looked sullen. 'Thirty.'

'I'll treble it,' the Roc said.

That settled it. The Pianist explained the Over Lord's orders while Prudence sat and exclaimed at what she was hearing.

'It was my job to do you in. Then Vince would bring up a luggage basket and we'd dump your corpse in it.'

Avtar said sharply, 'Did you say *Vince*?'

It was so *obvious* once he'd been told: Vince was working for the Over Lord and the Spy Master. Everything that Vince had done that day slotted into place as soon as he knew that. Particularly when Scar said, in a shocked voice, 'The god! I told Vince you were a Ghosty Boy.' So the Over Lord must have ordered Vince to murder the Baker.

The Roc raised an imperious hand for attention. 'But why kill my daughter?' The Pianist tried to look contrite, but no one was taken in. 'She was to have been spared, but then she was caught with a dumb Messenger Boy they are certain is this King Avtar character. Our young Ghosty Boy here is lying. He's not Avtar.'

The Roc looked as pleased as a cat with cream. 'Dear, dear,' he said. 'Bang goes our agreement to free Khul.'

All Avtar could say was, 'I *am* Avtar.' But it sounded perishing feeble!

'Then prove it. Here's my throat. If you're the king, let's see you do the King's Touch. Heal it.'

It made Avtar so angry that he understood at last the huge anger that ate away at his sister. Before he could stop himself he said, 'Don't be a fool. I'm no miracle worker. The healing is *sighants*. And your lot destroyed every shred of it when you attacked us. Silly man.'

The Roc went pink. 'I beg your pardon!'

But everyone else was trying not to smile. Then Fidelis surprised Avtar again. 'I'm afraid your agreement with Avtar still stands, Papa. This boy here doubles up as a dumb Messenger Boy. Perhaps they're short staffed. He gave me a message this very afternoon. I recognise him. He's Avtar all right. You're honour bound to free Khul.'

The Roc gave her an extremely sharp look, but Fidelis looked him straight in the eye and said, 'Papa, we are in danger of our lives, sir.' It was a fair old clash of wills.

Then the Roc said, 'A man must always do as his daughter says.'

Prudence tittered politely at his little joke. No one else did. They were waiting to hear him say it. And he did. 'I'll free Khul for your sake, Fidelis. On the same terms. If he withdraws Khul's insult to the Empire.'

'Agreed,' Avtar said. 'I apologise. Khul apologises.' And he rushed on before the Roc could change his mind again. 'Vince is on his way up here, sir. We'd better be ready. He's very big and very efficient at knifing people.'

The Roc took command at once. He made a speech pointing out that they couldn't rely on his loyal cavalry's support because they all had collie-wobbles. The Over Lord, however, had four hundred fit guards at his disposal. 'The odds are against us,' he summed up, 'but with the exception of Kitten on the Keys here,' he prodded the Pianist with his gun, 'we gallant few stand together, shoulder to shoulder; and, therefore, I shall leave the City immediately with my daughter. The question is – how?'

Avtar wracked his brains. It was vital they went so that the Roc survived to keep his promise to free Khul. But he was blowed if he could think how. Unexpectedly, the Pianist said sulkily, 'Round it up from ninety to a hundred and I'll tell you how.' The Roc gave him the kind of minuscule nod used at an auction.

'Vince and I,' the Pianist said, 'had orders to load your body into Porcini's car as part of her luggage.'

'The Sun, you did! Why?'

'Scandal. You were supposed to bring your wife. Remember?' The Roc frowned. Fidelis said, 'Oh come on, Pa. It's obvious. It was meant to look as if you'd murdered Mama and run off with Madame Porcini. You know; an "affair", it's called.' Prudence gave a tiny mortified scream that Fidelis should know about such things, let alone talk about them, but the Roc slapped his thigh. 'Got it,' he said. 'They were out to discredit me completely: a scandal as well as a murder. Anyone left on my side – the Empire's side – would be so disgusted they'd cross over to the Over Lord's faction at once.'

'Clever plan,' Scar said. The Roc gave him an icy look, and Prudence said reprovingly, 'Hush, you monster.'

The Pianist went on, 'You could still leave in the car – but alive,' and practically held out his hand for the money. Scar cut in. 'No. The Over Lord will see you get into it. He sees everything.'

'Anyway,' said Avtar, 'they've planted a time bomb on it.' The Pianist looked very surprised. 'A bomb? Why?'

By now, Avtar had worked it out. 'It was to look like an accident – as if that newfangled car thing had just exploded. But really it was to prevent Madame Porcini from discovering the Roc's body and exposing their plot. She'd be blasted to bits.'

The Pianist said, 'But they guaranteed Porcini's safety. They said they'd place an Exile Order on her. She'd vanish abroad and everyone would assume the Roc had gone with her.' He was so indignant he just had to be telling the truth.

Then he said something that interested Avtar. 'There's a world out there beyond the blasted Empire that's longing to hear Porcini; so I agreed.' That "world out there", Avtar thought, could be the place for him and Melior.

The Pianist waved his fist under the Roc's nose. 'Typical of you Empire types! You're only going to blow up the greatest singer of our time. But what's one diva more or less to your lot in a power struggle?'

The Roc puffed his cheeks in dismay. 'A bomb,' was all he said, which Avtar thought was a perishing useless contribution.

He turned to Fidelis. 'You understand, do you?' He spoke to her as if no one else were there – or in the world, for that matter. 'Even if you succeeded in driving out of here, you'd still be blown to smithereens half way across the plain. Whatever you think of me, or of what I've done, please listen. Don't get into that motor car, for both our sakes.' She widened her eyes slightly as a warning that they shouldn't look as if they knew each other too well. She nearly made him laugh, but he cobbled a humble "Forgive me for speaking so frankly, my lady," onto the end of the sentence.

The Roc noticed nothing. His shoulders sagged. Even his beautiful moustache sagged. 'There's no way out of this City for us, Fid,' he said to his daughter. 'Quite worrying. We're like rats in a trap.' For once, Avtar felt sympathetic. Fidelis put her arm round the Roc. 'While there's life, Pa.' She looked at them all defiantly. No one likes to see their father hit zero in public and she didn't want them thinking her papa was weak. But the Roc continued to sag. In the end, Avtar came to her rescue. He smiled at her. 'We'll think of something,' he said.

The Roc looked him over. 'When I was a bit older than you, when I was a young officer...'

Fidelis interrupted. 'The Sun, Pa! Is this the time for one of your military school stories?'

As she spoke, the French windows crashed open. The curtains were blown horizontal by the wind, the bedroom door slammed shut in the draught and the French windows banged together again. Everyone except the Roc jumped sky high. He went rambling on as if nothing had happened. 'One of the things we learned,' he said, 'was elementary bomb disposal.'

A plan swept into Avtar's head. 'Listen,' he said. 'This is what we do.'

CHAPTER TWENTY—EIGHT

The night didn't work out as Melior had hoped. No sooner had her passengers staggered into the house than the Chief Medical Officer's batman, an obsequious Policy Maker, stopped his master at the foot of the stairs before he could follow his wife up. 'A message from the hospital, sir,' he said.

'What is it? What is it?' moaned the Chief Medical Officer, hugging the banisters for support. The man lowered his voice so that Melior and his Policy Maker attendants didn't hear. 'A suspected outbreak of diphtheria, sir.'

The Chief Medical Officer clutched his forehead. 'Surely you mean dysentery, man?'

'No, sir.' The batman's training forbade him to cause a panic amongst the listening servants. 'I mean the other D word, sir,' he breathed. 'Highly contagious. They need a quarantine authorisation from you, sir.'

The Chief Medical Officer groaned again and tottered into his office, where he wrote a brief note and stamped it with his seal. 'Take that,' he whispered in agony, 'to the hospital. See to it in person.' And he walked with fast, tense little steps into the hall.

'Yes sir,' the batman replied. He stood to attention, stiff as an ironing board, next to Melior, in the hall while the Chief Medical Officer was borne upstairs and escorted out of sight by his attendants. They heard a yelp of "Oh no!" from the Chief Medical Officer, and cries from his helpers of "Phweughooh! The Sun!" and then a door slam. Only then did the batman relax. 'Morag,' he said. 'Master wants you to run round to the hospital with this note. Off you go.'

She couldn't believe it. He was sending her back into the arms of the guards and the clerk. She didn't refuse: he'd throw her out for that. She took the note obediently. 'Hark!' she lied to him. 'Master's calling.' The batman instantly assumed a respectful expression and ran up the stairs.

He was back in a minute, but by that time Melior had gone to the hospital – or so he thought. He didn't notice that the Chief Medical Officer's military cap, which he'd left on the hall stand, had also gone; and so had his carriage.

* * *

Melior drove the Chief Medical Officer's carriage through the half drowned city waiting for dawn. She was safe, but she and the horse were drenched. Most of the street candle lamps had gone out, so it was hard to find her way. She tried to take shelter under the crossways and little viaducts that were part of the maze of the City's streets and passageways, but she had to keep on the move. She could hear her captors pulling the City apart trying to find her. As soon as they came within earshot, she urged the tired horse on again.

Once she pulled up out of the deluging rain under the stone arch of an overhead walkway, opposite the machinists' hostel. Some of its windows still had a candle burning in them. She worked out which one of them was hers and Triss's room. She was going to chuck a stone at it to attract Triss's attention. But she didn't. Even though she longed to say a proper goodbye, it would land Triss in terrible trouble if they were caught.

A massive crack of thunder echoed under the arch, and lightning hit the street ahead with a loud snap. The horse gave a frightened scream. The reins were dragged from Melior's hands as it bolted into the dark. She had lost control. On and on they careered through the streets. The carriage rocked and swivelled behind her. Spray flew up on either side and she clung to the driver's seat as the horse galloped on. A solitary candle lamp on the corner of a derelict shop lit up the cobbled street ahead and she saw that the storm had turned it into a racing torrent. It poured downhill. She thought – this is the end of me. She called to the horse, begging it to calm down – it didn't even hear her. Someone else did, though. A gangly figure stepped out of the dark and snatched the horse's head. Love may be blind but it's very perceptive and Brad, out hunting for Morag, had recognised the slight figure in a military hat gripping the driver's seat for its life.

He hung on to the bridle although he was scared stiff of horses and it hurt his wounded arm. The wooden shaft of the carriage hit him hard in the small of his back, and his feet were almost off the ground as the horse plunged down the lane. Wavelets of water broke round his shins, but he still hung on. The horse's eyes were rolling with fear, and froth dripped from its mouth; but at last it came to a standstill in the sheeting rain and stood, blowing and snorting and shivering, with the water swirling round its fetlocks.

'Thanks.' Melior was breathless with fright. She peered down at her rescuer. He was a Messenger Boy. A waterfall of rain poured continuously off the peak of his cap and his amazing ponytail had stuck between his shoulder blades like a drowned snake; but she still recognised him. It was the awful pest Brad. 'The god!' she said. 'Is there anywhere you *don't* get?'

She gathered the reins and moved the horse on, but the pest Brad loped alongside with the water surging over his shoes. He whispered that he had a message from her brother. That scared her. How did he suddenly know she had a brother? She scowled down at him from under her cap. 'I have no brother. Clear off.' Then he pulled out the heart-shaped roll her brother had showed her. She wondered if her brother's torturers had given it to him and sent Brad after her. How else could he have the roll? 'Watt sent this,' Brad said. 'To prove I'm all right.'

'Heart-shaped rolls,' she jeered. 'You can pick up one of those anywhere.'

'Dough Balls! It's only me as makes these. I's the only one in the Bakery as does.' He looked so ridiculously offended it almost made her smile. He smiled back eagerly.

'Get lost,' she said and walked the horse on. This time he didn't follow. She'd got rid of him at last. 'Watt said you was an untrusting cow!' she heard him call after her. 'Whose elephant fell in the water?'

'Mine. No, his,' she said quietly. She stopped the carriage and waited for him to catch up. Brad climbed up beside her. She flicked the reins and they moved on through the teeming rain. 'What's the message?' Brad explained about the Product Convoy. 'I was already headed there,' she answered when he'd finished. 'Now go away.' She pulled up to let him get down. Brad didn't budge. 'Your fatty-faced clerk would kill me over you. I'm coming too'

She smiled at him. It lit up his life – temporarily. 'No, you're not,' she said.

'Well, flip you,' he replied. 'I'm coming anyway.' She nodded. Without knowing it, Brad had passed one of Melior's tests.

'Did he really call me an untrusting cow?'

Brad patted her shoulder. 'Who'd call you untrusting?' he asked. 'Or a cow?' he added, just in time. 'Watch out,' he said. 'I think we're here.'

The houses had petered out now, and the lane had merged with a broader road that led to the Main Gates. Melior drew up a short distance from a low building running parallel with the road. It was a long, roofed-over platform that served as a loading bay. There was a sweep of flattened land on the other side of it. Bits of the houses that had been knocked down to make the clearing were still standing around the perimeter like forgotten bones.

The clearing was cindered over and the convoy of wagons was parked on it in a horseshoe shape. The lighting was good enough for them to see a new brick building at the far end of the horseshoe and the blurred movements of men sitting at tables behind its steamed up windows. Brad guessed they were the drivers waiting to move off when day broke. Further off was another long block of stabling that must house their teams of horses.

The wagons were identical: a six-wheeled wooden cart with a high-hooped, canvas-covered frame that protected the load. There was a hinged tail board at the rear that could be lowered during loading, then swung up into place again and fastened with a metal peg. The remaining opening, at the back, could be closed off with a roll of canvas that dropped like a blind from the top of the wagon's frame, then laced up to the canvas sides to secure it.

Only one wagon was left to be loaded. It was parked with its rear facing the platform, its tailboard down and the canvas blind rolled up. There were packs of the sort of dark blue uniforms that Melior had spent the past few years sewing together stacked by it, but there was no one around loading them.

Melior and Brad sat side by side on the driver's seat and considered the open wagon. Melior glanced about. There wasn't a sign of life in the street: just the rain bouncing on the road and long rumbles of thunder. She looked at the wagon again. 'Do you think Watt's in there already?'

Brad was uneasy.

'Dunno. It feels too good to be true. Like someone's inviting us into a trap.'

Melior said in a low voice, 'There's an arrangement with the Head Driver. I got the impression he smuggles people out. Let's go.'

Brad put a restraining hand on her arm. 'I'll look it over first.' He jumped down and ran the length of the platform doubled over so he couldn't be seen from the other side. When he judged he was level with it, he leapt up onto the platform and stepped into the rear of the wagon. Six Policy Maker guards fell on him.

Melior heard a single shout and was just able to make out a dark, scuffling movement on the threshold of the wagon, which rocked slightly. Then she heard the clerk's voice call out, 'Have you got her?'

'No, it's a dratted Messenger Boy,' a guard replied.

Melior lost no time in turning the carriage round. Then she sat there. Her every instinct was to drive off into the dark and leave Brad to fend for himself. But she sat there.

Brad swore and squeaked 'Hold on there' to a guard who held his wounded arm in a lock. 'I've got a message, haven't I?' He swore again, and the guard laughed and let him go. Someone lit a lantern.

Brad found he was sitting on the floor of the wagon with six armed men crouched round him. The rain kept up a constant tattoo on the canvas roof. An Inmate woman, dressed in a white nightdress, had been strung up to the wagon's framework by the arms and feet. He could hardly see her face she had been so badly beaten. But Melior would have known that it was Triss.

'What's your message?' One of the guards jabbed him in the ribs with the butt of his gun. 'Not allowed to say,' Brad answered promptly. 'It's Policy.'

'We saw you come in on the Chief Medical Officer's carriage,' another said. 'Have you brought the confirmation?'

'Confirmation,' Brad repeated noncommittally. He was way out of his depth. Not only that, he could see the clerk walking down the loading platform towards him. It would be the finish of him if the clerk saw him.

'Are we quarantined?' another guard asked him.

'Couldn't say, fellows,' Brad replied. Which was true. 'The message is for the Head Driver, isn't it?'

'Get out of it then.'

They shoved Brad out onto the platform and turned purposefully towards the woman, who gave a cry. The light went out. The cry was the most frightening noise Brad had ever heard. He ran on long shaky legs across the cindered clearing towards the drivers' building, pretending to deliver his message.

Melior saw the lamp in the wagon go out and then watched Brad cross the clearing in complete disbelief. What was the stupid boy doing? Then she heard screaming coming from the wagon. The god! Was it Avtar?

She craned further round the side of the carriage to look back at the loading bay through the rain. She could see the clerk now, standing on the platform. He was leaning against the rear of the wagon and looking inside, and he was smiling. She shouted gruffly in her best Policy Maker accent, 'Look, lads, by the Main Gates. The Sun! It's her.'

The clerk yelled into the wagon and then ran to the edge of the platform. He hesitated, thought better of jumping, and sat down on his bum and slid over the edge. Then he ran down the road towards the Second Defence Wall and the Main Gates. The six guards came out of the wagon at the double and hared after him.

Melior turned the carriage and drove alongside the platform. She hitched the reins through a tethering ring and ran over to the wagon. It was pitch dark inside. She felt for her precious matches. They were still dry. In the flare of the struck match she saw Triss sagging from the frame where she was tied. Melior could tell she was dead. The bayonet head that had killed her had been dropped on the wagon floor. Melior whispered, 'Oh Triss. My poor Triss. This is all my fault.'

The match burnt out and the clerk said from the opening of the wagon, 'See what happens, Morag, to people who don't obey?' He was holding an oil lamp and smiling at her through his dripping wet hair. 'I'd know your voice anywhere, Morag,' he said. 'You didn't fool me.' His currant eyes glowed. 'Give up,' he said. 'You can't win. You're my wife now. You didn't know that, did you?'

She shook her head. He moved towards her and she looked up at him in that proud, sad, fierce way that made him love her. He put the lantern down and drew her towards him, and Melior plunged the bayonet deep into his stomach.

She watched him die without any remorse. He had killed the only friend she had in the whole world – Triss – who had risked everything to care for her and who had lost everything because of her. He had blundered into their lives and destroyed what little they had to call their own.

And now she had taken her revenge.

Brad, poking an anxious face round the side of the wagon, had to hold onto the canvas and swallow hard so as not to vomit at the sight.

Melior said, 'I have made myself a widow. Get his coat. You could do with a Policy Maker jacket.'

It was a revolting idea, but it was a good one, too, and he did as she said. The jacket was still warm from the clerk's body.

Melior tore a piece off the hem of Triss's white nightdress and soaked up the pool of blood the clerk was lying in. Her face was set. 'Come on,' she said, and they left the wagon. Brad helped her to roll down the rear panel of canvas to close up the back and Melior wrote on it with the cloth in letters of blood:

'Not much chance of his climbing aboard that now,' she said. Together they settled on the driver's seat of the carriage. 'Walk on,' she told the patient horse.

'Where now?' Brad asked. It was the first time he'd realised that their escape route had been cut off. 'We're stuck here now,' he said. 'Aren't we?'

'We must try and find my brother,' was all she answered.

The biggest fork of lightning yet zigzagged out of the storm and lit up the entire sky. They saw huge sepia clouds racing behind the castle up above them. At the same time, the thunder crashed in on them. Melior said, 'Steady there,' to the horse and Brad pointed up at the castle.

'Look!'

CHAPTER TWENTY–NINE

'I'm all for shooting the fellow.'

'I've got kids,' the Pianist appealed from the bathroom floor, where they'd trussed him up with Fidelis's long-suffering stockings.

'You should have thought of that before,' the Roc replied, and held out a commanding hand for the key.

'Perhaps I'll keep it,' Avtar said. 'You'll only nip back and do him in.'

'Too right,' the Roc agreed heartily.

So Avtar pocketed the key once he'd locked the Pianist in and steered everyone out of the apartment to the head of the little stairs.

It was much darker and colder out there, and the wind howled as though it would break through the walls. Avtar whispered that the Roc was to fetch a bag of toiletries from his room. But the Roc said he was going back to stick a bolster in Fidelis's bed to look like her corpse. 'They are expecting Fid to be murdered,' he whispered. 'Could be our undoing if the Spy Master does a body count. Send Prudence.'

'I'm half killed already,' Prudence objected. 'Who's to know what the heck might jump out on me?' So Avtar sent Scar with her.

Once he was alone with Fidelis, it was hard to know

where to begin. So much had changed since they had sat and talked behind the curtain. They were friends now, he hoped, but they were still enemies too. How could two friends be on different sides? And how could you tell when you were being friends and when you were foes?

Fidelis said formally, 'Your Majesty,' and curtsied. He laughed quietly, and bowed back. 'My lady,' he whispered. 'And I'm no king, thanks to your father. I hope you understand why I couldn't tell you who I was.' He smiled. 'You might have let me drown if you'd known.'

She didn't smile back. She asked quietly, 'Why did you come and warn me about the Over Lord? It put you in such danger. Did you come in return for my pulling you out of the Reservoir Tank?' He hesitated, unsure how she would take to the idea that he'd come because he liked her.

'Was it a sort of payback, like politics?' she persisted.

'No. It was because I didn't want to see you dead, even though we're on different sides.' Fidelis *did* smile then. 'For that matter,' he challenged her, 'why did you throw your weight behind me, and not behind the Empire? It's as much your doing that Khul is free as it is mine.'

'Oh!' she said airily, as though she were suddenly on safe ground. 'That wasn't politics either. I *had* to stick up for you. One must always stand by the family and you're family, Sire.'

'No I'm not. And forget the "Sire".'

'Yes you are. Your mother was a distant cousin of my mother, which makes you and me even more distant cousins. What's that if it's not family?'

'How?'

'Your mother was from the Old Country.' He could see she was trying not to laugh. 'Your *face*, Avtar! Didn't you know?'

So he was half Policy Maker! When he thought about it, it felt horribly likely. It would explain his Policy Maker accent: he would have learned to talk from his mother. She'd been so fair, too, like most Policy Makers. That's why the Baker and Triss had gone to such trouble to hide his and Melior's hair. Blonde hair was a big pointer to who their parents were. He'd always thought of his mother and father as just that – parents. He hadn't even noticed they were different races. Why should he? Most people in Slave City were. People had come from all over the Empire to take refuge in Khul. But to be half Policy Maker! That shook him. Which half was which? And why didn't half of him hate the other half?

Fidelis's grey eyes were brimming with amusement. 'It's not so bad being one of us.' But it wasn't that which was upsetting him; it was Fidelis herself. He had wanted her to say that she'd sided with him over Khul because he was in the right, and even because she liked him too.

Fidelis was watching him in a very peculiar way now, and he realised he'd got his special grin on to stop him saying what he was thinking. He took it off hurriedly. She looked extremely relieved to see it go. 'I don't want you dead either,' she said. 'So be careful of my father, Avtar. He means every word he says. He's put you outside the protection of your crown and City. He's done that for a reason.'

'When did he tell you that?'

'He didn't. I guessed.'

'You're as good at this as he is. How exactly did we insult the Empire, by the way?'

She looked grave. 'The old king sent it a lump of mould and a list that was a string of filth.' Avtar laughed. His father had been generous. He'd sent them the "Yellow Magic". 'It's not funny, Sire.'

'No, I don't suppose he thought so either.'

'I'm sorry. It's a terrible thing we did. I know that now. But be careful, Avtar. My father says he wants you a hundred miles away. Make it more.'

'Easier said than done. He certainly outmanoeuvred me.'

'He's the Roc. He's had a lot of practice. You were fantastic; like a king. But he hates your mother.'

'Why? She handed over the City to him.' Now that he knew his mother had been a Policy Maker, it made complete sense that she had. 'What more does he perishing want?' he whispered angrily.

'The Sun!' Fidelis exploded. 'Don't say that you of all people...'

'Sh!' he whispered fiercely.

'Sorry,' she whispered back, just as fiercely. They both peered about the landing nervously. There was no one. Just the darkness and the moaning wind. 'So am I sorry,' he whispered. 'No point in us having a row.' He grinned. 'Even if we *are* related.'

Fidelis nodded and whispered more calmly, 'I was only going to say that I can't believe that the queen's own son has swallowed the Over Lord's story.'

'What story?'

'That she was a traitor.'

'You're saying that she wasn't one?' he desperately wanted to believe her, but where was the proof?

'Lady Zoë says she wasn't, and she's in the know.'

Who the flip was Lady Zoë?

'Her husband is a Counsellor,' Fidelis whispered. 'And he told her the whole Council agreed to the story. It was a pack of lies.'

So it was no wonder he'd struggled to accept his mother's treachery. He'd had to force himself to believe it was true – but it wasn't. His mother hadn't chucked him away like mouldy bread and left the City in ruins. She was innocent. Avtar just about managed to say 'Thank you...' But the rest of it got lost. He turned away. The trouble with crying was that it could become a habit.

Fidelis said gently, 'You must miss your mother very much.' He nodded, still not up to speaking. 'I know I miss mine,' she said. 'Even though she's not a patch on yours. Mine's a tough nut. Ask Pa.' It made him laugh and she joined in, glad to have cheered him up.

'But if it wasn't the queen,' he asked, 'who did betray the City?

Fidelis frowned a little as she thought about his question. 'No one.'

He stared at her in surprise. This girl had a mind like a jigsaw puzzle. 'How do you work that out?'

'It's a classic tactic.'

Tack tick! Another new one! Was it to do with nails? Bugs?

'You put the blame on someone who can't answer back,' Fidelis continued. 'And the people vent all their anger on them instead of the Empire.'

'You really *are* good at it,' he said wryly.

'It's politics,' she replied in a thin voice. 'Nothing personal.' But he could tell she was embarrassed that she understood the Over Lord's thinking so well. 'Did Lady Zoë say anything else?' he asked.

'Not really. Something about jealousy, I think. But

then we had to go down to a disastrous ball.'

'We must…' He'd been going to say "We must talk about this more" but if his plan for her escape succeeded, this was the last time they would ever see one another. He changed it to "We must hurry". But she had thought of it too.

'Where will you go?'

'I've someone to meet up with,' he said evasively. 'We'll decide then.' He didn't intend to reveal his sister had survived too.

'Of course.'

He couldn't have guessed from her polite reply how miserable she felt. This "someone" he was meeting was obviously much more alluring than she was.

Prudence and Scar came back with the toilet bag. And the Roc popped out of the apartment with a whispered "All done". He dabbed his throat. 'I even dressed it up with a little gore,' he said with a reproachful look at Scar.

'Let's go.' Avtar was nervous now. 'Quiet as mice, everyone.'

They could not have made more noise. Sacks of flour would have descended the little staircase more quietly! They creaked and thumped across the Great Room as though he were leading a brigade of walking wardrobes. Then the Roc dropped his gun. It went spinning across the floorboards with a noise like a giant egg whisk, and they all had to crawl about in the dark trying to find it. Avtar thought they would drive him mad before they even reached Porcini's room, which was where he was leading them. He thanked the god for the covering noise of the storm.

He didn't take the lift for fear of meeting Vince. He led them down the South West Tower. It was furthest from the Over Lord's and the Spy Master's quarters. They shuffled behind him as nimbly as a herd of oxen. Frightening glimpses of guards, scouring each floor for Avtar, reminded him that he was on the run too.

They'd reached Porcini's level when they met six guards head-on, coming up the steps. Scar pulled his knife out of his boot, but the Roc slipped his gun into Avtar's hands, took a big breath and strode down towards them.

The men stopped and goggled at the sight of him. Their eyes kept returning to Prudence in her nightgown and the Roc in his. Everyone knew the Roc was a bit of a lad on the quiet, but this was hardly on the quiet. And what about his bleeding throat?

The Roc swept into action as if he were on the battlefield, not caught on a staircase in his nightclothes by soldiers who were probably on the Over Lord's side. 'Well done, chaps,' he said warmly. The men straightened up and looked patriotic. 'Glad to see you've got a grip on the situation.'

One of the guards stammered, 'But we haven't found him yet, sir.' The Roc addressed the ceiling. 'Found him? Found him?' he blared. It was a ploy Avtar knew well. The guard immediately supplied a lot more information. 'King Avtar, sir? We must take him alive, sir. There's a big reward.'

'Oh, Pa! These poor, poor men,' Fidelis said. The Roc shot her an anxious look. What was she up to? Fidelis clasped her hands in pity. 'Avtar's been captured already. Some of your colleagues pulled him out of the Reservoir Tank.' The guards were indignant. 'Nobody told us.'

The Roc took his cue. 'Disgraceful! I'll see there's a handsome consolation paid.' Fidelis gave the guards a real Roc's daughter's smile.

'Couldn't these weary soldiers have a rest now, Pa?'

The Roc said he thought that was a dashed good idea, and ordered the search for Avtar to be called off. 'Tell the rest of the troops,' he barked, 'then back to barracks, every man-jack of you. The drinks are on me.' And the guards took off down the steps, two at a time.

The Roc wiped his forehead with his flounced cuff. 'Hmm!' was all he said, but Avtar could see he was dead scared. He didn't blame him. So was he.

They crept towards Porcini's room without a guard in sight. 'Brilliant!' murmured Avtar to Fidelis. 'You've cleared the Over Lord's men out of our way.' And she brightened up no end. They tiptoed past bedroom doors. Occasionally the noises of someone enduring the Thunderbags remedy outdid the storm, but there wasn't a soul about – until they reached Madame Porcini's room. A small group of soldiers were crouching, making chirruping noises through the closed door.

Their Captain took in their group's appearance and asked the Roc, 'Are you and my lady in difficulty, sir?' He stared unpleasantly at Scar and Avtar. 'Are these two lads giving you trouble?'

'Not at all.' The Roc was all cordiality. 'What are you chaps up to?'

'We're the relief search party for her ladyship's dog, sir.' But then he said, 'I'm not happy with the look of this, sir. I'm calling the Over...' His nostrils flared. 'Phorr!' he said weakly. Span was limping towards them.

It was the first time Fidelis had ever been truly pleased to smell him. She picked him up and waved him round the group, who scattered. Prudence lost no time in asking the Captain, 'You know that King Avi character's been copped, do you? Your boys are missing free drinks in the garrison.' And soon the corridor was deserted. But Madame Isabella Porcini's bedroom was locked and awaiting fumigation, according to a notice hanging on the handle.

'Now what?' the Roc asked testily. Avtar shoved his hands in his pockets, trying to look unfazed. They all watched him expectantly. Being the leader, and having a plan, definitely had its drawbacks: the people you were leading expected you to solve whatever extra problems came up along the way. They put you in charge of *everything*, even the unforeseen. He felt the keys in his pocket and tried them, just for something to do. The one from his father's dressing room, that he'd dropped all those years ago, opened it.

The Roc made a terrible fuss when Avtar asked him to shave off his moustache. But Avtar propelled him into the bathroom, and Scar put the door back on its hinges. 'Cripes!' Prudence exclaimed when she saw the mess Vince had made of it. And the Roc wondered aloud, 'Did Porcy have one of her tantrums in here?' It was all too clear that the Roc knew much more about Porcini than he ought to know. Fidelis bit her lip, and Avtar guessed she knew what was going on too.

He was filling in the details of his plan to the others when the Roc called him into the bathroom to lather the soap for him. Avtar was surprised the man could shave himself; he seemed to be incapable of everything else. When the Roc emerged moustacheless, Fidelis said brightly, 'It suits you, Pa,' which alerted the Roc and everyone else to the fact that his daughter was capable of lying.

The Roc was looking browbeaten by now, but there

was more to come. Prudence stripped his nightshirt off with a prim 'With your permission, sir.'

'What's all this?' he shouted as Madame Porcini's travelling dress was thrown over his head. 'Hush, Pa,' Fidelis said, adding a velvet cloak. 'It's our only chance.' Then Prudence placed Madame Porcini's reserve wig on his head, which Avtar had discovered along with all her other understudy items. Perhaps the tantrums were the reason why she kept two of everything.

'More petticoats,' Avtar instructed. The Roc glowered at him.

'All right for some,' he grunted, wriggling his way into the frothy mass of lace that Prudence prepared for him.

At length, Prudence stood back and they all looked him over. 'Well?' the Roc demanded belligerently.

'There's something sort of missing,' Avtar said.

'Yes,' they all chorused. 'There is.' The Roc gathered up his skirts and stomped over to the dressing table mirror; then he rushed into the bathroom and came back with two bath towels. He glared at Scar. 'Give us a hand, then.' Scar leapt into action, pummelling and coaxing one towel down the Roc's front and the other round his midriff, until the Roc was satisfied.

'Now?' he asked them all breathlessly. They stood back again and looked him up and down. 'Well?' he asked. 'Do I look like Porcini? That's what you want isn't it?' They nodded silently.

It was Prudence who was the first to go. To her well-bred servant's horror, she gave a snort of laughter at the Roc – panting from his efforts, a tall, rotund figure with a heaving towelling bosom and a magnificent head of hair. Soon Fidelis and Scar were weeping with laughter as well. Avtar kept shushing them, but it was hopeless and eventually he was laughing too. It was sheer nerves; they were all so frightened, it had to come out somehow. Better to laugh than scream!

'What?' the Roc kept asking them. 'What's so funny?' And they all went off again. Scar appeared to laugh noiselessly, but when he breathed in he made a braying noise, which made everybody laugh more. Fidelis had to bury her head in the chaise cushion, and Span found the last of the biscuits while no one was looking.

Then Avtar had an inspiration and wrapped Madame Porcini's smoky stole around the Roc's head and shoulders. Everyone stopped laughing at once. 'Ah!' Fidelis and Prudence said. 'That's done it.' It was true: the Roc looked a passable version of Madame Porcini.

Fidelis, Prudence and Span climbed into Madame Porcini's largest luggage basket and pulled down the lid, while Avtar and Scar went to hide in the bathroom. 'You'll be fine, sir,' Avtar assured the Roc. He wasn't as confident as he sounded. The Roc looked nervous.

The Roc rang the bell and waited. Avtar was counting on no one knowing that Madame Porcini had been taken to hospital. Sure enough, two Inmate porters answered the bell to carry her luggage down to her car. The Roc said in a grand falsetto, 'Bathroom, boys.'

They looked surprised, but trooped obediently into the bathroom. After a short pause, Avtar and Scar emerged, wearing their uniforms. Scar's was a perfect fit, but Avtar's jacket was down to his knees and he'd had to roll up the trouser legs.

Then there was a hitch: the luggage basket was too heavy. Scar could manage his half but Avtar, who was exhausted by now, couldn't even get his side off the ground. The Roc was all for hoicking Prudence out and leaving her. It was hard for Avtar to keep his temper with him. Prudence had just saved the man's life; yet here he was, prepared to dump her. He clenched his fists and haggled with the Roc. Scar pulled out his watch and warned it would soon be daybreak. Fidelis settled the row by suggesting they took the basket to the ground floor empty, and got in at the last minute. 'All right, all right.' The Roc was looking more flushed and agitated by the second. 'But let's get on with it.'

But Avtar wasn't finished. He'd already fixed that Scar should leave by the way he'd come in. He'd even managed to stop Scar from kissing his hand while they arranged a rendezvous outside the City walls. Now Avtar had to break it to the Roc that he had an extra passenger. But the Roc agreed at once to give him a lift until they were clear of the First Defence Wall. And, to Fidelis's deep satisfaction, Avtar revealed, 'I've got to meet a Ghosty Boy and his girlfriend.'

They took a servants' lift to the ground floor, then carried the basket as close as they dared to the door onto the Parade Ground. Fidelis, Prudence and Span climbed in while Scar went on ahead. There was a long pause. Avtar's heart was thumping so hard he thought the Roc must be able to hear it. At last Scar was back, dragging the unconscious sentry by his armpits. Avtar whisked open a door marked "No Unauthorised Entry", and Scar bundled the sentry through it.

Avtar said pointedly to the Roc, 'Good luck, sir.' It was time for the Roc to go to the Main Door where he was to wait for the car to drive through the tunnel and pick him up. He strode out of the lobby and then strode back again. 'Same to you.'

'Take smoother steps,' was all Avtar replied. 'Walk like you're a cream puff on wheels.' And off the Roc sort of skated, smoothing Porcini's skirt as he went.

"Tell Wamsy never forget Porcini." Avtar had delivered Porcini's last message to the Roc while he helped him shave off his moustache. He'd also told him how the Spy Master had confiscated their messages to one another to engineer a quarrel between them. The Roc had scraped away in silence while Avtar explained that the Spy Master had done it to keep them apart. Avtar spelt it out: 'To make sure that the two of you didn't spoil their plan by spending the night together'. The Roc had blustered something about Avtar keeping a civil tongue in his head, but Avtar had told him, 'Shut it, Roc, there was a Messenger Boy murdered in his bath over it.'

The Roc was wondering if he should have trusted his daughter to Lenita's boy – and Span too, for that matter. He hurried towards the Main Door. The Sun! He'd been in some tight spots before, but never one like this. He remembered to do the cream puff walk which, all in all, he thought was rather an accurate description of Porcini in motion; though what the Roc achieved had more the look of a bouncing éclair.

The car drew up as Avtar and Scar emerged from the castle. Scar was fascinated by the busy windscreen wipers. The chauffeur called out, 'I'll take her up into the tunnel. That'll keep the pair of you dry while you load up.' It was a useful idea. Loading was the most dangerous part of Avtar's plan; that was when the Over Lord might become suspicious. If they were hidden in the tunnel, he wouldn't be able to see them at all.

With Scar taking most of the weight, they bumped

their three passengers round the arcade. The motorcar's headlights lit the far end of the tunnel brilliantly. By contrast, the lamps hooked up on the stone walls shed a dimmer light to the rear, which suited Avtar's plan.

The next part was difficult. It was vital the chauffeur believed everything was as normal. He'd only to raise the alarm and they'd have a garrison of four hundred soldiers down on them in seconds.

Avtar leant through the chauffeur's window and struck up a conversation to keep his attention off Scar. Scar's job was to transfer everybody from the basket into the back of the car. Avtar told the chauffeur that Madame Porcini was in a fair old state and could hardly speak – which prepared the way for the Roc's terrible imitation of her voice. 'She's drunk,' the chauffeur replied. 'That's what she is.'

Avtar resisted the impulse to spit in his eye and carried on with the plan. He asked innocently, 'One of those two lights at the front of this thing is flashing on and off. Is it supposed to?' The chauffeur swore and got out to have a look. Avtar went ahead of him, but he could hear a tremendous rustling coming from the rear. Couldn't they do *anything* quietly?

He glanced back. The tunnel was too narrow to open the car door wide enough. Scar was in a sweat and someone was stuck half in the basket and half in the car. He could see quantities of yellow organza, so it had to be Fidelis. The chauffeur couldn't possibly miss all the activity, so Avtar tripped and let his fingernails scrape the whole length of the bodywork. By the time the chauffeur had finished bawling him out for the scratch, Scar was putting the empty luggage basket on top of the tool chest. That meant everyone was inside as planned

319

and lying like sardines on the floor. All they had to do now was to tie the basket on the back. The Over Lord would think it contained the Roc's corpse. In fact, it would be Avtar inside.

The chauffeur studied the lights for a minute. 'You're seeing things. These lights are perfect.' He gave Avtar the strap to secure the basket. 'It will never stay put, though.' He smirked with pleasure. 'It's bigger than her usual basket. The old nightingale's so sozzled, she's sent you down with the wrong baggage.'

Avtar joined Scar at the rear of the car. The chauffeur was right. The strap was nowhere near long enough. He'd made a fatal error in his plan.

The Roc, waiting on the steps of the main entrance, was nearly levitating with frustration. He could see the car's lights in the tunnel. What was the hold up? The Butler had arrived to hold an umbrella over his head and the Roc was all too aware that his Porcini disguise wouldn't stand close inspection. What in the name of the Sun was keeping them so long?

The Over Lord was wondering the same thing, and spoke urgently into his speaking tube. The Spy Master woke up with a start, threw on an oilskin and rushed down to the Great Room and onto the balcony. He looked out into the rain. He could see Porcini down there, waiting under an umbrella. He could see the lights of the car too. He went to investigate the delay at the double. At which point, the Ghosty Boys set up their lamenting song again. And the Roc lost his nerve.

With a glass-breaking screech of "Wait here!" he interrupted the Butler's description of how moved he had been by his singing, hauled up his skirt and sprinted across the courtyard to the car. The chauffeur tried to get out and salute him, but the Roc waved him back to his place and squeezed to the rear of the car. 'What the deuce is the matter?' he panted. Avtar showed him.

'The Sun!' the Roc said. 'What do we do?'

'Change the plan. Defuse the bomb now, instead of outside the City. The basket will fit if we put it directly on the luggage rack and dump the toolbox here.'

'We could do with some more light,' was all the Roc said, and he lifted the basket off. 'Tell the chauffeur Porcini's looking for something,' Avtar whispered at Scar.

'Her galoshes,' the Roc advised.

'Galoshes?' Scar had never heard the word.

'Then go,' Avtar said. Scar didn't need much urging. The Roc had already selected a spanner and undone the bolts that held the toolbox to the supporting frame. The time bomb was menacingly audible. 'Hear the brute tick,' the Roc said in an awed voice. Avtar showed him how the false top lifted out, revealing Vince's bomb.

The Roc plunged his pink, sausage-style fingers in amongst the wires that connected up with the timer. He fiddled and fumbled. Avtar shut his eyes. He only opened them again when the Roc said, 'Done. All came back to me. Like riding a bicycle.' He handed Avtar the toolbox. 'You get rid of the whole shoot, then hop in the basket and I'll tie it on.' Avtar ran the chest to the garrison end of the tunnel and left it there.

The Roc was putting the basket in position when he looked up and saw the Spy Master watching him from the mouth of the tunnel. Without hesitating, he wrenched open the car door and clambered in, trampling on Prudence in his hurry.

'Drive on!' he bellowed at the chauffeur. The car

buzzed forward and the Spy Master had to jump to one side. Avtar watched it drive off without him in total disbelief. Then the basket toppled off the back into the tunnel.

'Oh Pa!' Fidelis was almost crying. 'We can't leave him. Please Pa. Please! Stop the car. They'll capture him. They'll hurt him.'

'There, there. I know, I know.' The Roc held his daughter firmly out of sight as they travelled at speed through the First Defence Gates. 'Deuced disappointing. I'd rather hoped to take him all the way home with us in that basket.' Fidelis was so shocked she could only say, 'Oh Papa!'

'Politics, Fid. Nothing personal. Useful young chap. He may deny it but he's got the King's Touch all right. If that lad can't cure people, then I'm a common foot soldier.'

The Roc peered through the rear window. Leaving behind the empty basket was disastrous enough, but the Spy Master had been holding a bath towel and looking at it thoughtfully. The Roc had lost some of his padding. He prayed silently that the Spy Master would not pick up on the clue. A troop of crack horsemen from the garrison could easily catch the spindly little car, even if it got clear of the City.

Avtar was thinking exactly the same thing as he watched the Spy Master at the other end of the tunnel. The Spy Master, who was half blinded by the headlamps, ran and unfastened the basket. The consternation on his face when he saw it was empty actually made Avtar laugh out loud. He called to the Spy Master, 'Want to know where the Roc is, don't you?'

The Spy Master smiled back at the laughing servant,

blotched with light images, at the end of the tunnel. 'I take it you know?' Avtar nodded. He needed to spin this out for as long as he could to allow the car a head start. 'I'll give you three guesses, Spy Master.'

'Or how about a deal? Your life for his – Avtar?' But Avtar had already whirled round to run and the Spy Master's knife only dug into the ground by his flying feet. The stupid trouser legs began to unroll, so he had to hold them up., It slowed him down, and the Spy Master gained on him.

He ran, as he'd never run before, to the Bakery. Most of the two o' clock shift were standing round the Baker, who was still seated at the table. They were singing their lament and crying. Others were trying to get some bread made, but the Baker always measured the ingredients. Without him, they were lost.

They all stopped what they were doing when Avtar flung himself into the room. He raced up to the Baker and touched his arm. 'Sorry,' he panted. 'Thank you.' Then he opened the flour vat and dived in. The lid crashed closed.

A minute later, the Spy Master arrived with some guards. He gave the frightened Ghosty Boys an enchanting smile. The furnace roared gently in the background. 'Where is he?' Nobody answered. The Spy Master's smile broadened. Lightning flickered through the Bakery and the Ghosty Boys gathered round the dead Baker in a little flock, as though he could somehow still protect them.

The Spy Master plucked one of the twins out of the group and held him up by his ponytail. 'Sim, isn't it?' he asked kindly.

'Som.' The boy could barely speak. The Spy Master

pulled Som over to the nearest oven and kicked the fastening up with his booted foot. The door swung open. He held Som in the scorching heat and beamed at Sim. 'If I don't get an answer, this little twin of yours goes straight in the oven.' Sim didn't reply.

The thunder almost drowned out Som's scream as the Spy Master pushed his head into the oven. Sim ran and pulled at the arm holding his twin. With tears pouring down his face, he pointed at the flour vat.

The guards opened the lid cautiously, as if an alligator might slide out. The vat was full to the brim with flour. The Spy Master fired his revolver into it four or five times. Clouds of flour spouted up and settled on him. A guard sneezed. Two more sliced into it with their kukris, but the vat was plainly full of nothing but flour. The Spy Master turned on the Ghosty Boys. They'd vanished.

With a brief order to push the Baker's body into the furnace, the Spy Master left with some guards. He saw Brad's blood on the ground at once. Just like Vince had, he followed its trail. Flurries of flour floated off his oilskin as he padded swiftly through the deserted corridors, while the thunder beat about the sky.

The Spy Master stood in the centre of Porcini's room looking attentively at every object, right down to the biscuit crumbs on the carpet. The towel? Why did Porcini strew towels in the courtyard? He tried the bathroom door. Locked. His guards kicked it down. Two men in their underclothes lay on the floor of the ruined bathroom. A Ghosty Boy's uniform lay next to them. A search yielded a key and a thin ribbon of paper. It was blotched with ink. He could make out the words "unexpectedly beautiful castle". No help.

The Spy Master was moving like a hurricane out of

hell now. He shot to the top of the castle and crossed the Great Room. Lightning laid bars of light across his smiling face as he ran to the staircase and took the steps three at a time. The light was still on in the Roc's room. The bed was empty. In the girl's room, the nightlight burning there revealed the hump of her body in the bed. There was blood on the pillow. So all was well there. But was the Roc dead or alive? More to the point, *where* was he? And how, of all people, was Avtar the only person in the world who knew the answer? He'd splinter every bone in the young king's body to find out.

He leapt down the staircase again as more unanswerable questions crowded into his mind. Why the towel? How did Avtar disappear? How had the scarred shepherd vanished into thin air in the Ante-room? He stopped abruptly as a memory of the Roc's idiotic tale of a disappearing bread roll came to him. 'Ah!'

He smiled and took the lift to the ground floor.

CHAPTER THIRTY

Avtar sat on the service stairs spitting out lumps of damp flour. Things were grim. He'd been awake for about twenty-two hours now and for most of them he'd been trying to get out of the City; but he was no nearer than he had been when he was here six years ago.

He wasn't surprised that the Roc had dumped him: people run when they're scared. He had run himself when the Spy Master had called him by his name, so no, he wasn't surprised, but he was angry. It was typical Policy Maker behaviour. He wondered if the Roc had left him here on purpose so that he could go back on his promise to free the City. That condition, banishing him from Khul, meant that he could, unless – and Avtar felt leaden with the thought that had been driving him all day – unless I can get out of the City.

He tried to imagine what Fidelis made of her father leaving him behind as she drove across the plain to home and safety. He hoped she was sorry. But then she was a Policy Maker too, so she probably wasn't sorry at all. Hadn't he learnt today that love and treachery were twins? There again, he'd had to unlearn it because his mother and the Baker had proved to him that that wasn't true. Either way, he'd never ever know now how Fidelis felt. He knew how he did, though. He said out loud, 'Oh shut up, Avtar!' because his thoughts were upsetting and embarrassing him, and went down to look at the drain Scar had told him about.

He'd left the trap open. And, just like Scar had described it, there was the cord attached to the hasp. None of today would have happened in the way it had if Melior and he had found the drain together. Of course, if he wanted to, he could simply take off down the cord now and forget about Melior and Brad. He dismissed the idea. He'd promised to meet them, and they might wait for him.

He looked at the cord more closely. It was thick and heavy and had probably been hooked into the walls of the service stairs to make a kind of steadying banister. It was funny that: he didn't remember feeling a rope on the wall when he'd been on the stairs when he was small. Had someone ripped it away and used it to climb down the drain before he'd got there? Then he saw that the first section wasn't a cord at all; it was a torn off sleeve. The rope was too thick to go through the hasp, so someone had torn off their sleeve, pushed it through instead, and tied it to the rope. The fabric was blue with silver patterns – Lal's fabric. It must be Lal's sleeve, then. So it had been Lal, his sister, who had whispered his name here six years ago, and not the thing he'd been so frightened of all this time?

If only he'd answered her, he would have escaped with her. She would have looked after him. She always had because she was the eldest. It struck him suddenly that until he was born, Lal would have thought she would be queen of Khul one day. He'd never thought of that before. Melior had been jealous of his kingship, he remembered, but not Lal, even though she'd lost the crown to him. He knew what losing a crown felt like. It was as though you had lost your own meaning. That took a lot of forgiving.

Suddenly he was in darkness. He hadn't registered that the blue lights were on until now, when they'd gone out. He heard a scraping, slithering noise behind him and jerked round to face it. The cord he was holding snapped away from the hasp. He forced himself to speak. 'Scar?' he called. His voice came out small and frightened, and the thing slithered nearer and nearer. It hadn't been just Lal here. There was something else, too. His terror of the thing on the stairs almost paralysed him, but he jumped to his feet to run. It got him, though, before he could.

It squeezed him, squeezed him so hard he couldn't draw breath. His face was pressed into suffocating, soft, wet folds. He felt the cord drop from his fingers into the drain as the thing squeezed his ribs, and he struggled uselessly for air. Then it dragged him up a few steps, holding his arms so tightly that the bones felt ready to split.

The light went on again and he could see enough to realise his face was pressed into a naked stomach. He looked up – at Vince. Vince's shirt was open and the sweat dripped off him. Vince looked back at him closely, then he struck him hard around the head and the blood trickled into Avtar's eye.

Vince said, 'Avtar, isn't it? Well, that's just to get us started, Avtar.' Vince held his arms with one huge hand and shook him. Avtar couldn't speak; the breath was being shaken out of him. Then Vince thwacked him back and forth against the rocky walls and his mind started to disappear into a fog. Vince shook him again and slapped his face. 'Wake up, little king. I'm wanting you to feel every second of this.'

Avtar said faintly, 'What are you doing here, Vince?'

Vince slapped him again. 'Followed you through the flipping bathroom wall. Changed your colours, haven't you. You were a Ghosty then.' Vince took hold of Avtar's jaw and stared into his face. 'But I'd know you anywhere now. Spitting image of your father, if you put a head of hair on you.' His thumb dug into Avtar's cheek. It hurt so much it felt as if Vince was prising out his teeth. 'Tell me,' Vince said, 'where the perishing way out is.'

However much Vince hurt him, he mustn't tell him. The minute Vince got out, he'd turn him over to the Over Lord and the Spy Master. So he smiled as much of his slobbery grin as Vince's thumb would let him. If it killed him, he had to keep quiet. Vince rumbled on. 'Wipe that smile off your face, Your Majesty, and tell me the way out or I'll tear your tongue out of your flipping gob. Then you'll know about being dumb, King Avtar.'

Avtar said as best he could, 'If you let go of my face, I might be able to tell you.' Vince did let go, but he kept a tight hold of Avtar's arms.

'I've been crawling round in the stench for hours,' he said. 'The walls groan and grizzle here, and there's something else here, something living as lurks here. But no way out. Show me the way out.'

'I can't.'

Vince threatened to hit him again.

'But we'll think of something,' he said quickly.

Vince lashed out. Avtar's voice was tight with pain. 'Yes, I do know one way.' Vince unbuckled his belt and threw it in a loop over his head. The smell from Vince's armpit as he did it was loathsome. He tightened one end of the belt round Avtar's neck like a collar and held onto the other end. He felt like a dog on a leash. Vince gave it a savage jerk. 'Show,' he said, and Avtar led him round to the south west side.

On the way he dared to ask Vince, 'Why do you do it? Why do you work for the other side?'

'Shut it,' Vince replied. 'I work for the right side. They're *my* side.' His freckled nose wrinkled with distaste. 'You're nothing but a jumped up slave.' And Avtar saw what he'd never seen before. Vince was half Policy Maker, like he was. In a sense, he and Vince were two of the same kind. They'd taken different sides, that was all. 'I'm just as good as you, King Avtar. Better.' Vince twisted the belt round his neck to a stranglehold. 'But I weren't born to the job like you, more's the pity. Look at you! What kind of a king would a boy like you have made? You wait. Old Vince will have this City hopping.'

Avtar could hardly speak, the belt was so tight round his throat, but he sort of croaked, 'Was it you then, Vince, who betrayed the City?' He hadn't argued with Fidelis when she had suggested that no one had. His father's haunting question "Where were the guards?" scarcely seemed evidence that someone had. But here was Vince so obviously expecting to be the king, it looked as if he'd been promised the crown eventually in return for treachery. 'Was it you?' he croaked again. Vince giggled. It was a grotesque little noise. 'Guess.' He smiled his twinkly smile. 'If you can. But you Royals! You're all the same. Thick as pig shit.' Vince glared at him, suddenly angry. 'You're sidetracking me, you cunning brat,' he shouted, and shook him hard. 'Why's we stopped?'

'Because we're here, Vince.'

They'd reached the entrance to the room beneath the Offering Table. Vince made Avtar go ahead of him, then lay on his stomach and eased his bulk along the burrow-like entrance with his elbows. It meant he tugged even more viciously at the collar. After much grunting and cursing, Vince got through and they emerged into the room.

A single golden lamp at floor level cast their shadows onto the walls – a giant and a midget.

Vince eyed the strange "going nowhere" stairs. 'What's this?' His voice was menacing. Avtar said quickly, 'I'll show you. We go single file up these steps. Look.'

He climbed the stairs. His heart was beating fast now. Vince came close behind him to keep hold of the length of belt round his neck.

Avtar said, 'Careful now.' And Vince stood still while Avtar explained, 'I'm going to draw back a metal panel.'

'Go on then, for the god's sake,' Vince grumbled, and Avtar drew back the panel slowly and gently. Vince observed his every move, looking up at him from watchful little eyes. 'Now I'm moving another panel,' Avtar said, opening the smaller shutter like Melior had to take the bread roll. At once, they heard a crash of thunder from outside and Vince gave a grunt of joy. 'Steady,' Avtar warned and Vince froze.

Then Avtar whipped out the rope ladder and hung onto the rungs. He swung in the air and kicked Vince hard in the face. Vince staggered backwards down the stairs, still holding the belt. Avtar was nearly strangled until Vince fell on his back, and let go of him.

He ran to the entrance, but Vince was already

331

sprawling after him and had him by the ankle. Avtar pulled out the Roc's revolver that he'd never returned. He didn't know how to fire it, but he drew back the trigger.

The noise was deafening. Vince lay dead still, his huge hands clapped to his ears. His freckled face was crumpled with surprise and fear. Avtar said, 'Stay there. Don't dare follow me, Vince, or I'll kill you, as sure as you killed the Baker.'

He backed into the little tunnel so he could keep watching him. As he did, he noticed Melior's neat pile of peach stones and fruit cores just by his left hand. She'd tried to eat a melon too, but without a knife she'd only made a bruised dent in its tough skin. There was a thick, white, fluffy mould growing in it. He took it with him.

The Spy Master heard the shot. The sound came up through the Offering Table as he stood in the rain with a storm lantern, pondering the disappearing roll. He felt around and found the small gap where the little panel had been removed. 'Who's there?' he called through it. He heard scuffling and cursing and then, to his astonishment, Vince's nose and one eye filled the gap. 'It's me,' Vince raved at him. 'And that Avtar kid is somewhere in here with me. Get the place surrounded, sir. And for the god's sake...' Vince corrected himself, '...the Sun's sake, get me out of here.'

* * *

Avtar ran, but where to? There was nowhere safe to run to now. He kept a watch out for Vince in case he risked coming after him. But how many bullets were left in the gun, he wondered, and could he actually kill him.

His long trouser legs unfurled over and over and he

had to keep stopping to roll them up. He'd just reached the kitchen entrance when they came down round his feet and tripped him. As he fell, his finger pulled the trigger of his gun and fired two shots into the edge of the door. It gave him a bad fright, but then he saw that the door had come ajar.

He pushed it, but it wouldn't open any further. He summoned every scrap of his remaining strength and gave it a mighty shove. The door squealed open and what felt like ten thousand plates slid off the shelves that had been built across the disused entrance to the service stairs and smashed onto the floor. Avtar stood on the threshold of the China Room, ankle deep in broken crockery with the melon under his arm.

The Cook appeared in the doorway. 'Glory!' she exclaimed, taking in the chaos. Then she raised her hands at the sight of Avtar's gun. He said, 'I'm Avtar. The Baker said I was to come to the kitchens.'

She said, 'Make haste. The Baker and me have a device that'll help you.'

'The Baker's dead.'

'The god! I'll do it alone then.' Her eyes filled with tears.

'Don't,' Avtar said. 'You'll start me.'

'I'll let you out of the kitchen window.' She wiped her eyes on her apron. 'This is the best night for Khul to find you alive, and the worst to have to send you on your way.'

Avtar crunched across the room after her, but he stopped her by the door and passed her the melon. 'Give this to the Butler if you don't mind. With my love.'

'It's the white mould,' she whispered. 'Oh Avtar, you've brought it back to us.'

'Tell him that the doctor knows what to do with it next.'

She nodded and then fished a sky-blue silk square out of her apron pocket. 'This is yours. Only Khul's king has the right to this particular blue. 'Tis your crest embroidered on it, so take a hold of it. It's yours. Your birthright.'

Avtar took it – the last shred of his kingship.

They went into the kitchen, watched by a pair of curious kitchen boys. 'You boys,' the Cook said, 'go and tell the rest we're ready. Look out for my signal. Afterwards, help yourselves. A cake each from the pantry.' They sped out of the room.

The Cook opened the low window. The mule cart was out there with the piano loaded up and covered with soaking wet sheets, waiting to be tied into place. The driver was sheltering patiently from the rain under his mules, whose heads hung low in their harness. Then a Policy Maker guard, posted there by the Spy Master, appeared in the window frame. 'What's all this?' he said nastily.

CHAPTER THIRTY-ONE

The Spy Master's men were at work. Lights and pickaxes had been brought, and they attacked the Offering Table. First one struck, then a second, then a third. Chips of white stone that gleamed like ice in the lamplight flew out from under each blow, and splashed into the puddles in the courtyard. No one moved to stop the assault as the pick axes ran a deep crack right across the centre.

And the storm gathered strength.

Thunder crashed overhead and lightning ripped open the blackness to drop into the City in a brilliant whiplash of raging power. It ran along the castle, zigzagged down onto the Parade Ground and struck the toolbox with the cartridge and the churn of gunpowder that had been so carefully prepared by Vince. The tunnel blew sky high with a *wump* that set every horse rearing in terror, and the Offering Table was blown inwards. The Spy Master just had time to open the gate to the Rose Garden before it slammed in his face. Vince died too as a ton of stone came in on him.

The whole castle shuddered. The fountain under the dance floor was shaken into action and water spouted upwards, jiggling the floorboards loose, which floated round the Inner Court like matchsticks. The castle shook and set off the booby traps laid by the Policy Makers in the Inner Way, triggering them into explosion after explosion. Windows broke, and the Great Tank below the Court began to leak.

Water seeped and then rushed down into the prison, and the guards ran for it. The tiniest boy in the Nursery Cage did what he'd not dared to do before and wriggled between the bars to freedom. He climbed up, took the keys from the hook on the wall and opened every cage door to let the other prisoners out. The valve in the Reservoir Tank on the roof opened as the water drained out of the Great Tank, letting more and more water swirl down into the heart of the castle.

* * *

Avtar and the Cook crouched on the kitchen floor, protecting their heads with their arms from the dust and silt that the explosion shook down from the ceiling. Soot rained down onto the embers of the fire.

The guard barring Avtar's way through the window ran to see what had happened. Avtar grabbed two drying-up cloths and tied them below his knees so the legs of his trousers stayed the right length. Then, helped by the Cook, he climbed through the window. He landed hard in the gritty yard. The god! He was tired out. He called to her.

'There's a pianist locked in Lal's bathroom. Let him out later.' He threw the key up to her.

'Go,' the Cook screamed. 'I'll back you up.' Avtar flew across the yard to the gatehouse and the First Defence Gates.

He had a fair idea what had caused the explosion. He

thanked the god that the guards on the gate had crossed the courtyard to fight the fire that had broken out in the hay store above the tunnel. The tunnel itself was blocked with slabs of masonry and rubble. People were leaping recklessly from the windows of the room where the boys with the peashooter had stood. Avtar didn't like to think what might have happened to crazy little Felix.

The new wrought iron gates were closed when he got there and stood like a mesh between him and his escape. In front of them stood the Over Lord in full military uniform, holding the Pianist like a shield, gripping him with his arms behind him.

'Get out of my way,' Avtar said.

The Over Lord was whiter than ever from the shock of the explosion. 'I take it we have King Avtar here?' He shook the Pianist, who made a frightened little affirmative noise. 'With tea cloths for garters! Very regal, I must say!'

Avtar wouldn't be drawn. 'I said get out of my way.'

'Certainly.' But he didn't. 'Presumably you and your red-headed accomplice caused this explosion?'

'Funnily enough, it was you who caused it.' He knew he should shoot – shoot them both. The Roc wouldn't have hesitated. Kings were supposed to swap someone else's life for their own as often as it takes – and then sit down to a good dinner. But he'd been readier to kill the Over Lord when he was seven than he was now. As for the Pianist, he almost felt sorry for him. 'Are you going to get out of my way?'

'Of course we are, my dear chap.' The Over Lord shook the Pianist, who nodded like a puppet. 'As soon as you tell me where the Roc is.'

'So you can kill him?' He was trying to think of

ways round the Over Lord, but he was so tired now and the Over Lord was so strong and the Pianist such a frightened bundle. The Over Lord said as calmly as if they were discussing the weather, 'That wouldn't trouble you, would it? If I killed him? After all, he did kill your father.

'I seem to remember it was *you* who killed my father.'

'On the Roc's orders.'

'But you *did* it.'

'My apologies. So where is he?'

And still Avtar couldn't think how to get him out of the way. The Over Lord took his silence for defiance and changed his approach.

'This will interest you, King Avtar. The hospital says that Porcini's condition is improving rapidly. Your doing presumably? The King's Touch?'

It was good news about Porcini, and a bit odd, too, because the doctor had been so gloomy about her chances. But all Avtar said was, 'Idiot!' The Over Lord looked furious, but managed to ask quite pleasantly, 'How come she's recovering, then? Are you saying you can't cure people? Haven't you got the gift?' Avtar didn't answer. He *could* cure people, but not in the way the Over Lord thought. The Over Lord gave a nod of satisfaction and the plume on his bright helmet shivered. 'Thought so. You've got the gift all right.

'Now, let's get down to business. You tell me where the Roc is and I'll give you your City back. No strings attached. Everything just as it used to be before the Empire came along. One word from you and you're crowned King of Khul. Long to reign over your grateful people.'

It was a better offer than the Roc had made – much

338

better for him personally. But if he gave the Roc away, he'd give Fidelis away too. Could he sacrifice her like she seemed to have sacrificed him? It would mean a peaceful life. He wouldn't be on the run ever again.

The Over Lord said, 'What's the matter? Have you lost your wits?'

Avtar took off his special grin. 'Listen mate. Your Big Cheese chums call you a brilliant strategist, but there's another word for it: it's "liar". The Pianist has filled you in on the Roc's deal with me, so you've bettered it. Or pretended to. I've seen you smarming round the Roc while all along you intended to murder him and now you're doing the same to me. Except you'd keep me alive in some flipping dungeon so you could use my magic touch or whatever daft name you call it. You're a liar from your tin lid of a hat to the soles of your big boots that some Inmate kid has spent his life polishing. Everything you've ever said has been a lie.'

The Over Lord bowed his head submissively. 'I'd like you to think better of me than that, Sire,' he said. 'Give me a chance to prove that I am capable of doing the right thing by you. I propose an exchange of information. You tell me where the Roc is and I'll tell you about your mother, Queen Lenita and what she did six years ago.'

Avtar interrupted him. 'I know what she did. You lied about her too.'

It was not the answer the Over Lord expected. For the first time, he looked thrown. He'd run out of arguments. He shrugged in resignation. 'And now I suppose you'll kill me. But if you intend to use that gun, you should try holding it the right way round.'

Avtar looked down at the revolver. As he did, the Over Lord drew his own. The first thing Avtar knew about it was the report when the Over Lord fired at him and the Pianist kicked the gun out of his hand so the bullet flew wide.

'The boy's worth ten of you,' the Pianist said. 'He stopped the Roc finishing me off, even though he didn't owe me any favours. And he loves his City. You hate it.'

Without a word the Over Lord knocked the Pianist down and drew his sword on him.

'Don't.' Avtar levelled the gun at the Over Lord. 'Don't kill him. He's got kids.'

'You sound just like your father, Avtar. Soft-hearted. Is that why you dressed the Roc's daughter up as Porcini? Felt sorry for her? Good idea, though. Nearly had me fooled. I've just dispatched a troop of cavalry to fetch her back. I thought his daughter's screams would bring the Roc out of hiding if nothing else did.'

Avtar tried to think clearly. How much start had the car had? Could it out-run the horsemen? He was so tired now and the thought of the soldiers pursuing the motorcar made him feel as if the guts had been dragged out of him. They would all be killed. Everything he'd achieved for Khul was in ruins. And he'd failed Fidelis.

The Over Lord was looking at him closely now. 'Ahhh!' he said. 'You're fond of her aren't you? Dear me, King Avtar, fraternising with the enemy were you? Just like your bitch mother.'

Avtar pulled the trigger on him.

There was a useless click. He was out of ammunition. 'Bad luck,' the Over Lord said and lunged with his sword.

But the Pianist trapped the Over Lord's foot under one arm and stabbed him in the calf with his dagger. Then he stabbed him again. The Over Lord twisted round with a scream of pain and drove his sword into the Pianist's body. He wrenched out the blade, red with the Pianist's blood, and turned it on Avtar.

But the Cook was as good as her word. She'd lit a fuse from the embers of the fire and set it fizzing and sparking to the powder inside a stew pot perched on the window ledge. Now blue light fountained over the ledge and poured into the wet yard. Blue stars snapped and banged into hundreds more stars. That was the signal.

The Baker and she had worked tirelessly. They'd gathered every firework left over from the old festival days and trickled their contents into every available container – anything from casseroles to coffee cups. Now kitchen boys, messenger boys and chambermaids, boot boys and butcher boys, laundry girls and ghosty boys, posted at windows and in turrets all over the castle, put a match to their saucepans, cups, frying pans and bread tins and set the castle alive from top to bottom with running blue fire and a million exploding stars.

For the people fighting the fire it was awesome; for the mules waiting for the Pianist, it was the last straw. They'd stood up to the explosion, but the blue crackling fire was too much. They backed and reared away from it, braying with a sound like the end of the world. The cart lurched steadily backwards and backwards towards the gatehouse, gathering speed as the driver lost his hold. At the last minute, the piano rolled off the back, smashed through the gates and fell to pieces with a thrumming discord.

Avtar, whose reactions were sharp as a razor by now, jumped back into the shelter of the gatehouse. The cart went over the Pianist. He said, 'Tell my sons I...' but he was dead before he could finish. Avtar didn't see what became of the Over Lord. Both mules were sitting back on their haunches with dazed expressions on their long faces, almost blocking the open gateway. Avtar squeezed past them with a grateful pat on the neck and was off down the street like an arrow. Not a single guard on the First Defence Wall was looking in his direction.

By now, Inmates were coming out of their houses to stare at the blue light and the orange flame blazing up at the castle, despite the drenching rain. Avtar pushed his way through small crowds and came into the main street as a medical carriage cantered past him.

'Brad, Brad!' His voice cracked with the thought that Brad might not have seen him, but the carriage drew up and he dragged himself up the hill. He opened the little carriage door, and crawled in and lay down. Melior appeared at the window.

'The Product Convoy's out,' she said. 'I'm going to the Main Gate. I've got a quarantine order from the Chief Medical Officer. They may just buy it.'

'This might add a good touch.' Avtar groped in his pocket for the white medical mask that Porcini's stretcher-bearers had given him that he'd been careful to keep. As he handed it to her, something else fell out onto the carriage floor. Melior didn't notice, and he picked it up quickly. She smiled at him. 'I'll put Brad in with you,' she said. 'Act like you're dying.'

'That shouldn't be too difficult,' Avtar replied. But she'd gone. He looked at the thing in his hand. It was a gold locket.

Brad climbed in alongside him. 'The Name!' he said when he saw Avtar's beaten face. He helped him lie out along the seat while Melior turned the carriage and set off for the Main Gate.

Avtar looked back. The castle was still running with blue light. It was just like his seventh birthday cake. He would never be able to thank the Baker and he would never see the Cook again; but as long as he lived and was Avtar of Khul he would be grateful to them and he'd always remember his beautiful castle alive with light. He turned back to Brad and gave him the locket.

'Be a pal. Open it up for me.'

Brad knew when not to ask questions. 'There's tiny writing.'

'Show me.'

It read: "Forget me not. Fidelis." It hurt to smile. But he did. He wrapped Fidelis's locket in his royal square of blue silk and put it back in his pocket carefully. Then he remembered the troop of soldiers riding to catch up with her.

Melior pulled up at the Main Gates. Avtar and Brad lay like the dead and listened. A guard hunched under a rain cape came out to them, swinging a lantern. He stood well back when he saw the mask on Melior's face. He waved the lantern towards the castle. 'What the deuce is happening up there?' Melior replied in her best Policy Maker accent. 'I reckon the party got out of hand. But there's worse to come.' She held out the Chief Medical Officer's letter for him to inspect. 'Quarantine order,' she announced. He was about to take it from her when she said, 'Plague,' and he withdrew his hand quickly. 'I'm taking these two patients in here down to the old reed cutter's place.' The guard took a large step further away from the carriage. 'They're making an isolation hospital there,' Melior explained. Her voice took on a sullen note. 'They're paying me time-and-a-half, but they'll be lucky if…'

But the guard had already hurried to the gate. Bolts shot back, keys turned, bars were lifted and the great doors parted – and Melior drove them all slowly and steadily out of the City at last.

* * *

'Can't you patch it up man?'

Fidelis could hear her father's voice was raw with the strain. She shivered in the wet and the cold. They'd come hardly any distance at all when the puncture had happened.

'I've told you,' the chauffeur insisted. 'Not without the toolbox, and somebody's run off with it.' The Roc went on hammering at the spare wheel with a stone. He made a wild figure in his wet dress and magnificent wig. But the spare wheel was bolted into its casing and he needed a spanner to lift it off.

Fidelis glanced behind her. It was already light enough to make out the dark cone shape of the City. At sunrise they'd be visible to the sentries on the walls; they'd be sitting ducks. 'Don't you think we should walk?'

'Agreed,' the chauffeur said. 'Back to the City. This whole thing stinks. All of you in fancy dress. I'm going.' And he took off into the greying darkness. Fidelis looked anxiously at her father and Prudence. Without the chauffeur, they really were stranded. Only he could drive.

Then Span climbed out of the car and, with a parting whiff, struck out southwards like a louse deserting a corpse. They could do nothing but follow him. Fidelis knew her dancing shoes weren't going to last long, and Prudence in her soaking wet nightgown looked frozen.

But at least the rain had stopped. The Roc swung his skirt over one arm and muttered, 'The Sun for a horse!'

Like an answer to his request, they heard horses' hooves drumming behind them. Fidelis looked back and saw the top of the City glow brilliant blue, a sparkling summit of blue fire. There was a scream somewhere back in the dark from the chauffeur, and men shouting, then a gunshot and then the hooves again. In seconds the Over Lord's twenty horsemen were upon them and a blaze of confusing firing began. Some of the Over Lord's troop fell and the rest wheeled their horses and fled back to the City.

'The Sun, Jameson!' said a voice from the half-light. 'What *are* you got up as?' Fidelis snatched the wig off her father's head, and Prudence took it and stuffed it up the sleeve of her nightgown. 'Mama!' Fidelis shouted. 'Oh Mama!' And she felt tears of relief pricking her eyes.

'Alma!' her father exclaimed as her mother trotted up in her carriage, where Span was already sitting comfortably. The Roc peered past his wife through the soft dawn light. 'And you've brought an army with you! Good show!'

'After your SOS, my love, naturally, I came armed.'

Fidelis recognised the message at once that her mother was holding out. It was the thin strip of paper she had found in the little desk in her room. She must have muddled up her own message to her mother with this one – "They are trying to kill us. Come. Hurry, my sweet, to service." By a huge stroke of luck, she'd sent it to Mama. And at last Fidelis saw what she was reminded of by the way the Ls of the signature were written: they were like stairs.

She took the paper before the Roc could say a word. 'Oh Mama,' she said, scrunching it in her palm, 'Pa has been so brave and you have been so clever.' The Roc lifted his wife out of the carriage and kissed her, and said his wife had saved his life and the Empire too.

Then an officer marched up and saluted the Roc without batting an eyelid at his unusual clothes. He said the Roc's favourite charger was saddled and ready for him to lead the advance on the City. The Roc kissed his wife again, put her back into the carriage and strode away.

Her mother called to her to join her in the carriage. They must retire to the rear of the action. But Fidelis leant against her mother's carriage and thought about Avtar. She was happy for her parents, but no one had mentioned Avtar's part in their escape from the City. No one had said that, but for him, they would be dead now. Avtar had saved their lives, and in return they had left him behind to die. She knew that she would never ever get over losing him. Prudence seemed to understand. She came and put her arm round her. 'My lady, look toward the river.'

* * *

Avtar felt the carriage slow down, and he sat up and looked out of the window. The rain had stopped and there was a line of silver at the bottom of the sky ahead of him. It was dawn. Then his stomach flipped over with fright. Horsemen were riding hard towards them through the first light. Then he heard Melior give a joyful cry, 'Scar! Oh Scar, my dear, you're all right!' And Scar came trotting to meet them, riding on a big grey horse and leading two others.

He was delighted to see them. 'I didn't know we were going to be four,' he apologised to Brad. But Brad said there was no way he was riding one of those things anyway so it was decided that he'd get up behind Melior, and he seemed pretty pleased with the arrangement.

They unharnessed the horse on the riverbank and pushed the carriage into the water, where it floated away into the brightening light. Brad winced as Melior kissed the horse goodbye on its nose. Then they left it contentedly cropping the grass.

'Where did you get the bridles?' Avtar asked as Scar gave him a leg up.

'Nicked them from the stables before I left,' Scar replied, and gave his braying laugh. Everyone else laughed too, except Avtar. He was free, but was *Khul*?

A breeze picked up and blew their horses' manes, and they sat and looked at each other in silence. Melior shivered. 'Where now?' she asked uncertainly. Avtar saw her hands were shaking. 'Thanks for getting us out, Melior,' he said gently. 'You were fantastic.'

'But I haven't got us all out,' she said. 'I think Phoelo is still there. Yes,' she said, in response to their startled faces. 'Phoelo is still alive, although he thinks he's called Felix.'

Avtar was appalled. Crazy, swattable little Felix was his brother. He couldn't bear to tell them that he was a Policy Maker now, so he said, 'Yes, he's still there,' and went on quickly. 'I'll get him out.' Brad gave a yelp of dismay. Avtar grinned. 'Not right this minute, dafty. The god knows when or how, but I will, I promise, Melior.'

She leant across her horse and kissed his cheek. It was practically the most surprising thing to have happened that night. He noticed then that they were all looking at him expectantly. He was the perishing leader again. 'I've heard Uncle Haakron escaped and is alive.' Distant rifle fire interrupted him.

'Shouldn't we be getting a move on?' asked Brad in a frightened voice.

'It's the Over Lord's troop of cavalry.' Avtar tried to sound calm. 'They're not after us.' He mustn't think of Fidelis.

Rays of light spread upwards from the horizon on their right, as the sun rose. It turned the clouds a glaring orange, and flooded light over the plain and a huge army, riding on Khul. Avtar strained his eyes. The wild figure in a dress and shiny helmet, galloping at the head of his cavalry, could only be the Roc. He watched them streaming towards the City, scarlet banners flowing, and felt for Fidelis's locket in his pocket. If the Roc was alive, perhaps Fidelis was too.

'Look at the Topmost Tower,' Brad said. 'Someone's raised the white flag.' So the Over Lord's people weren't going to put up a fight.

'We should go now,' Avtar said.

'Which way?' Melior asked.

'Far north. That's all I know.'

Scar pointed to the hills behind the City. 'That way, then, over the river.'

Avtar straightened up and nudged his horse on. 'There's a crossing of sorts. Remember it?'

They turned their horses' heads into the wind and trotted forward. No one in the castle saw the trio of horses half wade, half swim the narrowest part of the river and pull themselves up onto the opposite bank. And only Fidelis saw one rider among them lift his arm in a farewell salute to his City before he broke into a gallop, riding north, parallel with the dawn.

And though Fidelis was crying now, she said, 'He's done it! Khul is free.'

THE END
OF THE BEGINNING...

Ursula Jones was born on the road to Wales. She trained at RADA and works as an actress. She has written TV scripts and plays for children, and her picture books have won the gold Smartie Award and the inaugural Roald Dahl Funny Prize. She lives in London and on the edge of a forest.

Acknowledgements

My thanks to Wally Handsley for sharing his
memories of his work as a lab assistant to
Alexander Fleming, and to the late David Duff
for his invaluable technical advice.
Thanks as well to Dr Peter Christian for his
help with things medical.
Finally, thanks to Tari Mandair for all he did,
and particularly for the loan of his name.

U.J. 2012